perfectly
damaged

E.L. MONTES

PERFECTLY DAMAGED
E.L. Montes
Copyright © 2014 E.L. Montes

Cover designed by Regina Wamba from MaeIDesign
http://www.maeidesign.com/

Edited by Megan Ward and Alison Duncan
http://www.meganwardediting.com/

Formatting by Self Publishing Editing Service

ISBN-13: 978-1499382648

For the ones who have
always felt alone,
like there was no more fight left in them…

&

For Isabella…

The most powerful thing of all is to believe in yourself, and
you'll never be alone.
Falling through the cracks sometimes doesn't make you
weak; it just means you'll be that much stronger in the end.
You're perfect exactly the way you are.
Never let *anyone* take that away from you.

"When the Japanese mend broken objects, they aggrandize the damage by filling the cracks with gold. They believe that when something's suffered damage and has a history it becomes more beautiful."
– Barbara Bloom

prologue

8 months earlier

I'm not sure how I got here. It's dark and chilly outside. The moon's light casting down around me is all I have to guide me through. I'm lost and afraid, trembling as the thundering rain assaults my body with every move I make. The faster I run, the harder the heavy drops stab my skin. But I continue to plunge my bare feet into the cold, muddy ground as I try to get away.

I can hear someone calling my name. It's a familiar voice, but I can't stop. My heart spirals out of control as I force one foot in front of the other. I have to run faster, get away from that person, get away from that voice. A scream tears up out of my throat, and I force myself to sprint through the graveyard. I lose my footing, slipping and falling in front of a tombstone. My body's covered in thick, heavy mud as I try to bring myself up. My hair is soaked, drenched and hanging over my face like a drape. Swiftly brushing the dark strands aside, I look up. My heartbeat drives full force before it comes to a screeching halt as I read the carving on the monument: RIP Brooke McDaniel.

"NO!" I scream at the top of my lungs.

No. No. No.

My body jerks up as I gasp for air. Skin damp with sweat, knuckles white, fisting the bed sheets, my chest heaves as I try to calm my breathing. It takes me a few seconds to collect myself.

A dream. Just a dream. About what?

In a complete daze, my mind struggles to remember. Darkness. Thunder. Mud. Running. And then… Brooke! Snatching my phone from the nightstand, I jump out of bed and run to her room. I place a shaky hand on the knob, but that's as far as I can go. I'm stuck. I know what I'll find on the other side, and it frightens me. After a few breaths, I find the courage to open it. And it's just as I expected: *nothing.*

Filled with all the things that defined her, her room is exactly the same as she left it. My eyes sweep across her large bookshelf, which is overflowing with hundreds of books. I fight back a sob as my gaze rests on the sitting area where she spent countless hours immersed in a story. I shiver, taking in the now-faded posters of her favorite bands pinned all over her pale yellow walls. Her favorite book quotes, stenciled on the wall over the headboard of her bed, bring back memories of days we spent endlessly talking about them and the authors who wrote them. Pink, purple, and yellow paint her room; colors that blend together in a beautiful and sophisticated décor that only Brooke could design. Picture frames filled with images of us, Mom, Dad, and Charlie cover her desk. All of these items are valuable to *me*. All of them mean something to *me*. But all they are…is exactly that. Tangible items, filling a room that feels nothing short of vacant.

Chin down, shoulders slumped, and heart breaking, I can't control the warm tears running down my heated cheeks. I'm praying, hoping this time it'll be different. But it's useless. Allowing the pain to overtake every nerve for just this moment, I hesitantly tread over to her bed, fall on top of the plush surface, and wrap myself securely in the comforter. She loved this stupid purple quilt. I remember the day she barged into my room with the soft lilac fabric in her hand, smiling brightly at the deal she managed to score at the mall. Her wide green eyes were filled with pride, her perfectly plump pink lips curled into a beautiful smile.

Why do I torture myself? Why do I allow myself to feel this pain?

I feel absent without her in my life. I need her back to feel whole again. I need her to bounce into the room with her passionate, wholehearted persona and bring light to my storm, the way she always used to. But that's not going to happen. Brooke isn't going to barge through that door.

And as much as I know this will do nothing but worsen the agonizing pain, I grab my phone and speed-dial Brooke's number. It rings. I bring the cell to my ear.

"Hi, this is Brooke! Leave a message after the beep." Her lively voice leaps through the speaker, followed by a long beep.

Again. "Hi, this is Brooke! Leave a message after the beep."

BEEEEEP.

Again. "Hi, this is Brooke! Leave a message after the beep."

AGAIN.

I torture myself over and over until I'm exhausted.

3

Exhausted by crying, by feeling alone, and by being lost. I listen to my sister's voicemail until there's nothing left in me. Nothing, until the dullness of the early morning hours creeps in and I can't keep my heavy lids open any longer. As I drift into my short coma, I wish, as I have many nights before, that I won't wake, that I'll vanish in my sleep because it's the only way to just forget.

To never again...*feel*.

early June

Grief never goes away. It haunts you, taking over your mind, body, and soul. Before you know it, it has won.

chapter 1

Jenna

I sit in the waiting area of my psychiatrist's office, vacantly staring at the glass coffee table. As usual, my thoughts trail off and I question myself: What am I living for? Every day is a struggle, wondering if I'll have another episode. My life is a constant reminder of how big a failure I am. I try to picture my life each day and how it could've been if I wasn't diagnosed with my mental illness. I absolutely despise who I am.

I've changed. I'm colder and more distant, numb to all those around me.

It's the only way to stop feeling. If I don't allow any emotion into my heart and soul, I have a better chance of surviving in this cruel, fucked-up world. Well, more like existing. In the end, it's the only way to protect myself. People don't get me; hell, half the time I don't get myself. My so-called loved ones fear me. And the funniest thing of all? They have no idea how much I fear myself.

Sure, there are times I run or curl into a tiny ball, rocking back and forth until it all goes away. But that's when I'm alone. I try not to allow anyone to witness my weaknesses. No one will ever understand it, nor will they accept it. Each day I wake up trying to fight through it, trying to forget until something triggers me to crumble again.

My phone alarm goes off, and I reach into my purse, thankful for the distraction from my thoughts. My eyes scan the room, taking in the woman across from me and her arched accusatory brow. She's obviously unhappy with my phone interrupting her reading. I cock an eyebrow in silent, smart-ass retort as I swipe across my phone screen, shutting the ringtone off.

I dig into my purse, determined not to give her any more of my time, and remove the container holding my medication. The cap pops off and I tip over the orange plastic tube, examining the tiny pills in the palm of my hand. Some days I skip them—days that I think are good and I'm capable of getting through without them. Other days I take them with no questions asked.

On this particular day, I'm not sure what to do. I'm confused. Can I handle this on my own? Is today just another day? It's been a week since I last took one. Although the voices will always haunt my thoughts, the hallucinations have been absent for a very long time. Until last night, that is.

Uneasiness kicks in and my vision gradually clouds over. The pills are now lost in a fuzzy haze. Here it is, another episode. *Breathe, Jenna. Just breathe.* My breathing grows shallow, and I clasp my hand tight around the capsules. My flesh is burning as sweat condenses on my skin. Any moment now, it will start collecting across my hairline, on my neck, at the small of my back. I'll feel it beading up and soaking through the fabric of my clothes. My chest is tightening; it's as if someone is reaching in, gripping my heart with their bare hand, and squeezing every inch of the muscle.

"I wouldn't take them if I were you."

My dazed head spins, facing the one who has intruded on the beginning stages of one of my meltdowns. She's seated beside me on the other end of the sofa, exuding a strong confidence that's unique to her. I take in a slow, shaky breath and try to reconcile the girl before me with reality. She arches an eyebrow while examining a chip in her polished nail—as if thinking she'll need a fresh coat soon. Her crossed leg lightly bounces in place. Finally, she peeks through her long lashes and settles her light green eyes on me. After she takes in my dismayed expression, her bottom lip juts out into a pout. "What's wrong, Jenna?"

"You shouldn't be here, Brooke," I let out in a harsh whisper. "Why are you here?"

Brooke's eyes widen and she swiftly scoots over, positioning herself beside me. "I'm here because you need me. You're lost, Jenna. I want to help." Her delicate features are fixed in confusion. "Aren't you happy I'm here?" I don't answer. She blows out a frustrated sigh and my bangs lightly drift at the airy gust. "Don't lose who you are, Jenna. It's okay to feel, even for this one moment."

I shut my eyes tightly, inhaling and exhaling three soothing breaths. "You're not real."

Come on, I can do this. I'm strong enough.

Shut it down, Jenna.

Don't feel.

Don't feel.

Do. Not. Feel.

"Nonsense." She brings a gentle finger along my moist cheekbone and wipes away a tear. A tear I didn't realize had escaped. Dammit. "Look at me, Jenna." Her finger traces down my jawline, hooks under my chin, and tilts my face up. "There's no need to shut yourself down. I'm here. I'll always be here. You know that, right? Jenna? Look at me," she urges.

"No!" Brooke's jaw drops slightly and her eyebrows furrow. She's both shocked and hurt. I hurt her. But I don't care. She isn't real. I look away and catch the same lady who was interrupted by my phone peeking over her book at me. This time her eyes are narrowed, and she's giving me a *this-girl-is-psycho* look.

You're not real. Get out of my thoughts. I chant in my mind. It's safer this way. No one can see me losing it.

Brooke moistens her lips. Her features soften, and then she leans in closer. Too close. "Oh, no? I'm not real to you anymore? Have I been gone that long that you've forgotten me? Do you see what they're doing to you? They're trying to make you forget me."

My head shakes softly. There's no way I could ever forget Brooke. Since we were little girls, Brooke felt the need to protect me, to guard me from others. Although we were only three years apart, Brooke became the mother figure I should've had. Our mother spilled thoughts into Brooke's head—that I was different, special, and that I needed a tad bit more attention than normal kids. Attention that resulted in numerous therapy sessions and countless prescriptions since I was too young to remember.

Who knew a child could be diagnosed with depression at such a young age, only to discover in her late teens that she's schizoaffective? I didn't, but that's what happened, and it's fucking embarrassing. Not just for me. No. It's embarrassing for my mother. Humiliating, actually. My mother's perfect little life, which she's worked so hard for by snatching up and marrying my wealthy father, is all she seems to care about.

Some say my mother won the jackpot. Others say it was love at first sight. And a very few say their marriage was a result of a one-night stand that led to pregnancy. There are three sides to the story: his, hers, and the truth. None of that matters, not when I have Brooke by my side…

But that's just it. I don't have her anymore. I'm alone. And before I'm reminded again of how excruciating it feels for her to be gone, I close my eyes, dig my fingers into my hair, and bend over in my seat, caging my head between my legs. No one can hear me, but deep within my thoughts I scream and cry out, *Get out of my head! Get out of my head! Get out! Get out! Get out!* My body shudders as I try to put away the pain and memories deep within the back of my mind, storing every bit of it in a sacred place that I mentally deadbolt and throw away the key to.

Suddenly, I jolt back from a soft touch on my shoulder. "Jenna, are you okay?"

"Dr. Rosario," I breathe out shakily.

My therapist for the past year narrows her eyes, examining me carefully. I stare at her wide-eyed. My chest rises and falls with uneasy breaths, and my arms are sprawled out with my fingers clenched into the sofa cushion. Dr. Rosario brings her hand cautiously to my knee, leaning in so only I can hear her next words. "Jenna, are you having an episode?"

"No," I lie quickly. "I feel sick to my stomach." That's not too much of a lie. "I think I caught a bug or something. Do you mind if I reschedule?"

She looks at me skeptically. With all her experience in this profession, she can tell when someone's having an episode. I guess my lie didn't work. "How 'bout you come into my office? If you still feel like you're going to be sick, we can end the session early. How does that sound?"

"Okay," I whisper. Seems like I don't have much of a choice. "I just need to use the restroom first."

Dr. Rosario stands. "Of course. You know where it is. Just join me in my office when you're ready."

I nod. Dr. Rosario smiles warmly then disappears into her office. I nervously look around. No sign of Brooke anywhere. She's gone. I collect my things, ignoring the stares from both the receptionist and the book lady, and head straight to the bathroom. With my back flush against the locked door, I steady my breathing.

You can do this, Jenna.

You know how some people say "one day at a time?" Well, in my life, it's more like one second at a time. The simple tasks normal people take for granted are very difficult for me. Like brushing one's hair or taking a shower or simply waking up and getting out of bed. These things need to be encouraged, pushed, because I'd rather stay in my room, tucked beneath the sheets of my bed where it's so much safer. I have no one to push me right now, so it takes me about three minutes just to talk myself into standing in front of the bathroom sink.

The silver-plated mirror reflects a pale, sickly-looking girl back at me as the water runs into the sink. I don't even recognize this girl. She's so young, yet, with the dark circles beneath her eyes, she looks at least five years older than she actually is. I want to cry. I need to cry, to just let it all out. The anger builds inside of me while questions about what I'm slowly turning into take over.

Some days I allow my thoughts to run wild, to consume me, and keep me hidden within myself. No matter how strong of a person I struggle to be, the fact still remains—even the strongest fall through the cracks sometimes. But for right now, I do what I've trained my mind and body to do when I have just enough fight left in me. I take my medication, swallow back the tears, straighten my shoulders, tame my disheveled chocolate-colored hair, and lift my chin. Today, I will gather what little strength I have left and not allow myself to be defeated.

Not quite feeling like a brand new woman, I walk into Dr. Rosario's office and take a seat on the white leather sofa, which I've grown accustomed to. Four years of psychotherapy, five therapists, and one admission to an inpatient institution later, my parents found Dr. Rosario. They feel strongly about her abilities and said I have an actual chance of recovery with her, whatever that means.

Dr. Rosario sits across from me, at ease in her matching white leather armchair. She opens my file and roams through it as her slender finger adjusts her glasses at the bridge of her nose. The only sound in the room is her fingers flipping through the pages. It's beginning to irritate me. My legs bounce in place. I nibble on my inner cheek as I wait. The silence claws at my skin. I like quiet, but not this kind. Not when there's someone else occupying a room with me. Not while I'm waiting for what she'll ask or say next.

What the hell is she thinking anyway? It never takes her this long to begin one of our sessions. Is she analyzing what she witnessed a few minutes ago? If that's the case, I'll be bullshitting my way through the next forty-five minutes, hoping that at the end of it she believes I'm getting better.

Her brown eyes meet mine. Finally. "So, Jenna, tell me how you've been dealing with your symptoms lately."

Is she serious? Why doesn't she try living with schizoaffective disorder for four years? Then she can tell me how she deals with it. "Good."

"You haven't experienced any episodes in the past week?" she prods.

I swallow back the truth. "No. I actually feel like the new medication may be working."

Dr. Rosario smiles. "That's great, Jenna." She scribbles down on a note pad. "Are you having any side effects from the antipsychotics?"

"I feel nauseous at times and have a loss of appetite. I also feel sleepy all the time, just tired."

"Ah. Do you feel that the constant need to sleep has to do with the depression part of the disorder?"

"Maybe." I shrug, looking down at my folded hands in my lap. I spot the gold, heart-shaped charm (inscribed with *Sisters Forever*), which hangs from the bracelet snugged around my right wrist. I cherish this bracelet. It's the one item that keeps me going. Brooke gave it to me at my high school graduation. Every year since then, she's added a new charm. But not this year.

"I'm going to prescribe you a higher dose of the antidepressants. We'll see if that'll help with your fatigue. Is that all right?" Dr. Rosario asks, disturbing my memories.

I keep my head low, trying to fight back tears as I cling to the tiny heart-shaped charm. I nod. "Okay."

"Great. Now, let's discuss a few things you can work on this week."

I nod again, allowing Dr. Rosario to go on, but her words sound off distantly as my mind is somewhere else. As usual, I react and answer at all the right times, so she thinks I'm engaged in the therapy, maybe even getting better. I have to make her believe it, or at least make myself believe it, because at this very moment I'd rather be in my room, entombed in my sheets, and locked away.

After my visit with Dr. Rosario, I take a long walk around town. It's the only way to clear my mind, to breathe. Anything to get rid of the hallucinations and the voices in my head. For once, I just want to feel normal. No one will ever understand it, not unless they're going through it. Eventually, my legs tire and give out, and I'm forced back home—a place I dread going to.

"Jenna, come here, sweetie," Mom calls as I enter through the front door. She is nothing if not predictable. Sometimes I really believe she has a tracking device on me. I mean, how else could she know exactly the moment I get home? How else could she pelt me with questions and jabs and reminders and meaningless information the second I walk through the door?

I somberly head toward dad's home office, which is the direction her deceptively saccharine voice came from. I stand by the entrance, taking note that she isn't alone. My mother looks like a queen sitting on her throne behind the massive cherry wood desk. Her silky smooth, natural red hair falls just above her collarbone, not a strand out of place. Her makeup is flawless as ever; never has my mother gone a day without her face made up just so. Come to think of it, never has my mother gone a day without dressing up either.

Her red lips twitch into a slight pout at my appearance. We're the opposite of one another—day and night. Where she wears dresses and skirts, I wear jeans and shorts. Where she wears overly expensive designer heels, I wear sneakers or flats. The only makeup I use is the dark shadow and liner around my eyes and a bit of lip gloss.

I'm sure it took every ounce of my mother's strength not to make a snarky comment about my chosen attire in front of our guests. After all, I am the daughter of Gregory McDaniel,

CEO and co-founder of one of the largest financing and marketing companies in the tri-state area. So I'm certain ripped-up skinny jeans, black sneakers, and a Lady Gaga T-shirt, which features her practically naked on the front, doesn't fit into my mother's idea of what a perfect daughter's wardrobe should be.

"Jenna, sweetie," she says, forcing a smile, "these are the contractors that'll be working on the guesthouse. This is Mr. George Reed and his son, Bryson." She extends her arm gracefully toward the two men sitting across from her.

They turn in their chairs to greet me. The older man, George Reed, looks to be in his late forties or early fifties. The younger one, Bryson, appears to be roughly around my age, maybe a bit older. They both politely nod as I walk in and stand before them.

I respond with the same gesture, but after my mother's disapproving, narrow glare, I reach my hand out to each of them. "It's a pleasure to meet you both."

"The pleasure's all mine." George Reed shakes my hand sternly.

"Same here," Bryson says with a smile.

"Should we get started, Mrs. McDaniel?" George directs to my mother.

With a delicate wave of her hand, she lets out a giggle. "Please, George, call me Laura. And yes, we can begin now that Jenna is here."

I'm caught off guard. "Oh, I wasn't aware I was allowed to be involved in this little project of yours." My words blurt out rapidly in a harsh tone, but it's too late to take them back now.

Mother bites her tongue and a tiny, firm grin forms on her face. "Of course I want you involved with this project.

Please have a seat, darling." Darling? Ha! We stare at each other for an awkward, short moment.

I try to find sincerity through her act. And would you look at that? I come up empty. Since I don't want to make a show in front of our guests, I swiftly sit in an empty chair beside Bryson and nod for them to go on.

George clears his throat and then spreads the blueprints on top of the desk. My mother squeals with delight. She scoots to the edge of the executive chair and leans in to have a better look. Bryson sets a laptop beside the prints, revealing a 3-D mock-up image of what the guesthouse will look like upon completion. "As you requested, Mrs.—Laura," he corrects himself and goes on, "we designed the exterior of the property to be the exact replica of your home."

Mother brings a hand to her chest and inhales an awed gasp. "I love it." As much as I hate to agree with her on almost anything, I have to admit, it looks really good. They've managed to take our eight-thousand-square-foot home and transform it into a two-thousand-square-foot replica.

Bryson nods and continues, "I'm glad you do. Now for the interior, we've designed a two-story home as you requested. The architect was able to add in all of your wants and needs without complications. If you decide there's anything else you'd like to add, we'd need approval from the architect before moving forward."

"No, everything here is exactly how I had imagined it would be. I'm sure it'll be beautiful. Mrs. Cunningham mentioned how amazing your work is, so I know I'm in good hands." The Cunninghams are great friends of my parents. Mr. Cunningham, formerly known as Senator Frederick Cunningham, graduated grad school with my father. They're now frequently seen together at the local golf course.

George strokes his dark grey goatee. "Laura, we understand that you want this to be a two-month project, but we usually ask our clients to give us an extra month. This gives us some leeway with ordering materials, weather conditions, and any delays or restrictions with the building permits. Again, this is just in preparation for any unforeseen circumstances that may arise."

"Yes, of course. So you're looking at a deadline of mid-September?"

"Roughly around that time. We're pretty quick workers, so I'm sure we can have it finished by the end of August, providing there are no setbacks. We can start as early as Monday morning."

"Terrific. Jenna, is this time frame agreeable to you?"

Both George and Bryson turn their gazes in my direction, waiting patiently for my approval. Why did my input matter so much to her? This entire thing was her idea. One day she woke up and said, "I want a guesthouse!" And *bam*, she made a few phone calls and now we're here. Instead of making a fuss in front of our visitors, I simply nod.

"Will it be just the two of you?" I'm not sure why I ask exactly; it just seems like a big project for two men to take on alone.

George chuckles. "Oh no. There'll be several of us. My nephew, a few other hard workers of mine, and some subcontractors like plumbers and electricians when the time comes."

"Oh. Okay, then," is all I say.

Bryson shuts off the laptop and rolls up the site plans. "Awesome. We'll fax over the contract and see you on Monday."

My mother stands and shows our guests out. Before she returns to ignite an argument about my ill-mannered behavior or disappointing ensemble, I scurry out the back of the house, past the side of the colonial-style structure, and into the three-car garage.

"Where the hell are they?" I mumble beneath my breath. "This is ridiculous." I huff out as I continue to rummage through the neat pile of plastic containers. It's been over an hour since my searching escapade began.

A red container labeled Christmas.

An orange container labeled Halloween.

A blue container labeled Fourth of July.

There's even a pink container that reads Easter with bunny ears drawn beside it. Every damn holiday is labeled on a color-coordinated container. Who needs Martha Stewart when there's the OCD Laura McDaniel around? My mother makes certain that things are never left undone or unfinished, that everything is always in its rightful place. But for some reason, my two boxes are gone. I distinctly remember placing them in here almost seven months ago. I search every corner of the garage, every shelf, every cabinet. Nothing.

"What are you looking for?" my mother's breathy tone pokes from behind me.

I take in a lungful of air before turning around and facing her. "Where are my boxes?"

She leans against the entryway of the garage door. "Why on earth are you looking for them?"

"Last I knew they were my things."

Mom tugs a hand through her perfect hair and her shoulders deflate as she sighs loudly. "Dr. Rosario—"

"Dr. Rosario said I could start again."

A stunned expression lines her soft features. "Oh. Well, then. I placed them in the shed." I nod and move swiftly past her, but before I can exit she reaches out and grabs my arm. Her touch is warm and soft. I shut my eyes at the contact. It's abnormal for her, for me. "Jenna," she says softly, "I'm trying to make things better between us. I know our relationship isn't ideal, but I am still your mother. I do care for you."

I manage to open my eyes and focus on her troubled expression. Care? Interesting word choice. "Is that all you wanted to say?" I ask coldly. My mother's stare lingers, turning hard as the muscles around her mouth tighten almost imperceptibly.

"Jenna, you know these cold little remarks are not helping. I'm trying to make an effort here," she bites out.

"How? By having us design a guesthouse together? I'm not sure if I should laugh or cry." Her hand drops to her side, releasing me and my arm from her uncomfortably intimate attempt to connect.

That's the end of that.

My two boxes are neatly stacked at the far right of the shed. They're both pretty heavy, so I have to carry them separately to the back patio by the pool. Once they're both out, I open the one labeled Jenna's Work first. I reach in and take out each abstract painting one by one.

A soft smile tugs at the corner of my lips; warmth settles over me and soothes my chest. I don't remember the last time I felt like this. There's something about art that brings joy to my heart, always has been. It's peaceful and beautiful. No matter how downright raw or gritty the appearance may be, there's always a story behind it. As much as others try to figure it out, the true meaning remains with the artist alone. The paintings in this dingy cardboard box hold my secrets, my life, and my journey. They're *me*...painted in different textures and colors, splashed with different emotions.

Bliss. Fear. Love. Desire. Loneliness—most of all loneliness.

Every one of my emotions is trapped in one large box.

After examining each painting, I place them back and open the second box, which holds blank canvases, paintbrushes, and wooden pieces that, once placed together, create an easel. The fleshy pads of my fingers graze along the bristles of the brushes and tingle with the desire to pick one up and start again. But I can't. Dr. Rosario thinks I'm ready to start painting again, but there's something within me that lurches every time I think about it. Art brings out strong feelings for me, feelings that I'm not ready to face. I decide to hold off and put the boxes away for now.

As if on autopilot, I find myself turning around and locking my bedroom door behind me.

In my room I'm safe.

With my headphones plugged into my ears and my music blasting, I'm away from everyone and everything, in a place where I can forget the world.

chapter 2

Jenna

Today is a good day.

I woke up feeling better. Days like this I feel brave. Brave enough to conquer the world—even from inside my room, which is where I spend most of my time. I'm not sure if it's the nightmare-free sleep or the fact that I'm able to paint again that has me feeling slightly optimistic today. *Paint.* I'm tempted to glide a brush along canvas, but I can't fully find the inspiration to go for it. Before, I used painting as way to cope with my feelings; now, I'm just afraid.

Fear is one of my most battled emotions. Fear of the unknown, of never knowing where each step I take will lead, terrifies me. For others it's a rush, a thrill—the beauty of taking risks. For me, a risk can ruin me. It's the reason why I grapple with every decision I make, constantly fearful that any and every choice will affect my life for the worse. To avoid triggers and potentially damning consequences, I keep hidden, locked behind my door.

Maybe tomorrow I'll find some more courage. But for now, I'll continue to sit by the window with my legs comfortably crossed, watching the pool boy snatch debris with an extended net. My eyes scan over his sweat-dripping body as he reaches his arms out and slowly sways the mesh from side-to-side, just along the top of the clear water. His biceps flex as he taps the edge of the net along the concrete, dumping the debris aside.

Swish. Tap.

Swish. Tap.

Swish. Tap.

I'm not sure why I find this to be so very entertaining, but it's the highlight of my morning—which proves just how lame my life actually is.

The pool boy is making my life a bit more interesting by adding chemicals to the water when my phone rings.

"Hello?" I answer, not bothering to check who's calling.

"Hey, slut. What are the plans for today?"

It's Charlie. She's the person most people would call my best friend. She was originally my sister's BFF and more like a second big sister to me, but after Brooke's death, Charlie and I bonded. She loved Brooke like a sister; no secrets were left unsaid between the two of them. At first, after Brooke was gone, I tried to keep my distance from Charlie. I didn't want to be bothered by anyone, especially not someone who reminded me so much of Brooke. But Charlie was persistent. She constantly called me and showed up to my home uninvited. It was quite annoying at first, but eventually I gave up and allowed her in.

Charlie has some *interesting* traits: she's blunt, has a great sense of humor, and uses profanity more than any other person I know. To top it off, Charlie has a very bad habit of taking any and all conversation and making it about sex. And I'm not just talking about sex in the general sense; she goes as far as making sure her hoo-ha is brought into the conversation somehow. Yep, that's Charlie. But you learn to love her—or hate her as I do eighty percent of the time. We have a love-hate relationship.

"Hey, Charlie." I lean my forehead against the window, and my skin cools at the contact. "I'm thinking of a lounge day. Read by the pool and relax."

"Sounds good to me. I'll be over in a few hours," she invites herself, as always. Charlie huffs through the speaker, adding, "I have to take Nick to the mall. You know, big sister duties and all."

Charlie is the eldest of four. She's always towing around her little brothers and sister. "Okay. See you later," I respond.

"'Kay, bye!"

In my black bikini, cover-up, and flip-flops, I tread down the grand spiral staircase. The front door swings open just as I reach the bottom step. My father walks in with his cell glued to his ear. It's pretty common to see him like this: cell in hand—usually crammed between his head and his shoulder—making deals, constantly on the go. At the edge of the staircase, I lean against the railing and study him as long as I can before he realizes I'm watching.

Dad shuts the door with his foot as his rich, deep voice echoes through the foyer, "Stanley, I don't care what it takes to seal the deal. We've been working on this account for over a year. If Mr. Whitman wants a penthouse, give him a fucking penthouse." His face is etched with irritation as he places his suitcase on the marble floor by his office door.

I continue to admire him silently. Gregory McDaniel is a man who exudes power. His title as CEO of The McDaniel

Corporation speaks for itself. The moment my father enters a room, everyone and everything in it instantly gets smaller, dwarfed by his mere presence. He may frighten others, but never have I seen my father as anything but that—*my* dad. With my mother or me, the tough businessman and CEO instantly turns into a big pile of mush. Just as he does right now, when his eyes scan the foyer and meet mine. His mouth twitches into a huge smile. "Stanley, just take care of it," he says sternly as he winks and walks my way.

"Hi, Daddy."

He leans in and presses his lips to my forehead. "Hello, beautiful. Going for a swim, I see." His arm finds its way around my shoulder and he pulls me in close, guiding me as we walk together.

"Yes. Would you like to join me?"

"Sorry, sweetheart, I have a conference call in five minutes and then a hot date tonight." He winks.

I smile, knowing his *hot date* is indeed my mother. Regardless of what others interpret my parents' relationship to be, I've only ever seen one thing between them: love. That's one of the things I love most about my father—the love he has for her. The way he looks at her and the small, intimate gestures he manages with ease, all proves how much he loves her. And as much as my mother and I can't see eye-to-eye ninety percent of the time, I appreciate the love she has for him too. Love like theirs is rare; it happens once in a lifetime. It's the kind of love others envy.

"Jenna, what is this?" my father asks. My gaze follows his pointed finger to the round mahogany table in the center of our foyer. Beside the large pear-shaped vase, filled with fresh long-stemmed yellow roses, is a medium-sized black toolbox with a silver inscription: Reed Construction.

"Oh, that belongs to the contractor who's going to be working on the guesthouse. They must've left it behind after Mom and I met with them yesterday."

"Very well." He kisses me on the cheek and turns to enter his office. "Have a good swim, sweetheart."

Two hours. That's how long it takes for my fingertips to wrinkle like tiny prunes. I'm drained from repeatedly swimming laps. It's time to call it quits. Although the sun has set, the air is still muggy, and I pull myself out regretfully, wishing I could stay in the cool water a little while longer. My phone blinks on top of the towel, but I ignore it after seeing that it's a missed call from my mother, probably checking in to see if I burned the house down. I'm sure of it.

I toss my phone aside, grab the towel, and begin drying myself off. I brush the towel over my shoulder and biceps and down toward my wrist. My wrist. My naked wrist. The bracelet is gone.

Every muscle and nerve in my body grows raw as I panic. I drop the towel and search the lounge chair anxiously. Nothing. My eyes scan over the cobblestone patio around me. Nothing. I trace my steps back to the edge of the pool. Nothing. Where can it be? I need that bracelet.

I *need* it.

I *need* it.

I *need* it!

I'm going to cry; my vision turns hazy as my lungs tighten in anticipation.

An item glistening at the bottom of the pool catches my attention and I blink my vision clear. I can't make out what it is, but there's something there. Without another thought, I dive in. My hips and legs sway as I speed down to the bottom. After a few seconds, I reach it, but it's just a damn penny. A penny. I continue to search around, but there's nothing else down here. I want to scream.

My lungs burn, and I can't be certain if it's my rage or a lack of oxygen causing the pain. How could I be so damn careless? As my mind races, my legs grow increasingly numb. Terror is setting in. I'm rapidly losing the ability to swim back up to the surface. If I could breathe, I'd be hyperventilating right now. I'm having a meltdown underwater. I can feel it; I'm about to break. I pull my legs into my chest and wrap my arms around them tightly. I wish I could say this is the first time I've been in this situation, but it's not. I know all too well what I need to do to calm myself down and get the hell out of here. With my eyes firmly shut, I try to focus on something blissful as I hold my breath. The silence beneath the water is soothing, peaceful even. Down here, there are no voices haunting my thoughts.

A calm, pleasant feeling finally settles over me.

And it's taken away from me in an instant. One second I'm enjoying the silence, and the next I feel a vice-like grip around my arm tugging me upward. I break the surface, shocked and gasping for air, and swallow a mouthful of chlorine water. It burns my nostrils and lungs.

"What the hell?" I cough out. My hands and knees slam against the concrete that borders the pool.

"Are you okay?" a gruff voice huffs out.

Who?

What?

Where?

In a daze, I look up to see a man, completely drenched,

leaning over with his hands on his knees. His head is hung low and his whole body rises and falls slightly as he tries to regulate his breathing. I scatter to my feet, jump back, and glare at him. "Who the hell are you?"

His head lifts and... Blue. He has the most beautiful blue eyes I've ever seen. They're a pale, misty blue with thin streaks of grey and flecks of shimmering gold surrounding the pupil. Thunder, lightning, one hell of a storm—that's what I see when I look in his eyes. Yeah, he's a walking storm, all right, and his hypnotizing eyes grow darker as he narrows them in annoyance.

He huffs out as he straightens, revealing broad shoulders and an over six-foot frame. "I'm Logan?" The way he says it makes it seem like I should know who he is. I raise my brows and urge him to continue. "I work with my uncle." I shake my head again. "Reed Construction," he finally says.

"Oh." I wet my lips and the taste of chlorine assaults my tongue. "What are you doing here?"

His face has morphed into full annoyance at this point. "My uncle called your mom. He left his toolbox here and needs it for a project tomorrow. Your mother said she'd let you know I was on my way."

"Oh." That would explain the missed call. I wipe away the few soaked strands of hair plastered against my forehead. The naked wrist crossing in front of my face sidetracks me. Dammit, I need that bracelet. I turn around and walk to the edge of the pool, leaning over to scan the clear surface. There's nothing there to see.

Discouraged, I turn back to the wet man. "What the hell was all that about?" I snap, nudging my head toward the pool.

"I saved your life," he says irritably.

Saved my life? Is he kidding? I snort, crossing my arms

over my chest. "You nearly killed me. Because of you, I swallowed a gallon of water. I could've drowned."

Lance or Logan—whoever the hell he is—reaches into the pool and pulls out a floating red baseball cap with a blue letter P stitched in the center of it. Clearly a Phillies fan. "You've got to be kidding me." The worn cap twists in his hands as he drains the water from the fabric. "You were under there for almost three minutes. I jump in, save your life, and this is the thanks I get?"

He shakes his head and tosses the baseball cap over it. It isn't until he reaches for the edge of his white T-shirt that I notice his arms—arms that are fully sketched in dark artistry. I try to make out some of the images, but they bend and twist with others, making it impossible to decipher what's what without staring. My eyes shift away from his tattoos and take in his physique. As he wrings his drenched shirt out in front of him, I catch a glimpse of a toned stomach. His wet clothes mold to every muscle of his impressive shape. Even so, it doesn't matter if he's good-looking or not. I'm still annoyed. "I didn't need saving," I mumble.

His head kicks back as he snorts. "Yeah, I'll remember that next time. Can I just grab the toolbox and be on my way?"

Right. The toolbox. Which is in the house. After one last scan of the pool and surrounding grounds, I glare at him and walk to the lounge chair. I toss on my cover-up, grab the towel and my phone, and lead him to the foyer. The only sound accompanying us is the squishing of my flip-flops along the marble floors. I throw my hand out, indicating the completely out-of-place toolbox sitting on the table. "Here it is."

His fingers grip the handle and he lifts it to his side easily. "Can I exit through here?" He points at the double doors. "My truck's parked out front."

"Yep." I walk over and open it for him. As he's walking through the door, I hear a car pull up the driveway. At first I think it's my parents, but once I see the familiar black sedan my heart starts to race.

Shit.

"Wait. Lance, come here." I grip his bicep. My fingers curl around the hard, toned muscle. The car door slams. My anxiety level's spiking, and I pull him closer to me.

Blue eyes wildly scan my face and look down at my death grip. He gives me a look, a *this-woman-is-crazy* look. "What are you doing?" He jerks his arm in an effort to pull away.

"Hold me—no—kiss me," I urge, yanking his arm to force him down. Unfortunately, he's not budging. What. The. Hell. My foot stomps once to the ground as if I'm having a five-year-old tantrum.

"What? You're a psycho," he says.

"No, please. Just *please*, Lance." I quickly glance over and see Matthew exiting his car.

Lance shrugs off my grip. "First of all, my name is Logan. L-O-G-A-N. Logan. Second, I'm not holding you, and I'm most definitely not kissing you."

Dammit, he's one of those. The good-looking ones always are. "Okay. I get that you're gay and all—"

A sharp raised brow cuts me off. "I'm far from gay."

Oh my God, Matthew is now making his way up the pathway. My attention back on Logan, I slam my hands to my hips, surely giving the impression that I'm younger than my twenty-one years of age. "Okay, well prove it," I challenge.

"You're kidding?" he asks, but I'm pretty sure my expression tells him I'm anything but. His lips curl into a lopsided grin as he considers this test I've given him. Blue eyes slowly and seductively roam my face. He takes me in as if he's trying to figure me out. News flash, buddy, no one has ever figured me out. Logan's stare drops to my mouth, lingering, and then a sense of dominance clouds over his features. I'm surprised. His stare is enticing, flirtatious, and goddamn sexy as all hell.

He sucks his bottom lip in, slightly scraping his flesh against his teeth with a seductive grin. That's hot. *Yes, I've officially lost my mind.* He places the toolbox down. Then, in the blink of an eye, he reaches his arm around my waist, hauls me in, and slams his lips to mine. Urgent, hard, and quick drives of his tongue steal all thoughts from my mind. I quickly inhale and my hand finds its way up and around his neck. He's a good kisser. He tastes like an apple-flavored Jolly Rancher, which is usually the one flavor I ditch in the pack; after this it may become a favorite. I think a moan just vibrated through me. *Get your act together, Jenna. You've been kissed before.* Our tongues begin to settle into a slow rhythm with long, soft strokes.

Lost momentarily in the sensation of our kiss, I feel his hand cup my ass, securing me in his sturdy hold. His soft lips, molding perfectly with mine, and the strong, confident movements of his talented tongue more than prove to me that Logan, Larry, Lance—whatever his name is—most certainly is *not* gay. Far. From. It. His fingers tighten on my ass when he pulls me in closer, and a groan vibrating up from his chest causes a throbbing pull deep down within me.

Someone clearing their throat for a second time registers through my daze. For a split second I feel a bit reluctant to pull away from the kiss. And if I didn't know any better, I'd say Logan feels the same way. That is, until I see his expression. Our eyes lock briefly before mine break away. He looks angry. His forehead is wrinkled and his lips, so adept at kissing me just moments ago, now form a thin line. Then he turns to face Matthew.

I swallow, slightly shake my fuzzy head to compose myself, and turn as well. "Matthew." I force a smile. "How are you?"

Matthew awkwardly reaches up and scratches the back of his head. "I'm good. I've been trying to reach you." He glances over at Logan. "Hey, man. I'm Matt." He reaches out and offers his hand.

Logan takes it. "Logan," he answers smoothly, but it seems like there's a hint of irritation in his voice.

There are a few seconds of uncomfortable silence as I try to clear the kiss—a kiss I can't believe I forced—from my still foggy mind. I attempt but fail to utter a freaking word. Finally, I blurt out, "I'm sorry, I've just been really busy. And I meant to call you, but I lost track and…"

Matthew lifts his hand, palm facing me. "No need to explain. I understand." Disappointment clearly written all over his face, he continues charmingly, "Well, I see that you're busy, so I'll leave you to your day. Take care." He nods, turns around, and walks back down the pathway.

Relief. As guilty as I feel, a rush of relief seeps through me. Matthew, son of the Cunninghams, and I were set up by my mother before Brooke's death. Though I think Matthew is a really sweet guy, I refuse to date anyone my mother tries to set me up with. No, thanks.

A chuckle from beside me forces my attention back to Logan, the talented kisser. He shakes his head in a disapproving way. "Poor guy. I feel kinda bad for him, and I don't even know who the hell he is, other than that his name is Matthew. So what'd you? Break his heart?"

Screw him. He doesn't know me from a can of paint. How dare he judge me? "You don't know me. You can go now."

"Gladly." Logan reaches down and grabs the toolbox. He straightens, takes a step forward, and then quickly turns back around. "Oh, and Jenny—"

"Jenna. J-E-N-N-A," I correct him, placing a hand on my hip.

"That's right, *Jenna*. Hmm." He lets my name sink in for a few seconds. I'm sure he's stirring up judgments by placing me on some type of stereotypical list of his. "Anyhow, you're welcome."

I cross my arms underneath my breasts; he glances down at them, and back at me. "For?" I ask.

"For saving your ass." He lifts two fingers. "Twice I might add." He winks, turns his back to me, and before I can respond, he's walking down the path. I watch him closely. He strides in a powerful and self-assured manner, only slowing when he reaches his truck to place the toolbox in the back. Then he hops in the driver side, looks over at me, and flashes a genuine smile with a slight nod of his head. I fight with all the strength I have not to smile back at him. He chuckles, shaking his head at me, then nods one last time. His truck roars to life, and then he speeds off.

A Truck. Tats. And a cocky attitude.

Typical.

Where the hell is Charlie?

chapter 3

Logan

I lean back against the booth and enjoy the rest of my beer. Our redheaded waitress serves us our food. She must be new. There's no way I'd have missed those large swollen tits and that ass, rounded so perfectly in those skin-tight jeans. Santino wastes no time removing the top bun to his sandwich. He grabs a handful of fries from the basket and piles them on top of his burger. He points at another basket. "Can I have two of your onion rings?" he asks Bryson, who hasn't had a chance to even touch his own food yet.

"Go ahead," Bryson mutters, and he drops his head against his hand. I squint my eyes at my cousin, speculating on what could possibly be wrong with him. He seems out of sorts, lost in his own thoughts. Without hesitation, Santino reaches across and grabs three rings, instead of the two he asked for, and piles them on top of the fries. Then he drowns the entire loaded sandwich with ketchup.

"Anything else, guys?" the redhead asks us, but her eyes are glued on me. She leans over the table, her tits centimeters from my face, and reaches for the empty beer bottles. There's plenty of space for her to maneuver around, yet she chooses to lean toward the very left side of the booth, right where I'm seated. She smells nice. Like clean linen and not the flowery-fruity shit most women overuse.

"I'll take another beer. Thanks," Bryson responds dejectedly.

"Me too," I add. My eyes focus in on the two melons stuffed behind her black fitted, deep-cut shirt. The name of the bar, Wasted, stretches across her chest in big, bold white letters, and I let my stare linger for a few seconds. After all, she's giving me a peep show. When I drag my eyes back to hers, she smiles shyly. She's playing the innocent role now. There's something to be said about a woman that plays bashful, especially when she throws her tits in your face. Lucky for her, I enjoy a good chase, so I play along by flashing a smile and giving her a wink.

She flings her hair off her shoulder, smiles coyly again, and then sways her hips as she leaves to grab our beers. "She so wants you bad, dude," Santino blurts out with a mouthful of his loaded burger.

I ignore his remark by turning my attention to my cousin, who's been sulking the entire twenty minutes since we arrived at the bar. "What the hell's your problem?" I finally ask him. Bryson looks up. His lips twitch as if he's going to speak, but he just shakes his head as a way to say, "Nothing." But I know my cousin. Very well. "It's that bitch again, isn't it?"

He scoffs, "Seriously, Logan? Stop calling her a bitch." He goes into full protective mode over the girl he's been dating for the past year.

The waitress brings back our beers, but I pay her no attention. All of my focus is on Bryson now. Before I respond, I take a long pull of my beer, drinking down patience. "In my book she is."

His nostrils flare. "Look. I know she can sometimes be a bit tough to handle, but don't disrespect her. It's bad enough she realizes that no one likes her."

"What I don't fuckin' understand is why you choose to protect her." I lean in over the table, squaring my shoulders, trying to keep the anger from distorting my features. "She's a bitch, Bry. She treats you like shit all the time. She talks down to you and cheats on you. Then after, she cries for forgiveness and you take her back like a little bitch. And then she does it all over again. That, my cousin, is what I consider a *mega-bitch*."

"She must have a golden pussy," Santino interjects. His face twists in shock, like he can't believe he actually said that out loud. Bryson glares at him.

If she does, it's a wide, golden, disease-infected pussy, I'm sure of it. I wouldn't touch her even if someone threatened to torch my dick until it incinerated and there were nothing left of it but ashes. I know it'd hurt like fucking hell, but I'd sacrifice my precious dick so it would never be near her. I wouldn't care if we were the last two people on earth and the only way to save the fucking planet were to reproduce. My dick would not be touching her. Get the hint? I just don't understand why, out of all the people I know, Bryson continues to put up with her bullshit. She's no good, and my cousin deserves better.

"If we don't change the subject, I'm leaving," Bryson says in a pissy tone. He can be such a damn girl sometimes.

The last thing I want to do is piss him off. We're family. Sure, we've fought lots of times growing up. Even roughed each other up here and there. But for some reason, Bryson has this strong infatuation with Mega Bitch. The last time we had it out over her, he didn't speak to me for months. And we work together, so imagine how fucking awkward that was for everyone else. Especially Santino, who's close friends with the both of us.

"Fine," I say, but then I decide I can't just leave it as is. "Let me say one more thing." Bryson rolls his eyes but nods for me to go on and get it over with. "Mark my words. I will never be that strung out over a girl. Ever."

Bryson shakes his head. "Whatever, man. It'll happen to you sooner or later. And when it does, I'm going to have front-row seats as you pour out your little Logan heart for all to see."

I snort. "That's never happening."

I've dated before, plenty of women. And every time a chick and I made our relationship more than just sex, I was never unfaithful. Why hunt for the meal when it's already cooked and waiting for you at home? That's my motto. But my exes know me. They know I'm not a clinger, nor am I the jealous type, and I couldn't give two fucks what the hell they wear. I'm also not one of those freaky, possessive alpha-male types that demands to know where their woman is at all times. I consider myself laid-back. My exes consider me indifferent.

But that's neither here nor there. All I'm saying is that— okay, maybe I didn't give a shit half the time, but I was always faithful. Did I ever have a true interest in furthering a relationship? No. It just always turned out that way, more from convenience than anything else. It wasn't that I didn't like or respect my girlfriends, I did. I just didn't really want anything more from them. So with that said, shouldn't I at least get some type of honorary certificate or something? It can read, "This honorary certificate goes to Logan Reed, who's not so much of a douchebag after all," and I can pin that shit to my wall.

Santino mumbles something with his mouth full. I don't understand shit he just said. "Come again?" I ask.

He guzzles back his beer to wash down his last bite. "What's this new job we're starting on Monday?"

Bryson cuts in; he knows more than I do. "The McDaniels' property. We're working on a two thousand-square-foot guesthouse beside a pool."

Santino whistles. "I swear these rich people have so much damn money, they can't think of anything else to do with it. Give me some of it; I can put it to good use." He leans back in the booth, smiling at himself.

"Yeah, you'd use it all on girls, food, and booze," I say.

Santino nods. "This is true. Maybe I should start playing the lottery."

"Anyway," Bryson adds, "they want their daughter, Jenna—I think that's her name—involved one hundred percent. Supposedly, it's a surprise for her twenty-second birthday in October. She doesn't realize Mommy and Daddy are basically building her a house."

Santino squints. "In their backyard?" He laughs. "That's not really letting her spread her wings. Is she at least hot?"

Yeah, she's hot. I'm instantly reminded of last night when Jenna and I tongue fucked on her front porch—after I saved her life and she basically bitched me out for it. In a weird way, it was kind of hot. Having a sexy woman in a bikini tell me off and then beg for a kiss? Hot. First impressions are very important, in my opinion. And she put down the fucking wild card on that one. I didn't know what to make of her, but after she implied that I was gay, I had to show her how straight I truly am—nothing against gay guys and all. Everyone has their preferences, and mine are simple: women.

And Jesus Christ, can Jenna kiss. I can still taste and feel her lips. I did it to prove a point, but after our lips made contact I was done for; I couldn't control myself at all. She was hesitant at first—even though it was her idea. She got the push she needed, though, when I shoved my tongue into her mouth. She let out a slight moan, which only fed my fire. My hand found its way to her perfect little ass, and the rest—well, let's just say if that douche, Matthew, never interrupted us, I probably could've gotten her past a few bases right there on her front porch.

"Yeah. She's hot," I answer Santino.

Bryson looks at me. "How would you know? You weren't at the meeting with Pop and me."

"Your father asked me to pick up the toolbox you left behind. Let's just say I was properly introduced to her."

"Ooh," Santino lets out excitedly. I nod at him, letting him know that whatever thoughts he's thinking right now may or may not be true, depending how far his thoughts are going.

"Logan, you know the rules." Bryson kills the slight buzz I have from my third beer. He always has to turn his ethical-professional-bullshit cap on.

"Yeah, yeah." I wave him off. This night is going nowhere. I look around the place and spot the redhead, who's leaning against the bar, staring directly at me. She waves with a smile. I grin back and stand. "I'll be back," I tell Bryson and Santino and head her way.

"I can't help but notice we have a problem." I slide onto a stool right next to her and get an eyeful of those big—

"Oh? And what is that?" She says in a sexy tone, looking straight ahead.

"We can't keep our eyes off each other."

Redhead's back is flush against the bar. A smile creeps up the corner of her lips. Turning her head, she looks at me.

"That is a problem. What are you going to do about it?"

I lean in closer. "I think I have a few things in mind. What time does your shift end?"

She doesn't blink. Leaning in fully to me, her lips almost touch mine. "In a half hour," she breathes out.

"A half hour it is then."

"Your orders are ready, Tammy," Tony says from behind the bar. Redhead, who now has a name, turns around and grabs the filled tray. She winks and then carries on.

I check her out as she walks away before straightening in my seat to face Tony. Tony is Uncle George's good friend and owner of this small bar. Tony shakes his head at my victory grin. "You're in the wrong business, son." He tosses a towel, aiming for my face, but I catch it in time.

"Yeah, and what kind of business should I be in?"

His stubby hands lay flat on top of the bar. "Male escort."

We both chuckle at this. It's ridiculous. "You have to be a pretty boy for that shit. I'm far from it."

"You'd be surprised. More and more girls are into this." He waves a hand between us, shrugging in the process. "Scruffy, bad boy, tattoos. It's a cliché role."

I snort. "Is that what I am? A walking cliché?" I shake it off. "I have sex for pleasure, not for money."

"Touché. How are you guys getting home?" he asks while removing the cap of a summer lager. He passes it to me and I tilt the bottle in salute to show my gratitude before taking a sip.

"Santino drove with Bryson. I have my truck."

"Are you guys all right to drive?" I grip the beer bottle, trying to mask my irritation.

I was in a good mood until he asked that question. I know this is what Tony does. He makes sure we're okay. He's been here for most of our lives and cares for my family—especially Bryson and me—as if we're his own. But with the two-year anniversary of my brother's death right around the corner, I feel offended. Maybe it's the three beers kicking in or the fact that I'm still fucking annoyed due to the mega-bitch convo with Bryson. I'm not exactly sure what it is, but my emotions are quickly stirring. "I'm not Sean," I finally blurt out, staring straight ahead and clenching my fist on the bar.

Tony's features transform into shock. "I didn't mean it that way, son. You know I wouldn't. I'm just looking out for you guys. I would never cross that line, Logan. I hope you know that, right?"

Fuck me. I feel like an even bigger douche bag. I guess I don't deserve the honorary certificate after all. I wave my hand. "Yeah, I know. Don't worry about it. That was out of line for me to say. I'm sorry, Tony."

I thank him for the beer again, return to the booth with the other guys, and sip on the rest of my last beer until Tammy's shift is over.

What the hell! This time I royally screwed up. My uncle is going to kill me. Even after the long speech he gave me a few days ago, I just can't listen, can I? "You have to be more responsible," he said. "You can't have your cake and eat it too," he said. "Simply put, you need to grow the hell up, Logan." I'm sure drinking the entire weekend and picking up a girl from the bar—who I fucked until she'd forgotten her own name and is currently sleeping in my bed at this very moment—was not part of his let's-save-Logan speech.

Grunting, I run a hand over my face, hop out of bed, and

toss on jeans and the first T-shirt that doesn't smell. Tammy, from the bar, is still here. I'm already late, so I quickly prod at her shoulder. "Get up."

She stretches with a yawn. "What time is it?"

I walk back into the room with her clothes. "It's time for you to leave," I say, tossing her things on top of the bed.

She flashes her eyes open and groans, quickly shutting them again. "Ah, shut off the light!"

"No lights are on. That's daylight coming in. I need you to get up and leave. I'm running late for work. Hurry up."

Tammy sluggishly sits up, places her arms through the sleeve of her shirt, and narrows her stare at me. "Could you be any ruder?"

"Please," I say. There. Is that polite enough for her? If it were any other day, I would've let her stay awhile. I would've even bought her breakfast, but if I'm any later, my uncle will fire me for sure this time.

Ten minutes later, I hop into my truck, start the engine, and head for Haddonfield, New Jersey. As I enter I-95 from the Woodhaven ramp, my phone goes off. Shit. It's Bryson. "What's up?" I answer, merging into the left lane.

"Where the hell are you?"

"I know." I glance in my rearview mirror and then back to the road ahead. "I'm running late." My foot presses down on the gas pedal. It's over a forty-five minute drive to Haddonfield from Philly, depending on traffic. I need to speed the hell up.

"You're fucking lucky Dad's not here. He had a consultation for another job in Royersford this morning. He just texted me that he's finishing up now and will be on his way. I suggest you get here—fast—before he does."

There is a God. I gun it, pushing the speedometer to

almost ninety. "Thanks, Bry. I owe you one."

A snort erupts through the speaker. "Yeah, one of many. And you better not be speeding. If you lose your license again, I won't be your personal chauffeur this time."

I let him slide on that one and we end our call. Over the past couple years Bryson has done more for me than anyone else. He's more than just my cousin; he's my brother and best friend. We grew up living next door to each other, learning the importance of family from an early age. After Sean died, our relationship could have gone either way, but thanks to Bryson's support and loyalty, we're closer than ever.

Finally, I reach the McDaniels' home and pull into their massive driveway. I cut the engine off, hop out of the truck, and hustle toward the back of the house. I'm walking along a pathway that leads past the scandalous front porch—just the sight of which brings a smug grin to my face—around a small pond, and through a landscaped grove of trees when I nearly trip over my own two feet and face-plant onto the perfectly manicured lawn.

The source of my smug grin only moments before is right ahead of me, and she hasn't seen me yet. Jenna. Her back is to me as she makes her way down the path, so I do what any guy would do and take a moment to appreciate what's in front of me. Her cinnamon hair is tossed in a high bun on top of her head and a loose blue shirt falls off her left shoulder. Very tight jean shorts reveal the curves of her very fine, perfectly shaped ass. An ass I had the pleasure of groping just a few days ago. She seems to struggle with carrying a large box. I, being the gentleman I choose to be at times, jog to catch up with her, but before I can reach her, the box slips from her hands, spilling all the contents to the ground.

"Fuck!" she shouts. Her head swivels as she surveys the

mess, and she huffs once before bending over to pick up what appear to be painting supplies.

I smile. She's in the perfect position for me to fully check her out. So I do. Again. After my peep show, I kneel down and grab a few paintbrushes from the ground. "I wouldn't have expected the first word popping out of your mouth to be fuck. You just don't seem like that kind of girl."

Brown eyes pin mine. "Yeah? And what kind of girl do I seem to be?" Her eyes tell me she's amused, but her tone tells me otherwise. Does she ever smile? This is the second time I've seen her, and both times she's given me dirty looks—attractive dirty looks, but dirty looks all the same.

My lips form a lopsided grin. "Hmm...dammit. Yeah." I nod, sure of my assessment. "You seem more like a dammit kind of girl."

Jenna rolls her eyes. She quickly gathers the rest of her art supplies and tosses them into the box before standing and resting the package on her left hip. "Too bad you don't know two fucks about me."

I laugh. I have a major smartass on my hands. That's okay; it's just going to take a little longer to lighten this one up a bit.

I've been around a lot of women, so I'm able to tell one type apart from another. Jenna's type is daring. They're smart, snarky wiseasses. They live for a challenge and love being right. But they're also—no matter what—women. And women can be sweet-talked at any moment.

I lean into her. She steps back. I smile.

There's just enough sun to fully take her in. Jenna's eyes, *man*, they're something. It's not the cute button nose, the soft, plump lips that I had the pleasure of tasting, or the even, golden skin tone that compels me. All of these features are

E.L. MONTES

striking, sure, but her eyes... Jenna's eyes are exotic, stunning. There seems to be an untold story hidden behind those large, almond-shaped beauties. The mystery of those eyes...

I lean my head in close to her. Really close. Jenna's lashes flutter, with wide eyes stunned. An extensive grin spreads across my face. "Ah, but if my memory serves me correctly, I know exactly how you taste." Her breath catches; she seems to be at a loss for words. Score. I lift my hand and twirl one of the paintbrushes I'm still holding. "And it seems to me that I just learned you like to paint." Her eyes narrow and her nostrils lightly flare as she snatches the brush out of my hand. She opens her mouth to say something but shuts it when we hear someone else call my name.

"Logan?" Bryson walks up beside us. Eyes still on Jenna, I straighten my shoulders, flash her a knowing grin, and then turn to face my cousin.

"What's up?"

He raises a questioning brow and glances over at Jenna. "Everything okay?"

"Yeah. Let's get to work." I clasp his shoulder and start walking, guiding him toward the site.

"What was that about?" he asks quietly.

I turn my head and look at Jenna who's still standing there breathing heavily with the box glued to her hip. I wink at her and turn right back around. "Nothing. I was just helping her with a few things she accidently dropped."

He grips my shoulder and leans in. "Logan, not here. This is work. Keep it like that. You understand?"

I shrug off his hold. I know what he means. I don't like it, but I understand. "Yeah, I understand."

It's not like we'd have more than just that one kiss on her front porch anyway.

44

chapter 4

Jenna

Logan looks back at me as he walks away with the other contractor. He shoots me a wink before turning his attention back to the path. "Nothing. I was just helping her with a few things she accidently dropped," I hear him say.

Exactly. *Nothing* is going on between us, and Logan better keep that in mind the next time he invades my personal space. A few days ago, I asked for it; I knew what I was getting myself into. Well, I wasn't expecting for his kiss to be so powerful and scorching hot. Still, that was on my terms. I was in control. Sort of. I couldn't foresee that I would enjoy the taste of him, the smell of him, the way he held me firmly against his chest, how strong his arms felt wrapped securely around me, or how, for a short moment within that one kiss, I forgot who I was. The world around us was completely still. I was lost in the arms of a complete stranger. That's what bothers me most: him. He bothers me. I know nothing about him, so how the hell could he make me feel so alive, so at peace, so...safe?

It's infuriating, not to mention unrealistic. The whole thing must have been a fluke brought on by the anxiety of everything that occurred prior to seeing him: the scene in Dr. Rosario's office the day before, losing the bracelet, him diving into the pool, Matthew walking up when he was the last person in the world I wanted to see. Logan was there, and I took advantage of that by kissing him. But I kissed him to get rid of Matthew; I didn't realize kissing him would rid me of all my thoughts as well.

The stubble of his growing beard was rough, yet the kiss felt soft.

His arms were confident, yet I felt vulnerable in his hold.

His touch was unfamiliar, yet it felt right within the split seconds of that kiss.

The memory shivers through me. I shake it off, adjust the box in my hands, and continue on my route toward the shed.

Thirty minutes later, I'm standing before three easels, all holding a different canvas painting. Old ones, of course, since I still can't find the desire to actually create anything. Maybe by taking time to admire my previous work, I'll find a sense of inspiration again. All three of the pieces in front of me have a sacred place in my heart. Each has its own story, its own venture and journey, which represents a specific time and place in my life.

My eyes settle on the first one and I chuckle softly. It's one of my very first pieces. For my tenth birthday, my father purchased my first art set, complete with several sized canvases, paintbrushes, and colors.

As any little girl would, I hugged my father tightly, shouted my thanks, and ran to my room to begin my artistic adventure. I was never a pink hearts and flowers kind of girl, so hours later, I presented him with what I thought at the time was a masterpiece. Splashes of red and orange with swirls of grey and blue colored the canvas. My father ogled the small painting with seriousness reserved for courtrooms and boardrooms. I stood before him with my hands clenched behind me, rocking in place. The waiting was excruciating for a ten-year-old. I remember thinking: *Will he like it? Does he think it's hideous? Am I good enough?* Those feelings instantly faded the moment my father looked at me with wide brown eyes and a genuine smile. "It's the best painting I've ever seen."

I doubt it was the best, but it made my heart warm at the thought. A month before that same birthday, he took me to an art show where I witnessed the artist create her work from the start. Brooke was sick with a cold and unfortunately stayed home. My father held my hand as I watched closely with wide eyes from behind a rope. My mother stood beside my father with her hands folded neatly before her. The artist, in her safe, small circle, stared at the canvas intensely for what seemed like hours. Then she began to scream and shout, dipping the brushes into different colored containers and splashing them against her large canvas.

The entire drive home, my mother nagged that the show was a waste, that the performance was awkward and bizarre. I didn't know it then, but looking back now, I guess I'm just as awkward and bizarre as that artist was. When her face grew angry as she tossed the red tint, I felt her *pain*. When her tear-filled eyes grew narrow as she splashed black, I felt her *emptiness*. When she stood before her finished work, breathing rapidly with eyes shut, blue paint still dripping off the edge of the canvas, I felt her *loneliness*.

I guess my first piece was an attempt to mimic hers because I felt every little bit of her emotions. As a child, I really didn't know what those emotions meant, but I know I felt each one acutely.

As I remember every detail of the second painting, goose bumps rise on my arms and I cross them in an attempt to hug myself. This image was inspired by the first and only love of my life. Grey covers the entire sixteen by twenty inch canvas. Red with the hint of a few white strokes creates two faces—a masculine profile staring down at a feminine face. She's afraid and slipping away from everything and everyone, but the moment her eyes lock with his, she instantly feels safe, no longer in the dark world she's lived in all her young life.

At the age of seventeen, I was more than just the problem child that my mother couldn't handle. Suspension after suspension from my fair share of girl fights—at the elite private school my parents sent me to—didn't place me anywhere near the Daughter of the Year category. After a fight with Blair Bitch, my archenemy, I was sent on one of many visits to the principal's office. My hair disheveled and face steamed in anger, I sat and waited for my turn to receive my punishment.

As I tried to calm myself, legs shaking and fingers tapping, the hall doors opened. Dark nearly black eyes pinned mine. They met me at eye level as the owner of those eyes sat beside me. He nodded, and his unkempt hair fell over his right brow. "So what're you in for?" he asked. I answered, giving him every detail of my encounter with Blair. He burst into laughter and I joined in. The best part? He blurted, "The bitch deserved it." The rest is history.

But *history* is exactly that.

I fell hard for Eric. He gave me what every girl desired—a sense of feeling loved. I had no doubt in my mind that Eric loved me. I felt it with every thread of my being. We were young and naive. I surrendered myself to him one hundred percent—mind, body, and soul. I gave him all of me. My first experiences in many aspects of my life were with Eric. His love, his touches and caresses… It was more than just the passion he poured out to me, though, that made me love him. Eric understood me, just like Brooke. He didn't judge me or look at me how others did.

Not until he witnessed one of my episodes. It was in the beginning stage, before I even knew what was wrong with me. I was afraid, and my mind was going crazy with racing thoughts and voices. I questioned everyone that approached and everything that surrounded me. Eric couldn't handle it. It scared the hell out of him. Instead of helping me through it, instead of showing that his love for me was true, he left me. Alone. When I was at my worst.

That was when I vowed to never let others, especially those who don't truly know me, see me in a weak state.

I blink the blurriness out of my eyes and allow my tears to roam free. *I'm alone in this shed. There's no one watching*, I remind myself. My lip begins to quiver as I edge closer to the third painting. I swallow and stare blankly at the unfinished piece. This was the last time I connected a brush to canvas. It was a month after Brooke's death and I needed to pour out my anger the only way I knew how. But that was the day of my first hallucination.

When you lose the only person who made sense in your life, the only person who helped you fight your battles, the one who helped you with your struggles, the only person you felt sane around, your entire world comes crashing down. And that's not even the best description. You become vacant, hollow. You can't breathe. The world around you is a complete haze; nothing is clear anymore. You're constantly fighting to live

because you were only truly living when they were around.

How can she be gone? One day Brooke was here, in this very room, laughing and teasing me about my eye shadow being too dark. Then the next day, she's gone, never able to share that smile on her face with the world ever again. She didn't deserve it. I hate what they did to her. Hate it.

The fresh memory stabs my thoughts, the way she was found, left for dead. I feel nauseated. Quickly, I grab the trash can by the desk, bend over, and dry heave into it. There isn't much coming out of me since I've barely eaten anything in weeks. Once I think I'm done, I place the can aside, sniff back my tears, and stand. The easel by my bedroom window is calling me, the blank canvas begging me to pour out my heart. With shaky legs and an unsettled stomach, I manage the short walk across the room. My fingers tremble as I reach for a brush, mix the white and black pigment, and slowly raise it to the canvas.

Before I know it, the brush is gliding along, creating. A dark grey sky represents my new life, how it'll never be sunny again. Reddish tones develop into an ocean, a storm. The red represents my pain and suffering. The storm represents my anger. Anger because she'll never live to see graduation, to walk down the aisle and have the wedding she always dreamed of. She'll never find love or bear children of her own. These things were taken from her.

Full-blown tears stream down my face, but even through my blurry vision I continue the strokes of the brush. In midstride, a low, familiar voice stops me in my tracks. "Jenna." Hair on the back of my neck stands on end. A chill roars through me, and I shake my head. No. This can't be happening. I've heard voices before, unknown voices. But this one is far too familiar. Slowly I turn to face it. My body shudders as all of the air from my lungs disappears. *Brooke. Brooke is sitting on the edge of my bed.* She looks sad, helpless.

I try to find a way to breathe as she stands. *"It's okay, Jenna. I'm here."* Brooke reaches out a hand. I stare at it in disbelief.

How can... How is this even... I can't even blurt out a simple thought.

"Brooke?" I swipe away the tears so I can have a better look. *Even if she isn't real, I get to have this, but I have no idea for how long.* "How are—" I wet my lips, soaking in this moment. "You're alive?"

She nods gently. "I can be, if you let me."

"What does that mean? Of course I'll let you. I want you alive, Brooke. I've missed you so much. I love you. Let's tell Mom and Dad." I reach out to her, but she pulls back and shakes her head. "What's wrong, Brooke? They'll be happy you're here and safe. We thought we lost you."

"No. They can't know. This has to be our little secret."

My brows furrow in confusion. "Brooke, they're devastated. They argue all the time. Mom won't stop crying, and Dad is barely home anymore. We need you. You're the one that kept this family together. Please."

"I'm sorry, Jenna. I can't do that."

"Why?"

"Because then they'll lose both daughters."

"What?" I blink, trying to make sense of what she said, and she's gone. Just like that. *Where did she go?* I look around anxiously, searching for her in the closet, behind the curtain, under the bed. *I had a small taste of having her back and now she's gone. Again. Maybe she changed her mind? Maybe she ran off to tell Mom and Dad. Excitement rushes through me. I* open the door and run down the hall, entering every open door and leaving just as quickly when I don't see her. I jog down the staircase, rushing to my father's office. My parents are in here, but there's no Brooke.

"Sweetheart, are you okay?" My father searches me with his eyes from behind his desk. He looks worried, like he can sense my anxiety.

"Yeah," I whisper as I glance at my mother. She's standing beside him with a document in her hand.

"Can we help you?" My mother asks warily.

"Uh…" I step forward and dart my eyes around, but still no Brooke. I focus back on them, on their narrowed, curious eyes. My lips are dry, so I moisten them before asking, "Did you see her?"

My mother places the document down on top of the desk. "See who?"

"Brooke." At the sound of Brooke's name my mother's eyes change and I instantly regret saying anything.

"Jenna." My father stands, his voice eerily calm. "What are you saying?"

Oh God, oh God, oh God. Can they handle it? What if they don't believe me? Oh God. My eyes flash from my father to my mother and back to my father in quick succession. "Brooke was here. She's alive."

"That's enough!" Mom screams, startling both my father and me, and before we know it she's coming after me. Dad grips her arm to stop her. With angry eyes, she turns her head and glares at him. "I'm tired of this, Gregory! Sick and tired." Her lips tremble as she tries to pull away from him. I stand frozen, tears running down my cheeks. "Don't you see it? It's painful enough to go through this grief, but I will not stand by and have her…" She raises her hand in my direction, pointing *at me as she locks her furious eyes on mine. "Have her lie for attention. Brooke deserves better than that."*

Attention?

"Laura." Dad pulls Mom closer, cages her face with both hands, and forces her to stare back at him. "She's sick, honey."

Sick?

Mom bursts into tears, shakes off Dads grip, and runs out of the office.

"Daddy," I cry. Oh God, I feel sick again. "What's wrong with me?"

"Oh, baby." In three strides he's in front of me, holding me in his arms and trying to protect me from all harm. I bury my face in his chest, shut my eyes, and try to picture myself as a five-year-old little girl again—when my father's arms were the safest place to be. Where in his arms I felt free from harm, like nothing could take me away. As hard as I try, I'm not that little girl anymore, and nothing can save me from me. I break down and allow the pain of the last thirty days to pour out onto my father's neatly pressed shirt.

"Why is this happening to me?" My voice is muffled against his chest.

He pulls me in tighter, rocks me in his arms, and hushes me to sleep.

Hours have gone by. I'm lost in the past as I stare at the last incomplete canvas. I remember every detail of that day, though I've tried to forget it. That's the day I stopped painting. It brought back too many memories, too much pain—pain that I don't want to resurface. How does Dr. Rosario expect me to start again and get better if painting is the very reason it all began? The hallucinations didn't stop because I stopped painting. They still come and go, leaving confusion and anxiety in their wake. And not all of my hallucinations are of Brooke— I have scarier ones too. I'm just afraid if I paint again, my condition will worsen. Sometimes I can't figure out why I'm like this. Yeah, yeah, it's a chemical imbalance, but it's also hereditary. My grandmother is schizophrenic. It skipped my mother and jumped right to me.

Footsteps and the clearing of a throat alert me that I'm no longer alone. I try to pull myself together by running my hands over my face and wiping away any smudged liner left behind by my tears. With a forced smile, I straighten my shoulders and turn to face...*him*. "Are you lost?" I ask.

Logan's smile fades, but I don't think it's due to my rudeness. "Are you okay? You look like you've been crying."

"Something was caught in my eye." I wave it off as if it's nothing. Crossing my arms, I raise a brow. "Again, can I help you?"

He's hesitant at first, as if he doesn't want to let it go, but he shakes his head and moves on. "By any chance do you have a measuring tape?"

"Really? You're the contractor. Shouldn't you be a bit more prepared?"

The corner of his lip tugs into a tiny grin, but clearly he seems to be annoyed. "Yeah, you're right. It's stupid, actually. We brought all the main equipment needed for today, but Santino forgot to pack the box with our measuring tapes. The one I had just broke. We just figured we'd ask before running off to the nearest—" He pauses and then waves a hand. "You know what, forget I asked. Sorry to waste your time." Logan turns to walk out.

Well crap. Can I be any bitchier? "Wait," I blurt out. He turns around to face me. "I think my father may have one in one of these boxes." I point toward the left side of the room to a shelf filled with equipment and neatly stacked boxes. To make up for being a complete bitch, I walk over and begin searching through some of the boxes. I can hear his footsteps move around behind me.

"These are good. Did you paint them?"

Small talk. I despise small talk. What's the point? Why can't he just stand here, wait for me to locate this damn object, and be on his way? "Yeah, they're mine," I mumble.

"Pretty cool," he replies. Finally, I find the measuring tape. I straighten and turn to face him. He's directly in front of the third painting. With his head tilted, he crosses his arms and examines it. "This one isn't finished. Are you working on it?"

"Here it is!" I shove my arm out, jabbing at the air impatiently. Logan turns around. His eyes land on my hand, and he smiles before looking back up at me.

He takes a few easy strides in my direction. Now before me, he reaches out and grabs the measuring tape. His hand covers mine, fingers slightly gripping my hold. I look up at him. A hint of worry clouds over his stormy eyes. "Are you sure you're okay?" I study him, watching him cautiously. Why does it matter to him if I'm okay or not? He doesn't know me. I shouldn't be any of his concern. Maybe he genuinely cares for others. Our hands are still clamped together, and he steps in closer. "Jenna, I want to apologize about earlier."

"About invading my personal space?" I ask a bit harsher than necessary, hoping it covers up my heavy breathing. I can't help it. Something about his strong, broad build overwhelms me.

He flashes a gorgeous crooked grin. "Well, yeah. I'd also like to talk about that kiss."

I swallow. My throat is really dry, and my heart rate is spiking. "Um, yeah. I'm sorry about the kiss. It was a mistake."

His thumb caresses the back of my hand, still locked onto the damn measuring tape. "Are you sure?"

"Sure about what?" I'm suddenly lost in his stormy blue eyes.

"About the kiss being a mist—"

"Well, well, well. What do we have here?" Logan and I quickly turn our heads toward the voice. It belongs to Charlie, who's casually leaning against the door to the shed with her arms crossed. A mischievous grin is plastered to her face. "Please, don't let me interrupt. I'm kind of enjoying the show." She winks at Logan. "Hey, hot stuff."

I shove the measuring tape into his chest, step back, and face Charlie. "There's nothing to interrupt. Logan was just leaving." Although I'm staring directly at Charlie, I can feel Logan's eyes on me. It's quite distracting. I exhale deeply, cross my arms, square my shoulders, and try to focus on my friend, who seems to be enjoying my discomfort far too much.

"Yeah, thanks for the tape. I'll get back to work," Logan says. As he moves by me, I momentarily shut my eyes and allow myself to breathe in his lingering scent. He leaves a trail, a mixture of fresh linen with a hint of spice. It's not as strong as two days ago—when his arms were wrapped around me and his lips hovered over mine as our tongues twirled in slow circular motions—but it's still there, slowly lulling me into a trance.

"Oh, you have it bad, girly," Charlie utters. I flash my eyes open, searching around. I sigh in relief, realizing Logan's no longer in the shed. My eyes meet Charlie's as she walks toward me with her blonde curls bouncing around her cherubic face. She's chuckling at my dumbfounded expression. "I don't blame you, though. He's tall, hot as all hell, and did you see those arms?" She nods approvingly. "I bet he can lift you up in two split seconds and fuck the hell out of you in midair. Air humping. No wall to hold you up or anything. Mmmhmm." She crosses her arms over her chest, steps in front of me, and gives me a stare down. "And why are you dressed in lounge gear?"

"Charlie," I warn.

"Jenna." She mimics my tone and expression perfectly. I shake my head and turn away, heading for the open box by the first easel. I start packing up the items on the floor. "What's up?" I ask.

"We had plans for a girls' lunch date. Please don't tell me you forgot again?"

Crap. I did. My mind was too busy focusing on these paintings and the memories that resurfaced. I lost track of time. "I'm sorry, Charlie. It's been a rough day. We can still go out, have a late lunch?"

I look beside me. She's nodding, but her main focus is on my paintings, which are still sitting on the easels. "Sure. Late lunch sounds good." She turns her head to meet my gaze. "Want to talk about this?" Charlie asks, thumbing the paintings. She knows exactly what caused my rough day.

"Not today." I brush off the topic. I never want to talk about it. Charlie understands me and I appreciate her for that. There are times I do need to get a few things off my chest, things that are too difficult to bear on my own. But as I said to Charlie, not today. I can handle it on my own. "I'm going to shower and dress. Will you be okay hanging around until then?"

She waves me off. "Yeah, yeah. Go, will ya! I'm starving."

Once I finish a quick shower, I dress down in skinny jeans, a white fitted T, and royal blue flats. Most days I wouldn't care if my hair were tossed up in a messy ponytail or bun and I had no makeup on, but Charlie's attire is a bit over-the-top. What the hell? Maybe spending a little extra time on my hair and makeup will make up for my lack of fashion, next to Charlie, of course.

Afterward, I go downstairs in search of Charlie, but no one's around. I'm sure my mother's off shopping, and my father is definitely working. I go out back to see if Charlie is lounging on the patio. Not only is she out here, but she's at the construction site by the pool—where the guys are—giggling at something one of them said.

They must be loving the little blonde bombshell in her tight—and very short—little khaki dress and high gold strappy heels.

As I approach them, I can hear Charlie a bit clearer. In a flirtatious tone she utters, "Oh, you guys are too funny." The guys around her are all smiling and enjoying her company, as usual. I don't blame them; she's a beautiful girl. If I went that way, I'd probably be all over her as well. I look around and spot Logan. He's a bit farther away from the crowd with Bryson. They both have a shovel in hand. Bryson is digging into the ground while Logan stands in front of him, using his shovel as a support to lean against. They're in their own little world, laughing about something.

Logan looks up and we briefly lock eyes. He nods once at me, smiles, and then turns his head back to Bryson, continuing their conversation. It's a small gesture, but it makes me feel something—a flutter in my stomach. I shake off the feeling, clear my throat, and reach my hand out, tapping a finger on Charlie's shoulder. She turns with a smile. "There you are. Ready?"

"Yep."

"Cool." She adjusts the owl-shaped charm hanging on her gold necklace. She never takes it off. It was a gift from Brooke in celebration of their ten-year friendship. It reminds me of my bracelet, which is still missing from two nights ago. My chest pains at my carelessness, but I snap out of it before I start to spiral. Charlie looks over her shoulder and waves at the three men who were eating up her charm.

"Think about it!" One of the three, a good-looking, olive complexioned guy with black hair and dark eyes, points at her.

Charlie begins to walk backward away from the guys. With a giggle, she shrugs both shoulders. "We shall see." In one bouncy jump, she turns around. Her extremely cheesy grin spreads wider as she loops her arm through mine.

I wait until we're a bit farther from the site, closer to the front of the house, before asking, "What was that about?"

"Oh my God, did you see him? His name is Santino Ramirez. He was born in Puerto Rico, but raised in Philly. That's why he doesn't have the Spanish accent. Anyway, he's twenty-seven, no kids, and fucking hot. Boom!" I shake my head as we reach her car. I'm pretty certain she learned his entire life story in the thirty minutes it took me to get ready. She unlocks the doors and we hop into her Volkswagen. As I'm sliding into the passenger seat, she adds, "And, I've never been with a Latino before." Her brows wiggle. "I hear they're..." She slams the driver side door, settles in her seat, and spreads her hands widely apart, giving me an estimated length.

"Do you think of anything else?" She's clearly delusional. I swear Charlie should've been a guy. No one would ever think this tiny blonde woman would come up with half the crap that comes out her mouth. Ever.

Charlie starts the engine, snaps on her seat belt, then turns to look at me before leaving the driveway. "What do you mean?"

"Well, sex. Do you ever think of anything other than sex?"

Her facial expression says it all. It's as if I've offended her. I bite back a laugh. Charlie shakes her head, presses her foot on the gas, and takes off. "Jenna, we discussed this before. Some women read for entertainment. I prefer sex."

"You know, there are smut novels," I say.

"Yes, but I tried reading that stuff. I just get hornier, and then I'm all over the next guy. I need to calm my whoring down to a certain extent. If not, I'll be known as 'the One Who Sleeps With All.'"

She doesn't make sense half the time. I take a peek at her profile. "You do realize you're already known as 'the One Who Sleeps With All,' right?"

Charlie rolls her eyes. "That was so last year. I've changed a lot since then." I can't help it. This time I burst into a hard laugh. "What?" she asks. I can't answer through my laughing. "Oh whatever, Jenna. I can't help it. It's the RPD."

RPD—also known as Rapid Pussy Disorder. The term was made up by Charlie herself. She claims that even simple things like the fine scent of a man cause her pussy to twerk in a rapid motion. Rapid Pussy Disorder. Yeah, I know. It's stupid, but she swears it's true.

Finally calm, I ask, "So what did he mean by 'think about it?'"

"Who? Santino?" She makes a left and then a right at the next corner. "Oh, he gave me this." She reaches into her purse and hands me an orange flyer.

"It's a party," I respond, looking over the bold letters.

YOU'RE INVITED TO THE ANNUAL
REEDS' LAKE HOUSE SUMMER WEEKEND BASH
June 14-16
Beer. Beer. And more Beer.
Let's Party!

"Yep. And we're going."

My head jerks in her direction. "What! No, we're not going."

"Oh, come on!" she pleads. "It'll be fun. We'll be together."

"No. And don't roll your eyes at me."

"You deserve a double eye roll! You need to get out more."

This is ridiculous. We don't know any of these guys, but she wants to go to a lake house and party with them—for an entire weekend? "I get out, Charlie."

"Oh, yeah? When?"

"I'm out now, aren't I?"

She groans. "This doesn't count and you know it."

With my arms crossed, I lean back in the seat and stare out the window. "Sorry, but I'm not budging on this one. No."

She huffs one last time and pulls into the parking lot of our favorite local restaurant.

And that's the end of that conversation.

chapter 5

Jenna

The one person my mother tried to keep Brooke and me away from was my grandmother. She felt it was the only way we wouldn't find out the truth—the truth of her past. But after I received my schizoaffective diagnosis, she had no choice. Ultimately, coming clean about all of the mental health history in the family was her only option.

Born and raised in Philadelphia as an only child, my mother came from nothing. She loved her father dearly. He used to work endless hours as a mechanic to support his mentally ill wife. When my mother was only ten, her mother was admitted to a psych ward and diagnosed with schizophrenia after stabbing her husband—yes, my grandmother attempted to murder my grandfather because the voices in her head told her to. After Mom was left with no mother of her own, she fought to make sure she'd never have to go through the turmoil of her childhood ever again. She vowed to stay away from anything that remotely reminded her of her mother's illness.

Until me, that is. Until I inherited the fucking crazy gene. Mom didn't have to say it; the expression on her face every time she looked at me explained it all. Her every glance was filled with disgust, hurt, and disapproval. She tried to change after Brooke was gone, desperate to build a relationship with me, but by that time it was too late. I didn't need her. I needed Brooke.

Three months before Brooke's death, we went in search of our grandmother. Mom refused to give us any information as to which facility she was housed in. Brooke researched endless hours until we found her. She did it more for me than for herself. Brooke knew how difficult it was for me to go through this alone. Yes, I had her by my side every step of the way, but no one truly understood the demons that I fought in my head: *Every. Single. Day.* I needed answers. The only way we felt we could find them was by finding her.

But even after my first visit with my grandmother over ten months ago, I didn't find answers. I still haven't. Every time I come here, I hope to leave with some type of reason as to why I am the way I am, but I leave just as confused as I entered. My grandmother lives at The Brandy Mental Health Facility. It houses people with mental disorders who are incapable of taking care of themselves, or are a threat to themselves or those around them. Instead of stopping my visits after Brooke passed, something compelled me to keep coming on my own. Knowing that I'm no different than her, facing the harsh reality that she is, in fact, all alone in here frightens me.

It could be me sitting in that chair with my head bowed low and my body slumped from all the mind-numbing drugs. Her eyes may be the most disconcerting thing about her. They're empty, lost in the world inside of her. Soft music plays in the background of the visiting room. Anxiously, my eyes leave my grandmother and roam the area. There are only ten patients in the room—all different ages and genders—and my eyes zoom in on one in particular. She looks so young, maybe late teens. Long, dark locks of her hair spill over her shoulders. She's curled up in a ball on the chair, legs pulled to her chest, arms wrapped around them. Her face is buried in her legs, but her eyes peek out above her knees.

The girl rocks in place, humming along with the soft tune. A woman sits in front of her, chatting away. I assume this is her mother. I wonder what's going through the young girl's mind. Is she terrified that this may always be her life? At such a young age, does she feel nonexistent, even though she's clearly here? Does she see how everyone around her looks at her as if she's crazy, even when they claim they don't? Is she watching everyone else live a normal life while she's stuck in a world she sees and hears differently? I feel for her immensely. I remember being her age and having these thoughts. I still have these thoughts.

"W-well, h-hello, Jenna. How are you?" I hear from behind me. Turning in my seat, I spot Thomas.

I smile at him. "I'm doing well, Thomas. How are you?"

He grins brightly. Blinking rapidly, he responds, "I-I'm d-doing well. My son is v-visiting me today." Thomas has been a patient here for a few years. When I first came to see my grandmother, he was in the visiting room. Every day he waits patiently for his son to come, but it never happens. "W-want to play a game with me?" he stutters.

"I wish I could, but I'll be leaving soon. I have an appointment."

The sad expression on his face breaks my heart. "O-okay. M-maybe next time?"

For some reason, I have a soft spot for Thomas. I take a quick look at my grandmother, who's still out of it due to the medication they gave her. It's either sit here and watch her sleep for the last fifteen minutes of my visit or put it to good use and spend it with Thomas. "Cards?" I suggest to Thomas. His face lights up, nodding in excitement like a kid instead of a fifty-year-old man. He grabs a deck of cards from the table beside him and begins to shuffle.

Dr. Rosario's office is empty as I enter, so she takes me in right away. I watch her as she looks over my file. Her dark hair, highlighted with shades of caramel, is twisted into a low bun. Square-shaped designer glasses frame her thin face perfectly. Dr. Rosario crosses her right leg over her left, dangling her three-inch platform shoe in place.

She reminds me of the nurses that take care of the patients where my grandmother lives. They're good at what they do, sure, but they're detached, clinical. They do their jobs and go through the motions. They don't really care about their patients. And Dr. Rosario doesn't really care about me. Everything about her and this office screams she doesn't give a crap about my condition. She cares about the money my condition bestows upon her. She's paid very well by my parents to "treat" me. More like keep everything hush-hush.

Everyone from family to friends thinks I'm in therapy because I need to talk about my feelings after Brooke's death. None of them know I've been in therapy practically all my life. If word got out that the McDaniels' precious little girl, the only one they have left, is screwed up in the head, rumors would spread rapidly. And my mother wouldn't want that.

Dr. Rosario clears her throat. Lifting her head, she stares at me through her glasses. "Jenna, how was your weekend?"

"Good," I respond.

She smiles. "Did you do anything interesting?"

"No."

"Nothing?"

"No," I answer again.

There's an awkward few seconds of silence. She finally huffs out, "Jenna, in order for this to work out, you need to be a bit more active in these sessions."

"Active?"

"Yes. More involved. I ask you a question. You answer."

"I am answering, Dr. Rosario."

She uncrosses her leg, adjusts herself in the seat, and places my file down flat on her lap. "Yes, you are, but I'd like a little more. A bit more description would be nice. Do you think you can do that?"

"Sure." I cross my arms over my chest. She wants more description. I can handle that. I lean back against the three thousand dollar white leather sofa.

"Good." She nods. "Okay, so how was your weekend?"

"It was good."

"Did you do anything interesting?"

"No. I. Did. Not." I emphasize every single word—descriptively, of course. I understand this is a bit childish of me, but let's face it, she's counting down the time just as much as I am. Only thing is I'm counting down to get out; she's counting to get paid.

Of course, since she's been my psychiatrist for the last year, she knows how to push my buttons. She leans back with a daring expression on her face. "Did you have a chance to work on your painting this weekend?"

There. She's done it. She's hit a nerve. I shift uncomfortably and tear my eyes away to settle over her desk on the left-hand side of the office. It's an excessively large desk if you ask me. "No, I didn't have an urge to do so." She knows how to make me tick. Right now I'm ticking. "But I did look over a few old paintings," I confess.

"Good, Jenna. That's a start. How did you feel when you looked at them? Did it bring anything up for you?"

Another tick. "I felt and remembered things that I've worked hard to forget."

She nods in understanding and scribbles something down. "Most individuals try to forget certain events or parts of their life for various reasons. It's normal. We feel if we don't revisit these memories or feelings, then there's less of a chance for vulnerability or a potential breakdown. But I find when I go back and learn how to cope with these issues and memories, there's a better chance that I learn how to deal with them and know what to do if I'm faced with them in the future."

I laugh at the last comment, turn my head from the desk, and dart glares at her. My expression is serious now; I can hear the ticking in my head. *TICK. TICK. TICK.* It grows louder, faster. Soon I'll be ready to explode. "That's exactly what I don't want. I don't want to ever deal with any of it again. I'm trying to have it all go away." My hands drop to my thighs. "I don't need it. I'm comfortable staying in the small cave of my room, away from everyone, completely isolated. I'm fine with never going out, having friends, or ever meeting someone. I understand this is my life." I point at my chest, staring at her intensely. I'm trying to make her fully understand, but it's pointless. She never will. No one ever will. "I know that I'm going to be alone, so I accept it, Dr. Rosario. I'm one hundred and ten percent okay with knowing that I'll always be sick in the head. Some days will be good, and others will be extremely ugly—"

She shakes her head. "No, Jenna. You can live a normal life. There are numerous recovery stories from people with your same condition. We just have to work through it, and we can do that together."

Work through it? What the hell does she think I've been doing for the last four years? The fucking bomb explodes. Standing, I hover over the coffee table, which, lucky for her, separates the space between us. "No, Dr. Rosario! You don't get it and you never will because you don't know what I go through. You don't know what it's like for me. You can pump me full of as much medication as you like, send me to therapy seven days a week, and even try a new treatment. I will always have this"—I stab an index finger at my temple—"in here. The voices and the thoughts, bad and good. You're talking to me and so is someone else—sometimes more than one someone else." My head feels foggy. I take a few deep breaths and try to calm down. I will not cry in front of her. Turning my back to her, I gather my things from the couch quickly.

"Jenna, our session isn't over."

"It is for me," I scoff. "And I won't be coming back."

Dr. Rosario rushes to her feet, her eyes wary. She lifts both hands to caution me as I storm toward the door. "Jenna, think about what you're doing."

I've thought about this for a long time. It's time to try to do this on my own. "Thank you for the last year, but I think I'm ready to be on my own now."

"Jenna, please," she begs. "The most important part of treatment for someone with your disorder is to have a support team."

"I have one. Myself. I'm all the support I need." With that said, I turn on my heel and walk out of Dr. Rosario's office.

As I storm down the hall with tears prickling my eyes from rage, I wonder if what I just did is actually best for me. The moment I step outside and feel the warm air, I expect relief, to feel free somehow. This is what I wanted, right?

Instead, I feel more lost than ever.

I'm not exactly certain how long it's been since I stepped out of Dr. Rosario's office. Days. Weeks. Honestly, I lost count. Days like this are when I'm at my worst. Days without eating, without seeing daylight. Days when I ignore every call.

I'm entirely secluded.

My father is busier than ever. With his company in its prime, he's barely home to notice. My mother, well, she's off shopping or at the latest local housewives committee meeting, discussing the latest gossip. She barely takes note of my depressed days. And that's awesome. I'm happy that I don't have parents who watch my every move.

I do, however, have an annoying friend who won't leave me the hell alone. Like right now. Charlie is banging on my bedroom door at this very second. If I hear one more damn knock, I might get out of bed, unlock the door, and strangle her until every strand of her curly blonde hair frizzes.

"Jenna, if you don't open this goddamn door, I'll break it down!" More banging. "And just because I'm this one hundred and fifteen pound, five-foot woman doesn't mean I don't have the strength to get through!"

"Leave me alone," I mumble, rolling into my sheets. I cover my face with a pillow.

"That's it. You leave me no choice. I'm getting one of

the contractors out back to saw this damn door open."

What. The. Hell.

She will, too; that's the screwed up part. Damn her. And damn my mother for giving her a key to the house. Damn her again for being a pain in my ass. Dammit all! I roll out of bed, stumble toward the door, and swing it open. Charlie, with her arms crossed, raised brow, and pissed-off look, stands on the other side. I size her up slowly and turn, leaving the door open as I walk back to my bed. "And it's one hundred and thirty pounds at four foot eleven," I correct. Somebody's got to keep her honest.

She lets out a frustrated groan. "I am five foot." I'm not going to argue with her. Not now. I just don't have the strength. My body flops onto the plush surface of my mattress. Mummy style, I wrap myself back up in my sheets. The bed sinks in as she hops on. "I'm not doing this with you today, Jenna."

"And what is that?" My voice muffles against my pillow.

"This." She pulls at my sheets.

I pull back. "Leave me alone."

"No. You're getting up. You're going to take a shower, and we're getting out of here."

"No." I grip the sheets again, tugging them a bit harder this time around.

"Jenna," she hisses.

"No!" I spit back. "I'm going back to bed. I'm tired. I don't want to do anything."

She moves around on the bed. Then she jumps off, which is such a relief. Good. I'm glad I was able to—

Oh. No. She. Didn't.

She thrusts at my hipbone and I fall out of bed, my ass making a loud thumping noise as soon as it makes contact with the hardwood floor. She just tossed me off the bed. I'm pissed. Beyond furious, I jerk up, untangling myself from the sheets. Once I'm free from the fabric, I shoot a death glare her way. If looks could kill, she'd be one dead chick right about now. "You bitch!"

Charlie grips her hipbones and matches my glare from across the bed. "You can do better than that. I've been called worse." She stretches out her right arm, pointing in the direction of my bathroom door. "Now, I'm going to need you to take a shower. Throw on a bikini. We're going to relax by the pool and talk."

"I don't want to. What part of that don't you understand?"

She straightens her back and relaxes her eyes. "Jenna, I truly don't give a fuck. We're going swimming for the following reasons: a) I'm a hell of a good friend and I'm concerned about you; b) I'm hot as all hell from this ninety-degree weather; and c) my pussy is sweating and needs a dip in the pool. So go, now!"

"I hate you and you're disgusting."

"Mmkay. You can hate me all the way to the pool. Let's get going. I'll be right here, waiting for you."

Humph. I storm into the bathroom.

chapter 6

Logan

It's hot as hell out here. I'm used to working under the sun, but today I could fry an egg on the fucking concrete. We started work on the McDaniel project four days ago. Between me and the other workers, it's been successful. The foundation of the guesthouse is almost done, and I suspect by Monday we can begin the framing. With ten-hour shifts, our team has been known to beat its deadline.

"Lunch time," Bryson calls out. I drop the hammer in my hand and hear the loud thump it makes as it hits the ground.

I'm starving.

Mrs. McDaniel insisted we use her patio instead of having us hanging around on the back of our trucks to eat our lunches. Either way, I don't care where I eat. I'm a big guy and food is a necessity to keep me going.

When I approach one of the tables, I see that Justin, Danny, and Scott are already seated and digging into their sandwiches. An arm loops around my shoulder, and I tilt my head to look at Bryson.

A wide grin spreads across his face. "My aunt makes the best sandwiches around." He winks. His remark about my mother makes me laugh. It's true. They're simple lunchmeat sandwiches on fresh Amoroso's rolls, but something about them just tastes like fucking heaven on earth. My mother makes a point to prepare all of the lunches for Reed Construction employees.

"Yep," I agree. We take a seat at the table with the others.

Danny lifts his head and looks around, searching for something. "Where the hell is Santino?" he asks.

I give a one-shoulder shrug. "No damn clue, but he can eat on his own time," I say, digging into the bag and searching for my sandwich.

"Damn," Santino utters as he exits the sliding doors from inside. "No love whatsoever. It's cool, Logan. I see how it is. I was just using the bathroom."

I laugh once. "You know how I get when I'm hungry. I'm not waiting for no one." It's true. I turn into the fucking devil himself when I don't eat. I open the foil of my sandwich, ignoring everyone around me, and bite into the deliciousness my mother prepared. Santino finally joins us at the table. Uncle George had to leave early today for another doctor's appointment. Before leaving, he gave each man his assignment and put his son in charge.

Santino clears his throat. "Yo, I have to tell you about this chick I met up with last night."

"The blonde from Wasted?" Danny asks.

While chewing my lunch, I sit back and watch the conversation unfold. "Nah." Santino shakes his head. "Another chick." He waves his hand. "So there we are in my bed. Her wrists are tied to my bedpost. Her tits are bouncing as I'm banging her. I'm whispering sweet nothings in Spanish, and —"

"Spanish?" I ask.

Santino turns his head my way, his face clearly annoyed by my interruption. "Yeah. She wanted me to talk Spanish to her while we banged."

"But you don't speak Spanish," I remind him. He's probably the only Puerto Rican I've met who doesn't speak a lick of it.

Santino flashes a mischievous grin. "She doesn't know that."

I lean over the table, laughing at him. "So you basically chanted a made-up language and passed it off as Spanish?" He nods, and his smile grows wider. "And she bought it?" I ask. Santino nods again. The rest of the guys burst into a hard laugh. "I bow down to you, master." I stand up, raise both arms, and bow.

"All right, can I finish my damn story now?"

The patio door slides open and closed. All six of us turn to see who it is. Both Jenna and her blonde friend—whose name I think is Charlie—step out in their bikinis, each with a towel in hand. Jenna glances over, hesitant to move forward. She starts to turn back around, but her friend tugs at her arm just in time. My eyes flick over her face; it's a weird instant reaction for me. There are two hot girls practically naked before me, but I glance at her face? She ducks her head low, nervously pushing a strand of hair behind her ear.

When I last saw Jenna on Monday in the shed, it was clear that something was bothering her. The moistness on her cheeks and the red rim around her eyes clearly showed she'd been crying. I know I shouldn't have allowed it to bother me as much as it did. Women cry all the damn time, but Jenna seemed to be lost deep in thought. I've seen that sad, empty look a dozen times before in my mother's eyes—when she cries, when she thinks back on my father, and when she thinks about Sean's death.

"Ladies," Santino greets with a nod.

Charlie smiles brightly and walks over to our table, dragging Jenna the entire way. "Hey, guys. What are you all up to?"

Santino leans in and whispers to us, "Watch and learn, guys. Watch and learn." He turns, giving Charlie his winning smile, and begins spouting off stuff in some made-up language in an attempt to sound sexy.

Charlie smiles, pleased. "What does that mean?" she asks.

Santino looks at her with smoldering eyes. It takes every bit of me to not burst out laughing. "It means, 'I was thinking maybe you and I could be up to something.'" I was doing well biting back my laugh, but the moment my gaze shifts over to Jenna and I see her pressed brows and the look of disgust aimed right at Santino, I lose it. I burst into the hardest laugh I've ever had, which starts everyone else up. Laughter erupts around the table. Everyone but Santino is howling, but he just glares at us. That makes us laugh even harder.

"That's not what you said," Jenna pipes up.

Santino drags his glare her way. "Oh yeah? Then what did I say?"

"I have no clue," she replies. I snort louder. Her eyes meet mine, and for a second I think her lips are about to twitch into a slight smile. But just as quickly, they fall back into the thin line she's famous for.

"If you don't speak Spanish, it may sound like gibberish to you. So, yeah, that's exactly what I said." Santino states matter-of-factly.

Charlie snakes her arm around Jenna's shoulder, pulling her in closer. "But Jenna's fluent in Spanish."

Oh my God, this might be the best day of my life. I'm crying from laughing so hard. "Busted!" I cough out, pointing at Santino, who's completely dumbfounded at this point.

Jenna nods. "Esto es cierto." I'm not sure what she just said, but it's priceless. It's the cherry on top of this entire conversation.

Staggered and a bit played, Santino smacks his lips aside in a cocky way. He then changes the subject. "Anyway, you ladies still coming to the lake house party this weekend?"

Now this brings me to full alert. I wasn't aware Santino invited them. I don't care, but we typically keep the invites to a minimum, only inviting people we know and trust to our yearly summer bashes.

Originally, it was a family vacation getaway in the Poconos. My uncle built the home himself. I spent most every summer of my childhood at the small cottage by the lake. Sean, Bryson, and I looked forward to it every year. But as we grew older and my uncle's business expanded, our little family vacations slowly vanished. It wasn't until Bryson's twenty-first birthday, when he convinced his father to give him the keys to the lake house for a small get-together with friends, that our new summer tradition began. Let's just say that the "small" get-together was a major success, one we repeated most weekends that summer. Ever since, we've been throwing parties there on the weekends every summer, starting with Bryson's birthday bash.

"I'm trying to convince this one to go." Charlie points her thumb at Jenna. "She's not so keen on spending a weekend with you guys." I look over at Jenna, whose wide eyes have zoomed in on Charlie.

Santino gets up from his chair and makes his way over to the girls, nestling between Jenna and Charlie. He wraps his arms around the both of them. "I promise we won't bite, ladies. We'll be perfect gentlemen, unless you want us to have a taste. That'd be awesome too." He says, looking at Jenna.

She shoves out of his hold. "No, thank you." I can see her repulsion at the idea when she glances over at me one last time before marching to the opposite side of the pool. I watch as she tosses her towel on the ground and belly flops onto one of the lounge chairs.

"What's up with your friend?" Santino asks. "She's so uptight."

I'm still focused on Jenna when I hear Charlie say, "No, she's just going through a rough time."

"Is she always like this?" I ask. I met Jenna less than a week ago, and I've already seen so many sides to her.

"Like what, exactly?" Charlie asks.

My eyes meet hers. She's staring at me inquisitively, making me feel a bit uneasy for having been caught staring at her friend. I'm not sure why; I never feel uncomfortable or even a tad bit embarrassed—especially not in front of women. "Up and down. Like you're not sure what to expect when you're around her."

Charlie crosses her arms over her chest and drops her hip as she sizes me up. "Yes. She's always like that."

"Pfft. Cray-cray," Danny interjects.

Charlie jerks her head around and glares at him. She chucks Santino's arm off her shoulder and bends over Danny. Her small frame looms over him, creating a shadow across his surprised face. One small hand goes to his shoulder, the other rests on the edge of the table. "The next time you call my friend crazy, I'll show you just how crazy *I* can get. And never, ever say that to her. Do you understand me?" Damn. For a tiny thing, she can be deadly. Danny nods. "Good," she finishes. Then she stands and strolls off to join Jenna.

Bryson lets out a long, low whistle. "That was intense. What the hell was that about?"

"I have no idea," I respond.

The rest of the lunch hour we all poke fun at each other. Santino finishes the story he tried to tell when we first sat down, and a few of the other guys tell stories of their own. All the while, I sneak glances at the girls from across the pool. My eyes may be playing tricks on me, but I think Jenna's been sneaking a few glances over here as well.

"Hey. Maybe we should make amends?" Bryson nods toward the other side of the pool. "The last thing we want is my father finding out that Santino's sexually harassing our clients."

"Yeah. You're right. Let's get it over with so we can focus on finishing today's goals."

The rest of the guys head back to work as Bryson and I make our way over to the girls.

chapter 7

Jenna

"Are we going to keep doing this, Jenna?" Charlie whines. I continue to ignore her. The last thirty minutes were hard to get through since I can never go very long without talking to her, especially when she's practically in my face, hounding me. "*Jenna*." With my eyes closed, I adjust myself in the lounge chair, making myself a bit more comfortable. As hot as it is, I soak in the sun and allow myself to tan in peace, disregarding her. "Jenna!" she cries out again. I think I'm enjoying this. This is payback for forcing me out of my room and then embarrassing me in front of the guys.

"That's it!" I hear her wet flip-flops squishing across the patio. Before I can utter a word, Charlie's legs are straddled on either side of my hips. I pop my eyes open and she leans forward, her face inches from mine. Charlie grips my wrists, places them over my head, and humps me. She's literally humping me.

"What the hell are you doing? Get off me!" I struggle beneath her.

"Oh, yes!" she yells out, panting. "Fuck. You feel so good, Jenna." Still humping. "Oh, God...*harder*." She looks ridiculous. "You know how I like it, baby. YES!" Her back arches, her eyes roll to the back of her head, and then her body shudders as she acts out her fake orgasm.

Is she serious right now? "You're absurd!"

She releases my wrists from her hold and sits back on my thighs. I lift myself up with my elbows and look up at my friend's crooked grin. "Is that a smile plastered across your face, Jenna McDaniel?" I force my lips back to a thin line. "Well, I think I've succeeded. One point for me." She shoves her hips, one time, into mine. "Boom!"

"Get off me." I wiggle beneath her and push forward to move her off. But I can't. Her legs are practically glued to my thighs.

"Careful. My pussy lips are twerking again. I may go another round."

"I hope we're not interrupting?"

Charlie and I turn our heads toward the voice. Can this day get any more embarrassing? Both Bryson and Logan are standing there, Bryson with a curious raised brow, Logan with his arms crossed and an amused grin on his face. Great. "I mean, we can come back if you need your privacy."

Charlie, loving the attention, smiles mischievously. "Oh no, we're not afraid of public affection. Are we, baby?" She looks down at me and winks.

For a split second, I imagine that I have eyes that can shoot out painful darts, and I aim those eyes right at the center of Charlie's forehead. Since nothing is happening, I crook my neck, focusing on Logan and his charming blue eyes. He yanks my chain by lifting a hand and pointing his thumb behind him, silently questioning whether or not he should leave so Charlie and I can continue fooling around. Smart ass. He must have read my facial expression because his lips curl into a wide grin. An adorable grin. I shake my head. "No. It's fine. What do you need?"

Bryson takes a step forward. "We won't take much of your time," he says. "We just wanted to apologize on behalf of Santino. It was unprofessional of him to treat you ladies that way. We're sorry. It won't happen again."

"I don't mind," Charlie declares.

Bryson nods once. "Right. Either way it was out of line."

It's kind of sweet he cares enough to apologize. "Thank you. I appreciate that," I say.

Logan, who hasn't taken his eyes off of me, clears his throat. "We'd still like to invite you ladies to the lake house this weekend. It's an annual event, and if you come and stay, we'll make sure you have your own room." He's looking at me intently, almost intimately, as if this conversation is just between the two of us. "We also promise no more remarks by Santino or any of the guys. Just think about it." They both smile reassuringly and turn away, walking in the direction of the soon-to-be guesthouse.

Charlie hops off my lap, releasing the pressure from my thighs. She sits beside me with concerned eyes. Goofy Charlie has been turned off and now caring, loving Charlie is on. "Talk to me."

My head slams back on the headrest of the lounge chair. "I left Dr. Rosario."

She places her hand on top of mine. "That must've been tough."

"It was…*is*. I'm just confused by it all. I thought I would feel relieved, but I feel stuck."

"That's understandable. You've been with her for almost a year. When you adapt to someone, they become a part of your routine, a part of you. And when they're taken away, you feel a bit lost. No matter how much you think it won't affect your life, it does." She sighs and turns her head away from me. I can't make out her exact point of interest, but it seems like her gaze is lingering over Brooke's bedroom window, the one right beside mine. "Do you think this is for the best?" she asks.

"I have no idea. But I felt suffocated. I still feel suffocated, Charlie." I adjust to sit up. "For God's sake, I'm in my early twenties and my parents control everything I do. It's as if I have no say whatsoever in my life. Sure, they're never here physically, but they manage to control every little thing anyway: school, work, therapy. For once I just wanted to feel in control. They treat me like I'm incapable of doing anything. Like I'm a pet puppy who can't be left alone without destroying everything, so they keep me caged."

Charlie gives my hand a tight squeeze. "I know the past few years have been difficult for you, Jenna. Especially the last eight months."

"Don't," I interrupt flatly. The last thing I want to be reminded about is the last few months of my life. I'm aware of how difficult it's been. I've lived through it. But I'm still here, fighting through it, managing somehow. It can't be so bad if I'm surviving each day. It could always be worse, right? At least that's what I tell myself. It's the only thing that's giving me hope.

That's the end of the conversation. Charlie knows how much I can handle, and she's learned throughout the years not to push my limits.

She stands. "Want to take a dip? I can't take this heat any longer."

"Sure."

Sometimes I wonder how I became so lucky to have her

in my life. Neither one of us can replace Brooke for the other. She meant different things to each of us and we'll never be able to fill her shoes. But in some small way, having Charlie around helps me hold on to a piece of my sister that I'd lose otherwise. And I think it's the same for her. She's been there for me through and through for the past few months. It's taken up to this very second for me to realize it. Knowing that I'll always have her, that she'll always be there for me, makes me grateful. Like today. I needed someone to pull me out of bed and force me back to reality, and she was there.

Charlie sits at the island in the kitchen, chatting away as I whip up scrambled eggs and bacon. She hasn't left my side since last night. Being the good friend she is, she insisted we rent movies, eat junk food, and have a good old-fashioned girls' night. The last time I had a night like that was about a year ago—when Brooke convinced me to watch *Grease* for the thousandth time. She had a massive John Travolta crush and refused to believe he acted in other movies. I smile, remembering how Brooke would jump up and dance along with the scenes.

Charlie didn't realize it, but I needed her last night more than anything. I didn't trust myself alone; I could've easily fallen back into a depressive spell. It isn't difficult to succumb to my gloomy moods, but with Charlie around I'm able to avoid my racing thoughts for a short period of time. We stayed up all night, talking about nonsense and watching comedies. My mind was free of everything I've been dealing with the past few days. I even laughed. That's something I haven't done in a very long time.

Who needs Dr. Rosario?

"On the latest issue of *Cosmopolitan*: '100 Ways to Satisfy Your Man,'" Charlie reads, flipping through the pages of the magazine. "Now this is what I'm talking about. Ooooh…" She looks up at me, intrigued. "Did you know that a female can have several stages of an orgasm?"

I turn off the gas range on the stove and toss our breakfast onto plates. "And here I thought there was only one." I smirk.

"Well, it's been a long time since you…" She wiggles a finger, pointing toward my lower waist. "You know."

She always has to go there. I glare, warning her to cut it out. "Thanks for the reminder." She catches the plate as I slide it her way.

Charlie raises her hands, palms forward in surrender. "Look, last remark about this subject and then I'm finished." She waits for my approval. When I sit down across from her and silently start eating, she takes it upon herself to go on. Leaning over the counter with her hand cupped around the side of her mouth, she faux-whispers, "They have magical toys to help you reach any stage you desire."

Just as I'm about to toss a piece of toast at her, my mother steps into the room. "The last thing I want is to walk in on my daughter and her friend discussing sex toys," Mom remarks.

Why does this keep happening to me?

With wide eyes, both Charlie and I watch as my mother gracefully passes us, opens the fridge, and removes a container filled with green juice. She never misses a morning without having her self-made, healthy energy drink. She's wearing her workout gear and the silky strands of her red locks are tied back perfectly in a ponytail. "You girls are up early," she points out, pouring herself a tall glass of the green tar.

"More like still awake. We haven't slept yet," Charlie responds.

My mother nods in acknowledgement. "Ah. That explains the dark circles under Jenna's eyes." I laugh at her judgmental remark. This woman can ruin my day and make my blood boil within a split second. Why? Why does she feel entitled to say anything at all?

Angrily, I clink my fork against the plate, stabbing my scrambled eggs. I refuse to allow her to bring me down. I refuse to let her words ruin my perfect morning. With my mouth full, I keep my head low and enjoy my breakfast as Charlie tries to make light of the situation.

"So, Mrs. McDaniel, I see you're going for your daily run. Keeping the body in shape for Mr. McDee, huh?" My best friend never fails to amaze me, but at this point even my parents are aware of her bluntness.

"Charlie, we've been through this numerous times. I'd like it if you'd refer to me as Laura. Mrs. McDaniel just seems a bit old, don't you think?" Ha. I snort, silencing the room. I peek up to find my mother's piercing eyes narrowed in on me. "Is there something you'd like to share, Jenna?"

Because I feel it's my daughterly duty to be a total bitch when she is to me, I respond with an arrogant smile. "Well, Mother, last I remember you're not getting any younger. In fact, a fiftieth birthday is slowly approaching, isn't it?"

There it goes. My mother has a thin vein on her forehead that shoots across from the base of her left eyebrow and disappears into the right side of her hairline. When she's upset, it pops out a bit more than usual. When she's furious, it pulses. Right now it's popping, not quite pulsing just yet. But I know I hit a nerve. Well done, Jenna. Well done. She knows how to push my buttons, and I know how to push hers. When we're together, we're lethal.

My smile falters as I watch the look in her eyes slowly change from ticked off to competitive, challenging even. Her stare still glued to me, she finishes her drink, places the cup down, and flashes a knowing smirk. "Dr. Rosario rang." My heartbeat hammers rapidly at her statement. "You're going back. No question about it."

The stool screeches along the tile floors as I stand abruptly. My heart feels like it's struggling to break free of my chest. "I thought there was a confidentiality agreement between her and me."

My mother's smile brightens. It's a fake, mechanical, smile, like that of a Stepford wife. "Yes, anything spoken between the two of you is most definitely confidential. But when I'm paying for the weekly visits, it's her duty to notify me when and why she stops charging my account. It was an agreement we had."

I can't believe this. It's just another way for her to control me. "I'm not going back," I say sternly. I want to make her very clear of my intentions.

I'm. Not. Going. Back.

"Jenna, yes you are. These therapy sessions are good for you."

Good for me? "You have no damn clue what's good for me!" My face heats in rage as I lean over the countertop. My fingers grip the edge to keep me from lunging at her. "You waltz around here, claiming to know everything, but you don't. You don't even know your own daughter. I question if you even knew Brooke at all."

"Jenna, stop," she demands.

Uncontrollable anger rushes through me. "Or maybe that's it. You knew Brooke so much more than me. You paid so much attention to her that you failed to see that you had two daughters, not just one. You make it very clear, Mother, that I'm a lost cause, that I'm useless in your life, in this family, and in this home. You manage to make me feel everything ugly—not only on the outside, but also on the inside. You make me more broken than what I am."

"Oh, honey," she says softly, eyes filled with pity. "You need to stop blaming others for your failure."

"Mrs. McDaniel…" I hear Charlie gasp in pure shock.

I'm furious. She does this. She knows how to hit every single nerve of mine. She knows how to make me ill and disgusted with a simple look in her eyes. She knows how to work me up. The question is why. Why does she continue to do this? Why does she feel the need to control my life? Does it make her feel powerful knowing the control she has over me? Is it because she's so desperate to push me away she'll do anything to manipulate my emotions?

"Jenna…" Charlie's voice is distant. I barely make out what she's saying. The voices in my head are overpowering everything—even my own thoughts. "Breathe," I hear her say faintly. I can't. It's hard to breathe. My fingers grip the granite, my eyes are unfocused, and my body is trembling as I try to fight for air.

She doesn't love you, She never has, She hates you, Why would she love you, You're a pig, You're disgusting, She wishes it were you that was dead, not Brooke, She would've rather buried your body six feet underground, You're a waste of space, Why are you even here, Go kill yourself already and get it over with, She doesn't care what happens to you, She's never cared…

The evil voice continues to dominate my thoughts. Every time I try to fight through it, I falter. It roots itself down deep within. Running. Running usually works. I push away from the counter, turn around, and dash out of the kitchen, into the foyer, and out the front door.

You stupid fucking bitch, You're a joke, No one cares about you, They all think you're crazy, because you are, Just do it already, Kill yourself, Do it, Do it, Do it, Do it, Do it. DO IT!

I scream at myself to sprint through the voices. I need the voices to go away. I need them out of my head. They're invading my mind. Houses, trees, parked cars all dash by in my peripheral vision. They all seem to be zooming by quickly, yet I feel stock-still, like I'm in a slow-motion movie. I'm not running fast enough. Forcing myself, I push hard, one foot in front of the other, faster and faster. Each long block fades in the distance with each one I pass.

It burns: my shins, my chest, my throat. Everything. My breathing is ragged. Choking in air, I continue to dart down the street, round a corner and down another street. The quicker I run, the more my skin feels the harsh breeze of this early summer morning. I push forward, daring the wind to take me away—away from my thoughts, from my fucked-up life, from my screwed-up mother. Each taunting word from the voices forces me to keep going.

Minutes. Hours. I'm not certain how long it's been before I collapse by a corner. Queasy and drained, I bend over. Sweat coats my face, neck, and arms, and I have to grip my knees for support. The urge to vomit settles in. Breathing is difficult to do. Everything is blurry. I vomit, over and over again, hurling the little breakfast I managed to eat all over the green grass of the street corner. The same street corner where kids are now lining up to wait for the school bus.

"Gross," one of the kids yells.

"Are you okay?" another asks.

"She's not wearing shoes," a little boy points out.

I barf again.

I hear the school bus pull up. All the kids hop on, and then it drives away. There's no way any more bile can come out of me. Exhausted and weak, my body collapses to the ground. My heart is still hammering as I struggle to scoot over and lean my head against the pole of the street sign.

In a complete daze, I focus straight ahead at the house across the street. The image before me is...well, perfect. A white picket fence surrounds a beautiful brick home with matching white shutters. The neatly manicured lawn beckons me to lie soundlessly on its bright green surface. It's this temporary comfort, this temporary peace, which tugs at my consciousness. But it's beyond my reach. My eyes roam over to the left side of the lawn. Catching my breath, I admire the oversized pink dogwood tree. It gives the home a pop of color, a cheerful color. I look up at the terrace on the second level, which appears to wrap around the entire home. It looks like the perfect place for the owners to relax and enjoy a glass of wine or simply sit and enjoy the sunrise.

Picture-perfect.

My home, twice the size of this one, is twice as beautiful on the outside, yet on the inside, it's filled with darkness. Filled with taunting judgments. Filled with sadness. There's nothing flawless behind my house's closed doors. The image of the house is just a facade for those who pass by to smile at. It's an illusion engineered to make them think, "There's the perfect home with the perfect family and the perfect life." If only they knew the truth. The truth that haunts me endlessly, the truth that longs to break free. Instead, the truth is hidden behind flower boxes and shiny glass windows and wood and walls and lies.

Just like me.

I continue to stare at the home, trying to discover if there's something else behind the brick walls other than perfection. I can't be the only one in this world, in this state, or even in this damn neighborhood that's screwed up. My mind shifts to a few years ago, when I was just as confused as I am today.

I like it up here. As high up as I am, I'm not afraid. The roof is my sacred place to get away. No one knows this is my escape, not even Eric. Well, except for Brooke. The only reason she knows is because she followed me one day, which is a usual Brooke thing to do. Still, she swore never to tell, and she hasn't as of yet. I like it this way. Quiet. Even when cars zoom by in the distance or birds sing during the day or the crickets chirp at night, it's peaceful. Just me and my thoughts.

But something is happening to me. My thoughts are slowly being taken over by someone else. I hear voices; I don't know whose. It started with one voice a few weeks ago. The voice said awful things about me and even about Eric. Then it multiplied to two, then three different voices—all consuming my thoughts. The voices are draining me. I try to shake them off, pound my head with my fist, anything to get them out and make them stop. Nothing works. I can't ignore them...except when I run. I run and run until the voices vanish, and by then I'm exhausted and collapse.

The first night it happened, I was scared and alone. I was home, sitting in bed studying for the SAT exam. Everything had been going great. My grades were improving and I'd applied to several colleges, hoping to be accepted into the same university as Brooke. Eric and I were doing better than ever. I'd never felt such a high in my life, even with all the pressure from my mother to do better in school. But then darkness descended and clouded over my world. My mood instantly changed. I felt like someone was in the room with me, spying. I grew paranoid. Then the voice began. It called me stupid and other foul names. It spat out hurtful words. It made me feel disgusted with myself.

It's becoming more and more difficult to concentrate in school. The voices are getting worse. I don't know how to control them. Dinner with my parents is always bad. I can hear them chatting about their day, very distantly, but the voices are overpowering them too. It's hard to even hear my own thoughts. Because of this, I've been excusing myself from dinner every night. I think Mom is catching on, though. She's been watching me a bit more than usual.

Then there's Eric. He has no idea what's going on with me. I'm afraid to tell him. All of this is bottled up inside, and I'm going through it alone. I don't know any other way. I keep lashing out at him, which isn't fair, but I have no clue how to handle...whatever this is.

Why is this happening to me?

Earlier today, the voices were poking and prodding, yelling. Each day they're getting louder and speaking faster. I sat on the edge of the sofa at Eric's parents' home. Eric rented a movie and ordered pizza for our date night while his parents were out.

He sat beside me on the couch, wrapping his arm around my shoulder and pulling me in closer to him. Usually, I'm a puddle of mush in his arms, but today I felt off about him. He was on the phone for a few seconds in the kitchen, whispering.

When he came back to the couch and settled beside me, I tried not to let it get to me, but the voices were persistent. "Who were you on the phone with?" The question came out in a harsher and more demanding tone than I had intended.

He looked at me and shrugged a shoulder. "It was Jim. Why?"

"Jim?" I questioned.

Eric raised a brow. "Yeah, Jim. Is that a problem?"

"Yes. I know you're lying."

His eyes widened at the accusation. "Excuse me? Why on earth would I lie about being on the phone with Jim?"

Angry that he would lie to my face, I stood and pushed him away. "You were whispering in the kitchen, Eric."

His features etched in confusion. He raised a hand, palm up. "I have no idea what you're talking about, Jenna. I wasn't whispering."

"Were you really talking to her?"

"Who?"

"Don't act like I don't know what you're keeping from me."

He got to his feet and brought his hands to my shoulders. His body towered over me, and his eyes pierced into mine. "Jenna, listen to how you sound right now. What are you talking about? And who is 'she?'"

"The other girl you've been screwing with!"

Shocked, he let go of me and took a step back. "You're crazy."

Then the voices began to chant his words over and over again.

You're crazy, You're psycho, You're crazy, You're psycho, You're crazy, You're psycho...

It repeated in my head, and it didn't want to shut off. So

I ran out of his house. I ran all the way home. I ran up the stairs into my room and climbed out the window onto the roof. Where I am now.

I wish Brooke were here and not away at college. I'm not sure if I'd tell her what's going on with me, but at this moment, I need someone to talk to.

My thoughts are all I have and they're the last things I want to keep me company. I'm a prisoner of my own mind, trapped with the unknown, angry voices.

chapter 8

Logan

The music and lyrics of my favorite band pounce through the speakers. I'm in a good mood for two reasons. One: I managed not to beat up my alarm clock this morning, so I woke up on time, which means I'll be early for work. Two: Tonight is the first summer evening of our lake house party, and with every previous year being such a success, I have no doubt this year will be just the same, if not better. As always, the kick-off to the summer lasts an entire weekend. After the first summer bash, we throw a party every Saturday for the rest of the summer.

Twenty minutes away from the McDaniels' home, I slowly brake as I approach an intersection. What the hell? Is that a girl sitting on the corner...in pajamas? This isn't abnormal to me. Living in Philadelphia, I think I've seen it all. But here, in this neighborhood, it just strikes me as odd. I shrug it off, release my foot from the brake, and drive on. As I pass the intersection, my curiosity gets the best of me. Turning my head, I look out the window and have a much better view of the girl. It's not just any girl—it's Jenna. What is she doing out here this early in the morning?

She's been crying. Again. I can tell by the black tearstains down her cheeks. For the second time in less than a week, I've found this girl in tears. She didn't see me; she's too busy staring blankly across the street. What should I do? Should I just keep going and act as if I didn't see her? Or should I pull over, check up on her, and see if she's okay or needs a lift?

I can't keep going. It'll fuck with my head all day.

I pull over by the curb. Placing the car in park, I adjust the rearview mirror and watch her for a bit. Maybe she's waiting for someone. She doesn't move; she just continues to lean against the street sign and stare straight ahead. I look out the driver side to see what's so interesting. It's just a house. Another look in the rearview shows me she's still there, unmoving. I'm a half hour early. Maybe I can see if she needs a lift. Before exiting the car, I reach into the glove compartment and remove a few napkins left over from some fast food drive-thru trips. I step out of the truck and slowly walk over to her.

Jenna doesn't move when I step up beside her. She's lost in her own head, not even realizing I'm here. I sit down beside her, a foot away. I don't want to scare her, so I don't say anything. Instead I just watch her. It's as if she's hypnotized. She doesn't move or speak or blink. If it weren't for the up and down, even chest movements, I would think she wasn't breathing. There's that and the tears roaming freely down her cheeks. Yeah, she's definitely alive. Did some guy break her heart? Was it that Matthew guy? What could cause her to be this sad? Within a heartbeat I reach out, placing the napkin in her view. Her features quickly change from vacant to confused. She snaps out of her trance, tossing her head back and away from the napkin. Her eyes follow my hand, up my arm, and then land on my face. I give her a slight grin and a one-shoulder shrug to say, "Hey," but her features turn angry.

"What are you doing here?" she snaps.

Maybe I caught her off guard. "I saw you sitting here when I was driving by. I thought maybe—"

"You thought maybe I'm crazy, right? Is that what it is?" she asks as she shuffles to her feet.

Confused, I shake my head and look up at her. "No, I thought maybe you needed a lift or…" Fuck. Should I have kept on driving?

Jenna fidgets and digs a hand into her hair. "You look at me and you see that, right?" She points across the street at the house she's been staring at for God knows how long. I look back at her. What should I do or say? Is she having a girl breakdown right now? How do people handle shit like this?

I stand but keep my distance. I don't want to set her off. Maybe she just needs to get some stuff off her chest. I remain quiet, silently giving her permission to go on. She turns away from me, faces the home, reaches her hands out, and points at each item she describes. "It's flawless on the outside. Every brick neatly stacked, every corner properly secured. Every shutter handpicked. Every rose planted in its rightful place. It's fucking perfect. But what happens when the walls can no longer hold up, when they can no longer contain all the demons inside? Do they just explode from the pressure, finally setting free everything that's been imprisoned inside?"

She turns to face me. Her brows draw closer and her face tightens as she shrugs her shoulders. "Or do they crumble into dust, taking all of the secrets, all of the monsters hidden within, everything—including the truth—down with them?"

Wow. Before me stands a girl who seems to be dealing with more issues than just a broken heart. I give it my best shot. "Jenna, I think you have to decide whether to let it break free or bury it. If you want it to break free, you just have to let go and allow it to. What's the worst that can happen?"

She shakes her head. "No. Not when you're not normal."

"No one's normal." I raise my arms and gesture at myself while holding her gaze. "Take me for instance. I'm far from normal."

She carefully scans her eyes over me as one hand fidgets at the edge of her camisole. Her other hand combs through her hair as she asks, "Oh. How so?"

Shit. I toss my hand in the air, blurting out, "I take people for granted all the time. I'm a loose cannon. I take advantage of girls, who I'm sure don't deserve it. But I'm a dick, so I don't give a shit half the time." I walk in closer to her, and she doesn't move, which is a good thing. "I've been walking around trying to figure out what the hell I want to do with my life, but instead of actually doing something, I stand around and sulk about it." I have no fucking clue why I'm telling her all of this, but I keep going. "Ever since my brother, Sean, passed away a couple years ago, I've been at a standstill, just waiting for something to happen."

"Like what?" she asks in soft voice, and I notice that her eyes have softened dramatically.

"Life. I'm waiting for my life to happen, but I'm not actually doing anything about it." Whoa. I didn't even realize I felt this way. I mean, sure, it's been stuck in my head, but I've never said it out loud. I don't know what to make out of this.

"Oh." She breathes out, looking down at the ground. Her arms rest languidly at her side as she stands there quietly.

"The point is, Jenna, no one is normal or perfect like that house you see across the street. Everyone suffers from their own struggles, whether they're big or small. There's no such thing as having a flawless life."

With her head bowed, she whispers, "Not according to my mother."

I suck my teeth. "Well, no offense to you or your mother, but she obviously doesn't know shit."

A soft chuckle escapes her. She's actually laughing. It's a soft laugh, but it's a laugh nonetheless. Jenna looks up at me, and her moist cheeks slightly lift as a small smile spreads across her delicate features. "You should do that more often," I say.

Baffled, she asks, "What?"

"Smile. It looks good on you." And just like that it disappears. Her eyes tear away from mine to look anywhere else but at me. It's like smiling is frowned upon or illegal or some shit. I shift uncomfortably. "Want a lift home?"

She shakes her head. "No. I don't want to go home."

I look around. It's just the two of us out here, but I don't want anyone seeing her like this. "Would you like me to drive you anywhere? I don't mind."

"No. Well..." she hesitates. "Do you think I can use your phone to call Charlie? I mean if you have one, of course."

"Yeah, of course." I dig into my jean pocket and remove my cell, reaching out to hand it to her. She grabs it and turns her back to me. Seconds later, she has my phone against her ear and she's talking to her friend. I wait patiently as Jenna tells Charlie where she's located, and then she ends the call.

Jenna turns back around and hands over my cell. "Thank you. She'll be here in fifteen minutes."

I take a look at the time. I have ten minutes before my shift starts. There goes being early. "I'll wait with you."

"Oh no, it's fine. Please, I'll be okay."

I'll be damned if I'm going to leave a girl by the corner alone. I mean I can be a dick sometimes, sure, but my mother taught me some manners, dammit. I walk to the corner and sit on the curb. "Nah. Like I said, I'll wait with you."

"Okay." She takes a seat beside me. I hand her the napkins in my hand again. This time she takes them.

"Thanks." She wipes her cheeks.

"No problem," I say. And then it's quiet, too quiet. I clap my hands together and rest my elbows on my knees. "So what were you doing out here?"

"I went for a run."

I look at her, flashing a half smile. "You usually run in socks and pajama pants?"

"I just needed to get away."

My smile falters. "Can I ask you something?" She nods at me. "Without you getting offended?" She scowls, hesitant at first, but then she relaxes and nods again. "Why did your friend say you're not too keen on hanging out with us guys at the party this weekend? Is it because we're not on the same level as you are?"

"Same level?"

"Yeah, you know, wealth, education, shit like that."

"W-what? No. That has nothing to do with it. I just don't know you guys and to spend an entire weekend with strangers is not very safe, in my opinion as a woman."

I nod, understanding. Well at least I think I do. "Oh. So you won't be going?"

"No. I'm sorry. No offense or anything, it's just not my scene. The partying, drinking, and socializing…all of it, it's just not me."

"It's more than just that. It's a chance to escape, to be free for a couple days." I shake my head, remembering the memories of the past few years. "I guess because I grew up at the lake house, it's a bit more than just a party place to me.

Look, all I'm saying is if you need a break from your own head, the lake house is probably the best place to go. So if you end up changing your mind, you're more than welcome to come."

"Thank you. I appreciate that."

Just as I'm about to ask another question, her friend pulls up. Jenna stands and dusts herself off hastily, walks over to the car, and jumps in the passenger side. After buckling her seatbelt, she looks out the window at me. I sweep my hand up and wave at her once. She waves back with a small grin on her face, and I think she mouths, "Thank you," before the car pulls away.

"Are you kidding me, Logan?" Uncle George yells out. Yep, I'm late—by fifteen minutes, to be exact. Fuck my life. I walk past him, ignoring his glare. I grab my tool belt and wrap it around my waist. I nod at Santino who flicks his brows up in return. His expression is scared shitless for me. "Logan!" I take a deep breath.

"Yeah, George?" I ask, turning to face my uncle.

"Get over here. Now." He points a finger down.

So I'm going to get fired today. Sweet. Fired on a day that I was planning to be in early, a day that I woke up early for. The same day I tried to be a nice guy and help a girl out.

I approach him as he scowls at me something brutal. I've seen this look before, plenty of times, especially when I was a kid and got in trouble with Bryson and Sean. "Give me a damn good reason why I shouldn't let your ass go right now!"

I straighten my shoulders. "Because I was doing a good deed."

"And what was that? Screwing a girl you met at a bar, who may or may not have some type of STD?"

I tighten my jaw. "No. Helping a girl who was stranded a few blocks away from here."

"And what makes you think I'd believe that bullshit?"

I shrug. "It's the truth. You can accept it and allow me to get to work, or don't and let me go."

His eyes narrow. "Get your ass to work. But the next time you're late—"

"I know. I'm fired," I finish for him. Then I turn and walk toward the rest of guys, breathing a small sigh of relief as I go.

chapter 9

Jenna

"Charlie, I asked if you could pack a bag for me, not bring along my entire closet." I grunt as I drag my large suitcase up her stairs.

"Well, I wanted you to have options." She shrugs.

"*Thanks,*" I sass. I do appreciate that she took the time to pack my things. There was no way I could stay in my house tonight. My mother would've driven me beyond mad. Thankfully, Charlie stayed after I ran off, waiting for me to come back. When she pulled up at the corner where Logan and I sat, I felt a huge sense of relief, but I also had to explain to her why Logan was there with me.

I lug my suitcase into her room, shutting the door behind me. Charlie sits down on her desk chair and stares expectantly at me. "What?" I ask.

"So are you going to tell me what's going on between you and this guy?"

I roll my eyes. "There's nothing going on. I don't even know Logan. He's just a guy who works for my parents that just so happened to be at the wrong place at the wrong time." I tread over to her bed; tossing myself backward, I land on top of her pink sheets and comforter. I'm exhausted. This has been the morning from hell.

"He seems to be arriving at the *right* place at the *right* time if you ask me."

"No one's asking you. Seriously, can we drop this? My morning has been rough enough."

"Fine." She taps her nails hard once on her desk, and then huffs. "You know what? No, it's not fine. Come on, Jenna. He pulled you out of the pool." I wish I never told her about that. Thank God I didn't tell her about the damn kiss. "Then I found the two of you in the shed, practically eye fucking each other. And this morning he just happens to be there after your mom goes into bitch mode and practically runs you out of the house?" I stare at the ceiling fan with no strength to fight back.

"We were not eye fucking," I respond lamely.

She snorts. "Whatever. If I didn't interrupt, I would've orgasmed with the stare the two of you were giving one another. That's not the point." Her chair squeaks. Five footsteps and a dip in the bed later, she's lying beside me and staring at the ceiling fan as well. "There's nothing wrong with having a little fun," she says softly.

"I don't want to have fun. I don't need to have fun. I'm happy not having any fun at all. You remember what happened when Brooke wanted to have a *little fun*?" I ask, deadpan.

"Low blow, Jenna. Low. Fucking. Blow." It takes a lot to make Charlie upset, and I just did. I feel terrible. She shifts to move off the bed, but I grab her arm and bring her back down, all the while keeping my eyes glued to the ceiling.

"I'm sorry. It was a low blow," I say.

Her heavy sigh fills the air between us. "It's fine. I just thought this party might help get you out of that shell of yours.

Loosen up a bit. Be free. But I understand why you wouldn't want to go. It's still too soon. I'm a terrible friend for even thinking it would help. So…I'm sorry."

Be free. Logan's words repeat in my head. *It's more than just that. It's a chance to escape, to be free.*

I want that. I really do, more than anything. I need a chance to just clear my mind, to relax without a worry in the world. A chance to break away from any thoughts of my mother, from any memories of Brooke. For just one day, at least, I want to be free.

"You're not a terrible friend, far from it. You're just looking out. And you know what? You're actually right. I need to let go a bit, be able to have some fun. I'm entitled to have fun. So all right, Charlie. Let's go." I can't believe I just said that out loud.

Charlie instantly sits herself up on her elbows. "All right?"

"Yes. All right."

"Eeeek! All right!" she squeals. Charlie jumps to her feet and starts bouncing happily on the bed.

The rest of the morning, Charlie and I shopped. Somehow she managed to drag me to the mall, much to my dismay. When she texted Santino to ask if we should bring anything to the party, he seemed extremely excited to hear that she was going. I'm sure he expects her to give him a little extra attention to-night.

After our shopping, she packed her luggage, and then we were on the road. Santino told her the guys were only working a half day and should be at the lake house by two this afternoon. She's been in la-la land all morning since I agreed to go. Now that we're actually on our way, my anxiety wants me to tell her to turn the car back around, that I've changed my mind. But I wouldn't be able to forgive myself for taking away her excitement. To be fair, she hasn't been out since Brooke's been gone. It didn't occur to me until now that Charlie needs this as much as she thinks I do.

"You look cute, by the way," she says, taking a peek at me from the driver seat.

I look down, examining my attire. "I'm wearing jean shorts and a black cami. There's nothing cute about it."

She continues to smile brightly. Not even my depressing mood swings can bring her down. "Still, your hair and makeup are done. I've always said it's not the wardrobe but the hair and makeup that should always be stunning. So, like I said, you look cute."

"You insisted I do them. I'm not sure why I listened."

Charlie turns to look at me again, and her eyes pop wide in warning. What did I do? She reaches out and swats at my hand, which is pressed against my cheek. "Stop biting the inside of your cheek. You do that when you're nervous. Are you nervous right now?"

I didn't realize I was doing it. I unclamp my teeth from the hold on my inner cheek. "No. I'm just...I don't know." I slam my head back twice in frustration. "I'm thinking, that's all."

"About what?" She looks straight ahead as she steers.

"About what you said, about Logan and me. For some reason I feel uncomfortable when he's around me."

"A bad uncomfortable or good uncomfortable?"

I adjust in the seat, admiring her profile. Charlie is beautiful, yes, but she's also so strong, so confident. I wish I had at least an ounce of the courage she has. "What does it matter? I'm just uncomfortable."

"Well, a good comfortable means you're just a bit nervous around him because maybe you feel something for him—more than knowing that he's just the guy who's working for your parents. A bad uncomfortable means you're afraid to be around him, that he makes you nervous in a bad way, like he could possibly harm you."

I take in what she just said. "No. I don't get the feeling he'd harm me."

"Okay. Good. Because if you felt that way, I'd turn this car around and go back home."

I smile. "You'd do that for me?"

"Of course. I would never place you in a dangerous situation. You know that, right?" She glances over, waiting for me to agree. I nod. "Good." Charlie focuses back on the road. I know she wouldn't put me in harm's way. I lean my head back against the headrest, feeling a bit more at ease, and listen to Charlie chat away for the rest of the ride.

Two hours later, according to our navigation system, we've reached our destination. I straighten in the passenger seat. Charlie drives down a long dirt path, which is supposed to lead us to the lake house. I look around, taking in the beauty of the outdoors. Who knew nature could create such perfection? It's like a work of art. Trees of all different colors and textures surround us, and the sun shines down in patches on the leaves and plants covering the forest floor. It's stunning, peaceful. I roll down the passenger window and lean my head out to catch the warm breeze on my skin and in my hair. Breathing feels effortless here. It doesn't feel like a task or a struggle.

Light strokes of the wind brush my face. I shut my eyes

and continue to just...*breathe*, letting the alluring sounds of nature fill my ears. It's quiet, like the only sounds in the world are the ones around me: leaves lightly rustling against one another in the breeze, buzzing of early summer insects, and birds chirping merrily. I haven't even seen the house or the lake yet, but right now, at this very moment, I feel at peace. I feel safe. It's the strangest sensation. So much time has passed since I've experienced it, it feels abnormal, yet right at the same time. I wish I could freeze this moment and stay here forever.

"We're here!" Charlie lets out a squeal. Her car comes to an abrupt stop, jerking me forward in my seat. I flash my eyes open as I throw my arms out against the dash. Wow. The lake house is much more than I pictured. I expected a tiny cottage—which would be fine—but I didn't expect this. A large two-story cabin sits proudly in a grassy clearing before us. The tall glass windows, wrapped around both the lower and upper levels, provide a perfect view of the inside. Just behind the home is the lake, encircled by tall trees.

Charlie and I exit the car. I stand just outside the passenger side with the door wide open, taking it all in. I hear the trunk open and close before Charlie interrupts my reverie. "Hey, want to help me out over here?" I turn around and see her struggling to roll both pieces of our luggage on the dirt driveway.

"We'll help out with those," Bryson calls out as he and Santino jog over.

"See you guys found your way," Santino says with a smile as he grabs a suitcase. Bryson grabs the other.

"Yeah. The GPS took us the long route, but we eventually made it," Charlie says, stretching her limbs. We're both a little achy from the three-hour drive.

Bryson smiles modestly. "I should have told you there

was construction on the main road so it would reroute you a different way. Sorry."

Charlie waves her hand. "No worries. It was great bonding time. Wasn't it, Jenna?"

"Yeah." I shut the car door.

Bryson jerks his head toward the house. "Well, let me show you guys where you'll be staying."

Charlie runs up between Santino and Bryson and starts chatting away as I follow closely behind. We reach the front porch and enter the home. It's exactly what you'd hope a lake house would be like: open, airy, and bright. The oversized sectional and two recliners in the living area give the space a more masculine look. There's no art on the wall, but there are a few large collage frames hanging over to one side, which I'm guessing are filled with family photos.

We follow the guys up the stairs and into one of the five bedrooms with two twin beds. They place our luggage down. "This is where you girls will be staying. I hope it's okay?" Bryson asks.

I slowly whirl around, meeting him eye to eye. "Yes. It's perfect, thank you."

He nods once. "All right. We'll let you girls get settled in." He glances at his watch. "It's only six. We have food in the kitchen if you're hungry. People will start arriving around eight."

"It'll be fun, girls," Santino says to us, but his focus is entirely on Charlie who's by the door, smiling flirtatiously in return. Bryson grips Santino by the shoulder and hauls him out of the room, shutting the door behind them.

I let out a large huff. "What are we doing here?"

Charlie gives me a distraught look and then places both hands to her hips. Here comes dramatic Charlie. "What do you

mean by 'What are we doing here?' You said it was okay, that
we should come. Please don't tell me you're having second
thoughts."

"It just feels bizarre. Earlier today I had an argument with
my mother, an episode. Now I'm here, standing in a room at
a lake house that's owned by the contractors working for my
parents." I toss a hand in the air. "None of that strikes you as
odd? Not even a little bit?"

Charlie drops her arms, walks over, and grips my biceps.
"Odd? No. Exciting? Yes. Loosen up a bit." She shimmies my
arms. "Tonight will be fun. I promise. We'll leave first thing
tomorrow morning if you're still feeling this way."

I raise a brow in question. "Promise?"

She brings a hand to her chest. "Promise."

"Okay, let's go downstairs, then."

"Attagirl!"

Charlie and I are introduced to the other three guys—Justin,
Danny, and Scott—who are also working on the guesthouse
for my parents. They seem like nice guys, though I can't help
but notice that Logan isn't around. No one has mentioned him,
and I don't want to seem interested, so I leave it at that. We're
all sitting around the kitchen table and the guys are telling us
how these summer parties of theirs work.

"And you have one every weekend for the entire summer?" Charlie asks, very entertained by their stories.

Bryson answers, "Pretty much. We started seven years
ago for my twenty-first birthday and it's been a thing ever
since." He takes a sip of his beer. All the guys and Charlie are
drinking already. I'm sure I'll be babysitting her the rest of the

night.

"When's your birthday?" I ask.

He looks at me from across the table and his face lights up with a huge grin. "Tomorrow, actually."

Charlie leans over the table, her breasts practically spilling out of her low-cut shirt. "Na-uh. Shut up!" He laughs at her and nods. "Well, happy birthday! We have to do something special for you."

I roll my eyes, shake my head, and look toward the living area just as the front door swings open. Logan steps in, wiping the dirt of his shoes along the welcome rug. My heart does a backflip and starts crashing around in my chest. I saw him this morning. He saw *me* this morning. I feel embarrassed now. The way I looked. The way I acted. He witnessed all of it.

"Logan, my man." Santino jumps up from the chair beside Bryson and spreads his arms, greeting Logan.

Logan nods at Santino and heads over to us. My face heats up and I avert my eyes. Can anyone hear my heartbeat right now? It's so loud.

"Hey, guys." He looks around the table, and I gaze up at him just as his eyes land on me. A shocked expression appears on his masculine features, and then he relaxes with a smile. "Glad you ladies could make it."

"Thanks. *Logan,* right?" Charlie asks.

"Yeah, it's Logan. Not Lance. Just Logan." He grins at me.

Oh. My. God. Did anyone else catch that? I look around furtively. No one's paying attention, thank God. My chest expands in relief.

Logan walks over to the fridge, right behind where Charlie is seated, and pulls out a beer. "What time you guys get here?" He shuts the fridge, turns around, and looks at Santino and Bryson, waiting for a response from them as he chugs down a beer.

Santino scratches the back of his head. "Um, around five. Right?" He looks over to Bryson for confirmation.

"Yeah, man, around five. My father keep you late?" Bryson asks.

Logan leans against the kitchen counter beside the fridge. I look down at my half-empty glass of water. This clear glass is quite interesting all of a sudden. "Yep," Logan replies, popping the P.

Santino laughs. "Well, what did you expect? You knew that bullshit lie about helping a stranded girl on the street wasn't gonna fly with your uncle. You should've just said you slept in. I think he'd respect that a bit more."

My heart just dropped. The stranded girl is me. I'm the girl he pulled over for this morning. I'm the girl he waited patiently with until Charlie arrived. I think I'm going to be sick. I look up at Charlie. She glances at me with a concerned look and flicks her brows as if asking, "Are you okay?" I nod and stand quickly, trying to keep calm. "Excuse me. I have to use the bathroom."

"There's one over by the living area." Bryson points toward the right of him. I dart straight to the bathroom and press my back into the door the moment I close it.

What the hell are you doing here, Jenna? My mind begins to race with thoughts. At least they're my thoughts for a change. This is ridiculous. It's times like this I wish I knew how to drive; I'd jump into Charlie's car, speed out of here, and never look back. As far as I can tell, the only people that know about this morning are Logan, Charlie, and me. If anyone else knew, I think I'd be sick. Beyond sick. People would start asking questions, and questions lead to more questions.

And unanswered questions lead to curiosity. I can't have that. It's bad enough Logan probably thinks less of me.

I breathe in and out evenly, stepping to the sink to dab my face with cool water. Once I'm pulled together, I step out. Charlie's face is the first thing I see when I open the door. She scares the living daylights out of me. "What are you doing standing there like that?"

"I heard you talking to yourself," she whispers, which is really a harsh non-whisper because Charlie is the worst whisperer ever.

Shit. I look around. The guys are no longer in the kitchen. "Did anyone else hear?"

"No." She drops her crossed arms. "They're in the back, getting things ready for the party. It's starting in an hour." She pauses. "Jenna, I know how you feel when people ask this, but—"

"Yes, I brought my medication," I interrupt.

"Are you taking them?" She sighs heavily. "Don't give me that look. I had to ask."

"Don't." I raise a finger to her chest. "Don't ever ask again. I know what I'm doing. This is supposed to be a good weekend. Don't ruin it by acting like *her*."

Charlie's shoulders relax. "I'm sorry. I shouldn't have asked. You're right. This is going to be an awesome weekend. Come on, let's go have some fun." She wraps her arm around my shoulder and hustles me out back onto a large deck where the guys are hanging around.

I'm supposed to be having fun right now, but all I'm trying to do is steer clear of Logan. I keep my distance. Every time I catch him staring at me, I look away. I stay close to Charlie and watch as new partiers arrive.

The party has filled out with over thirty people—all drunk, of course. Charlie is all over Santino. At least she's having a good time. Logan is playing cards with Bryson and a few girls at one of the tables. I guess he got the hint; he hasn't looked at me once over the past hour.

It's the perfect moment to escape, so I climb down the steps of the deck and look past the trees, toward the lake. No one's there, so I head to the waterfront. I reach the end of the dock and take a seat. With my feet dangling over the edge and my arms crossed, I inhale and exhale a fresh breath of air. The music from the house becomes distant. I zone it out, focusing on the image before me. I watch the sun set as blue, purple, pink, orange, and yellow paint the sky. The reflection bounces off the lake and ripples when a light breeze whips by. I try to picture myself home at this very moment. I'd probably be stuck in my room, but I'd rather be here.

I've probably been sitting here for about twenty minutes when I hear the dock's floorboard creak loudly. Startled, I turn around to see what it is. Logan is walking over with two beer bottles in each hand, a warm smile spread across his chiseled features. I swallow hard, taking him in fully for the first time. Every other time I've been around Logan, I've been too wrapped up in my own head to really pay attention. He has a great physique, tall and toned. His broad shoulders could belong to a linebacker. His arms, swollen against the sleeves of his T-shirt, are sinewy and tan. Brown hair, cut close to his scalp, is a perfect contrast to his clear blue eyes. He's wearing loose jeans that hang low on his waist, and his confident, carefree attitude is obvious in the way he carries himself. He's got sex appeal, that's for sure. I'm certain other girls can't resist him.

With every step he takes, the more ragged my breathing becomes. I'm nervous, and I have no idea why. I've been purposely avoiding him the entire evening. I think it's because he saw one of my meltdowns this morning. He probably thinks I was having some type of boy trouble or something. Little does he know he witnessed one of my mild episodes.

"Hey," he says as he reaches me. "Mind if I join you?"

Yes. "No."

He sits beside me as another light breeze blows by us. I inhale his scent. "So are you enjoying yourself?"

God, my eyes are closed. Did I seriously just close my eyes to breathe in his scent? I flutter my lashes open. Embarrassed and momentarily distracted, I blurt out, "Huh? Oh, yes. Yes, I am." He extends his arm, offering me a beer. "No, thank you. I don't drink."

"Never?" He raises a brow.

"No. Well, I used to. Not anymore."

Logan wrinkles his nose. "Bad experience, huh?" I answer with a nod and turn my head back to the lake. "Are you girls thinking of staying tomorrow too?" He cracks open a beer for himself and takes a gulp.

"Probably not. We'll probably leave in the morning."

"You should think about sticking around. We have a barbeque going on in the afternoon, and then we usually jump in the lake and have a few drinks." He chuckles. "Although you don't have to partake in the drinking." I try to hold back a smile. He leans forward and I look over at him; he's staring directly at me. "Are you smiling?" he asks with a large grin.

"I think it's funny that you used the term *partake*."

"I think it's nice to see you smile." His smile wavers, and he raises a brow. "Why do you do that?"

I look down at my feet swinging beneath me. "Do what?"

"You instantly stop smiling the moment I mention it. It's okay to smile, especially out here." I peek up at him. He spreads his arms wide, bottle in hand, and looks around. "No one will catch you."

"I'm not afraid of anyone catching me."

He nods, takes another swig of his beer, and looks straight ahead, across the lake. "Then what are you afraid of?"

Myself. "Nothing." I steer the conversation away from me. "It's beautiful out here. Thank you for inviting us. I'd probably be home watching TV or sleeping right now."

"Sleeping? It's only eight…nine…eight or nine." He takes a sip of his beer.

"Yeah, well I don't exactly live the high life." He laughs at my response. We look at each other. His grin is contagious; I smile back at him. It's a light smile, and I know I'm doing it this time. I just hope he doesn't mention it. Logan drops his stare to my lips and his eyes linger there. For a moment, I watch him watching me. My smile slowly fades, and I don't know if it's a nervous reaction or a physiological one, but my tongue darts out to wet my lips. When it does, he tears his eyes away, taking another gulp of his beer, and the moment is gone.

"So how long has your family had the lake house?" I ask, hoping to cover the awkward moment.

"About twenty years," he answers, but he doesn't look back at me. He's focused down on the beer bottle, twirling it in his hand.

"Oh, wow. That's a long time. It's beautiful."

"Yeah, it is. When my uncle George purchased the land over twenty years ago, he barely had two dimes to rub together." He shrugs, still twirling the bottle. "It was a deal he couldn't pass up. He used all his savings on the land itself and purchased lumber and other items little by little until he had enough to build a small cottage. Originally, it was a two-bedroom, eight-hundred-square-foot cabin, not the four-thousand-square-foot party house it is today."

I smile, trying to picture a small cabin where the large home now rests. "How did it get the way it is now?"

Logan brings the rim of the bottle to his lips and tilts his head back, chugging the rest of the beer. I swallow as I watch his lips curl into a smile around the rim. After he finishes, he places the beer down and looks up at me with a lopsided grin. "As my uncle's business increased and more money came in, he began expanding the home. When Bryson, my brother, Sean, and I were in our teens, my uncle came up with a new tradition. Every summer, we'd come here and help with expansions and renovations until it became what it is now."

"That's amazing."

"It is. The thing is…" He lifts one leg, leaves the other dangling, and twirls his body so that he's facing me but not looking at me. His focus is over his left shoulder, on the house set back from the dock. "You'd think three teenage boys would want to spend their summers partying around, but we looked forward to helping with the lake house every year. There's a piece of each of us in there." He nods his head toward the property. "I guess that's why we make it a point to still come. I mean it's not like it used to be, filled with family, but I guess people grow and change."

"Yeah. People do."

Logan reaches for another beer bottle and twists it open. "So what's your story?"

"I don't have one," I reply automatically, but my words come out flat.

"Everyone has a story, Jenna." My name on his tongue

sounds foreign, odd, but nice.

"Mine's not worth telling."

"I doubt that."

I snap my head over irritably. "Why are you so interested?"

He shrugs, trying to school his features despite my nasty outburst. "I just think you're interesting. That's all. Is that a problem?"

"Trust me, the last thing you need is to know anything about my life. And the last thing I need is someone else judging me. So save yourself and become uninterested. Okay?" I hop to my feet. When I look down at him, a sigh escapes me and I relax my shoulders. He was sweet this morning, and now I'm being a bitch. "Look, I'm sorry for that. Just ignore me, okay? Thank you for being friendly."

I turn to walk away. Halfway down the dock he calls out, "I didn't tell anyone it was you this morning." I stop, but I don't look back.

"Thank you," is all I can say. Before he has the chance to say another word, I walk away, following the path back to the house. I climb the stairs to the deck and pass the partiers, who are now in various stages of inebriation. Charlie is sitting on Santino's lap on a patio chair. He hands her another shot glass; she tosses her head back and takes it. But the liquor must be too strong for her to handle. It's either that or she's over her limit because she spits it back out, coughing.

"Oh shit." Santino laughs.

I storm over. "Come on, Charlie. You've had enough. It's time for bed." I grip her arm and she stands sluggishly, stumbling into me.

"Oh, come on! It's still early. The party just started!" Santino raises his arms, begging.

"No. She's had enough."

Bryson stands up. He seems to be the only other person besides me that's not stupid drunk. "I'll help you get her up the steps."

"Thank you," I reply. He tosses Charlie's arm around his shoulder, grabs her waist, and hauls her in the house and up the stairs.

As soon as Charlie is settled in one of the twin beds and Bryson leaves, I lock the bedroom door and place a chair securely underneath the knob. I check the tiny closet in the room. It's clear. Then I make sure the window is locked and the curtains are drawn before hiding myself underneath the unfamiliar comforter and forcing myself asleep.

chapter 10

Jenna

It's quiet in this room, quieter than my own bedroom. There's no sound whatsoever. No creaks of the floorboards. No rotating blades of the ceiling fan. Nothing. Not even the voices I've grown accustomed to are present. Complete silence. Except for my own intrusive thoughts, which are rapidly running through my mind like a hamster on a spinning wheel. There's no stopping my thoughts of Logan, my mother, and Brooke.

I hate that Logan is even on my mind. He's no one. No one at all. Yet here he is, present and accounted for, drawing almost every ounce of my attention. I hate it. I hate it so much I almost wish for the voices to come back. At least with the voices I know what to expect for the most part. I've adjusted to them controlling every memory, every thought, and every image. And the fact that I'd rather their presence than the chaos of my own thoughts scares the hell out of me.

My chest tightens at my realization and a moan slips out as I force myself to sit up. My eyes scan the room. On a nightstand between the twin beds, bright red numbers blink at me. 5:00 a.m. Great. I groan, rub a frustrated hand over my face, and gingerly step out of bed. Charlie is sleeping away and I don't want to wake her. Being as discreet as possible, I reach for my cell and tiptoe toward the door, where I remove the chair from under the knob, unlock it, and close it gently behind me as I leave the room.

What now? It's five in the morning and I'm standing in a dark hallway by myself while everyone else sleeps. I need to wash my face to cool off my damp skin. Bryson mentioned last night that there's a bathroom on the second level, but with all of the doors down the hall closed, I can't make out which door leads to which room. Screw it. I'll just use the one downstairs; the last thing I need is for me to sneak into someone else's room and accidentally wake them up.

After I use the restroom, wash my hands, and tie my hair back in a ponytail, I step out. Just as I close the door behind me, I hear a loud thump.

I look over toward the kitchen to my right. Bryson is standing by the counter with an apologetic look on his face. He mouths, "Sorry." Then he bends over, grabbing an item off the floor, and straightens back up. "You're up early," Bryson whispers as he waves me over. Looking down at my feet, I slightly sway in place and inhale shakily. What's wrong with me? He's not going to attack me. Exhaling, I relax a bit and walk toward him.

"So are you," I respond as I reach the table. I stand there with my hands crossed behind my back.

He holds up an iPod, ear phones dangling from the device. "Yeah, I'm getting ready for my morning run."

"Ah." I nod and take note of his workout gear: sweat pants, a sleeveless T-shirt, and running sneaks.

"Would you like some coffee?" He points to the pot brewing, and then places the iPod on the counter.

"No, thank you. I don't drink caffeine."

He smiles. Bryson is just as good-looking as Logan. They're probably the same height, but where Logan has low-cut brown hair, Bryson has shaggy, dark blonde locks. Logan has blue-grey eyes. Bryson has green. Logan's arms are covered in tattoos. Bryson seems to have just a few, not nearly as many as Logan. "You don't drink alcohol or caffeine," he remarks. A small chuckle escapes his lips. "You're probably the first person I've met who doesn't drink either." There's no point letting him know that caffeine and alcohol have a bad effect on my condition and sometimes worsen my anxiety. It'll just lead him to questions about my illness.

He backs away from the counter and pours himself a cup of coffee.

"You drink it black?" I ask him. He nods in response with a smile. "No sugar?" He nods again, this time pressing the cup to his lips. "That's gross." I wrinkle my nose.

He raises a brow teasingly. "Coming from someone who doesn't drink it and who's anti-anything delicious."

I drop my arms from behind me. Shaking my head, a low, arrogant laugh tickles my throat. I pull a chair from underneath the table and have a seat. "I used to." I smile matter-of-factly with my arms crossed over the table.

Bryson pulls out a chair as well and sits across from me. "So did you have a good time last night, aside from having to babysit Charlie?"

My fingertips tap along the table. "Uh, yeah. It was okay."

He places both hands to his chest, feigning a hurt expression. "I'm wounded, McDaniel."

I shrug. "Sorry. It's just not my scene. But the place is beautiful. The lake is peaceful. I do love the scenery."

"Nah. I get it." He lifts the mug and takes another gulp

of his coffee. "Well, if you decide to stay today, it's going to be awesome."

I just remembered something. "Today is your birthday, right?" He nods. I grin at him. "Happy birthday."

His smile spreads wide. "Thanks."

"How old are you?" I'm not sure why, but this small talk is distracting me from my own thoughts. Why not keep the momentum going?

"Twenty-eight," he replies.

I wonder how old Logan is. "You and Logan are the only ones related between all the guys?"

"Yep. Logan is my cousin. His mother and my father are siblings."

"Who's older?"

His forehead wrinkles. "Between his mother and my father?"

I laugh. Stupid me. I wasn't clear. "No, between you and Logan."

He flicks his brows in realization. "Ah. I am. Logan is younger by two years."

Which makes Logan twenty-six. Five years older than me. I shouldn't be so curious, but I am, so I take advantage and continue to ask questions. "Are the two of you very close?"

"Yeah. I'm an only child, but I grew up living' next door to Logan and Sean all my life. We were the Three Musketeers."

"Sean is Logan's brother, right? The one who passed away?"

He nods, clasping his hands before him cautiously. He's just sitting there, not resisting or backing away from my interrogation. I lean into the table a little. "How did he pass away?"

"Accident," he answers.

"What kind of accident?"

"Motorcycle crash." Whoa. A chill shoots down my back and I cringe.

In a lower tone, I ask, "How long ago?"

"Two years ago," he responds, just as low.

I look up at him. I know how it feels to lose someone you love dearly, especially a sibling. "Am I asking too many questions?"

Bryson nods.

"I'm sorry." Great job, Jenna. You're finally around people and you just don't know how to keep quiet.

"It's okay. Can I ask you a question now?"

Well dammit. I guess I really don't have a choice. I nod for him to go on.

"Why are you so curious about Logan?"

Whoosh. That felt like a blow to my lungs. I lean back in my chair. "I'm not."

He doesn't seem so convinced. "Yeah, you are. All these questions, they're mostly about Logan."

I shake my head. "No. They were about both of you."

Bryson presses his hands flat on the table, pushing himself up to stand from the chair, and grabs the now empty mug. "No worries. I gotta go for my run. It was nice chattin' with ya." He places the cup in the sink and heads out the back door.

That was just awkward. What the hell is wrong with me? I need to learn how to control my impulses. A buzzing noise catches my attention. My phone is vibrating. I pick it up and look at the screen: DAD. He never calls me this early. I swipe the screen and hurriedly answer the call.

"Hello?"

A deep sigh comes through the earpiece. "Sweetheart,

I've been calling you."

"You have? I don't have any missed calls."

"Yes. I—" Shit. He's breaking up. I look at the phone. Dammit. I only have one bar.

"Dad, hold on. I'm not getting any reception in here. Let me step outside." Now out on the deck, I check my bars again. All five are active. "Dad?"

"Yes. Where are you?" He sounds clearer, worried.

I relax my shoulders. "I'm with Charlie. I'm fine, Dad. I just needed to get away."

"You can't do that, Jenna. You know better." Here we go again. The lecture. I see a bench swing up ahead, hanging from one of the trees. I head for it.

"I'm twenty-one. I can come and go as I please."

"Not in your condition," he argues.

My condition? I freeze. I hate it when he and Mom make it sound like that. "What did Mom tell you?" Silence. I push my feet forward until I reach the bench. I take a seat and push back off the ground, leaning into the sway as I swing forward and back. "What did she tell you?" I ask again.

"She said the two of you had an argument and that you said a few hurtful things, which caused her to retaliate."

Wow. She manages to bullshit her way through everything, all the time. I laugh. "And you believe her?"

My father lowers his tone. "Jenna. Come home. We can talk about this in person."

"No." I can't believe this. He believes her. Short, quick breaths start to take over. Calm down, Jenna. Breathe easy. "You always take her side. Always. Why?"

"You know that's not true. I'm trying to help both of you."

"Because of my *condition*. Is that right?"

"Jenna." He breathes heavily. "I didn't mean it that way. You know I love you."

I do. My father has always been there for me. Even with the differences between my mother and me, he's tried not to take sides. But lately she's managed to win him over. I inhale and exhale a shaky breath. "I know."

"Good. Listen, I know you're in good hands because you're with Charlie. Take as long as you need. Just text me to let know you're okay. Okay?"

I nod before realizing he can't see me. "Yeah. Okay."

"And you know what?"

"What?"

"How about when you get back we set a date for just the two of us?"

A comforting warmth floods through me. We haven't had a day like that in forever. After Brooke's death, he buried himself in work. I think it was the only way he knew how to deal with losing a daughter. I don't blame him; I buried myself away from the world the day she was taken from us. "I'd love that." I choke over the words.

"Good. I love you, sweetheart. Be safe, okay?"

"Okay. Love you too, Dad."

We end our call. I sit back, lift my feet onto the bench, and admire the beauty of the early morning as I swing alone.

chapter 11

Logan

Seriously? It's six in the morning. I don't even get up this early for work, let alone on a fucking Saturday. This sucks balls. I grumble out of bed, head for the kitchen, and grab a bottle of water. I almost choke on it. I'm never drinking again. Never. The fuck. Again. My body can't handle hangovers as well as it did in my early twenties. I toss the empty bottle of water, completely missing the overloaded bin filled with empty beer bottles. Oh well. I need more water. Opening the fridge again, I twist the cap off the second bottle and guzzle it down.

After Jenna left me on the dock last night, I pretty much chugged the rest of the beers, hung out for a bit, then called it quits. Well, I called it quits *after* Santino forced me to take a few shots with him. Then he called me a pussy for calling it a night so early. But I was tired as hell, and tonight will be the party of all parties. Last night was just a warm-up.

Which reminds me. Jenna was acting kind of weird last night. Weirder than usual. I don't even know how to get through to her. She must be strangely uninterested in me—or a lesbian. For my ego's sake, I hope it's the latter.

The back screen door squeaks as it's hurled open and closed. Bryson walks in from the deck with his headphones plugged into his ears, sweating and panting. I'm sure he's coming back from his early run. He's committed to that shit. Every morning, seven days a week. He never misses a morning. Don't get me wrong, I work out, but it's always in the evening. Like I said before, this early morning shit is not my thing.

He looks over at me. "Hey!" he shouts over the music blasting in his ears. I lift my hand, gesturing him to lower his voice. He removes the plugs. "My bad."

"It's cool. Happy birthday, man." I walk over, lifting my fist in front of me.

He taps a closed fist to mine. "Thanks. Tonight's gonna be wild. I think there's gonna be over fifty people here."

Fifty people is a lot for our parties. We usually keep it low-key and to a maximum of thirty. "That's cool," I say. "You need me to pick anything up for tonight or you think we got it all covered?" I ask. I'm pretty much up, so I reach for the already brewed pot of coffee and pour myself a cup.

"Nope. We have plenty of burgers, ribs, and chicken for the grill. I think we have enough beer and liquor to last the entire summer." He laughs, but I know he's probably right. The entire shed is stacked with cases of beer.

"Cool."

Still trying to catch his breath, he asks, "What are you doing up this early?"

I gulp down half the coffee. "Pfft. I wish I knew. But I was out early last night, so that may be it."

"Ah." He nods.

"What?"

"I didn't say anything," he says, raising his hands.

"You didn't have to. Your face says it all. What?"

He grabs a bottle of water from the fridge. "I thought maybe you were keeping tabs on Jenna." What is that supposed to mean? "You know, since she's outside and all." He nudges his head toward the door.

I look out the window above the sink and scan the outside. I don't see anyone on the deck or the dock by the lake. Then my eyes catch movement by a large tree on the left side. She's on the bench swing. By herself. "What does her being outside have to do with me?" I look back at Bryson, who's slowly backing away into the living area.

"I don't know. Go and talk to her."

"I did. Last night. And she doesn't seem interested. And you seem kind of pushy. What happened to not flirting with our clients?" I shrug it off as no big deal. "Why are you smiling like that?"

"Well, I had a little talk with her this morning. She seemed very interested in you. She couldn't stop asking questions."

"Really?"

"Now who's smiling?" he asks.

"Dick." I look back out the window. "Maybe I can take her out a cup of coffee."

"Nope. She doesn't drink coffee."

"Does she drink orange juice?" I ask, facing him again.

"How the hell should I know? I need to shower. Peace." He flashes two fingers, turns, and then jogs up the stairs.

I don't know why, but Jenna seems different than the girls I've always interacted with. Girls I've pursued in the past never pushed me away. They've always been pretty flirty, willing. Jenna is distant, shy, and keeps to herself. Sometimes, if a girl is worth it, I kind of like the chase. I'm curious to find out about her, to slowly break through her defenses, in a non-stalkerish, friendly kind of way. I'm not sure that even makes sense. But I'm damn well gonna try.

"Well, isn't this your lucky morning." I announce as I approach her.

She slowly crooks her neck to look up at me. "How so?" Well, at least she's not pushing me away. Yet.

"May I?" I point at the empty space beside her. She nods. I sit down, stabbing a foot to the ground to give us more of a push on the swing. "I brought this for you." She takes the red Solo cup filled with OJ.

"This isn't spiked, is it?" she teases, but something tells me it's a serious question.

"There's only one way to find out." She lifts the cup to the tip of her nose and takes a sniff. I laugh. "I'm joking. It's pure orange juice with some pulp." She flashes me a sly grin, then takes a sip. After the first taste, she downs the rest of it. "Whoa. Take it easy there, killer. You don't want to OD on pulp."

"Funny," Jenna says. Then she looks back at the lake. "It's peaceful here." She breathes in deeply. "It feels easy."

Easy sounds like the wrong word choice, but I encourage her to go on. "Yeah? Easy how?"

She leans back, getting comfortable on the wooden bench—the bench my brother and I built together. "Just easy. Life feels like it's always hard. There's never a calm way to get through it, to just breathe. Every day brings the same challenges, the same routines…the same everything. And as much as I hope the next day will be different, it's not. It's just the same old cycle over and over again." She turns her head and rests her chin on her shoulder. "Sorry. Is this too much for an early morning chat over orange juice?" She giggles nervously.

"No, not at all. I sometimes feel the best mornin' talks are had over a fresh cup of OJ."

She laughs. "Logan?"

"Yeah?"

"Thank you. For yesterday morning. And I'm sorry about last night—you know, the way I acted on the dock. It wasn't right—"

"Hey, don't worry about it. And you're welcome. Again." I tease.

"Again?"

"I mean…" I purse my lips, lift both arms, and shrug. "I keep saving your life: the pool, that Matthew dude, and then from the evil, perfect house. I think we're meant to be. After all, how could you resist this body?"

"Wow. Are you always this into yourself?"

"Hmm." I tilt my head, pretending to be in serious thought, then nod. "Pretty much."

She nudges my arm. "At least you're honest."

I smile. "That I am."

"Well, if it makes you feel any better, thank you for all three."

"It does," I say. Jenna laughs again. Then my mind drifts back to her earlier statement. "If it makes you feel any better, I do feel that way sometimes. Like you mentioned about life being a constant cycle."

"Like you're trapped in a nightmare, where you're screaming for someone to wake you, but it never happens?"

I nod. It does feel like that at times.

Jenna's expression changes to compassion. "I remember you saying something like that yesterday. After you lost your brother, right?" she says.

Yesterday, as she stood in her pajamas on the corner, I

told her how after Sean's death, I felt like I was stuck, at a standstill. Me and my big fucking mouth. It's been two years since his death, and it still kind of fucking hurts to talk about him. But I do anyway. "Yeah. We were really close."

"I was very close with my sister before she passed," she confesses.

A jolt of shock rushes through me. "You had a sister who passed?" She nods. "How long ago?"

"About eight months now."

"Wow." It's all I can say; I can't believe she lost a sibling as well. In some ways, this explains a lot about what I've witnessed of her so far.

"Yeah," Jenna says quietly.

"Is it too early for me to ask how she passed?" She looks down and nods. I can understand. For the first year of Sean's death, it was difficult for me to talk about how it happened without it taking an emotional toll on me.

This little confession of hers sparks an idea. I stand from the bench and reach for her wrist. She looks down at my grip, then back up at me. "Come on," I say. "I want to show you something."

She doesn't resist. Instead, she reaches out and places her hand in mine. I hold her small, delicate hand the entire time as I lead her toward a large wooden shed. I leave the doors wide open, just in case she feels uncomfortable, and guide her in. Jenna looks around but doesn't say a word. She steps toward the first table and our hands lose contact as hers slips away. I kind of wish she'd held on just a bit longer. I would be lying if I said I didn't enjoy it, because I did. A lot.

Jenna slowly walks past each carved sculpture, lightly brushing her fingers against them as she admires each one.

"Did you make these?" she asks.

"No. Sean did. At first it was a hobby for him. Then he became really good at it. He did it as a way to cope with his depression." She looks back at me. Her features are pinched but unreadable.

"He suffered from depression?"

"Yeah." I move forward, standing beside her as I look over each sculpture. "He was dealing with a lot of difficult issues. Issues a regular teenager should never have to go through."

Jenna crosses her arms, hugging herself as if she's chilly. "What kind of issues?" she asks.

I swallow, wondering if she'll act like most everyone else who hears about Sean's story. "When he was younger, about seventeen years old, he was reckless and out of control. What teen isn't, right? Well, one night he was underage drinking and driving with a few friends in a car. He accidently ran a red light and hit two people crossing the street—a kid and his mom."

"Oh my God," Jenna lets out in a raspy tone.

"Yeah." I nod, tempted to leave it as that, but I decide to keep going. "He didn't leave the scene. He pulled over and called an ambulance. He waited there and held the kid in his arms until help came. But by the time they arrived, the kid had lost so much blood he was already dead. The mother suffered severe injuries, but she survived. Sean did some time in jail for it. Once he was released, he was never the same. Mentally. He couldn't get the image of that scene out of his head and knowing that his irresponsible behavior killed an innocent boy made him insane."

It's the first time I've spoken about Sean's history with anyone. Family and close friends who know of the incident never speak of it. When Sean was released from prison at twenty-two, everyone just tried to pretend it never happened. But Sean still lived with it every single day until the day he died.

I went on, staring intensely at one of the pieces—a half angel, half demon full-body sculpture. "Some say that Sean's death was an accident, that he lost control of his bike and hit the tree. He wasn't drinking. It wasn't snowing or raining. It wasn't dark out. It was a direct hit to the tree. As much as everyone wants to believe it was an accident, I know in my gut that he did it on purpose. It wasn't the first time he tried to take his life. It was the day before the anniversary of the kid's death. I think he couldn't handle it anymore, and I think he thought if all of us believed he died in a motorcycle accident, we wouldn't feel guilty. Guilty for not trying hard enough to get him help."

I back away from the table, face Jenna, and look down at her. She stares at me with puffy eyes. But there's no pity in them, just understanding. "Why are you telling me this?" she asks.

"I don't know." I shrug. "It just feels right. I've never talked to anyone about it, but I think knowing you can relate makes it easier." It does make it easier. Jenna knows how it feels to grow up in a household with someone all your life— your best friend—only to have them taken away from you in the blink of an eye. "I also wanted you to realize that even though the pain will always be there, I'm living proof you can get past this. Right now I know it feels impossible, but one day you'll look back and see how far you've come."

Jenna lifts her hand to my face and cups my jaw. There's warmth where she touches. Her eyes stare intensely into mine. I stare back, waiting for her to say something. My gaze drops to her lips—those perfectly pouty, pink lips—which she wets with a stroke of her tongue. She opens her mouth to say something and then shuts it quickly. "Thank you," she finally whispers as her eyes water. She tries fighting back the tears, but she can't, and a few escape.

"Come here." I bring her close, wrapping my arms tight around her. She buries her face in my chest, and I think about the pain we both share. More than anything, I wish Jenna and I were bonding over something else, that she didn't know what it feels like to lose a sister and I a brother. I rest my chin on her hair and hold her, giving her whatever comfort I can.

After we stand this way for what seems like forever, Jenna looks up at me, her tearstained cheeks flushed. She seems embarrassed by our small connection and pulls away from me. "I-I'm so sorry. I didn't mean to cry on you. I'm so very sorry," she says.

"Don't be. You needed it. It's okay to cry sometimes." I smile. "It's kind of nice chatting with someone who doesn't know me and doesn't judge me for a change."

She furrows her brow. "Why would I judge you?"

"Because that's what most people do when they hear what my brother was responsible for or the reason behind his jail time. They look at me with revulsion, or they whisper something like 'His brother is a murderer.' They make it seem like I did it."

Jenna sniffs, brushing her nose with the back of her hand. "You're not your brother, Logan," she says with a simple shrug. "And even at that, I'm sure he wasn't a bad guy. It sounds to me like he was a young kid that made a terrible mistake, and he had to live with that mistake for the rest of his life."

Does she even know that those are the exact words I needed to hear right now? "Thank you," I say.

Her pouty lips tug into a tiny smile. Damn. I'd do anything to touch those lips again. "You're welcome," she says. Then she turns around and walks out of the shed. I fight back the urge to reach out, grab her, and kiss her. Not like the kiss we had on her front porch when I first met her. Don't get me wrong, that kiss…well…it heightened all my senses and could have turned into much more than just a kiss. But it wasn't a real fucking kiss. I want to show her how much this one moment truly meant to me. Wow. I'm starting to sound like a little bitch.

"Jenna," I call out. She turns around.

"Yes?"

"Go out with me. On a date." From the look on her face, I can tell I've caught her off guard. She opens her mouth to speak but closes it just as quickly. "You don't have to give me an answer right now," I say. "Think about it."

"I don't think it's a good ide—"

"Do me a favor and just think about it first. Okay?"

She nods. "Okay. I will."

I arch a brow. "You'll think about it? Or you'll go out with me."

Jenna casually laughs. "I'll think about it, Logan."

And then she's gone.

chapter 12

Jenna

I can't believe I just cried my eyes out in front of Logan. What the hell was I thinking? Some of the things he said resonated with me so deeply that I allowed myself to show weakness in front of him. His empathy, his understanding, his loss completely shook my resolve. How pathetic am I?

There's a part of me that feels relieved—relieved that I was able to just let it out. He's a stranger. I don't know anything about him aside from the little I've seen. Even so, I feel a unique connection with Logan. When he revealed the details of his brother's death, I felt sympathy for him, but not in the way an outsider might. It was coming from a place of first-hand knowledge, from a place of compassion. I felt his pain, the struggle I imagine he went through, and his loss. I've lived through it.

There's another part of me that feels it may have been a mistake—a huge, stupid mistake. I don't want him to think that because we shared a moment there could be something more between us. Because there can't be. Of that I'm certain. Logan is probably a good guy. Or maybe he's not. Either way, he's a risk I'm not going to take.

I grab a bottle of water from the fridge and sneak back into the bedroom, quietly shutting the door behind me. I turn and see Charlie sitting against the headboard of the twin bed. Her shoulders and head are slumped over, but she looks up when she hears me. I smile. She rolls her eyes. "Don't take out your hangover anger on me," I say, treading over to her.

"I'm never drinking again." Sure. That's a famous line of hers. I hand her the bottle of water. "Thank you," she mumbles, snatching it from my hand. Charlie unscrews the cap and chugs back the entire bottle. She places the empty bottle on the nightstand beside her and leans her head back against the headboard. "Oh God. I'm going to be sick."

"I'm pretty sure you threw up all of last week's meals last night." I hand her the clean bucket from beside her bed and take a seat across from her on the bed I slept in last night.

Charlie settles the bucket between her legs and stares into it. "Where were you?" she asks as she concentrates on the green container.

"Downstairs. I couldn't sleep and didn't want to wake you."

She nods. "I woke up over a half hour ago. I didn't have the strength to go looking for you. I told myself if you didn't come back in fifteen minutes, I was going to force myself to search."

"Ha! I'm sure you would've made it," I tease. "Whenever you get yourself together and ready, we'll drive back. Take your time."

She groans. "Do we have to leave? I'm seriously in no mood to take a three-hour drive back home. It's not like you can take the wheel if I get sick."

"We're not staying another night, Charlie."

"Come on. I'm going to need a day to recuperate. I

promise I won't drink today. I'll keep it to just soft drinks. Don't make me drive back home like this." She pouts her lips and rolls her head back against the wooden headboard.

"Oh my God. I can't believe you're making me feel guilty."

"Do you want to face your mother today?"

"Low blow." And the brief reprieve I had without thoughts of my mother is now over. "Fine."

Charlie doesn't smile at my concession. She just sighs and her shoulders deflate. "Thank God," she says. Then she sinks into the bed, tossing the covers over her face.

It's noon. I sat in bed channel surfing on the tiny television until Charlie woke up. I couldn't leave the room and face Logan alone after what happened this morning. Charlie grumbled out of bed with only the word "food" escaping her mouth. I waited patiently as she showered and put on shorts, a tank top, and flip-flops. Now, we're finally heading downstairs together.

"There's my little alcoholic," Santino sings as Charlie and I step into the kitchen. All of the guys are hanging out in here. Danny, Justin, and Scott are seated by the table, dishing some food onto their plates. Bryson is by the stove, cooking, and Logan is leaning against the counter with his legs and arms crossed. His eyes are on me. Even though I just saw him a few short hours ago, my chest constricts. I look away.

"That's me," Charlie responds with her arms raised. She walks over to Santino. He pulls her into his lap and she lets out giggles.

"If you girls are hungry, we have plenty of breakfast."

Bryson points toward the center of the table where there are several plates filled with pancakes, waffles, bacon, and sausages. "Help yourselves."

"I'm starving!" Charlie turns to face the food, still on Santino's lap, and grabs herself a plate. She begins filling it.

"Jenna?" Logan says. I look over. He's pointing at one of the empty chairs for me to take a seat. I shake my head.

"No, thank you."

Charlie waves her hand. "She barely eats. I could never do it."

Santino looks over and says, "Are you one of those girls who force themselves not to eat because they want to keep a stick figure image? Because personally, I love me a curvy woman. The more curves, the better." He grips Charlie's hips and begins to bounce her. Her laughs fill the room as my irritation spikes.

"What? No. I eat. I'm just not hungry." I want to kill Charlie right now. She looks over at me, and her smile instantly disappears. She mouths, "Sorry."

Everyone digs in to their plates, except for me and Logan, who's still leaning against the counter all good-looking and cool, like he doesn't have a care in the world. It's annoying. I feel awkward now. Out of place. I let out a deep breath, force a small smile, and make my way out the back and toward the dock.

"I'm really sorry, Jenna. You know I wouldn't say anything to make you feel bad, especially about yourself. Right?" Charlie grips my shoulder. I look up at her.

"Yeah, I know. It's fine."

She smiles gently. "We're all going to take a dip in the lake and play a few games. You should join us. It'll be fun. Maybe it'll take you out of this little slump you're in."

"I'm not in a slump."

"Look, I know you don't want to be here, but can you at least pretend? You're acting like the antisocial kid right about now."

"I am the antisocial kid."

"Well, can you not be today? Let's have fun today."

I let out a draining breath, pause, then nod. We head for our bedroom and change into our swimsuits.

When we exit the house, there are several people hanging around in the back area—more than just the guys and us. There are girls in bikinis and guys in swim trunks that I haven't seen before. Some are on the deck, sipping on drinks. Others are by the grass. There's a net set up, so some are playing volleyball. There's a table set up with aluminum containers filled with food. My stomach growls, and I cover my belly with my hand. "I'm kind of hungry," I whisper to Charlie.

"I bet. You haven't eaten. Let's grab a quick bite then we'll head for the dock."

We step down the deck and walk over to where the food is. We both grab a plate. I prepare a burger while Charlie fills her plate with all sorts of things. When I look in the direction of the lake, I almost drop my food. Logan is there, wearing nothing but wet swim trunks that hang deliciously from his hips. I knew he was in great shape by the way his clothes fit him, but I wasn't expecting a GI Joe physique.

"Whoa. Check out your man. Did you expect to find that

E.L. MONTES

under his shirt?" Charlie says, pulling me out of my ogling session.

"He's not my man."

"Does he know that? Oooh. He's on his way over here. He must've spotted you." Oh shit. I look at Charlie, scared shitless. She smiles. "Don't be scurd." She winks. This is no joking matter. I can't handle him, especially while he's half naked.

"I'm not scared."

"I wonder how he's packing."

"What?"

"You know." She lifts a squirmy hotdog in one hand. "Weiner?" Then she reaches for something else. "Or large corn on the cob?" She wiggles her brows as she shakes both items. My face flames at the thought.

"Can you stop it? He's getting closer."

We both look his way. You know how when you're told not to look at something you automatically look at it? Yeah. I'm trying my hardest not to look down, but I can't help it. I take a gander below his waist, at his trunks pressing against his...junk. Oh my God. I blink and face Charlie, embarrassed. Did he see me checking him out?

"Oh, yes, definitely large corn on the cob. He's a keeper, Jenna. Go get ya man!"

"Shut up!"

She laughs. Logan is now standing in front of us. "Hello, ladies," he says.

Oh my God. Don't look at his junk. Don't look at his junk. Don't look at his—dammit I looked. Again. Breathe. Maybe he didn't notice. I straighten my shoulders and meet his eyes. He's smiling brightly. A little too brightly. Oh God. He totally caught me. Great. "Hi," I manage to get out.

"Want to play football with us? We play in the lake."

"Oh, tackle football in the water." Charlie nods with a big smile. My eyes widen, silently telling her no. She ignores me and nods again, making the decision for the both of us. "We like playing football, and it's a very touchy-feely game. Count *us* in."

"Great. After you girls fuel up"—he nudges his head to our filled plates—"we'll get started." Logan leans into my ear and whispers, "You're on my team." He grins then walks away.

"All right, these are the rules for the game," Bryson shouts from the water. I'm standing by the edge of the dock with my arms crossed, listening and trying to figure out how this is going to work. All of the guys are in the lake already. They're all taller than I am, so the water reaches just above their waists. For Charlie, who's tiny, it'll probably reach her chest, and for me, mid-stomach.

As Bryson goes on about the rules, I look around. Logan, Santino, Charlie, and I are on the same team. Logan and Santino are in the water about four or five yards away from the dock. Their arms are crossed as they listen to Bryson. Charlie's in her bikini, sitting Indian style on the dock beside me, her cover-up thrown carelessly beside her.

I've never played a sport in my life. Well, if you consider baseball in the backyard at the age of five a sport, then I guess I've played some kind of sport. But I've never played football. And although the rules Bryson's calling out aren't exactly pro-football rules, I'm still keeping my ears open to every single detail.

Bryson stretches his arm to show us our "touchdown" marker, which is a tree farther down the side of the lake. When he turns back around to face us, his face lights up and he yells out, "Babe!" I zoom in on him as his gaze focuses behind me.

Logan scoffs. "Great."

My instant reaction is to turn around and see Bryson's "babe" for myself. As if my life isn't interesting enough, the antagonist of my very own horrifying chick flick—Blair Bitch—is treading her way toward me. Blair Bitch, whom I spent four terrible years of high school with, is the same girl that I punched in the face, which led me to the principal's office, which led me to meeting Eric—the one and only love of my life.

Her green eyes go from squinty—as if she's trying to place my familiar face—to bulging out of their sockets once she figures out who I am. My stomach turns as she rushes over to me with her arms spread wide. Then her features twist sympathetically. I'm both shocked and frozen as she wraps her arms around me and pulls me into a very, very tight hug.

My arms are glued to my side while I try to regain my fuzzy thoughts. "Jenna! Oh my God, how are you?" She pulls away, holding me at arm's length. "I'm so sorry to hear about Brooke." She shakes her head. "It's just a shame. A big ole shame." She shakes her head again.

"Uh, thanks?" She didn't know Brooke, but everyone in our town and those who went to the same high school as we did were well aware of what happened to her. It was all over the news and media, which I made a point to stay away from.

Blair Bitch drags her palms down my biceps, past my forearms, and grips my hands firmly. I'm still trying to figure out what kind of alternate universe I just stepped into where my archenemy would approach me in such a manner, when she says, "I just want you to know I forgive you for your past aggressions, and I hope we can become really good friends. After all, we're not in high school anymore."

"Um, okay."

Bryson is now on the dock beside us. He leans in and pecks her cheek. "Hey, babe." Babe? Oh my God, it just registered. Blair Bitch is babe. They're dating.

Blair steps back and wipes her cheek. "Bryson!" she chastises. "I've spent all morning on my makeup."

"Sorry." He half smiles. "I didn't think you'd be coming. How do you two know each other?" He points between us.

Blair smiles at me like we're BFFs or something. "We went to high school together."

"Cool," Bryson says. "Want to play with us, babe? We're about to start a game." He lifts the football in his hand.

"No." She laughs. "You know I don't play any sports."

Bryson shrugs. "Just figured I'd ask. All right, you can watch, then." He turns and jumps into the lake, making a splash upon contact.

"Well, I guess I should get in there," I say, backing away, an awkward smile plastered to my face. This is weird. The entire scene is weird. I need to get in the lake. I remove my cover-up before jumping in.

Charlie joins me, and we swim farther from the dock before she asks, "Who is that?"

"That's Blair Bitch. We went to high school together. We weren't exactly friends," I say with my eyes on Blair. She's standing with a huge smile, waving over at us.

Logan swims up beside me, his face irritated. "Great. There goes my night. How do you know Mega Bitch?"

I laugh. "You call her Mega Bitch? My nickname for her in high school was Blair Bitch. I haven't seen her in four years, not since I graduated. I'm guessing things haven't changed?"

"Nope," he says, narrowing his eyes in her direction. "She's still a bitch."

"Good to know."

Bryson claps his hands. "All right, let's start!"

We're all scattered around. Bryson holds out the football and taps his hand against it. "Hut"—he looks to the right—"hut"—he looks to his left—"hike!" He tosses the ball toward Danny, and Logan immediately closes in on him. Logan jumps to midair and then grabs the football, taking it down with him under water. Seconds later he jumps up with the ball in his hand. I jump up clapping. "Go!" I yell out excitedly.

Never having played a sport before, I didn't expect it to be this fun. Logan hurries through the water, dodging the other guys. Justin throws his body forward, grips Logan by the shoulders, and tackles him under the water.

Yikes. Charlie and I jog through the water toward them the best we can. Logan finally jumps back up, football still in hand, and keeps going.

"Touchdown!" Logan yells out, splashing the football into the water when he reaches our touchdown tree.

Charlie and I scream and yell, jumping up and down. "YES!" We reach him, and he lifts both hands toward us for high fives. "That's how you do it." He winks at me.

"All right, all right. Lucky first shot. It's your throw," Bryson calls out.

"Jenna, you're going to throw the ball, okay?" Logan says to me.

Wide-eyed, I respond, "Uh, no. Have Santino or Charlie. I've never played before."

"I'll show you. Santino and Charlie are going to spread

out as far as possible, and you're going to throw the ball to them."

Charlie nods. "You can do it, girl." Then she swims farther down.

I look around; everyone is waiting for me. "What if I screw it up? I've never thrown a football before, Logan." I turn, facing him.

His mouth forms a full smile—an adorable, infectious, completely beautiful smile. "No worries. I'll show you." He turns me to face everyone, then presses his front to my back. My chest expands. He leans his head down and presses his cheek to mine. "Left or right?" he murmurs against my skin.

I sink into him. "Huh?"

He chuckles. "Are you left- or right-handed?"

I swallow. "Oh, I'm…" What am I again? "Right. Yeah, definitely right-handed."

"Are you sure?" I can hear the humor in his tone. I nod, distracted by my cheek brushing against his freshly grown facial hair.

"All right." He reaches for my hand, lifts it, and places the football on my palm. "How does that feel?" His breath cools my skin.

"Good," I mumble.

"You have to grip it a bit tighter," he says. My left hand grips his firmly. "The ball, Jenna. You need a firm grip on the football so it doesn't slip out of your hand."

"Oh." I press my fingers into leather skin of the ball. "Like that?"

"Yeah, good." His fingers press over mine, and then he slightly lifts my arm, with his right behind it, over our heads. I have to reach up on my tiptoes because he's much taller than me. Logan brings his left hand to my stomach, pressing me firmly against his chest. "Who do you want to toss the ball to?"

I flash my eyes open. Dammit, I didn't realize they were closed. I look around. All eyes are on us, waiting patiently.

"Charlie," I say. She's more open than Santino.

"Sure?" he asks. I nod.

"All right, I'm going to bring our arms back just a bit more. When I say let go, just let go of the ball and let it fly over to her. Okay?" I nod. "Ready?"

"Yes."

Logan does as he said he would, bringing back our arms then swinging them forward. He lifts me a bit higher with his left arm and yells out, "Let go!"

I did. The football darts toward Charlie. Her face is surprised but happy when she lunges for it. The guys from the other team immediately try to run for it, and as the play continues, all I can think about is Logan, his hold on me, the way his right hand drags down my arm, and how as he slowly brings me down to my feet, my body slides along his.

Then he pulls away. I hate that he did. I like the way I felt against him. I like the way his stubble felt against my skin. I like the way his arm felt around my stomach. I just like being near him.

Before I can reel in my thoughts, Logan's hand slaps my ass. I jump. "Good job." He winks; then he swims toward the rest of the group surrounding Charlie.

We lost the game. Win or lose, I had a really good time. It was getting kind of late and more partiers were arriving, so I took a shower, changed, and headed back down.

Charlie is sitting by the fire pit with Santino when I get out back. Logan is there as well. His eyes catch mine and I smile at him. He smiles back and waves for me to come over. I'm about fifteen feet away when Blair Bitch calls my name. I turn around.

"I wanted to talk to you." She looks over my shoulder.

"Okay. What's up?" I ask.

"Are you and, you know, Logan, like, a thing?"

"No."

She nods. "Oh. Because it seems like you are."

"I can assure you we're not. Aren't you with Bryson? Do you have a thing for Logan?"

She grimaces. "Um, no. I would never date Logan even if I was single."

She's got my full attention now. "Why not?" I ask.

She takes in a deep, dramatic breath. "Well, he's not exactly the commitment type. And he's slept with a few of my friends—who all had bad experiences with him. Not in bed! Just, you know, the way he treated them afterward. I haven't seen you in a long time, and I really want to make amends with you, so I guess this is my way of apologizing. I'd really love to be friends." She smiles.

"Yeah. Thanks. I appreciate that."

I decide to stay away from the fire pit and go for a walk instead.

chapter 13

Logan

Mega Bitch waves at me and smiles wickedly. What the hell? Because I know she has a tendency of making my life a living hell every time she's around, I can only imagine what she just said to Jenna. I know for a fact she's putting her devilish claws away right now because before she got to her, Jenna was coming my way. Now she's walking in the opposite direction, heading toward the bench swing. Great. I stand, ignore the questions about where I'm going, and head over to Jenna.

She's swinging alone. I plop my ass down beside her without asking, but she doesn't look at me. She keeps her eyes focused straight ahead. "Can I help you?" she asks.

Yep. Mega Bitch said something to tick her off. But I'm not one to beat around the bush. "I saw you talking to Blair."

"Yeah. And?"

"And she said something to you about me, didn't she?"

"No."

"You're lying."

She turns to look at me. "Why do you think she'd talk about you? To me, no less?"

"Because Mega Bitch and I despise one another. We

don't speak *at all*. We can't stand to be in the same room to-gether. And when we are, she manages to do anything and everything to grate on every nerve of mine. So after she stopped you just now, then waved at me as if she won some type of stupid fucking game, I knew she said something to turn you off. So spill it."

Jenna huffs out a long, draining breath. "She said you're not the commitment type."

"Half true," I confess.

"You slept with almost all of her friends."

"I slept with *one* friend of hers. After I realized the two of them were friends, I ended that shit real quick. Go on."

Jenna narrows her eyes. "You treat women like crap."

"In the short amount of time we've spent together, have I treated *you* like crap?"

"No. But you could be trying to get into my pants."

I smile. "What makes you think you're my type?" She quickly closes her mouth. "I'm kidding, Jenna. You're defi-nitely my type. Trust me."

"Well, you're not mine." For some reason that tiny insult makes me chuckle. "I'm serious," she adds. I nod, still smil-ing. She squares her shoulders and continues, "Logan, I'm just not that into you. At all."

"Okay, I get the hint. And because you're *just not that into me*, I'm guessing no date?"

She shakes her head and shrugs once. "No. Sorry."

"Well damn. There's no way I can change your mind? Not even this." I wave my hand over my face and smile charmingly.

She laughs and taps a fist to my shoulder. "You're a dork."

I chuckle. "That's a first."

Jenna's smile softens. "Seriously, though, can we be friends? Is that okay?"

Friends. I allow the word to simmer in my thoughts. "I'm not certain two people of the opposite sex—who are clearly attracted to each other—can remain friends."

"I have a feeling you're attracted to most any woman."

I raise a finger. "Nuh-uh, not Mega Bitch. I'm definitely not attracted to her."

Jenna laughs again, a bit harder this time. "Okay, you have a point. But you can do it. We can be friends. I have hope for you."

"All right, McDaniel. I can't promise I won't try to cop a feel here and there or try to kiss you or even try to make you fall for me. But I can most definitely try not to."

"You're funny," she says, her lips pursing to the side.

"It's part of my charm." Jenna shakes her head and leans back in the swing. I wrap my arm around her shoulder and pull her into my side. She freezes. "I'm a touchy-feely kind of guy, but I promise not to cop a feel on the first night of our friendship."

She nudges my rib with an elbow. "Jerk." Then she nestles closer to me. "Want to hear something funny?"

"Always," I respond, giving us another push with my foot. The swing takes off again.

"It's about Blair Bitch."

"You mean Mega Bitch?" I correct her.

"How about we combine the two and from now on refer to her as Blair Mega Bitch."

"Hmm…" I repeat the name in my head. "I like. Go on."

"All right. Well, Blair Mega Bitch and I weren't exactly BFFs."

"Thank God because you'd be swinging alone," I joke.

Jenna chuckles, then goes on, "We were actually the opposite. I hated her as much as she hated me. But it was high school. I think every teenage girl has at least one enemy in high school."

"Which I never understood. I thought all you girls stuck together. You know, girl power and all."

"Are you going to let me tell the story?" I don't respond, giving her clearance to go on. "Well, one day I was walking down the hall on my way to class and spotted Blair Mega Bitch with her clique. I ignored their usual stares and kept going. I didn't expect her to put her foot out and trip me as I passed by her."

"Wow. How original."

"Right? Anyway, I wasn't one of those antisocial kids that ran to the bathroom crying after being picked on. Instead, I was the antisocial kid that fought back. So I gathered my things, put them aside, straightened my shoulders, turned around to face her as she laughed her head off, and punched her straight in the face."

Right here, right now, I feel pride. So much pride. I can't contain myself. I pull Jenna up, face her, and place my hands on her shoulders, looking excitedly into her eyes. She narrows her stare, not exactly sure what I'm about to say or do. I breathe in and, in my best Will Ferrell impersonation, blurt out, "Did we just become best friends?"

Jenna smiles, nods once, and says in a deep tone, "Yep!" It's the worst John Reilly impersonation I've ever heard. I burst out laughing. She's seen *Step Brothers*.

Motherfucking score!

Then the most perfect plot of all fucking plots stirs in my head. I can be friends with her and slowly make her fall for me. "Do you like ice cream?" I ask.

She raises a brow. "Uh, yeah?"

"We're gonna go out for ice cream this week." I say.

"Logan. That's a date."

"Since when has going out for ice cream been a date? Kids go out for ice cream. It's friendly. Very, very friendly. In fact, to prove it's not a date, I'll even put my ego aside and allow you to pay."

Jenna laughs. It's the sweetest laugh I've ever heard. "You're trying to sneak in a date with me."

I raise my hand to my chest. "Promise. Not a date, just a friendly outing. Two friends, chatting over gelatos, sharing the same hate interest for a Blair Mega Bitch."

"All right," she says.

I smile.

chapter 14

Jenna

This weekend at the lake house was—well, I can't explain it. I just needed it. It was the perfect end to a screwed-up beginning. I won't admit this out loud, but I'm actually happy Charlie talked me into going. At first it was difficult for me to be social and open up, but Logan made it easy. No, I didn't open up one hundred percent about myself. But there were times this weekend when he brought out a side of me I hadn't seen for a long time. I miss that part of me. And even though I get this tingly feeling in the pit of my stomach when I'm around him—which is more than what a friend should feel for another friend—I like that we agreed to be *just* friends.

Because deep down I know he'll never want to be with someone like me. The real me. The *me* he has yet to see. The question is if I keep spending time with him, will I be able to keep that part hidden?

We're on our drive back to Jersey now. Charlie's chatting away as I lean back in the passenger seat. My eyes catch the reflection of my smile in the passenger window. Smiling. It's such an odd expression for me. And it's because of Logan. The way he treated me this weekend. The way I felt around him. He made me laugh, made me feel comfortable with being a goof, playful even. And for the first time in as long as I can remember, it was okay to feel those things.

I must admit, when I first laid eyes on him in my backyard by the swimming pool, I would've never pegged him for the friendly, gentle goofball—probably one of the biggest I'll ever meet—that he is. So what if I only spent a few days with him? I still can't imagine Logan being the person Blair Mega Bitch claimed him to be. If she's anything like she was back in high school, I'm certain it was just a ploy to get back at Logan—or me, for that matter—for one thing or another.

"You and Logan seemed a bit friendly this morning," Charlie prods.

I turn my head, facing her, "What do you mean?"

Charlie looks straight ahead, focusing on the long tree-lined road. "Well, for starters, he was practically all over you this morning…and it was kind of awkward."

I'm caught off guard. "He was not all over me this morning. And what was awkward?"

"Yeah, okay. He was sitting beside you with his arm over your shoulder, and you were leaning into him. The both of you kept whispering in each other's ears and laughing."

She's talking about when Logan and I were cracking jokes about Blair Mega Bitch during breakfast. "And what's so awkward about that?" I ask.

"It's not a bad awkward. It's just like, I don't know—it felt weird watching you like that. You seemed happy."

"It's weird to see me happy?" I retort. Charlie's little statement causes a flash of heat between my ears, and I'm sure my face is flushing right now. Have I been that out of touch with myself that I haven't even realized how miserable I've been? So miserable, in fact, that seeing me happy is out of place? Now I'm kind of angry with myself.

"No. No, Jenna. I'm just curious. The two of you were, well, out on that swing the entire night in your own la-la land. Did something happen? Are you guys, like, well…hooking up?"

I laugh self-consciously. "Hooking up? No. We realized we have a lot in common, that's all. And I told him I'd prefer to just be friends. He was fine with that. I don't know Logan entirely, but it's nice to have someone to talk to."

"You can always talk to me." Her voice is soft, perhaps with a bit of jealousy.

I reach out, placing a hand on her shoulder. "Charlie, I will always have you, and you'll always have me. You're an amazing friend. But you're the one who said I should stop being the antisocial kid. This is *me* stopping that."

She sighs, nodding. "You're right. I just want you to be careful, ya know? I want to make sure you're careful. That's all."

"I already told you I don't feel like he'd hurt me."

"I know he won't harm you physically, Jenna. I'm talking about emotionally. I don't want to see you get hurt, emotionally." I stare at her, taking in what she just said. I know exactly what she means. Slowly, I push my feelings for Logan aside. I tuck them away in the back of my chest, hiding them behind a large brick wall. Charlie peeks over at me. "Did you tell him? About…you know," she asks. She's referring to my illness.

I look straight ahead, and only the memory of a smile remains on my face. "No. And I'd like to keep it that way," I respond.

The sound of Charlie's tires screeching to a stop is much louder in my head than in actuality. My chest feels heavy as I look out the window and see my home. Home. What actually defines a home? Is it simply a place you reside, surrounded by four walls and topped with a roof? Or is home a place someone looks forward to returning to after being away for a long or short period of time? A place where someone can feel safe? A place that, if you were alone on a deserted island, you could dream about in order to keep your hopes for survival alive? Is that what home is?

For *me*? I dread home. Every bit of it.

I haven't faced my mother since I ran out of the house during my last episode. Fear of what will be waiting for me pulls at my chest.

Charlie reaches for my hand and brings it down from my face. I didn't realize, yet again, I've been chewing the inside of my cheek. "Do you want to stay at my house? You're welcome to stay as long as you like," she says softly.

I shake my head, let out a long shaky breath, and force a smile as I face her. "No, but thank you—for everything." I reach over, wrap my arms around her, and squeeze her in a hug.

"Of course," she mumbles into my hair. "Always, Jenna. If you need me to come pick you up, I'm only a phone call away. Okay?" I nod and pull away.

After collecting my luggage from the trunk, I wave good-bye to my friend and walk up the pathway toward the double wooden doors. The entire time, my mind races with various scenarios of what to expect on the other side. I freeze once I reach the first step of the porch. My hand grips the handle of the black luggage. My teeth skillfully maneuver the raw meat of my inner cheek, gnawing away. My heart thump thumps in slow motion, yet every nerve in my body is sensitive, on high alert.

Take a step, a soft voice in my head urges. I'm not sure if it's mine, but I do what it says. *Another step.* I do it again. *One more.* Now at the top, I move forward to the door. *Grab your keys.* I reach in my purse and dig them out, searching for the right one. I place it into the keyhole.

Click.

It unlocks. Cautiously, I tap a finger against the door. It swings open. I blink a few times and look straight ahead. It's exactly the same, except the black and white marble tiles in the foyer are shinier. The large round table is still there; the only difference is the color of the fresh-cut roses in the center. These are pink. It's quiet. Eerily quiet. Swallowing back my anxiety, I step in, close the door behind me, and quickly run up the stairs.

One Day Later.

"Hello?" I answer the call on the first ring.

"Hello, Jenna. It's Tiffany."

"Hi, Tiffany," I respond to my father's assistant for the last ten years.

"Your father asked me to call you. He wanted you to know he received your text, and it just so happens an opening for tomorrow is available. Would you like to have lunch with him at noon at the restaurant Moon?"

"Okay."

"Great! I'll schedule you in. I'll have a driver pick you

up around an hour and a half prior. How does that sound?"

"Sounds great. Thanks again."

The call ends.

Dresses are not my thing; I hate them. I just feel out of place and boyish when I wear them, which is weird, actually, since dresses are the most feminine attire women can wear. Most women feel sexy in them. I just don't. Yet here I am, standing before a tall mirror in my bedroom, wearing a pale yellow knee-length, strapless sundress. I could change into something a bit more comfortable, but since it's lunch with my father and I want to look my best and Moon's such an upscale place, my usual ripped-up jeans, loose T, and flats probably wouldn't be received too well.

I take in a soothing breath as my eyes scan over my reflection. My hands pat over the loose waves of my hair to smooth down any flyaway strands. There's nothing else I can do to perfect my appearance. It is what it is. I turn on the heels of my nude open-toe shoes and tread out of the room and down the stairs—very carefully, since heels aren't my friend either.

For the past two days, I've made sure to stay locked in my room to avoid my mother. I'm not ready to face her yet. Even though it's been four days since our last disastrous encounter, I just can't bear to see her. I know what will happen anyway. It's not the first time we've had an argument. When it happened before, we'd either ignore each other, as if the other didn't exist, or she'd ask me a question about something irrelevant, like the newspaper or the weather, when the silence between us became strangely awkward—anything to spark a conversation. Depending on my mood, I'd ignore her or respond with a low one-word answer. And then the next day, she'd act as if nothing had happened.

My mother and I never discuss our feelings or talk out our issues. We leave them behind us and move forward. Some say it's good for the soul to leave your troubles in the past, but I think that's bullshit. If you can't resolve it in that very moment, or even try to, how is it good for the soul? For me, moving on and ignoring the animosity that exists between my mother and me only darkens my soul and reaffirms my mother's rejection.

Well, screw that. I'm not dealing with her today.

With my clutch in hand, I open the front door and step out into the sweltering mid-June heat. My skin begins to prickle from the sun immediately. I continue down the pathway, at the end of which is my father's driver and a limo. In one hand he's holding the back door open for me, and in the other, a gorgeous bouquet of yellow roses. I can't contain the smile tugging at my lips. Every time Dad took Brooke and me on one of our father-daughter dates, he always had one of his drivers meet us, and they always had our favorite flowers: red tulips for Brooke, yellow roses for me.

A loud thump draws my eyes to the right. Logan is jumping off the back of his pickup truck when I spot him. He tosses a stack of two-by-fours over his shoulder and carries them across the lawn. My stomach twirls as I appraise him. His Phillies baseball cap is pulled down low, obscuring his eyes, but I can imagine the clear blue of them just fine. My tongue darts out, wetting my dry lips as I watch his sketched, bulging arms flex through his sleeveless shirt. He looks good with tats. Really good. For the better part of the weekend, we were up close and personal, but I still have no idea what kind of ink he's sporting. I couldn't risk him catching me studying his arms. There was just no way to do it surreptitiously, and it would have felt too personal to ask him about them. I didn't want to give him the idea I was interested after all.

Logan's head turns my way. He catches me staring and flashes a white, toothy grin. My heart skips a beat.

Shit.

"Hey, Jersey," he shouts. Then he drops the wood down in front of him and lightly jogs my way. Why am I so damn nervous? We had a good weekend together, but I shouldn't feel this fluttering in the pit of my stomach. "Hey," he says again with a smile. Small beads of sweat glisten on his upper lip and neck.

"Hey," I respond.

"You look really nice. Hot date?" he jokes.

I peek over to the driver, and then back to Logan, who follows my gaze. His smile falls a bit.

"Something like that," I respond. What the hell possessed me to say that? It's not like I'm trying to make him jealous or anything. But then again, it's none of his business. Maybe if he thinks I'm dating, he'll get the hint and won't ask me out again.

"Oh. Well, he must be one hell of a guy," he says. Then he fidgets with the rim of his cap, pulling it lower.

"Why's that?"

"Well, I mean, it's obvious. Look at me. If you passed up on something like this, the tool must be a hell of a guy, that's all." He's joking, but something tells me it's a cover-up. Either way I laugh because he has this amusing side of him that makes it difficult not to smile or giggle or find his charming sense of humor intriguing.

"You know, I've never met such an egotistical man."

"Pfft. Imagine how I feel. I have to live through it. It's not easy being me, Jersey."

"Jersey? Is this a new name for me?" I ask, amused.

"Yeah. I figure two friends like us should have nicknames for one another."

"I see. I don't like nicknames, but I think I can come up with something for you." I smile.

"Make it good, Jersey. You only get one shot at this. If it sucks, then you lose."

"I wasn't aware we were playing a game."

He leans in, his gaze dropping to my mouth. "I didn't think so either, since I'm not so keen on playing games. But there's nothing wrong with a little fun." His voice is low, rough. He's not talking about the nicknames anymore; he's talking about us. Before I can think of a witty response, Logan looks over at the car waiting for me. He straightens up and adjusts his cap again. "Well, I don't want to keep you," he says, suddenly upbeat.

I breathe in the chemistry wrapping around us. I feel it. I see it in his grey-blue eyes and right now, I want him to *keep* me. I want him to continue his attempts at flirting. I want him to make me smile, make me laugh, and bring back the side of me I've missed for so long. But then reality sets in. It whirls back around to the forefront of my mind, sweeping away any hopes I have of normalcy, of affection, of…love. Again, I'm reminded of all the reasons why Logan and I can't be more than what we are. I let out a slow breath, one I'd been holding since he leaned in close enough to kiss me. "Okay. Well, um, chat soon?" I ask nervously.

"Yeah, sure." He nods and turns away, walking back to the stack of wood assuredly. I watch as he bends over, picks it up, and tosses it over his shoulder. He doesn't look back.

The drive into Manhattan is better than I had anticipated, except for one thing—the entire drive all my thoughts trail off to Logan. I question whether I should just come clean and tell him about my "issue." At least that way if he wants to back off, he can. It won't bother me. I've only known him for a little more than a week. And we haven't shared anything more than what we've shared, which isn't much.

The car pulls up and stops in front of Moon. The driver opens the door for me and gives me his business card with instructions to call him when I'm ready to be picked up. I quickly take in the busy streets of New York and hurry into the restaurant. Being in and around large crowds, especially the hectic crowds of New York, makes me feel uneasy.

My anxiety kicks in as I step into the waiting area of the restaurant. It must be a busy day for the restaurant. It's jam-packed. I weave through all the people waiting to be seated and approach the hostess. "Hello, I have a reservation under Gregory McDaniel."

The hostess skims through the list. "Yes, he's already seated." She tilts her head toward a gentleman beside her. "Please take her to table 45."

The gentleman's gaze lands on me. With a smile he says, "Please, follow me." And so I do. I follow closely behind, focusing my eyes on the back of his head. "Here you are." He halts. I almost stumble into him, but I catch myself before I do.

My anxiety quickly dissipates as he walks away and my father turns to face me. His warm smile lights up his face. "Jenna, you look absolutely beautiful." He stands, places a peck on my cheek and guides me into the booth. He settles in as well, across from me. It's the same booth he always reserves—tucked in the far corner of the restaurant, beside a large window that looks out over Manhattan's skyscrapers. Although Moon is surely filled to capacity, our little corner feels private, like it's just the two of us in the crowded space.

"I'm glad you were able to make it," Dad says. He stretches his arm out across the booth and grabs my hand.

"Me too." I gently smile at him. "We haven't had one of these in a long time. It's nice."

"Yes. It was quite overdo, wasn't it?" He grins. The waiter approaches us and we order our usual. Dad leans back, unbuttoning the perfectly tailored suit jacket as his eyes pierce mine. "So, tell me, how are you feeling?"

"All right, I guess," I answer with a slight shrug.

"Jenna," he hesitates. "I don't want to make you upset"— which means he will—"but I want to speak to you about your mother."

Here we go.

My shoulders tense uncomfortably. "I'd rather not. I just want to enjoy lunch with you without Mom ruining my day, as always."

"Well, how about we just get it out of the way so we can enjoy the rest of our lunch? What do you say?"

"Fine." There's no escaping this conversation, so I give in. "What do you want to talk about?"

"First, I feel you owe your mother an apology." My eyes narrow to a harsh glare, and he lifts a hand to stop me from an outburst. "Before you say anything, I feel she owes you an apology as well. I'm not picking sides, Jenna. I love you both. It's very difficult for me to see two women whom I love deeply despise one another. She's your mother, and you are her daughter. I'm already swamped with work in the office. I have a potential client I've been trying to pull in for years that's finally beginning to cave. The last thing I need is to come home to the two of you acting like juveniles. I shouldn't have to deal with it. It's infuriating. Do you understand?"

I cross my arms over my chest. Is this what our little lunch date was for? For him to just educate me on my rights and wrongs? For him to judge my relationship with Mom, even though he has yet to witness just how cruel she can be? I can't help but laugh. "Yes, I understand," I say, hoping it ends this topic.

"Good. I arranged for the two of you to have a girls' spa day tomorrow."

"What?" I nearly shout.

"Can you at least pretend to be thrilled about it?"

"I'm sorry if I'm not bursting at the seams with excitement at this very moment. But I'm not ready to face a woman who told me I shouldn't blame others for my failures during one of my episodes," I blurt out. My father's twisted expression immediately has me feeling guilty for not thinking before I spoke.

"She said that to you?" he asks, his tone low, his eyes darkening in distress. Not toward me—he's disappointed in my mother. And I know I shouldn't care if he is or isn't, but when it comes to my mother and me, my father has a very soft spot. When he looks at her as if she's let him down, I can feel exactly how she feels. The burning whole within your chest. The shame of knowing that you've disappointed a loved one. It's how I feel every time she looks at me.

My mother, when she gets one of those stares from my father, does everything and anything to win back his affection. She would be nothing without my father. If she had to, she'd crawl through a pile of nails, walk through fire, and swim through a tank of sharks to win back his love. Because that's what you do for people you love, right? And she loves him. Truly loves him. And she knows if he ever left her, she'd have no one. She'd always be alone.

Maybe she's more fucked-up than I am.

Sometimes I wonder if she would be better off alone. Other times, I wonder why I feel bad for her in the first place. Is it because deep down she's still my mother and I'm still waiting for her validation? No matter what has happened between us, if she were ever to change, if she were to ever tell me she was truly, sincerely sorry and wanted to work on our relationship, I'd do anything to win that from her, to win the affection of my mother's love. But we've gone through this for so many years now, and she's always been the same with me. I've gone bitter. And my mother? Well, she has too much pride to ever ask to rebuild what's been damaged between us.

"Yes," I confess quietly, averting my eyes in shame. I lower my head and stare at my hands as I press my palms together, trying to absorb the dampness.

"I see," he says. "I wasn't aware—"

"You're not aware of a lot. You're hardly around anymore. So, yeah."

Silence.

I don't dare look up at him, though I can feel his stare burning into me. It's not normal for me to lash out at my father, or even talk back. I respect him far too much to treat him like I treat my mother. So, of course, the guilt sets in.

His phone buzzes against the table. I peek up as he reaches for it, hesitates, then swipes the screen and lifts the cell to his ear. "Honey," he answers, his voice calm and monotone, "I'm having lunch with our daughter." I swallow a large lump wedged in my throat. Dad keeps his eyes on me but continues on with Mom, "Yeah. We have a lot to talk about when I get home tonight." *Oh shit.* He's going to tell her about what I said. No. I can't deal with the aftermath. She'll be angry, she'll take it out on me by saying things, hurtful things. I can't handle this right now.

My leg begins to shake. Tugging on the skin of my lip, my eyes shift his way as I hear him go on, "I'm not discussing this with you right now; I want to enjoy lunch with my daughter. No. Tonight, Laura… Hold on." He pulls the phone away, glares at the screen, and then brings it back to his ear. "I have to take this call. I'll see you tonight." He swipes the phone, dismissing my mother, and goes on to the next call. "This better be good, Stanley—" Dad stops to listen. It must be good news. His lips curl into a smile, and it's as if my mother and I are no longer a concern. "That's amazing. I want the contract drawn up immediately, before he changes his mind. Yes. While you're preparing the contract, I'll make the necessary phone calls. I should be back in the office within"—he glances at his watch—"fifteen minutes."

Dad ends the call. He reaches for his wallet, pulls out a few hundred-dollar bills, and places them on the table. "Jenna, I'm so sorry—"

"It's okay. I get it. No worries. You're a busy man."

His smile is gentle. "I'll make this up to you. I promise."

A promise he'll never be able to keep, but I go along with it anyway. "I know."

Before I know it, he's up and out of sight.

Lips trembling, I bite down to focus on the physical pain rather than the emotional. There's an ache in my chest that I'm not sure how to soothe. Brooke would've known what to do; she would have made me laugh. I wish she were here.

I miss her.

I've suddenly lost my appetite. Reaching for my phone, I call the driver and ask to be picked up.

I wanted to keep going, to just drive and drive and never look back. But the driver was growing impatient, and I had no choice but to finally direct him home after four long hours.

We pull up in front of the house. I feel suffocated, stuck. I don't want to get out. This backseat has become a protective bubble over the last few hours, but time's run out and I have nowhere else to go. Charlie isn't picking up my phone calls, so as the driver opens the back door and reaches in to give me his hand, I reluctantly take it. "Thank you," I mumble as I step out.

"My pleasure, Ms. McDaniel." Sure it is. He nods, shuts the door, and steps back to the driver side. My back faces my home. I breathe in, trying to soothe my nerves and muster enough courage to turn around and go inside. The car drives off, and my breath whooshes out as I turn around and see her. My mother. A knot twists painfully in the pit of my stomach. She's standing with the door wide open at our front entrance. She must have heard the car and expected my father. From this distance I can't see her features, but I can tell by her slumped shoulders that she's disappointed. Then she lifts her head and straightens up, turns around swiftly, and slams the door closed. The resounding *thump* is so loud I can hear it clearly from where I stand.

I fucking *hate* her.

"How was that date, Jersey?"

My head snaps to the left. Logan is by his truck, packing

his tools away. I didn't realize how late it is. His shift must be over. I roll my eyes, not in the mood to joke or flirt or anything. My fingers clench the strap of my clutch as I focus directly on the double doors, behind which my mother awaits. Do I go in, dreading what's to come, or do I just walk away and give us both some space?

The second sounds like a better idea. I chuck off my heels, reach down for them, and then turn, walking up the slight hill of our long street.

"Jenna?" Logan calls out. I avoid him and keep going. Not running, not strolling, just walking at a normal, even pace with my focus determinedly straight ahead.

She's pissed off at you. She hates you. She's never cared about you...

Well, I hate her back.

You'll never live up to her expectations. You'll never be perfect—her perfect little girl...

My feet push forward faster now, keeping up with the voices trying to seep through my sanity, trying to take over. I realize now—and damn me for never putting it together before—that my mother is a major trigger for me. I don't know how or why I allow her to crawl so deep into my psyche, but she does and she always has.

Tires crunch over rocks alongside me. Looking over, I see Logan driving slowly in his truck with a smile tilting his stubble, irritatingly gorgeous cheeks up. Irritating because I don't want to look at him this way. I don't want to notice his handsome features and I don't want them to do anything to my heart or my chest or my head or anything. I just want him to go away.

"You know, I'm starting to get a feeling you like to be barefoot outside," he says.

I scowl at him, shake my head, and focus forward, not bothering to pay him any attention.

Logan chuckles. "How 'bout you hop in and we can go for that ice cream you owe me?"

"I'm not in the mood for ice cream," I say, deadpan.

"Even more reason why you should definitely go."

"Can you just leave me alone?" I continue along. My thoughts are racing. What I need is a distraction and he is not helping right now.

"No."

I stop and whip my head toward him. "No?"

He stares down at me as he sits up high in his truck, the whisper of a smile on his lips. "No. I'm not leaving you alone."

"What do you want from me? What does anyone want from me?" Anger bubbles up from deep within. I tighten my jaw and clench my teeth. "I just want to be left alone. Is that so damn hard to ask?" I'm not sure where it came from exactly. I'm just frustrated. Logan shrugs once, one hand hanging casually out the window, while the other grips the steering wheel. His worn-out Phillies baseball cap hangs low over his eyebrows. The rim shadows his eyes, concealing any emotions within them, which means I can't get a read on him at all. I hate it. Just effing hate it. "Would you take off that stupid hat?" I practically yell.

He laughs.

"What's so funny?"

"You," he says.

"Well," crossing my arms, upset with myself for getting worked up—especially in front of him—I retort, "I'm glad I can entertain you. At least you're a first."

His lips tug into a lopsided grin. "Come on, Jenna. I can

tell something is bothering you and in my experience, ice cream solves everything."

Now I laugh. I laugh because I'm exhausted. I laugh because I'm exasperated. And I laugh because I want to cry, but I don't.

I shake my head, temporarily releasing all of the emotions bottled up within me. Fine. If I want to get away for a while, maybe he can distract me. Maybe he can help rid me of this ache, even for just an hour or so.

chapter 15

Logan

Watching Jenna struggle up into my truck is an exercise in self-restraint. I'd love to wrap my hands around her waist and... Fuck me. I mentally kick myself in the ass. I should've gotten out and helped her, but the fact that she's even agreed to hop inside my truck to begin with has thrown me off. My mind has been wrapped up with Jenna since she left the lake house Sunday morning. I couldn't stop thinking about her. I actually looked forward to work on Monday just so I could see her. But I never did. Tuesday went by, and still no sight of Jenna. Until today, when I saw her all dolled up and beautiful—for another guy. Yeah, it stung, but I couldn't show her it affected me in any way. So, as always, I used humor to distract her from how I truly felt. But that's the thing—it shouldn't have affected me nearly as much as it did.

I make a mental note for next time to help her in and out of my truck.

Finally settled into the seat, she moves on to her next battle—this time with the seatbelt. She huffs and puffs a bit before clicking it in place and facing forward. Though she's looking straight ahead and isn't making a peep, it's obvious she's pissed off about something. I'm sure it has nothing to do with me because for the first time I haven't done anything. My mother's advice hums through my mind as I put the car in drive. She said when a woman is pissed, leave her alone to cool off, but never leave her side because if she's in need of a hug, you'll be the first person she'll find. So I turn up the volume on my radio and allow my favorite band to fill the silence.

As I drive, Jenna remains quiet. The last notes of one song fade as another begins. The melody of a guitar strums through the speakers. It's one of those songs that once it begins, you just know—you know the words are going to hit you hard, and the melody… Well, it's as if the melody weaves its way into your very existence, easing itself inside of you, altering your mood with its highs and lows. When the lead singer's powerful voice begins, you pray for mercy, because you know what it's capable of. It seizes every emotion you've ever experienced and wrenches them all to the surface, leaving you completely exposed. Exposed because sometimes we keep everything bottled up for a reason. But it's songs like this that have the potential to change everything. They can put everything into perspective and make you feel like the words and the song itself belongs to you and only you.

I love this fucking band. This band does that for me— every single time. The words and music course through me, and I have to sing along.

"Who's this?" Jenna asks, her tone soft. I shift my eyes toward her. She's blankly staring at the radio, taking in every word, hypnotized by the sound, the lyrics. She feels a connection too.

"It's City of Sound. They're an indie rock band from Philly. You've never heard of them before?" I ask, completely shocked. They're popular and have been around forever.

She shakes her head, her solemn gaze still stuck on my dashboard. "No."

"Oh. Well they're one of my favorite bands. This song is called 'What's the Point?'" The lyrics speak about life and whether it's worth it. With all the fucked-up things we all go through, what's the point of still living? There are times when you just want to give it all up. But then it goes on to say that maybe, just maybe, there's a purpose in your life and that purpose could be sitting right next to you.

The light ahead of me flashes to red, and I take this time to study Jenna. Her head rests against the headrest, and her eyes are shut. Brown hair tumbles down her shoulders and touches her hands as they rub along her biceps. Goose bumps cover her arms. I have the air conditioner on, but it's low. "Are you cold?" I ask.

"No. It's just…the words. They're dead-on. So dead-on. That's all."

I know exactly what she means. "I love their music. It's always powerful, real, and raw. Their albums got me through some tough shit in my life. I can't believe you've never heard of them."

Jenna tilts her head along the headrest, large beautiful brown eyes looking into mine. "I'm surprised I haven't either. Do they have more like this?"

"Ch-yeah!" She smiles at my response. "Do you want to hear one of my favorites?" She nods. I scan through the album on my radio until I find it. "This is 'Rain on Me.'"

Her lips curl into a grin as the song starts. Listening intensely to the words, she leans back again, closes her eyes, and allows the music to just seep through. After the first verse, she starts bobbing her head side to side along with the beat. She's enjoying it, feeling it. I can't stop smiling. It's like I'm listening to the words for the first time.

Jenna flashes her lids open when the song ends and looks at me. Her eager eyes widen at catching me staring at her, but then she blinks as she beams from ear to ear. "I love it. I want to hear more."

I chuckle. Whatever was bothering her before isn't on her mind now. "All right, here's another one of my favorites." I find the song and continue to drive.

"I can't believe you didn't let me pay," Jenna argues, her round button nose wrinkling as she slumps down into a chair.

"I told you, it wouldn't be fair to make you pay when you're not in the mood for ice cream, so it's my treat." I wink, settling in a seat across from her.

"You think you're just so smart, don't ya?"

"Well, I didn't get the highest SAT scores out of my entire senior class for nothing."

"Really?" she asks.

"No," I confess. "I had a terrible score." Jenna's cheeks color as she laughs at me. I smile charmingly and continue, "But I'm sure I could've done better. I didn't bother to study. There was no reason to. I already knew college was out of the question for me."

Her features shift out of curiosity. "Why was that?"

"'Cause I knew I had a set job with my uncle. I hated school to begin with. I hated studying, for that matter. I just didn't see the point."

"Is that what you always dreamed of doing? Working in construction your entire life?" She seems disappointed.

"Look, Jenna, not all of us have it easy. I didn't want to

try and scrape up money and then work three dead-end jobs just to pay for a diploma. I knew a piece of paper wasn't gonna get me anywhere in the end."

"I see." She looks down, dips her plastic spoon into her ice cream, and then brings it up in salute. "Here's to stupid, overpriced pieces of paper." She smiles, drops the spoon into her mouth, pops it out, and licks her lips afterward, letting out a slight moan as she does. "This is so good."

Fuck me. I wet my lips and look down, stabbing my spoon into my own bowl. I just can't. It's taking every fucking ounce of my willpower not to lean across the table and suck on her chocolate-flavored lips. This is going to be harder than I thought. "Yeah," I add. "I tried to convince Bryson to return his diploma after he freaked out when he received his first student loan bill. He said it doesn't work that way." I know it doesn't work that way, but it was my way of using humor to make a shitty situation better. A new noise brings my head up. Jenna's hand is covering her mouth. "Did you just snort?" I ask her.

"Oh my God, Logan. You're..." She drops her hand as she stares at me with bright eyes. "Very interesting. Yes, that's it. You're interesting."

"I'll take that as a compliment and not an insult."

She sucks in her bottom lip. I think she knows the effect those lips have on me. Shit, she could recite the entire dictionary and I promise you right now, it would be the most entertaining narration I've ever heard—as long as I could stare at those lips. "It's a compliment," she says.

"Well, well. Now we're talking..." Her eyes shift uncomfortably. "I'm kidding, Jersey. No need to get that scared look in your eyes."

"Whatever."

"So what about you? What did you major in at college?"

She slips another scoop into her mouth. "What makes you think I went to college?" I raise a brow, giving her a don't-give-me-shit look. "All right, I did. My major was business. Their plan was to have me work for my father's company, but things got in the way and I left school before I could finish."

"You don't have a degree?"

Jenna forces a tight smile. "Sorry to disappoint you."

"No, you're not disappointing me at all. It's just that I'm surprised. What kind of things got in the way?"

"I knew you'd ask that," she says, blowing out a long breath. "It's, um, complicated. I just had a lot going on in my head. You know, petty teenage girl problems." She brushes off the whole discussion with that last line, as if the interruption of her college career was no big deal, but I take it as a decoy. She's trying to cover up the real reasons behind it, but I don't push her.

"You said, 'their plan.' Who's they?" I ask.

"What?"

"The plan for you to go to college and work for your father's company. You said it was *their* plan."

She shakes her head, remembering, then wrinkles her brow. It was only a minute ago. She must be pretty distracted with her thoughts to forget so soon. "Yeah, I meant my parents. It was their plan."

"What was your plan? What did you want?"

Jenna's face twists as if I've asked something she wasn't expecting. "For my future?"

"Yeah." I smile. "What did you want to do or still do?"

She swallows and wets her lips, hesitating to answer the question. She finally blurts, "I wanted to teach. What? Why are you looking at me like that?"

I adjust my smile. "Nothing. It's just I could see that. You teaching."

"Can you?"

"Yeah. What did you want to teach?"

She shakes her head. "It's stupid, actually. A stupid pipe dream."

"Not to me it isn't. I'd like to hear it," I tell her, genuinely interested in her response.

"All right." She drops the spoon into her bowl and pushes it aside. "I wanted to teach art for young adults in their early and late teens—but not just any teenagers. I..." She looks down, staring at her now empty bowl, and brings a hand up to her cheek, pressing it in as if biting the inside. "I wanted to teach teens with mental illnesses, those who suffer from any type of mental disorder, whether it's depression, bipolar, autism, or," she looks up at me for the last one and whispers, "schizophrenia." She closes her mouth and swallows nervously as she watches my expression. I don't know what she sees on my face, but she must have deemed it okay to proceed because she continues, "A lot of teenagers who suffer from a mental disorder need an escape. Some use writing or music, and many use art as way to escape the monsters trapped in their head. I wanted to give them that escape, to be a mentor, an open ear, a person they can trust and feel safe with. I don't know." She laughs. "I told you it was stupid."

"That isn't stupid. That's...wow...it's fucking great."

"Really?" she asks uncertainly.

"Really. I wish..." I let out a huff. "I wish Sean had that...had something like that. I mean, I know he was in his early twenties when he was released from jail, but I kind of wish he had that..." I trail off.

She reaches across the table and grabs my hand. "Thank

you," she says, giving it a tight squeeze.

I smile with a nod. "Yeah, no problem. So..." I shake off my thoughts about Sean and ask, "Why don't you still do it? I've seen your work. You're talented, Jenna, and to use that talent for something good would be awesome."

"No. My parents, especially my mother,"—she rolls her eyes when mentioning her mother—"think art is a good hobby, not a career choice." She shrugs. "Besides, I don't paint anymore."

"At all?" She shakes her head. "Why? Shit, if I was even a quarter as talented as you are, I wouldn't throw that away."

"Logan, when I paint, I feel. It may not make any sense, but painting brings out a lot of emotions for me. I'm sure, like any artist—musician, writer, sculptor—the emotion just pours out. But sometimes, it becomes too much to handle. You know?"

"Yeah. And what's wrong with that? Do you know how many people keep so many bottled up feelings inside, there's no way to just let it all out, and they don't have a way to let it out. Why not pour it out into something beautiful? Make it a masterpiece, whether it's a piece of art, or a brilliant poem, or a soulful song? That's what makes it the best. When someone else can look at your work and see every single nuance, sense every individual emotion. Feel like they were there with you. I don't know about you, but I wouldn't waste that talent."

"Wow," she says, lost for words. "Are you sure you don't have any secret talents you're hiding from me?"

"Nah. I wanted to be a rock star when I was thirteen, but that was short-lived. When I realized I couldn't hold a tune, I had to give it up."

She laughs. Hard. I laugh too. Then she looks at me differently, as if she's seeing me in a whole new light. "I like you, Logan."

"Who doesn't?"

"You know, when someone gives you a compliment, just say thank you. Okay? Because you can ruin a moment like this." She snaps a finger.

"Thank you," I say.

"You're welcome."

I look across the street where the playground is. It's nice out and I'm not ready to take her home yet. I'm not ready for her to want to leave either. I want to keep her as long as I can. I want to know her better. I want to just… Dammit. I just want to be able to look at her for as long as I can. "Wanna go to the park and act like big kids?" I blurt out.

"Hmm," she contemplates. "Okay. I'll race you." She quickly stands, removes her shoes, and darts for it.

"Dude! That's so not fair. You're cheating!"

I swirl off my seat and run after Jenna, making sure there's no oncoming traffic as I pick up the pace. I catch up, sticking my tongue out as I pass her. She gasps and runs harder. "First one to the slide wins!" she shouts out.

"Bet!" I respond.

We both run harder. Shit, she can run. I'm all out of breath, but I continue to push through. My legs are way longer than hers, so my strides are wider. She beats me anyway, by a few inches. As she reaches the red slide, she turns around, and throws out her arms, breathlessly yelling out, "I won! Ooot, ooot!" She does a little dance.

I stop in front of her and bend at the waist, out of breath and raspy. "Did you just cabbage patch?"

Jenna lands her hands to her hips. "Yeah, why?"

"You need to get out more."

She laughs. "Well, you need to work out more.

Because…I BEAT YOU! OOOT, OOOT!" She dances backward all the way to the swing. "Oh, yeah. Oh, yeah. Oh, oh, oh!"

"Please don't ever quit your day job," I tease, following her and taking a seat on the swing right next to hers.

"I don't have a day job," she says softly.

"Is that a bad thing?" I ask, swinging beside her, still trying to catch my breath.

"Yeah. My parents won't let me work."

"How old are you again? You're not underage or anything, right?"

Jenna giggles. "I'm twenty-one. Damn. Is it that obvious I live under my parents?"

"Well, yeah. You're twenty-one and listen to almost everything they say. Don't you have thoughts of your own?"

She quiets. "Unfortunately, my thoughts are usually drowned out by others."

"Ah." I look over at her. She's staring straight ahead to where the slide and sandbox are. She's doing that thing again. "You do that a lot, the thing with your cheek."

Jenna looks at me. "Oh." She pulls her hand away from the side of her face. "Bad habit. I, uh, chew the inside of my cheek when I'm overthinking, or nervous."

"Are you nervous now? Do I make you nervous?"

She shakes her head. "No, I'm not nervous now."

"But I do…make you nervous?"

"A little," she confesses. "I mean I don't think you would harm me or anything. It's just…I like you and that makes me nervous. That's all."

"You're right, I wouldn't harm you," I say. "I like you too. A lot." I smile.

"Why?"

I shrug. "I'm curious about what goes on in that beautiful mind of yours."

Jenna rips her stare away, the corner of her lips twisting down into a frown. "Trust me, there's nothing beautiful hidden inside my mind. Nothing worth telling and nothing worth knowing."

"I disagree."

She blows out a long, heavy breath, as if fighting back an urge to argue with me. "Well, let's just agree to disagree, shall we?"

"Okay." I don't push her. "So how was your date?" I had to fucking ask. It's been killing me the past hour.

She chuckles. "My lunch date with my *father* didn't go as well as I'd planned."

"With your father, eh?" I can't lie; this news makes my ears ring with happiness. "That bad?"

"Here's the thing: I'm close with my father. I have a bad relationship with my mother, 'mommy issues' you could say. What I thought was going to be a great lunch with my dad turned into a lecture about my relationship with my mother. So yeah, that bad."

"Sorry."

"It's okay. Thanks."

I wet my lips, hesitant to ask this next question, but decide to go for the plunge anyway. "That morning I found you by the street corner in your pajamas, was that about your mother too?"

"Yeah. Something like that," she whispers.

"Want to talk about it?"

"No." She shakes her head. "I'd rather not. Thoughts about my mother put me in a bad place. I don't want to go there, especially not right now." Jenna looks over, a delicate smile etched along her beautiful, pale face. "I'm having a good time. I don't want it to be ruined."

"You're beautiful."

"Huh?"

Fuck.

Did I just say that out loud? Yeah, I did. Oh screw it; I might as well own up to it. "You're beautiful, Jenna. I'm a man and I'm not afraid to admit when I'm lucky enough to look at someone as beautiful as you."

She doesn't say anything, just stares back at me, her expression unreadable. Did I cross a boundary here? Should I not have said anything?

chapter 16

Jenna

My mouth has gone dry. Logan thinks I'm beautiful. Great. Just great. Exactly what I don't need. He's a great guy; I can really tell.

You know how there's that one person who stumbles into your life and you instantly have a connection with them? Someone who's a genuinely good person. Someone you just know you can build a great bond with, and it doesn't have to be in a romantic way either. It can be with someone you have no attraction to whatsoever, you just instantly recognize something in them and they in you. Like in another realm, in another life, you were meant to be together in some way. Whether with a mother, daughter, sibling, best friend, or romantic partner, it's a strong, unexplainable connection between two individuals.

That's how I feel with Logan. But instead of being platonic, the attraction between us is undeniable, which makes it that much more difficult to ignore. The pull, the tug, the electric current charging the air between us… It's constant. And I don't need it. Not now, maybe not ever.

"Logan," I start.

"Wait. Don't say anything. I get it. I just wanted you to know you're beautiful. I wanted you to hear it for yourself. I understand you just want to be friends. I understand this isn't a date, and I understand you don't care to ever go on one with me."

"That's not true. It's just…" I sigh and shake my head. This is so frustrating. "Can I be honest with you?"

"Yeah. I want you to be."

"I'm not exactly dating material." I laugh at how ridiculous I sound. "It's me. Seriously, it's not you."

"Oh no, not the good ole 'it's not you, it's me' spiel. I'm kind of shocked, Jersey. Usually that talk comes after people have started dating. You just like being ahead of the game?" He chuckles.

I don't find it funny. "It's not a spiel—I'm serious. And it's not just you—it's anyone. I'm not dating material for *anyone*. I'm—God, this is so hard to say."

"Then don't say it. I get it."

"No, you don't." I shake my head, fiddling with my fingers as a way to distract my thoughts. How would he look at me if I told him the truth? Could he handle it? "I have issues, Logan. That's all. Nothing more, nothing less. Just plain old emotional issues." I settle for that because he's not ready to know about me and I'm not ready to tell him.

"I can handle issues, Jenna."

My head twists to look up at him, and I smile softly. It's nice for him to say that, but I know the truth. "Not my issues. Just trust me on that."

Gripping the chains of the swing, he stomps his foot to the ground and pushes, slightly lifting his feet and leaning back to gain momentum. "You know, if this *were* a date, I'd feed you this long line of cliché bullshit about how everyone has issues and there's someone out there, regardless of what you may think, who can handle anything you're dealing with—because maybe that person needs you just as much as you need them. And then, my cliché bullshit would probably touch you somehow, make you feel some type of emotional connection with me, and possibly make you swoon, which would only allow me to go in for the kill and kiss you. But like I said, that's if this were a date. Since it's not, you're not so lucky."

I let out a hard laugh, rolling my eyes playfully. "Thank God this isn't a date. You saved me from your long line of cliché bullshit."

He chuckles. The corners of his eyes wrinkle slightly when his mouth spreads into a white, toothy grin. Those strong, chiseled features…they're kind of gorgeous.

God.

I like him. Logan. I like that he's not so intense. I like that he knows when to stop asking questions. I like how he turns a serious situation around and finds humor in it. I like his silly personality. I like that he's funny. I like that he makes me laugh. I like the crooked grin he gives me when he's being cocky. I even admit that I like that stupid Phillies baseball cap he wears all the time. It looks good on him.

Dammit.

I just like…him.

"Have I told you I was the fucking king of the monkey bars back in preschool?" he asks.

You see what I mean?

I bite my lip, resisting the urge to just melt for this man. He makes me feel young. I know that may sound ridiculous because I'm only twenty-one, but the past few years have aged me in inexplicable ways. But Logan, he makes me *feel* my age. I feel vibrant and alive when I'm with him.

I shake my head to answer his monkey bar question.

"Well, allow me to show you the moves that earned me the title."

He stands from the swing, reaching his hand out to me. I look up, smile, and grab it. The palm of my hand meeting his is a welcome sensation, and our fingers lock between one another's. We walk and I silently note how small my hand is in his large, calloused one. It feels perfect. It feels so right. It feels like they belong together.

Two lost pieces of a puzzle, finally meeting their match.

I'm so screwed.

Logan's truck slowly approaches my house. It was getting dark out, so we decided to call it a night. I've learned a bit more about him this evening, which only makes him that much more appealing to me. It's scary how two people can so easily fall into the get-to-know-you process, where they confess all these things they've never told anyone else. Except there's one tiny issue—a secret one of them is afraid the other might be turned off by. That's my reality. And I'm sure Logan has a secret too. He has to, there's no way he's the perfect guy he portrays himself to be. There's no way he's this open and honest about himself. He must be holding something back, just like I am.

Rocks crunch under slowing tires, truck shifts into park, a seatbelt *clicks*.

I look over at Logan. He twists in his seat to face me, a smile set on his face. "So, I had fun."

I match his grin. "Me too."

"What are your plans for tomorrow? I'd like to hang out with you again. Like around five, since that's when my shift ends. It's not like I have a far drive to pick you up or anything."

Laughing, I unbuckle my seatbelt, eyes still on him. "Well, if you were paying any attention over the past three hours, you'd remember that I have no life since I don't work or go to school. So yeah, my plans for tomorrow will probably be sitting by the pool or hanging in my room, watching awful reality television."

He wrinkles his nose. "Yikes. Bad reality TV is a waste of life if you ask me. Why do that when you can be doing something much more fun?"

"As in?"

"As in hanging out with me tomorrow. Same time. What do you say?"

I hold back a smile. "I'll think about it."

"You do that." God, he's so damn good-looking.

I tear my stare away, my eyes focusing on a small photo hanging from the rearview mirror. I didn't see it before. Then again, I wasn't really paying attention. I reach out and grab it, leaning in to have a better look. It's a picture of a younger Logan with his arms posed wide open and a big goofball grin on his face. I can tell it's him. He looks slimmer and shorter, but it's definitely him with those same vibrant blue eyes. Beside him, posing the exact same way, is a guy a bit taller and more muscular than Logan. The unknown guy is wearing a Phillies baseball cap—an exact replica of Logan's. "Who's that?" I ask, pointing at the guy in the picture.

"That's my brother, Sean, wearing his favorite *stupid* hat." My stomach sinks. Stupid. Stupid. Stupid. I feel like an ass. Pushing down my fear of making a fool out of myself, I look back at Logan. His smile is still there, just a bit wider. Reaching up, he tugs the rim of the cap. "Which is now my favorite," he adds.

"I…um…*shit*…" I shut my eyes, breathe in and out, then flash them open. "I'm sorry, Logan."

Logan chuckles, a low rumble deep within his chest. "It's fine. Seriously. I didn't get offended. Most people would, but I'm not like most people."

"No. You're certainly not." I shake my head, trying to rid myself of the humiliation of the moment. "If it were me, I'd probably punch you in the face."

He laughs again. "I kind of get the feeling you're not kidding."

"No. Not when it comes to something personal like that. To others it may seem like it's just an item, nothing special, but it's a keepsake for you. You know?" He nods. "I had a bracelet Brooke had given me as a graduation gift. I lost it the night you found me in the pool."

"Is that what you were freaking out about?"

"Yes. It's something I never left home without, and losing it was like losing a piece of her."

Logan's forehead creases in confusion. "Wait. Was it some type of gold charm bracelet or something like that?"

"Yeah, how'd you know?"

"Santino found one by the pool when we were prepping on our first day. He gave it to your mother."

"What?" My hands grip the dashboard so hard my knuckles turn white.

Logan looks nervous—or scared. I have no idea how I look right now, but I'm sure I look like I'm about to beat someone with a bat. "Yeah, your mother thanked Santino for bringing it to her and took off with it."

Red. All I see is red. I jump out of the truck and slam the car door.

"Jenna?" Logan shouts out, but I keep going. My legs have a mind of their own. I have no idea how they're moving, how they're pushing, because my head is empty. Completely deserted. There are no thoughts whatsoever, just one image I keep seeing over and over again: my mother's face.

Trembling, I open the door and dart into the house. My chest is heaving, my heart beating wildly, but my mind is clear.

Voices. Familiar voices from the office. I don't hesitate. I move toward them, smoothly gliding across the marble foyer, yanking the knob, and pushing the door open. My mother jumps, turning to face the entryway I just barreled through. My father's wary features shoot my way, studying me: my rigid posture, my hands opening and closing into tight fists at my side, my tense shoulders, and finally my bloodshot eyes, which are fixed and zooming in on her. The bitch.

"Where is it?" I threaten more than ask.

Mom seems startled by my approach. "Where is what, darling?"

"Fuck off, Mother!"

"Jenna!" Dad shouts.

Ignoring him, I move toward her aggressively. She steps back, afraid of what I might do. "The bracelet. Give me my bracelet. It's mine, not yours. Brooke gave it to me. Where is it?" I scream.

She brings a hand to her chest. "This is ludicrous. You're acting—"

"Give. It. To. Me."

"Where is the bracelet, Laura?" Dad demands.

Her appalled, open-mouthed, and wide-eyed expression

leaves me and lands on him. "Do you think I would keep it from her on purpose? Gregory, I would never do such a thing—"

"Do you or do you not have the bracelet, Laura?" he cuts in.

Wetting her lips, she moves her head side-to-side, staring at me, then him, then me again. Without another word, she walks over to the large bookcase. Removing a small trinket box, she opens the lid and lifts my bracelet out. I don't give her time to bring it to me. I stomp over, snatch it from her hand, and storm out of the office.

I hate her more than ever.

"I can't believe your mother did that. I'm sorry, but that was a shit move on her end," Charlie says, fanning a hand over her damp, heart-shaped face.

I lean back against the lounge chair. The sun is brutally hot today, but I allow it to beam off my skin as I lie with my eyes shut. "Yep. She doesn't matter anymore; I have my bracelet and, quite honestly, that's all that matters," I say, reaching for my right hand and allowing my fingers to smooth over the gold chain, now perfectly snugged around my wrist.

Last night I could hear Mom and Dad arguing but couldn't make out all of it. I did hear my name thrown in a few times, and on any other day I would have eavesdropped, but last night I didn't bother. I had my bracelet and I was too upset with my mother to even want to hear what she had to say about me. I know one thing, I'm really glad Dad cancelled that spa appointment he had scheduled for Mom and me. I didn't want to go initially, but after the bracelet fiasco, there wasn't a chance in hell.

"Yeah. Thank God," she says. "What the hell? It's hot as balls out. I'm taking a dip in the pool. Want to go in with me?"

"Sure." I lift onto my elbows. "It's too hot to even sunbathe."

We stand, tread to the pool, and dip in, allowing the warm, refreshing water to swallow us up. Charlie swims to the corner at the shallow end of the pool, which has a built-in bench. Sitting down, she bends her head back on the edge and closes her eyes. I follow, making myself comfortable beside her, our seats in clear view of the Reed Construction guys working on the guesthouse.

"What was the sigh for?" Charlie asks.

"Huh? Did I sigh?"

"Yep. A big ole dramatic one too." Her eyes flash open. Staring straight ahead, it doesn't take her long to realize the reason—or should I say the person—that prompted my sigh. "Logan looks good…"

"I guess?" My eyes study him from this distance. The Phillies cap is on his head, white earphones are plugged into his ears, and his golden tan is glistening in the sun. "Mmmhmm. I see where your line of vision is. Do you see that male goodness from afar?" Charlie sits up and goes on dramatically, "Are you admiring those fine-tuned, muscular arms? That glorious, gleaming golden tan? The beads of sweat dripping ever so softly from his rock-hard body? The way the veins of his biceps pop out when he flexes? His rough-worn jeans hanging low on his sculpted hips, leaving you to imagine what's waiting just a little bit lower? Ooooh, that was some descriptive shit right there. I should be a writer."

I roll my eyes. She is so over-the-top. But I must admit, she's right. What is happening to me?

Charlie fans herself, dipping her head back into the water. "Damn, I made myself hot with that scene. You know you were turned on. I can just see it now." She spreads her arms wide. "Charlie Murphy, erotica novelist, making pussies twerk nationwide. RPD, bitches."

"You're ridiculous," I say, splashing water her way.

Charlie shrugs. "Oops. Hottie coming our way."

I turn, and… Yep, Logan is heading toward us. Straightening my shoulders, I sit up, watching as he approaches.

Logan reaches the edge of the pool, bends at the knees, and meets us at eye level. "Ladies," he says with a smile.

"Logan." I match his grin.

"Hottie McHotterson." Charlie beams.

Logan squints his eyes at Charlie, uncertain as to how to handle her. I'm sure no one knows how to handle her. Then he looks at me. "Have you thought about it?"

"Thought about what?" Charlie interjects.

Logan answers, "Going out with me tonight. My shift is over in an hour and I figured I'd ask now so you can get ready. Or you can go in your bikini. Either way is good with me."

Charlie's lips curl into a devious grin. "Ah, going out, huh? Yeah, she's going." I go to speak, but she lifts her hand, stopping me before I can start. "Go and get ready, Jenna. I'll keep Logan occupied. So, Logan, let me tell you about this book I want to write."

"You write?" he asks, amused.

"Yep. And I can come up with some pretty damn steamy scenes. I'm thinking of writing an erotic—"

I grip her arm. "Yes, Logan. I'll go out tonight. I'm going to start getting ready. Charlie, come help me find something to wear."

"Oh," Charlie says, shocked that I'm actually asking for

fashion feedback. But I'll do anything to keep her from embarrassing herself. Who am I kidding? I'll do anything to keep her from embarrassing me. "All right. See ya, Logan." She winks at him.

Logan smiles, and his eyes find mine. "Cool. See you in an hour."

I nod, twist my body beneath the water, and lift myself out of the pool. Turning, I bend down, yank on Charlie's arm, and pull her out.

We're in my walk-in closet, and I'm seated in a chair with a towel wrapped around my chest. My hair's dripping water down my back as I watch Charlie rummage through my closet. Her features vacillate between shock and distress regarding the news I just told her. "Wait a minute. The two of you went out? Why am I just hearing about this?" she asks, skimming through the hangers.

"Because it happened out of left field. Besides, it was just a friendly get-together."

"You decided to mention Mommy Dearest stealing the bracelet, but you left out the fact that you were on a date with Mr. McHotterson?"

"Not a date," I huff.

"Whatever. So where did you guys go?"

I pick the skin at my lip as my eyes roam over my clothing. Though there's plenty to choose from, I feel like I have nothing to wear, which is completely unlike me. Any other day I couldn't care less about what to wear. But I keep shaking my head no to all of Charlie's suggestions so far. "We went for ice cream, then the park."

"Are you kidding me?" Her hand stops midstroke on a sundress, and she turns to face me.

"What?" I ask, unsure of the reason behind her wrinkled nose.

"Ice cream and the park?" I confirm with a nod. "What are you guys, like five?"

Rolling my eyes, I shift in the seat and cross my legs. "Whatever. I think he was sweet and we had fun. I had an amazing time…" I trail off with a smile, thinking about last night. Logan was the perfect gentleman.

"All right, then," Charlie says, mockingly. "Well, I guess no dress for you, since he might surprise you and take your ass to BounceU."

Funny thing is, after witnessing Logan and how goofy he can be with just a set of monkey bars, I'm sure BounceU would be right up his alley. "There'd be nothing wrong with us acting like big kids, jumping around in inflatable bounce houses."

Charlie coughs out a laugh. It's one of those incredulous laughs, one that lets me know she's humoring me. She knows that is not my scene, but maybe it could be. With Logan it could be.

"Wear this." Both of her arms jut out, a pair of white skinny jeans dangling from one hand, and a teal strapless blouse from the other. "It's cute, yet comfortable. What do you say?"

"Okay. I can do that." I stand, walk over, and grab them from her hands, dropping the towel and tossing the outfit on.

"Do you want to wear heels, flats, or sandals?" Charlie asks, twirling to face my shoe collection.

"Sneakers," I say seriously.

Charlie meets me with a pair of nude flats and hands

them to me. "Nope. I will not allow you to look a hot mess on this date."

"It's not a date."

"Whatever. Put on the shoes. I have to do your hair and makeup."

chapter 17

Logan

I'm on the front porch, leaning against the column as I wait for Jenna. Memories of the first time we met float forward from the back of my mind—especially that kiss, which happened to occur on this very porch. Dammit. She wants to keep things clean and friendly, but the thought of that kiss turns my thoughts to anything but. It's going to be very fucking hard for me to control myself tonight. I'll try to be good and respect her wishes, but I can't make any promises.

I hear rather than see the front door open. Leaning forward, I crane my neck and eye the double doors. Both Jenna and Charlie step out, and damn, Jenna looks…well, she looks fucking hot. Although I changed out of my dingy work clothes, I kind of wish I'd had time to go home, take a shower, and get completely ready. Whatever. Straightening, I shove my hands into the front pockets of my jeans. My heart staggers into a quick beat. What the fuck? I'm nervous. Why? It's not like I've never seen a fucking chick before. *Calm the hell down, Logan.*

Charlie's small figure struts up before me. I have to look down to meet her eyes, as if I'm staring at a ten-year-old. With her arms crossed, she sizes me up, scrutinizing. Then she whips her head back to glare at me. "You better be good to my girl, or I'll be making a few calls and you'll have a Lorena Bobbitt case on your hands." She shoots up a brow. "Or should I say…in your pants."

I wrinkle my brows. *This chick is kidding, right?*

"Oh my God, Charlie." Jenna stumbles forward, pushing Charlie with a swat of her hand. "Sorry about that, Logan. Shall we go?"

"Um, sure." I grab Jenna's hand and step forward, walking side by side with her down the walkway. I can't help but look back and sneak a peek at Charlie, who catches me. She gives me an aggressive two-finger eye point, making it clear that she'll be keeping her eyes on me.

"Your friend is very…" I trail off, trying to find the right words without offending Jenna.

"Weird? Aggressive? Direct? Dramatic?" she finishes for me. "You can choose one, but I'm sure all of the above apply."

"Yeah. Definitely all of the above."

She laughs.

We reach my truck. I, being the awesome gentleman I prepared myself to be, open the door and help Jenna into the passenger seat. She thanks me with a slight giggle after I give her a small bow and a knowing, lopsided grin. Then I jog around and slide into the driver seat. "I have something for you," I say, reaching into the backseat and grabbing the gift. Jenna's eyebrows slant with curiosity when I hand her a thin, square object wrapped in newspaper. She flips it around in her hand, wondering what it could be. "Sorry about the wrapping," I say. "It was last-minute and I didn't have any of that colorful wrapping crap. So I figured newspaper would do just the trick."

Jenna's pink, glossy lips twitch into a smile. "What is it?" she asks.

"Open it and find out."

Hesitantly, she runs her fingers over it, right above the headline regarding Philly's City budget cuts. Licking her lips, she swipes a finger under a flap, beneath the clear Scotch tape, peeling off the rest of the paper and revealing the album. I take in the charm bracelet resting on her right wrist. She got it back. Yesterday she seemed pissed the hell off with the news regarding her mother having the bracelet this entire time.

I want to ask about it, but then I remember how Jenna said talking about her mother is the equivalent of placing her in a dark hole, so I decide to not mention it—at least not right now. "It's City of Sound's *Greatest Hits*," I say. "I figured since you like what you've heard so far, you'd probably like to hear more from them."

Jenna tilts her head my way. Her large and beautifully brown eyes gleam in the early evening light. I hope she likes it. Her pouty lips are not smiling, but she's not frowning either. A vertical line creases between her brows. Her expression seems to be saying a million things, none of which I can decipher. While her eyes hold on to mine, she seems to be reaching deep, trying to read me, to figure me out or something. Finally, she brings a hand up, her fingers play with my stubble jaw, and then she leans in.

Shit.

She's going to kiss me. I can feel it. I can sense it. I calm my breathing, waiting, hoping for her lips to touch my...

Cheek.

Yeah.

Jenna's lips, sticky from some kind of gloss, land on the

left side of my cheek, just above my jawline. Pulling back, her face inches from mine, her lashes flicker as she meets my stare. Her thumb gently rubs over the kiss mark, removing the lip gloss from my face. "Thank you for the album, Logan. I love it."

Talk, dickhead.

"Oh, no problem." I breathe out, bringing my arm up to hang over the steering wheel, hoping it makes me seem smooth.

Moron.

Jenna settles back into her seat, clips on her seatbelt, and looks down at the album in her hand.

"I hope you're hungry because I'm taking you to the best mom and pop shop in Philly."

She looks up at me and smiles again. That smile alone is going to drive me insane tonight.

Pattie's is definitely not an upscale, fine restaurant, but if you want a good home cooked style meal, it's definitely the best spot in town. Besides, it's also close by the next place I want to take Jenna to, which I'm hoping she'll like.

I help Jenna out of my truck, slipping my hand into hers as we walk, and we keep it that way. She doesn't pull away and neither do I. I like it. It just feels right. Hand in hand we step into the overly packed, rowdy, small restaurant. I lean down, my lips touching the curve of her ear. "Sorry, I didn't expect for it to be crowded on a weeknight. But the food is great. I promise you'll like it."

Jenna doesn't say a word. Her eyes sweep over the small surroundings; she seems to be uncomfortable. Her body slightly shudders, and she leans into me, almost cowering as a way to keep close. Her fingers start working at her lip as fear slowly creeps into her eyes. Lifting my hand, I place my palm along her lower back, and twirl her around so her front is facing mine; I pull her toward me without resistance. In fact, her breathing seems to instantly calm, her shaking stops.

And then it starts to makes sense. The day I saw Jenna by the corner street sign and asked her about coming to the lake house, she mentioned how large crowds make her uncomfortable. And when she did make it to the lake house, she was always apart from everyone, distant, always tucked away, alone. To anyone else, it might appear that we're just two people getting cozy because of how crowded it is in here. But they wouldn't know that I've just put together another piece of the puzzle that is Jenna McDaniel.

Jenna lifts her eyelids, blinking as she looks up at me. There's a small understanding between us. No words are spoken; they're not needed. I can feel her discomfort here, and she can sense that I know. I nod once, lifting my hand to the side of her face and rubbing my thumb along her rosy cheek. "Wanna get out of here?" I whisper. She answers with a small nod. "Okay," I say. I turn around, take her hand in mine again, and keep her close as we exit the place.

We're settling back into my truck, and I turn the ignition on. I don't pull away, though. If she feels this uncomfortable here, there's no way she'll like the next place. "I was going to take you to this small indie art show, but I think I purchased the last two tickets, which means there'll probably be a lot of people there."

"Oh." Jenna's voice is small. She looks away, her hands fidgeting in her lap.

"Yeah."

"I'm sorry, Logan. It's just...I have anxiety around large crowds," she whispers, bringing her head down, embarrassed.

"I figured."

"I know it's weird. I'm sorry."

I chuckle softly. "It's not weird, Jenna. Trust me, I know people, and they can be creepy fuckers sometimes. I'd freak out too, but I want to keep this badass act up as long as I can."

She laughs. Good. "You're so not a badass. You may look it, but you're more of the good guy hiding behind the bad boy image."

"Dammit. And here I thought I had everyone fooled. I need to work harder on this image thing." I scratch the back of my head, trying to figure out what to do for the rest of the night. "I know this twenty-four hour diner that serves the best potato pancakes you'll ever have in your life. It's near my apartment. It's usually crowded for breakfast or at like two or four in the morning, when drunk asses crave munches. But around this time, it's usually dead. Wanna go there?"

"Okay."

Jenna orders the banana French toast and a side of one potato pancake, which I told her was a bad idea because once she tastes it, she'll want another. I order my usual, the big man breakfast meal, which comes with two of everything: eggs, pancakes, sausage, bacon, and potato pancakes. Yeah, I'm that hungry. I'll devour my entire plate and then some.

Like I figured, the diner isn't too busy. There's probably a handful of people in the entire place. Jenna and I are seated at a booth in the far back. Though I can tell she feels a bit more comfortable, I still find her looking around. She's keeping an eye out for something, but I don't know what. It's not weird, just different. Her mind always seems to be preoccupied with other thoughts.

"Is it weird we're having breakfast for dinner?" she asks.

"Nope. Best time to have it, if you ask me," I say, drowning my pancakes in syrup.

A slight moan escapes those pretty lips of hers when she takes her first bite of the French toast. "You're right. Best time to have it. I've never had breakfast at any other time, never for anything other than breakfast."

"Well, I like to break the rules sometimes. You know, to keep that bad boy image alive and stuff."

Jenna leans back in the booth, patting her belly. "I'm stuffed."

"You barely ate," I point out.

"I ate half of it. Sorry I can't clean off my plate like you." She giggles. "Thank you for bringing me here."

"No problem. It's my pleasure, really."

And just like that, it's like she's somewhere else, blankly staring at her plate. She lifts her hand to the side of her face, pressing on her cheek.

"What are you thinking?" I ask.

Jenna blinks, then looks up at me. "That I don't know you. That you seem really nice. That I want to know more about you."

"Okay. What do you want to know?"

"Everything. Where you grew up, your family, your likes and dislikes, everything, Logan."

I nod, leaning back in the booth. "All right. Uh, let's see, where can I start? Oh! Once upon a time—"

"I'm serious!" She laughs.

"So am I. Let me tell my story." She rolls her eyes, then

nods. I go on. "Where was I? Ah, yes—once upon a time, there was this small, snot-nosed, pain-in-the-ass kid named Logan Reed. His mother couldn't handle him. No one even wanted to watch him because everyone believed he was the devil's sidekick, if not the devil himself."

Jenna lets out a laugh, adjusting herself a bit to get more comfortable. She crosses her arms on top of the table and leans in. I continue, "But for some strange reason, his mother still loved him. So when it came to his mom, he was a bit of a pussy, or to say it nicer, he was a momma's boy. His only father figure was and still is his uncle George because his biological father was serving time in prison."

"Really? I'm sorry, Logan," Jenna whispers.

"Yeah. It's cool, though. I can't complain. I've lived a good life. I had a family that always stuck by one another. I was always loved, still am. Just because I didn't know my father, doesn't mean my life was ruined. I didn't blame him for anything. I may have missed out on a lot of things, but not having him in my life doesn't define who I am now."

"Where is he now?"

I suck in a deep breath. I had sometimes wondered if I should've reached out to my father, but before I even attempted to make a decision, it was too late. "Dead. He died in prison of a heart attack or something like that. He was doing time for drugs. Not just little shit. He was involved with a crime organization, busted in the middle of a huge drug deal. I wasn't even born yet; my mother was pregnant with me when he got arrested. Gotta love the eighties.

"Anyway, I was never a part of my father's family. You can't miss what you've never had. I don't even have his last name. My mother gave me her maiden name when I was born and paid for Sean's last name to be changed when he was a kid. My mother worked hard to make an honest living, hoping her sons wouldn't end up like their father."

"I know your brother was arrested and did time. How about you?" Jenna asks, tilting her head, waiting for my response.

"Have I ever done time in jail?" She nods. "Nope." I answer.

"Were you ever arrested?"

"Enough about me. Let me hear something about you."

"Logan," she says, stressing my name as it rolls off her tongue.

Fuck my life. "Yeah. I was arrested. Once," I confess.

Jenna's eyes widen. "For what?"

"DUI," I respond blankly.

"But your brother and the reason behind his jail time… Why?"

Huffing out, I scoot forward, lean over the table, and fold my hands. "Look, after Sean's death, I lost it. I was pissed. Angry at him. At myself. At everyone. I wanted to feel numb and liquor and weed wasn't doing the trick. I'd never done drugs before. I mean, I'd smoked pot before, but never any hard-core shit. So, I met up with a few friends who did all of that. My boy Joe said he had something for me that would get the job done. It was this tiny grey pill. Some new drug dealer, experimental shit. It was a mixture of different drugs; they called it the blackout dose. He warned me it was strong and to wait until I got home. I did.

"As soon as I got home, I tried it. It took probably fifteen minutes before it hit me. I don't remember anything after that. I completely fucking blacked out. Go figure. What else should I have expected with a drug named that, right?" I shake my head, going on. "I woke up twelve hours later. It didn't take long before I got addicted to it and needed it to sleep every night. But I always made sure I was home before I took one.

"Then, one shitty day or night—I don't even remember—after I left a bar, I was completely wasted. Even though I was drunk, I still felt everything. The memories of Sean were too hard to bear and I just wanted to feel numb again. I got behind the wheel of my car with no business being there in the first place. I remember digging into my pocket, popping the pill in my mouth, and driving off.

"After that I woke up in a hospital, groggy and in a daze. I felt lost. I had no idea how I got there. Then the entire night began to piece together. The first thing I remember thinking was that I'd killed someone. I'd done the same thing Sean did. I killed someone. But I didn't. Thank God, I didn't. I just killed myself."

"What do you mean?" Jenna asks.

"I died. At least that's what the doctor and my mom told me. Apparently, when I drove away from the bar, I didn't make it too far before I blacked out and drove straight into a light pole. I had a few broken ribs; my arm was literally broken in half, hanging. I dislocated my hip and fractured my skull. But I had my seatbelt on."

I laugh at that. "My fucking seatbelt. There must've been an angel with me that night because I don't even remember putting it on. I remember popping the pill and then driving off. Not the seatbelt. Anyway, I'd lost a lot of blood by the time the ambulance came and took me. I was bleeding internally. My rib had punctured a lung. When I got to the hospital, they took me into surgery immediately. I died on the table for approximately forty-two seconds.

"Some say when you die, you see a light. I didn't see shit, nothing but blackness. And then, by some miracle, I was revived. After that, I didn't want to experience the blackouts anymore, especially after seeing how much pain I caused my mother. I was being so selfish, trying to rid the pain without realizing there were others who were suffering too. So I got my shit together.

"After I got better and left the hospital, I was arrested for destruction of city property, DUI, and other stuff. I was bailed out within hours, but the charges stuck. Since it was my first offense, I had to do six months of a rehabilitation program and my license was suspended for a year. Actually, I just got it back six months ago."

Yeah. Now she'll probably run as far away from me as possible. That was my past. I'm not like that anymore.

Jenna's features distort in confusion. "You don't do drugs or anything anymore?" she asks.

"No."

"But you drink?"

This is difficult to explain. "Yeah, I do. I'm not addicted to alcohol. I know that's what an addict would say, but I'm not. I never was. I drink from time to time, socially, but I don't turn to booze to solve my issues. When I'm dealing with something, I work out instead. I take out all my frustrations at the gym."

"Oh," she says.

I lean forward, lowering my head in an effort to coax her into looking at me. Her eyes meet mine. Finally. "Tell me what you're thinking right now. Tell me if what I just told you changes your opinion of me. One thing you'll learn about me, Jersey, is that I'm very honest and I don't like to sugarcoat anything. What you see is what you get. And I'd like it if you could be that way with me as well, okay?"

"All right." She straightens her shoulders, her eyes

boring into mine. "What do you want to know?"

"What are you thinking right now?" I ask.

"That you're not perfect," she responds, deadpan.

I snort. "I've never claimed to be."

"I know. I like that about you."

"You like that I'm not perfect?" I ask, waiting for her to clarify.

"Yes. It makes you real, authentic. I'm not perfect either."

"So are you saying you have a dark side you're withholding from me?" I ask playfully, but the look in her eyes transforms my smile into a thin line. "What are you not saying?"

"Judgments are given so easily; learning about a person and their struggles is far more difficult."

"You're right—judgments are easily given. But I'm not judging you, Jenna. I would never do that. I genuinely want to learn about you. If you allow me to, that is."

She seems to be struggling with her own thoughts. Her eyes are downcast as she brings a shaky finger to the side of her temple, rubbing it as if her head aches. "Excuse me. I have to use the restroom," she says before she stands and walks away.

Jenna

Pacing back and forth inside the bathroom, I try to breathe. I'm having an anxiety attack; at least it feels like I am. Why is it so hard to just come out and say it? Logan could walk away right now and it wouldn't hurt too bad, would it? Then again, he shared personal things with me about himself, which

I'm sure wasn't easy for him to do.

"I'm schizoaffective." I say it out loud in the empty bathroom. "I'm schizoaffective." I allow it to roll off my tongue.

I can't do this.

How will he look at me? Logan says he won't judge me, but I know the truth. It's never easy to look at someone the same way after hearing news like this. It's different when you tell someone you're dying because of an illness. Then, you just get the sympathy treatment. When you tell them you have a mental illness, especially when it's associated with schizophrenia, you get the is-she-going-to-jump-out-and-stab-me-because-she-must-be-crazy look.

It's the same look my mother gave me when I was diagnosed. Maybe it was like reliving her childhood all over again, I don't know. Either way, she couldn't bear to even look at me. My own mother turned on me. What makes me think Logan will be any different? He has no ties to me; he can just up and leave and never look back. My mother had no choice but to deal with me.

Dammit. I feel dizzy. I grip the sink to keep my balance and then look up at my reflection in the mirror. Look at me. All this makeup, my perfectly styled hair, these clothes neatly paired together—it's all just one big cover-up. No matter how hard I try to perfect being normal, I will never be able to. There's not enough foundation or eye shadow or even clothing in the world to conceal who I really am. And even if I were to fool everyone around me, I could never fool the villains inside my head. I will always be me: Jenna McDaniel, the girl with more issues than she can carry. No man will ever be able to handle them. Not even Logan Reed.

Logan

When Jersey comes back from the bathroom, she seems distracted, distant. She's barely said a word in the last ten minutes and I'm beginning to wonder if I said or did something wrong.

The waitress dropped off the check and I paid cash, leaving the money on the table. "I'm thinking maybe we can go to a movie, since the art show didn't work out." Shit. Stupid ass, a theater will be just as packed with people. "I mean we can go back to my apartment to watch a movie."

That didn't sound right either. *Just shut the fuck up.* Jenna is back to feeling uncomfortable. I can tell as she shifts nervously. *Great, asshole.* "Or I can take you home. Either way, whatever you want." I try to save my sorry ass, but I don't think it did any good.

"Sure. I don't mind going to your place."

"Yeah?"

"Yeah. I'd like to see how Logan Reed lives. I'm sure it'll be very amusing."

"It's a thousand-square-foot, one-bedroom apartment. Nothing special. Bachelor pad to the fullest, trust me. Oh, and there are copious amounts of video games."

She finds this funny. "You know, I had a feeling you'd be a gamer. After spending time with you, it just seems like you."

"If you keep figuring me out, Jersey, we're gonna have to end this friendship. It's getting out of hand."

At least she gets my humor. Most women find it arrogant and not funny at all.

"All right, I'll go to your apartment, and if I find anything un-badass, I promise to keep it to myself. Under one condition."

"What is that?"

Jenna's face turns serious. "I need your address. I need to text it to Charlie. Please don't think I'm weird or anything. It's just that I'll feel safer if someone knows where I—"

I cut her off, reciting my address. I can understand this. I don't ask her anything or the reason behind it. After all, I don't want her to feel unsafe in any way. She pulls out her cell, and I can tell she feels embarrassed to ask if I'm being truthful. So instead of reciting the address again, I pull out my wallet and hand her my driver's license.

Jenna looks down at the plastic card; it takes her a few seconds to finally grab it. She punches my address into her phone and sends it off to Charlie, who kind of scares me a bit if I'm being completely honest.

Jenna is by the entryway just outside of my apartment; I'm inside with my hand on the knob, holding the door wide open. She looks down, focusing on the shift of her weight from one foot to the other, as her fingers find one another and start to fidget. I wait patiently. I don't rush her or push her or say a word. I just allow her to think. The more time I spend with her, the more I'm curious about what makes her this way— the nerves, the paranoia, and how she's always lost in thought. There's a lot more to Jersey than she's letting on, and I want to know what.

My foot stomps down on the doorstopper to keep the door open on its own. I let go of the knob and shove my hands into the front pockets of my jeans. "I can leave the door open," I say, my voice low.

She looks up, her eyes tracing my features and roaming down the length of my body. Her vision lands on my hands in my pockets, and then she drags her gaze toward the doorstopper. She takes in a silent, deep breath, drops her arms to her side, and steps forward. I turn, my back facing her, and walk farther into my place. I can't hear her footsteps, but I definitely feel her following closely behind me. My hands still in my pockets, I take a seat on the sofa.

Jenna stands by the end of the couch, her head hung low, but her eyes watching my every move. Very slowly, I remove my hands. I don't know why, but I don't want her to think I'm going to attack her or something because that's how she's acting right now, as if I'm going to attack her at any second. I lean forward, grab the remote from the oak coffee table, and lean back just as quickly.

Crossing her arms, she looks around my living space, taking in every detail of my spot. I sit there and just watch her, remembering what she said about the perfect house and what lies within. As her eyes roam past the large flat screen mounted on the wall, I wonder if any of that is on her mind now. Her vision brushes down to the entertainment stand, which holds both of my game consoles and three piles of video games. A soft smile pulls at the corner of her lips. I grin too. Just watching her as she examines my place feels awkward. A good awkward, though. It's like she's collecting all the artifacts of my world and filing them away in that mind of hers to examine later.

Those perfect lips, which I always seem to come back to, press into a straight line as Jenna's stare circles the room, drifting over the plain, artless white walls. She twirls a bit, facing the galley kitchen. Then she turns back around to face me. "Your place is so normal."

I can't help but laugh. "Were you expecting whips and chains?"

"No. It's just...I don't know what I was expecting. It's just simple, like you. You know?"

I shake my head. "No, I don't know. Won't you tell me?" I pat down on the cushion next to me, gesturing for her to sit down.

She does, right beside me. "You were definitely right about it being a bachelor pad. No art on the walls, not even a picture frame." She chuckles. "But I like it. It's definitely you. A place can tell you a lot about the person who lives in it."

"Very interesting—and what does my place say about me?"

"Ha. You'd love to know, wouldn't you? I'll keep that to myself," she teases as she lifts her leg up onto the couch and twists her body to face me. Her arm hangs over the back of the sofa. She's acting playful again. All of her body language says she's beginning to feel comfortable, thank God.

"Wanna laugh at Kevin Hart's pain?" I ask.

She nods with a small smile.

We watched two stand-up comedies back-to-back. I stayed on my end of the sofa, and Jenna stayed on hers. We poked fun at the comedians, laughed at a few jokes, and laughed even harder at the funnier ones. All in all, it was a good night.

Afterward, I took Jenna home. She kissed me good night on the cheek, and I drove away.

My mind is reeling over Jenna. She's smokin' hot and very mysterious and secretive, which, to a certain extent, I actually like. I'm beyond curious about the things she seems to avoid talking about. I push those thoughts away, deciding that if she's ready to tell me more—if there is more—I'll be waiting, but I will not push it out of her.

chapter 18

Jenna

If I could meet anyone from a past time, it would probably be Vincent Van Gogh, and it's not only because he was a brilliant artist. It's more because, in a way, I'm able to relate to his mental illness—he was known to have suffered "hallucinations of sight and hearing." If he were living in this era, his symptoms would be diagnosed as schizophrenia. He also suffered from depression. He used painting as a way to cope, or I guess as a way to escape.

As I lie here on the dock by the lake house, with my elbows bent and hands beneath my head, I admire the night's canvas. The sky reminds me of one of Van Gogh's most famous paintings, *The Starry Night*. I'm reminded of this painting because everything about tonight is perfect: the cool breeze, the breathable air, the way the moon casts over the trees and gleams down on the lake. If Van Gogh were here, would he have attempted perfecting *The Starry Night*?

When I was in college, I minored in art. One of the things I learned about Van Gogh is that he admitted himself into an asylum, but not for fear of others, more for fear of himself. I became obsessed with researching and learning about him, about his life, and his art. I read hundreds of articles about him, and still it wasn't enough. I wished I were able to have been in his head, to have spoken to him in person. He was brilliant: a talented artist, yet he suffered from a disease that slowly crippled his mind.

Van Gogh died from a self-inflicted gunshot wound to his chest. When his brother Theo came to his side after hearing of the incident, Van Gogh's last words to him before his death were "the sadness will last forever."

"The sadness will last forever."

When I read his dying words, I cried, not out of sympathy, but because I understood what those words meant. It's something that cannot be controlled or escaped from. Depression is evil. Before you know it, it takes over and there's no escaping it. Van Gogh died a sad and broken man, yet he left a legacy with his paintings that will last forever. Still, I want to know—when he painted, when he admired the sky at night to paint it from memory during the day, was he troubled in those moments? Because right now, this beautiful scenery is doing wonders for my state of mind. Right now, I am peaceful, content; there's no possible way I could be sad. How will I feel when I remember this moment tomorrow in the daylight?

Footsteps make me alert, but I don't move. I already know who's coming toward me. I texted Logan about an hour ago, letting him know I'd be on the dock, waiting for him. He was working overtime on the guesthouse when Charlie and I drove up to the lake earlier today.

The past couple of weeks, things have been really good between Logan and me. We're slowly developing into something more, which scares the hell out of me. Ever since the ice cream get-together and watching comedy at his place the next day, we've been inseparable. After his shift, we usually go out somewhere, whether it's driving around, walking through the park, or just to his apartment. We've been spending all our free time with one another.

"Always by yourself, Jersey. I think you like being all alone," Logan says, almost whispering. It's so quiet it seems like more of a statement for himself than for me to hear.

"Have you not learned anything in the past couple of weeks?" Still in the same position, I tear my stare away from what could be a Van Gogh masterpiece to a uniquely Logan work of art. A smirk spreads across his gorgeously chiseled features. He lifts his hand to frame his chin, his thumb rubbing along the stubble. I've come to recognize this pose as his version of *The Thinker*.

"Well, we have been spending a lot of time together, so I guess you're not too much of a loner." He settles to lie down beside me, and puts his hands behind his head as well. "What are we looking at?" he asks, looking up.

I tilt my head to look up as well. "I'm admiring a Van Gogh. *The Starry Night*."

He chuckles. "Oh, wait. You're talking about that painter dude who went crazy, right?"

"Not crazy. He suffered from a mental illness, Logan."

"Um, if memory serves me correctly, he cut off his own ear. I'm pretty sure that's some form of crazy."

"Yes. Yes, he did cut off his own ear," I admit, but I don't give in on the crazy.

"And didn't he, like, shoot himself? That's another form of crazy."

"All right. Enough about Van Gogh. How was your day?" I ask, changing the topic. Obviously, this "crazy" talk and how he perceives a mental illness will only add fuel to a very small fire building within me, and I don't want this night to go wrong. Not tonight, not with a view like this.

"Oh, you know. Same shit, different day," he says nonchalantly.

"Ah."

"Well, I was mostly thinking about you," he confesses quietly.

"Me?" Tilting my head, I meet his gaze.

"Yeah." He smirks, charmingly so. "I just thought about how you'll be surrounded by so many people here today. It's a pretty big crowd tonight."

Right. The party, which is happening behind me and which I've managed to tune out for the past few hours. "It's okay. That's why I'm out here on the dock, away from everyone."

"I know. But still, it'd be nice if you could interact with the crowd, maybe try to work on that shyness of yours."

I look away. "It's not shyness."

"Then what is it?" I don't answer, so he goes on, "Yet another thing you don't want to talk about. I get it, Jersey." His nickname for me is quite annoying, but I'm beginning to get used to it. "Fine. If you won't talk, then we're going to play." He stands up, gripping my arm and lifting me in the process.

"Play? W-what are you talking about?" I stand up straight, looking up at him.

"We're going to play beer pong."

I widen my eyes reflexively. "I don't drink, *remember*?"

"Yes, that's why I'll be doing the drinking." He thumbs his chest, smiling widely at me.

I cross my arms, drop my hip, and smack my lips. "Sorry. I've never played before. Guess you're out of luck."

Logan reaches down, places both his hands on my shoulders, and smiles. "You're gonna learn today." He impersonates Kevin Hart. Logan takes my laugh as an okay, twists my body to face the lake house, and leads me toward the party.

The rules to beer pong—well, I think they may be made-up by the guys—are that there are two teams of two people each with six Solo cups on each end of a rectangular table. Each cup is filled halfway with beer. Each player gets one Ping-Pong ball and one throw per round. The object is to get your ball into one of the opposing team's cups. If the other team shoots the ball into one of your cups, you have to chug that drink and vice versa. The first team to sink their ball into all the opposing team's cups wins. The team that loses has to drink the winning team's remaining filled cups. But there's a catch. The losing team has to take three shots of vodka as well.

This is what I call alcohol poisoning just waiting to happen.

"All right," Bryson announces from the other end of the table. "Since Jenna doesn't drink, we'll shift the rules slightly. Jenna and Logan are on the same team, but Logan does all the drinking. Jenna tosses the ball. Same with Blair and me."

Logan and I are against Blair Mega Bitch and Bryson. I'm hoping to do an amazing job because I want to beat Blair point-blank. Also, I really don't want Logan drinking all that alcohol by himself.

"Does everyone get the rules?" Bryson yells over the loud music. Logan and I nod. So does Blair. "All right, Blair, you're first. Do me proud, babe."

My teeth find my inner cheek and chew as I take in every

movement Blair makes. She positions her body as if she's about to perform a squat. She puts her game face on—serious. You would think she's in a real championship match. She lifts her hand, fingers gripping the tiny orange ball, and flexes her wrist back and forth to loosen it up.

Logan's hand finds its way to my waist, his lips lightly brushing the curve of my ear. "Don't be nervous. You'll do great," he whispers encouragingly.

By this point, our table on the deck is surrounded by partiers. And if Logan's hand didn't feel so damn right against my waist, I would've brushed it off. Instead I leave it there. Blair Mega Bitch finally tosses the ball, and I flinch as it taps the edge of one of our cups then bounces off. I smile in relief.

"It's okay, babe. That was just a warm-up," Bryson encourages her.

I go next and miss too. Blair and I go back and forth two more rounds, missing, until she finally makes the first shot. Logan grabs the cup and, with the ball still in it, chugs the beer down. He smiles at me, flashes a wink, and nods his head before saying, "It's all right. I've played this dozens of times. It doesn't faze me." But it fazes me.

I take extra measures to focus and it works. I make the next shot. I turn to face Logan, jumping up and down as I do. His wide grin and gleaming eyes show his affection for me.

I bite my lip, face Blair's scowl, and put on my poker face.

Game on.

"All right…this is good, we still have a shot. You got this, Jersey," Logan slurs. I raise my brow, completely and utterly sure that we're going to lose. We lost the first round, which made the boys competitive, so they decided on best out of three. That's a lot of drinking on their part. We won one round and Bryson and Blair won the other. This is now the third round and both Logan and Bryson are completely trashed. The opposing team definitely has better odds. They only have one cup left to win and I have three.

I toss the ball and make it in a cup. Bryson drinks. Blair takes her turn, tossing and missing. I go again and make the second in. The crowd around us—all highly intoxicated as well—whistles and cheers loudly. Bryson chugs. This is our last chance. One cup left for each of us. I want to win because there's no way Logan can have another drink. I'm afraid he'll pass out. Several cups of beers and three shots is no good, even for a heavy drinker.

Nervously, and with complete focus, I aim and shoot. Dammit. I miss. Blair takes her turn, shooting and landing it. While everyone, including Blair and Bryson, shouts and screams—a bit overly dramatic if you ask me—all I can do is look at Logan, who has the largest grin smacked across his handsome face. He sloppily lifts his right hand up to give me a high five. "We didn't win," I say.

"So?" He shrugs. "You played and that, *my* Jersey Girl, is a celebration in and of itself."

He just called me *his* Jersey Girl, emphasizing the "my." I can't help but smile. Bryson, now beside us, places their last cup next to our last cup along with three shot glasses filled with vodka. Logan's hooded eyes graze over the shot glasses and he cringes. I'm not sure why, but something in me just can't do it. I just can't let him. I quickly grab both red Solo cups and chug down one of the beers.

More whistles and cheering.

Beer is disgusting. I can't fathom why people actually drink this for enjoyment.

I chug the second without another thought, gagging a bit at the end.

"W-what are you doing, Jersey?" Logan stumbles forward.

A hand tugs at my arm. "Yeah. What the hell are you doing, Jenna?" Charlie's beside me now, looking at me like I have five heads.

I shrug her off, smirk, and grip two of the three shot glasses. Saluting Logan, I tell myself this is for him. I bring the glass to my lips, tilt my head and gulp down the burning liquid. Logan laughs at my face, which I'm sure is twisted in disgust. "Jenna...you don't have to drink it," Charlie says.

"I'm blending in, just like everyone else," I say, taking the second shot, which I almost spit back out. I feel a burning in the pit of my stomach and wonder again why people drink this for fun.

Wetting my lips and already feeling sick to my stomach, I reach for the third shot glass, but a hand stops me. I look up at Logan, who slowly shakes his head. He grabs it for himself instead and gulps it down. I hear Charlie mumble something under her breath as she stomps off. I'll deal with her in the morning. Right now, I can't keep my eyes off of Logan and the look he's giving me.

There's no humor. Just Logan and his stormy blue eyes, scorching deep within me, trying to figure something out. He slowly steps forward. I tilt my head back to look up at him as his eyes scroll down over my face. *What is this look, Logan?* He rests his hands on my waist and gently pulls me in, my body against his. "Why did you do that?" he murmurs, low enough so only I can hear.

"Because believe it or not, I care enough that I don't want you to have alcohol poisoning," I try to joke. But I fail miserably, too consumed with how close Logan is and how his hands curve comfortably along my hips.

"You care about me?" He's still giving me that unknown look.

Something is stuck in my throat and I try to swallow it back. "Um, I care enough about the alcohol poisoning thingy." *Thingy?*

He leans down, his face centimeters from mine. "I care about you too," he tells me. And I don't know if it's the way he's looking at me or the words he's saying to me or the fact that everyone else seems to have disappeared or a combination of all of those things, but I can't help the way my heart soars at his declaration.

"Y-you do?" I stumble over the two words.

"I do."

Don't kiss me. Please do not kiss me. He leans in closer. My chest burns, and I'm not sure if it's the aftershock of the vodka or my nerves causing it.

He smells like liquor and beer and Logan.

Please kiss me.

And he does. Three small pecks, but not where I expected. The first one lands on the tip of my nose—a small, simple peck. I shut my eyes at the contact. The second one presses along my forehead. It leaves a warm and tingly feeling and my chest expands. The third tickles my chin, lingering a little longer than the rest.

It wasn't what I expected—and I'd be lying if I said I wasn't hoping for a kiss similar to the first one on my front porch—but these three small kisses mean so much more.

They're beautiful and gentle and simply Logan. They

outshine the first kiss on any given day.

"Jenna?"

"Yes?" I yawn, my head dizzy from the liquor. I'm snuggled against Logan's chest. It's a little past three in the morning. Every one of the partiers has left except for the ones who crashed because they were too drunk. We're lying beside one another on the large, comfy couch. His fingers are gently running through my hair, and it feels so good.

I like this.

I like cuddling with Logan. I like lying on Logan's chest. I like the fact that our legs are tangled with one another's and it feels completely comfortable.

He breathes out a heavy sigh. The smell of beer and vodka invades the thin space between us, but I don't mind it. "I want us to be more," he whispers.

More?

Oh no, Logan. Just…no. I knew it. I was afraid of this. As much as I'd love to be able to give him what he wants, I can't. My thoughts roil with the idea. I'm too much more. He has no idea how much more I am—and not in a good way. He won't be able to handle me, my issues, my illness, and especially how damaged I am. I'm just too much.

And more is the last thing he needs.

Finally tilting my head up, I look at him. His eyes are shut, his lips slightly parted. Just like that, he's fast asleep.

For the past hour this morning, I've scrolled through my

phone, pondering whether I should or shouldn't text him. Matthew has sent me a few messages since the day he landed on my doorstep unannounced and Logan was there to save the day. After each text was met with no response, he must have finally gotten the hint because he simply stopped messaging me altogether. The last text I received from him was over a week ago, asking if I wanted to go out for a friendly coffee date.

When Logan said he wanted more from me last night, it scared the hell out of me. Maybe he was just drunk and it was the liquor speaking, but that's a chance I can't take. I'm not sure if going out with Matthew is the best option. I used Logan to get rid of Matthew. Now I might use Matthew to push Logan away. The thing is I don't want to push Logan away; I want us to keep what we have. It's simple and perfect. But the *more* he wants will only complicate things. Letting out a frustrated breath, I type a text, send it off, and then head downstairs where the others are.

"Well, well, well. If it isn't Ms. Drunkster herself," Santino jokes. He's seated by the kitchen table with Charlie on his lap as usual.

I moan, brushing him off as I take the only empty seat, which is beside Logan. He smiles and pushes a full glass of water and a bottle of aspirin toward me. I open the cap of the bottle and pop two pills, gulping them down with the water. Everyone is minding their own business, chatting away. Logan leans in, quietly asking, "What happened to you this morning? I woke up and you were gone."

"I had to use the restroom, and I felt so sick I just went to bed upstairs. I didn't want to chance it if I had to vomit. Sorry." I really needed to just get away. To think. Alone. Without being in his arms.

He reaches up and brushes my bangs aside in understanding.

"Would the two of you just hook up already?" We both turn our heads and face Blair Mega Bitch. She rolls her eyes. "Don't give me that look. We all think the two of you should just do it already," she says, tossing both arms in the air in frustration.

"We're just friends," I say. My phone buzzes. I open the text that came in and read it.

"Well, with friends like the two of you, who needs fuck buddies, right?" she goes on.

"Jealous?" Logan retorts.

Blair's eyes spread wide, then she laughs. "Of the two of you? Hell no. It's just disgusting. The tiny whispers, giggles, cuddling, but no kissing or sex? Pfft. The entire scene makes *me* have blue balls and I don't even have balls."

Logan opens his mouth to retort, but I cut him off by saying, "Well, like I said, Logan and I are just good friends. In fact I have a date on Tuesday."

"With who?" Logan whips his head around, eyes glaring and lips slightly parted.

Shit. Why do I suddenly feel nervous? Most of all, why do I feel guilty? "Matthew." I say it so low, I don't think he hears me, but his twisted features tell me otherwise.

"*Matthew*?"

I look around at everyone. I guess I'm secretly hoping for help, but everyone turns their head and pretends not to be listening—except for Blair Mega Bitch, that is. The smirk on her face just proves she's enjoying all of this. I'd like nothing more than to smack it off her face.

"Yeah. We're going out on Tuesday for a late coffee date. Is that a problem?" I face him, arching a brow.

"Nope. Not at all," he says smoothly. I study him. Interestingly enough, he seems to be okay with it.

Logan

Is she fucking kidding me?

Matthew?

The same dude that stopped by her place when she forced me to kiss her so she could get rid of him?

Do I have a problem with it?

Nope. Not at all.

I'm completely fucking cool about it.

She can go out with Matthew.

I couldn't care less.

I couldn't give two fucks.

Matthew?

Fuck Matthew and Tuesdays and shitty fucking coffee dates.

Jenna

It's Tuesday, six in the evening. Matthew took me to a quiet coffee shop nearby my house. Over the past hour he's been going on and on about starting grad school in the fall, and how his parents are proud of all his achievements, and how he graduated top of his class, and how he wants to be involved with politics just like his father and hopes to one day be president of the United States, but before he can move up, he has to start from the bottom, so his first goal is to be a senator within six years and blah, blah, blah.

None of this interests me.

Physically, I'm here with him as I nod and smile. Emotionally, my head is wrapped up in Logan. He sent me a few texts last night. They were simple, as simple as Logan could be.

LOGAN: Excited about your coffee "date?"

ME: "Date?" Yeah, I guess I am.

LOGAN: Yeah, "date." I mean who takes a girl out for coffee as a date?

ME: Believe it or not, it's very common.

LOGAN: It's stupid.

ME: What would you do for a first date?

LOGAN: Take her out to a diner and then back to my house to watch a comedy ;-)

ME: Sounds like a nice date. Lucky girl.

And then I regretted texting it because it was flirty and I didn't want to give him the wrong impression. So I changed the subject to something completely random, talking about the weather and how it's going to be extremely hot in the coming week. He must have gotten the hint because he played along.

"Are you okay?" Matthew prods.

"Huh? Yes. Well, not really. I have a headache."

"Would you like me to take you home?"

I know this is so bad in so many ways, but I ask anyway. "Do you mind driving me to a friend's house in Philly?"

"No, not at all."

I smile.

Logan

I'm enjoying my second beer, playing a video game, and trying to focus on anything other than picking up my phone to bug Jersey Girl. I know she's on her "date," so I'll just wait. But waiting is a bitch. I'm just about to break my own rule when the doorbell rings. I groan. *Who the hell could that be?* I'm not in the mood for visitors. Reluctantly, I stand from the couch and make my way toward the door, opening it while I take a sip of my beer. My eyes meet with Jersey Girl's brown gems and I act natural. I don't want her to see how much her being here actually excites me.

Jersey's eyes trail down my shirtless body and the PJs hanging low from my waist. Then she looks back up and smiles at me. "Can I come in?"

I step aside, still holding the door open for her, and close it after she steps in. "How'd you get here?" I ask, following behind her as she makes her way into my kitchen.

"Matthew."

Matthew. I'm happy her back is facing me so she can't see the way my expression sours at the mention of his name. "You asked your date to drop you off at another guy's place?" That makes me smile.

"Nope. I told him it's a friend's place. I didn't stress it was a guy's place," she says, opening my refrigerator. "I'm so hungry."

Jersey looks good. She's wearing tight jeans—which accentuate her ass perfectly—and a loose yellow blouse that brings out the color of her eyes. Her hair is done in long waves that fall just past the middle of her back. I love when she wears her hair like that. It looks good on her. She's bent over, her head in the fridge, and I can't help but picture all of the things

I want to do to her. In the kitchen. On the couch. In my bed. Then something flares in my stomach as an earlier thought prods my mind. She got dressed for another guy. She got dressed for another guy and it pisses me off. I lean back onto the counter, crossing my legs and trying to compose myself.

"What the hell, Logan? You have nothing in your kitchen except for old Chinese food and a bag of large marshmallows." She shuts the fridge, turns around, and faces me with a pout.

She's so damn cute. "Don't downplay marshmallows." I say, uncrossing my arms and legs. I open the fridge and grab the bag of marshmallows.

Jersey lifts herself up onto the counter and sits beside the stove, facing me. She watches as I grab a fork and plate and turn on the gas stove. I stab a marshmallow onto the fork and roast it over the fire.

"You're roasting a marshmallow on your stove with a silver fork?" she asks.

"Yep."

She shakes her head. "I'm hungry for real food, Logan."

"Matthew should have fed you. I'm sure you didn't have any coffee either, since you don't drink caffeine."

She stares at me for a few seconds before responding, "I had a water."

I shake my head. Douchebag didn't even know that much about her. "I'll feed you after you try this."

"Okay." She nods.

She watches the white puff light up in flames. I slowly rotate the fork until the marshmallow turns charcoal, then I blow it out. I let it cool down before bringing it up to her mouth. She looks down at it first, hesitant. Then she wraps her lips around the fluff and closes them over the fork, taking the gooey sweetness into her mouth. And fuck is that sexy. I wish it were something else her lips were wrapped around.

"Mmm. Delish," she says.

"Told ya, Jersey Girl. Don't knock it 'til you try it."

"Food. Please," she demands.

"All right, all right. I'm gonna go throw on some clothes."

"Why? I don't mind if you go like that," she jokes.

I smile. "I bet you don't. Wanna go to the diner?"

She nods, her gaze lingering over my chest.

I shake my head, laughing as I head to my room.

July

As much as I try to repair my damaged soul, it's useless.
How can you fix me, when I can't even fix myself?

chapter 19

Jenna

It's dark out. I can barely see…

No. My head turns to the right.

I'm cold from the rain. My breathing is uneven as I search around…

No. My head moves to the left.

I'm so scared. I can hear the boots trudging through the mud. They're getting closer. I run…

No. White-knuckled, my fingers grip the bed sheets.

I run faster, harder. Out of breath and lungs burning, I run, not looking back, just pushing forward…

No. Go away. Just go away.

I lose balance, slip, and fall. With shaky hands, I try to lift myself up. My gaze meets the tombstone.

No! My eyes flash open.

The dream. It's the same nightmare over and over again. When I think there's no way it'll come back, it proves me wrong every single time. It usually happens when I'm under a lot of stress, when my life is chaotic. Like now—or at least I *think* it is. I don't know. I'm more confused than I've ever been.

I wet my dry lips and sit up, leaning my head against the headboard. There's nowhere to run or hide. I'm trapped in this room. My eyes quickly scan the space. The creeping feeling that someone is watching me crawls over my skin, and I nervously peer into the dark corners, praying someone isn't lurking there, waiting to attack.

My large bedroom feels small all of a sudden, like the walls are caving in. I've felt safe behind these walls for the last twenty-one years of my life, but now they're betraying me.

My stomach churns and my throat starts to close, as if an invisible hand is slowly choking me.

I'm suffocating.

I need air or water or an escape. I just need to breathe. Find some way to just breathe. I push the sheets off. It's so damn hot in here; I brush away the sticky strands of hair from my face. Talking myself into it, I allow my legs to dangle off the side of the bed. I'm dizzy, my mouth is dry, my chest is tight—I need to call someone. I reach for my cell phone on top of the nightstand. With a shaky finger, I skim through the short contact list. Charlie is away on vacation with her family for the Fourth of July week.

I'm stuck. The walls are zooming in. Closer. I breathe in and out, three soothing breaths.

Logan.

He's been an amazing friend over the last month, but the more time we spend with one another, the closer I feel to him. Too close. And I'm frightened that one day he'll pull away. He'll pull away as soon as he knows. I suspect he has an idea of what's wrong with me. Even though I feel better about myself when I'm around him, I sink right back into reality when we're apart. The reality where Logan can never be mine.

Mine? What is wrong with me? He's not an object I get to claim; he wasn't handed off to me or gifted or purchased. Logan remains the sole owner of himself. But shamelessly, I still want him to be mine.

"Hello?" Logan's voice, low and raspy, prickles through the speaker. I look down at the phone in my hand. *Oh God*, I didn't realize I hit the call button when I saw his name on the list. "Hello…Jenna?" I hear again, his voice sleepy.

I quickly bring the cell to my ear. "I-I'm so sorry, Logan. I didn't mean to wake you. Please, try to go back to sleep," I whisper.

He yawns. "It's cool. What time is it?" He pauses. I look at my clock just as he recites the time. "It's almost two in the morning, Jersey Girl. Are you all right?"

The sound of his voice is soothing, especially when he says the nickname he made up for me. It's something I've grown accustomed to over the past few weeks. "Yeah…I just had a bad dream."

"Another one, huh?" he says, his tone a bit clearer now. I can hear his bed squeak, as if he's adjusting himself to sit up.

Last weekend at the lake house, Logan and I fell asleep on the couch in the living area. That couch has been known as our spot for the last month. We'd stayed up most of the night watching movies while everyone else sat out back partying. I didn't realize I'd dozed off until Logan gently shook me awake. He said I was shaking and whimpering in my sleep. Even though I knew, I couldn't tell him what my dream was about. I did tell him, however, that it's a nightmare I've been dealing with for a very long time. He didn't question me, thank goodness. He rarely does. But waking up to Logan made me feel safe. I guess that's why I subconsciously called him just now.

"Yeah," I say. "The same one."

"Wanna talk about it?"

"Not really. I guess I just needed to hear your voice," I confess. "It calms me."

He chuckles. The sound of the low rumble deep within his chest shoots a warm liquid through my heart, and a tug starts at the corner of my lips. "That's good to hear," he says.

"Yeah," I say, trying to think of something else to keep him on the phone a bit longer.

"Jersey Girl?"

"Yes?"

"Want me to come over? I mean, I know your father is away on a business trip and your mother left for that stupid spa retreat with her friends. And Charlie's on vacation with her family. You're all alone in that house. I know you're probably afraid."

He's right. I am alone. I've never felt more alone than I do now. "I am scared, I guess. But I don't want you to drive here at this time. It's late—or early… Whatever. I'll be okay."

"I don't mind. Tomorrow is the Fourth and I'm off. If I leave now, at this time, there shouldn't be any traffic. I can make it there in thirty minutes. Only if you want, of course. I don't want you to feel uncomfortable."

"You don't make me uncomfortable, Logan."

His silence says he doesn't believe that. Have my reactions to certain things convinced him otherwise? "Well, the offer is still there," he says.

"Okay." I finally cave in. I want him here with me. I'm afraid of this house, of my dream, and of my own thoughts. I want Logan to clear all of it away, like he always unknowingly does.

"All right, see you soon."

We end our call. I hop out of bed and walk into the bathroom. I look like crap, so I wash my face, brush my teeth, and comb my hair. Then I tread down the stairs and wait at the bottom step, in the foyer by the door.

I just sit and wait.

The doorbell sounds, startling me a bit. I stand, rubbing the numbness out of my behind from sitting on the marble stairs, and then shut off the alarm and open the door. With sleepy eyes, Logan smiles adorably at me and scratches the back of his head. His hair is a bit longer than when we first met. Right now, the right side is crushed flat against his head while the rest is wildly all over the place. A little giggle escapes me. "You have bed hair."

Logan's mouth slants into a crooked grin as he brushes his hand over the wild locks. "Well, I did hop out of bed and run to your rescue. Give me some credit, huh?"

Even at almost three in the morning he's an ass. I playfully shove my hand against his shoulder. "All right, big guy, no need to be all cocky." I smile. "Come on in." Stepping aside, I give him room to shuffle in. When he does, I shut the door, lock it, and punch the code into the alarm. "Are you hungry or thirsty?" I ask him.

"Nah. You?" he asks.

I shake my head. "Well, um, I guess we can go up to my room."

Logan nods once. It's not like I'm nervous or anything. I've been alone with Logan a lot in the past few weeks, especially in his apartment. But he's never been in my bedroom, and I've never been in his. A bedroom is kind of a sacred space. Asking someone to go in with you could give the wrong impression—especially for us. Will he be able to see right through me and know the exact person I am by my possessions? I shake that thought aside. I trust Logan, so I walk up the stairs, and he slowly follows behind me.

As I enter my room, I look around. Suddenly I'm insecure of my things. I wonder what he's thinking as he takes in the cave I spend most of my time in. Is he judging the light grey walls and sleek black furniture? What about the built-in bench by the window? It's filled with three stuffed animals my father gave me as a child, and I just can't seem to let go of them. Does he think them juvenile?

I walk carefully toward the bed, turn to face him, and then plop down cross-legged on the center of the mattress. Logan's eyes roam over the shelving unit by my desk, which is filled with old art sketches and oil paintings. "Did you sketch these?" he asks with his back to me.

"Yeah. A long time ago."

"Damn, Jersey Girl. I knew you were talented with the oil paintings, but these are very detailed. They're amazing."

"Thanks."

Logan drops the clear plastic shopping bag he walked in with on top of my desk. Through the bag I can see jeans and a white fabric, which I'm guessing is a T-shirt. He turns around, facing me, and comes my way. My heartstrings thrum when he reaches the edge of the bed and slightly lifts his shirt, reaching for the button of his jeans. He looks up. "I hope you don't mind? I usually sleep naked, but I'll keep my boxers on this time." He winks with a grin.

Naked? "Uh, no, that's fine." My voice, I'm sure, is a bit shaky.

Nodding, he drops his jeans, then grips the edge of his shirt, lifting it up and over his head. Each groove and line of his ab muscles flexes in the process. I swallow hard. I've seen him practically naked in swim trunks. This isn't a big deal. *Just think of swim trunks and quit ogling him.*

My traitorous eyes navigate over his broad chest, which is just begging to be touched, down his perfectly sculpted abs, also begging to be touched, and past the V of his hipbones, which I wouldn't mind running my tongue along. Then comes…his package. The fabric of his grey boxer briefs, snuggly wrapped around his impressive size, has my breath quickening and my mouth watering. All my self-control abandons ship and my thoughts betray me as images of Logan climbing into bed and covering my body with his explode in my mind. The only thing I can see are his blue-grey eyes filled with lust, penetrating mine as he drives his cock inside of me.

Oh my God.

I tear my eyes away, flushed and embarrassed by where my mind just went. Trying to shake away the shameless thoughts, I scoot over to the left side of the bed, giving Logan room to join me on the right side. I feel the dip in the mattress as he settles in. I can't look at him again; I feel like I've been caught red-handed. The yellow and blue polka dots scattered around my pajama bottoms are extremely interesting all of a sudden. I trace each one along my thigh. God, I look like a five-year-old in PJ bottoms and a white cami next to his extremely adult, manly body clad only in boxer briefs.

"Everything okay?" Logan prods.

I make the mistake of looking up. He's in my bed, half naked with his head propped against the headboard. His waist and legs are beneath my covers, but his upper body is in full view, completely on display. I sigh again. "No. I mean…" I shake my head. "Yes. Yes, everything is okay," I fumble. Obviously I've forgotten how to speak

"Well, come here. I feel lonely over here."

Nodding, I scoot back so I'm leaning against the headboard like he is and drag the comforter up to my waist. My hand smooths over the steel blue fabric. The color reminds me of Logan's eyes. Funny, I never put that together before now. "So what shall we talk about to keep that pretty little head of yours clear of bad thoughts?"

Tilting my head along the cushioned headboard, I cross my arms and meet his gaze. "What makes you think I have bad thoughts in my head?"

"You must have bad thoughts before bed if you keep having the same bad dreams over and over again. Something keeps bothering you. If you actually let me in and talk to me about it, it may help." There's a slight hint of annoyance in his tone, which in turn annoys me.

"I have let you in, Logan. Other than Charlie, you're probably the only person I have ever let in, besides Brooke."

He shakes his head. "Don't try to humor me. You don't and you know it. You beat around the bush with me. You never tell me what's bothering you. You won't tell me how you feel. It's like you skip over it, and I allow it. I accepted it because I thought you needed time, but now I'm not so sure if it's time you need. I feel like you'll always keep everything bottled up inside."

"Wow. If that's how you truly feel, then why are you even here?"

He bites down, jaw clenching. Through his teeth he mutters, "Because believe it or not I actually care about you."

"No one asked you to," I spit out, crossing my arms and looking away.

"Well, it's a little too late for that, huh?"

"What is that even supposed to mean?" I ask. Logan lets out a mocking laugh. I scowl at him. "What's so funny?"

"You. Me. Us. Everything!" He raises his hands for dramatic effect. "Look at us. We're arguing like we're a damn couple."

"Yeah. Well, we're not."

"You've made that very clear," he retorts bitterly. Then he scoots down into the covers and roughly turns to his side, giving me his back. So I guess we're done with whatever this was—disagreement, argument, misunderstanding?

Yes, it was harsh. I know it was. But we're not a damn couple and I don't want him to think we are. I'm just…I don't know. I'm frustrated now—frustrated at myself for being such a bitch and frustrated at him for wanting more, for making me want more too.

I stand and pad over to the light switch by the door, mulling over the shitty turn that the last few minutes took. The small lamp on the nightstand casts the only light in the room now.

Slipping back underneath the bedsheets, I rest on my side with my head on my arm. I stare at the back of Logan's head while my mind wheels in circles trying to fill the silence. He's in my room, and I know he's mad, and I want to know what the hell is currently going on in his head, but I don't dare ask because it isn't fair. How can I ask him what's going on in his head if I can't even tell him what goes on in mine? Now I understand his frustration.

"Art was always my thing, even as a child, as far back as I can remember," I start off quietly, my gaze lingering on Logan's rumpled brown hair. His shoulders slowly lift and drop with his even breaths.

Silence. Then, "Yeah?" He speaks but doesn't move.

"Yeah," I reply and keep going while I have the guts to do it now. "It's difficult for me to share or show my feelings. It was the same when I was a kid. I always drew, pencil to paper, and later discovered painting. Art was the only way I could express my emotions. I could create something beautiful without the risk of getting hurt." I laugh at the thought. "I know it may sound stupid."

Logan shifts, rolling over to the left side of his body so he's facing me now. He stares at me, his head gently resting against the pillow. Not a trace of humor can be found on his face. "It doesn't sound stupid at all," he says.

"Maybe. Maybe not." I shrug. "The more I relied on my drawings or paintings as a way to cope with all my bottled-up emotions, the worse I got. It triggered something else, and I withdrew even more into myself. It got so bad that the one thing I was truly passionate about slowly became an enemy.

"My heart gradually shut out all those who cared for me, making me numb. Painting became the only way I could effectively communicate. I poured all of my frustration into my paintings, so much so that when I got overwhelmed to the point of a breakdown, I exploded. One huge destruction. I couldn't paint fast enough to handle everything, and I couldn't handle painting or drawing without crying, without falling apart. It hurt too much. Once it came to that, I told myself I wouldn't do it again. So I shoved most of my paintings and all my art supplies into a large cardboard box, metaphorically storing away all my emotions. I couldn't handle it anymore, so I just stopped."

"How long has it been since you last painted?"

I try to think back on it. "A little over nine months. My last painting was a month after Brooke died. I never finished it. It's the only painting I've never finished."

His eyes glisten as if a memory just sparked. "That one painting in your shed, when I walked in and asked for the measuring tape... That was the one, wasn't it?" he asks.

I nod. "That was the first time since I stored all my paintings away that I looked at all of them. My psychiatrist thought I was ready to start again, but I didn't feel ready yet. I don't think I'll ever be ready."

So many questions linger in his stare, but he doesn't ask. Instead he makes a statement. "You're so talented, you can't let that go to waste."

"Do you like to build?" I ask him.

"Yeah," he answers, a bit thrown off by the question.

"Why?"

"Just...because I do." He shrugs.

"No. There's a reason why."

He thinks for a moment. "Because knowing I took part in creating something that others can enjoy is rewarding somehow."

"Exactly. That's how I felt for a very long time, fulfilled at the end of each piece I'd created. But then it turned into something else. Something darker. I was no longer fulfilled; I was angry at everything and everyone. My anger slowly turned into something more and then, before I knew it, creating art wasn't fun anymore. Every time I tried, it triggered something else." I shut my mouth and then open it to tell him. Tell him what it triggered. Tell him about my disorder. Tell him who I truly am.

Then Logan scoots in closer, reaching his hand over my waist and bringing me into him. We're both in the middle of my mattress. My hand easily lands on his chest, and his rises to rest on the base of my neck. "You *will* create art again and when you do, you'll have that feeling back at the end of each piece. Because I believe in you and your work and the person you are."

"I don't think I'm strong enough to handle it," I confess, and I truly don't think I am.

He brings his head to mine. His lips touch the tip of my nose, my forehead, and finally my chin. Our little thing. Ever since the first time he's done it, he's never stopped, and I will never let him. I'd rather have a thousand little Logan kisses like those than no kiss at all, because when his lips lightly caress my skin, he's mine and I'm his.

He rests his forehead against mine. "You're stronger than you think, Jersey Girl."

"I hope so," I whisper.

I wake up to the smell of buttery pancakes and bacon. Logan steps forward at my bedside, a plate in one hand and a glass of OJ in the other. He rests the glass on my nightstand. His smile is contagious, forcing me to smile back as I sit up.

"Good mornin', Jersey Girl. You slept like a baby."

"That's the first time in a long time I've slept like that in my own room."

He smiles, handing me a plate. "Breakfast in bed," he announces proudly.

I grab the plate, placing it on my lap. Two pancakes, three strips of bacon, and scrambled eggs. "You actually cooked?" I ask in disbelief.

"Yeah. Unlike at my place, your folks actually had something in the fridge." He sits on the edge of the bed beside me, studying my features.

"Thank you. Um, I usually don't eat breakfast, though."

Logan lifts his leg up on the bed and twirls his body so he's face-to-face with me. "How 'bout this—if you eat up, I'll give you a hint about a little surprise I have in store for today."

"Surprise?"

"Yep."

"What kind of surprise?" I ask.

His lips curl up into a grin. "Eat up." I stab my fork into the fluffy cake and take a bite. "There you go, Jersey Girl. Let's get some meat on those bones."

"What?" I mumble through my mouthful. "I'm not skinny."

He chuckles. "Eat up, will ya?"

I quickly scarf the rest of it down until my belly's aching and on the verge of exploding from being full. But it was worth every bite to see the satisfied look on Logan's face as I took my last swallow. That's the best breakfast I've had in a really long time.

"This is not fair! You made me eat all that breakfast and you haven't given me one hint!"

We've been driving for almost two hours now. First, Logan had to stop by his apartment to grab a few things. He asked me to wait in the car, which I did. When he came back out, he held a black book bag over his right shoulder. When he entered the truck and I asked what was in the bag, he tossed it in the backseat and told me it was none of my business.

"I gave you a tiny hint already," he says.

"Telling me to bring a change of clothes and dress comfortably with sneaks is definitely not a hint."

"We're heading toward the lake house."

"Is that the big surprise? The lake house?"

He laughs at my unenthusiastic tone. "No. We'll be there tonight to hang out. Bryson, Santino, and a handful of people will be there. It won't be packed since everyone is with their families for barbeques and fireworks and crap like that."

"Why aren't you and Bryson with your family for the Fourth of July?"

"Because my mother hasn't celebrated the last two years; it's too close to Sean's birthday. Uncle George usually hangs out with his buddies. It's not really a big holiday for us."

"Oh."

"But I can tell you where I'm taking you is nearby the lake house." He steers the wheel as he turns his head to take a quick peek my way. His smile brightens. "Oh, come on, Jersey."

"Come on what?" I ask innocently.

"What's that face for? I expect you to be enthused by the mystery of this adventure."

"Honestly? The lake house isn't a huge surprise. I wouldn't have scarfed down my breakfast for—"

"Oh, have a little faith." Logan shakes his head at me in mock disappointment. "I only said it was *by* the lake house. It could be the most epic surprise of your life for all you know." I cock my head to study him. He catches me staring and smiles.

"Okay. Fine," I relent. "I'll give you the benefit of the doubt. This could be the *best surprise ever!"* I joke, slamming my hand to my chest and batting my eyelashes at him.

"See? Now you're getting it, Jersey."

Logan parks his truck in a large dirt-filled parking lot surrounded by tall trees. There's a handful of cars spread out in the lot. I unclick my safety belt but stay inside, scooting toward the dashboard and crooking my neck to get a better look.

We're parked at the base of a trail into the woods, but these woods aren't like the ones by the lake house. Those are open and airy and you can see at least a mile. These woods, even though it's sunny and bright out, feel dark, secretive. Hundreds of tree trunks hide what's beyond.

Run.

Sweat coats my skin, trailing behind a sheet of goose bumps. My fingers grip the edge of the seat as I stare ahead. I stare and stare, waiting for him to jump out—the person watching me. I can't see him, but I can feel his eyes penetrating through the trees, across miles of wildlife, through the windshield, and straight into me. He's waiting for me to step out of the truck.

Run.

"All right, Jersey let's do this—"

Logan stops midsentence. Shuddering, I slowly turn my head to him. He's beside me with the door wide open. His eyes cautiously take in the fear in mine. "Are you all right?" he asks.

I'm not. Everything in my stomach is churning, my mind is racing, and my heart stammers in my chest. I'm not all right. I'm scared and though I don't know the man that I'm afraid of, I can't help that I am. I don't want to be anywhere near him.

Logan's hand finds its way to my cheek. The warmth from the contact instantly soothes me. I lean my face into him, wishing I could shrink and curl into a tiny ball and live in the safe haven that is Logan Reed's palm for the rest of my life.

"*Look* at me," he urges kindly. My eyes flutter open, mesmerized by stormy blues as they fill with concern for me. "We can leave," he says, acknowledging my discomfort.

You always ruin everything.

Shut up, I tell the voice in my head.

You do! Just because you've ruined your own life, doesn't mean you have to ruin it for everyone else, You're pathetic...

Straightening my shoulders, I suck in a shaky breath and fight back the urge to burst into tears. As much as I hate the voice, it's right. I ruin everything for everyone.

Slowly, I shake my head side-to-side. Logan's brows draw in, "You sure?" I nod. He's not convinced. "I don't know, Jersey—"

"I'm fine!" I croak. Clearing my throat, I finally say, "Seriously, I just thought I saw something, that's all. I'm fine now. I promise."

Logan stares at me, hyperaware of every bit of my anxiety. He turns his head toward the evil woods. I focus on him, breathing a little heavier than normal. Finally his eyes are back on mine and everything is okay again, if only for a moment. My lips tremble into a shy grin.

"All right, then," he says. "Let's get to it." He reaches his hand out for me. I grab it without hesitation and hop out of his truck.

Logan intertwines his fingers with mine, tightening his grip as he pulls me in closer to him, but our bodies remain inches apart. Using his free hand, he shuts the passenger door behind me.

I take in all of his actions. Even if they mean *nothing* to him, they mean *everything* to me. The way his body towers over mine—it makes me feel safe. The way he pulls me in close enough to breathe in the smell of Gain fabric softener lingering on his fresh T-shirt—it sets my senses whirling. The way our bodies touch without actually touching, my chest centimeters from the middle of his stomach—it only intensifies the magnetic pull between us, slowly luring me to him.

I'm falling deeper and deeper into an ocean filled with nothing but emotions for Logan Reed. I'm the anchor sinking to the bottom. Reality is the life vest thrown in to rescue me. But in my life, I don't want to be rescued from reality. I want to drown in this small world created with Logan. I want to breathe it all in, let it fill me up, and drift away. I don't care how much it'll burn or the amount of time I have left before my lungs stop working. I want to just feel this way for as long as I can.

What is this feeling? I have no idea, but I know that it hurts and heals and nurtures all at the same time.

"You see over there?" Logan says, his tone low, almost a whisper, but the words sound loud in my head, pulling me out of this trance I'm in.

Fluttering my eyes open, fighting back the urge to cry—I have no idea why I have this urge, but I do—I lift my chin and meet his gaze. He looks down at me and his forehead wrinkles with worry. Quickly I force a smile, hoping to distract him. "You see over there?" he repeats, his head nudging behind me.

It takes me a moment to work up the courage to look over my shoulder. Farther down, a few feet away from his truck, is a huge wooden, worn-out sign that reads Coven Pocono Nature Trail in bold red, chipped paint.

"Is that where we're going?" My question comes out soft. I'm not sure he's heard me until I turn my head back to him.

Wetting his lips, he lets go of his grip on my hand. I'm upset at first because I need his touch. I need the contact. And he gives it to me by bringing both of his hands up to cradle my face.

I'm safe again.

"Jersey Girl," he whispers and I shut my eyes. Now and forever, I will always love that name. I don't care how much Charlie makes fun of it; it's mine. All mine. Logan gave it to me and it will forever be *only* mine. "We don't have to go in. I just... I don't know. I wanted to show you how beautiful it can be. It may look scary and dark on the outside, but on the inside there's so much more. So much potential, so much room to grow."

Swallowing back a hiccup lodged in the center of my throat, I meet his gaze and nod.

He smiles.

Logan drops his hands from my face and takes ahold of my hand again. We step forward, side-by-side, toward the entrance of the trail. I lean in closer to him, and my eyes focus on our sneakers crunching against old fallen branches and leaves underfoot.

Logan stops abruptly just before we walk into the trail. "I almost forgot," he says, slinging the backpack in front of him and catching it between his knees. With his left hand still tangled with mine, he struggles with the zipper using his other hand. Once it's halfway open, he opens the flap. "Can you grab the camera in there?" he asks me.

Raising my brow in question, I do as he asked, digging my free hand in to remove an all-black, older Canon model camera with the extended lens perfectly intact. It's sturdy and a bit heavy in my delicate hand, but I keep it secure while Logan zips up the book bag and swings it back into place behind him.

"What's this for?" I ask.

"We're going to take photos."

"Photos?"

"Yep." He nods. Then he wraps the strap from the camera around my neck. It drops heavily, dangling over my chest.

"Why?"

"You'll see." He moves forward, turning to see what's keeping me in place when I don't move. His features relax. "Do you trust me?"

I nod.

"How much?"

"With all I have," I admit.

He steps back to me and tilts his head lower, pursing his lips and then giving me SLKs (Special Logan Kisses). Nose. Forehead. Chin.

My body instantly relaxes and before I know it, we're in the woods, walking down the trail. At first it's just like any nature trail—tall trees, leaves and branches shielding the sky, a hint of sunlight beaming through.

My fingers grip Logan's hand tight as we tread on. I look all around us: up, left, ahead, right, over my shoulder. No one is in sight. I let this roll through my mind a few times before I relax again.

We continue to walk in silence for about twenty minutes when Logan stops midstride. I look up at him. His head is tilted back, staring up as his shoulders move steadily with his breaths. "Do you see that?" he asks.

I look up, trying to figure out what he's looking at, but I don't see anything, well, except for the branches and leaves above us. I look back to Logan who has let go of my hand and is now bending at the knees. He lies down on his back, crosses his legs, and then folds his hands over his stomach.

I step up beside him, looking down as he smirks up at me. "What are you doing?" I ask.

"Admiring."

"Admiring what?"

He taps the ground beside him, gesturing for me to lie next to him. I look around us. We're in the middle of a trail with no one in sight and he just wants to lie down? It's weird, but Logan always has a reason behind his actions, so I just shrug it off and get comfy beside him. Positioning my body the same as his, I adjust the camera on top of my chest so it doesn't tip over to the ground.

We gaze at Mother Nature above us. The vibrant colors of tea-green leaves, lemon chiffon sun, and celestial sky blue artistically paint the perfect image. It's soothing and perfect. I take in a deep breath and just marvel at it. I wish I could capture this and keep it forever.

Then I remember the camera. Reaching for it, I remove the lens cap, switch it on, and bring the eyepiece in view.

Click. Click. Click.

I stop midclick, tilting my head to find Logan with a full-tooth grin, still looking up. "Why so happy?" I ask him.

"Just because." He shrugs.

Click.

He tilts his head to look at me.

Click.

His smile weakens. "Stop snapping pictures of me!" He moans.

I giggle. He looks cute when he's upset.

Click. Click. Click.

"I'm going to rip that camera out of your hands and return the favor."

I stick my tongue out at him and adjust the lens to snap another shot when pink shoelaces appear in the frame right beside Logan's head. Slowly, I lower the camera and follow the shoelaces up two little legs to a small body and curious round face.

"Momma, look!" A little girl—no older than three—points down at us. I sit up. The mother runs up and quickly grips her daughter's hand.

"I'm so sorry," the lady says to us.

Logan chuckles as he sits up. "No problem."

"Momma, I'm big girl," the toddler says, wrinkling her nose as she tries with all of her strength to pull her hand away from her mother's.

"Yes, Lana, a very big girl. But big girls need to hold their mommy's hand. Besides, I'm not ready to let you go. You think you can do that for mommy?"

"O-tay," the little girl says, defeated. Then she jumps up and down. "But come on! We go on adtwenter."

"Yes, Lana. Let's go on the adventure." The woman treads forward with her daughter, looks back at us, and mouths "sorry" one more time.

I watch as the mother and daughter walk side-by-side, the toddler's tiny sneakers stomping and hopping around as she talks away—her words barely understandable—and the mother nodding, laughing, and just enjoying her daughter. A smile pulls at the corner of my lips. I lift the camera, zoom in on the two of them, and take the perfect shot.

"All right," Logan announces with a single clap. "You ready to finish the rest of our adtwenter?"

chapter 20

Logan

Jersey Girl and I spent a little over two hours on the nature trail. At first she was a bit hesitant, but after a little push she really enjoyed herself. She took pics of everything and anything we hiked by, which is perfect for what I have planned.

When we finally arrived at the lake house, we did our usual: ate, jumped in the lake, and then showered—separately—but the thought of how Jenna would look naked, with her hair soaked underneath a showerhead, did cross my mind. Just for an instant. All right, you caught me. Who the fuck am I kidding? It was on my mind for my *entire* shower. The only excuse I have is that I'm a guy.

Right now, Jenna is getting dressed in her room while I'm in the kitchen, grabbing a beer. The back door swings open and Bryson steps in, his arm wrapped around his not-so-better half, Blair Mega Bitch. She slightly nods my way, flashing an arrogant smirk, and then treads her slutty, potentially disease-infected self toward the living area. Honestly, I'm shocked I haven't heard any more stories about her cheating, yet. It's only a matter of time, though. After all, it's only been a couple of months since her and Bryson patched things up.

"What's up, Bry?" I say, uncapping the beer and taking a swig.

"Nothin' much. We're just getting in. How long you been here?" he asks.

"Jenna and I got back a couple hours ago from that nature trail Mom used to take us to. We hung out a bit when we got back. Now she's upstairs getting dressed. She should be down soon."

"The Coven trail?"

I nod.

"Damn. I haven't been there in forever," he quietly reminisces. "What made you go there?"

Shrugging, I say, "I wanted to show Jenna."

"Ah."

I pause midsip of my beer, narrowing my eyes. "What's the dumb smirk for?"

"Nothing." He raises his hands, palms forward. "You're so defensive."

"Don't fuck with me, Bry. I know you better than anyone."

Bryson leans against the counter and crosses his arms over his chest. He still has that shit-eating grin across his face. "Well, I'm just here admiring you, my little cousin," he says. I raise a brow. He continues in a mocking tone, "Mr. I Will Never Get Strung Out Over a Girl. *Ever.* But from where I'm standing—front row, I might add—you're so fucking strung out I think you lost your balls along the way."

"Fuck off."

Bry laughs. "I'm serious, dude. You have a strong thing for this chick and you're not even together-*together*. What happens when you are?"

"What the hell does 'together-together' even mean?"

Bryson arches a brow. "Come on, Logan. You know what I mean. You guys act more like a couple than Blair and me, but at least we...*you* know."

"No, I don't know. Enlighten me," I say, interested in what he means by this "together-together" crap.

"Do I have to spell it out for you?" he prods. I stare blankly at him. Bryson huffs. "S-E-X. Sex, Logan. Blair and I are intimate. You and Jenna are not, but the way the two of you act, you might as well be."

"We're just friends," I clarify, my tone stern. I'm not sure why I'm feeling defensive, but there are two things Bryson said that I don't like. One, Jenna is not just some "chick," and two, I'm not strung out. That's fucking ridiculous.

"The moment you two realize how you feel about one another—because, let's face it, it's obvious to everyone around you—the easier it will be. Trust me." He straightens, dropping his arms to his side.

I open my mouth to say something, but shut it just as quickly when Jenna walks in. "Hey, guys," she greets. Her hair drapes over her shoulders, still damp from the shower. As my eyes eat up the pair of denim shorts and white tank top that hug her frame, I swallow back the truth. The fucking truth that's been in the back of my head for the past couple of months. The truth that I've buried because I know she doesn't want more than what we are. The truth that Jenna and I will never be anything other than just friends.

"Hey, Jenna," Bryson says, his eyes still glued on me, giving me the you-know-what-to-do look. Then he nods his head and turns, joining his girl in the living area.

Jenna takes a few steps until she's standing only a few inches from me. I chug the rest of my beer, keeping my eyes away from her, and place the bottle on top of the counter after

I'm done with it. She pushes her body against mine, lifting her arms and wrapping them around my neck. This shouldn't make me uncomfortable. This is normal for us. But after what Bry just said, my thoughts are racing wild, and it's fucking confusing.

Finally, I shift my gaze and look down at her. "About what Bryson just said..." she mutters.

My heart stammers as my eyes widen. "You heard that?"

"Most of it," she confesses. "I walked in and heard the part where he talked about how our feelings toward one another are obvious to everyone else." Her lips pull into a shy grin.

Thank God she didn't hear the beginning of it. I look down on her and she seems calm about it all. I wonder what she's thinking. Is she going to finally confess that maybe Bryson is right? Sighing, I place my arms around her waist and pull her in a bit more. This doesn't faze her. Again, it's normal for us.

Jenna grabs the side of my face, her fingers grazing the stubble of my growing beard. I like it, the way her hand feels when she touches me. I like us this way, close enough that I can dip my head a few inches and kiss her. I like how comfortable it is for us.

"Logan, don't pay any attention to Bryson. He, along with everyone else, just doesn't understand our relationship and that's fine. As long as we know what it is, why does it matter what others think?"

I bite back what I really want to say and settle for, "And what is our relationship exactly?"

She smiles like it's the most obvious thing. "Best friends, of course."

I laugh and she does too, but I'm sure she's laughing for

an entirely different reason than I am. She probably finds humor in our chat. She probably thinks I'm laughing because, of course, *duh*, it should be obvious we're best friends. But that's not why I'm laughing.

I'm laughing to cover up the fact that I want to bash my fist through the kitchen cabinet because never in my life did I ever think I'd be placed in the fucking friend zone.

And that fucking sucks.

Jenna and I are sitting beside each other on the couch, her hand in mine. Santino is sitting on the floor, leaning against the sofa. Bryson is on a La-Z-Boy chair with Blair on his lap. It's a slow night, which I don't mind. It's nice to have a small group and have a relaxing night once in a while.

Jersey Girl hasn't said much since the kitchen scene. I'm sure she hasn't given it much thought either. I look down at her. Her head is resting against my chest; her breathing is calm. I smile as she traces small shapes on my hand: a circle, turns into a triangle, then transforms into a square, then finds its way back into a curvy, nonexistent object. My eyes drift in Bryson's direction. I catch him staring at us, and he flashes me a told-you-so grin. I narrow my eyes at him, which he counters with a chuckle. Blair turns her head to see what's so interesting. As soon as she sees it's about Jenna and me, she instantly rolls her eyes. Then her expression changes, her eyes brighten, and a smug grin pulls at the corner of her lips.

"Jenna, I almost forgot to mention," Blair says animatedly. Between the suspicious gleam in her eyes and the current of malice underlying her words, I can only imagine what Blair's about to say.

Jersey Girl lifts her head from my chest and looks in Blair's direction. Mega Bitch twirls her body on Bryson's lap to fully face Jenna. "Yes?" Jenna responds.

"Guess who I recently ran into?"

I'm glaring at her now. Whatever Blair's up to is not with good intention. It's written all over her face.

"Who?" Jenna asks cautiously.

Blair allows the anticipation to build for a moment before blurting out, "Eric."

From the way I'm seated, I can't see Jenna's expression. Her back faces me, but she shifts uncomfortably. Then she straightens her shoulders, I suspect to show Blair she hasn't gotten to her. *That's my girl.* "That's nice," she says evenly.

"Yeah, it is. I mentioned I've been spending time with you here." Blair giggles. "It's funny, he asked if you were still a nut job. I had no idea what he meant. I told him you seem normal to me." Blair pouts, mocking a sad puppy dog look. I have the urge to smack it off her face, but lucky for her I don't hit girls.

My eyes shift from Blair to Jersey Girl when her hand squeezes mine and her leg slowly begins to bounce. "Thanks," Jersey Girl responds.

"No problem. Oh, and he looks good! Did you know he's engaged? Crazy. Yeah, he seems to be doing really well for himself."

"Good for him," Jenna says with a straight face.

"Isn't it?" Blair digs in.

"Yeah," Jenna whispers. Then she stands, excusing herself as she walks away. She doesn't run or storm out; she just simply walks through the kitchen and out the back door.

I glare at Blair. "Wow," I say.

"What?"

"There are times I don't think you can be any more of a bitch than you already are. And you manage to prove me wrong every single time." I stand and walk off toward Jenna. In the background I hear Blair asking Bryson if he's going to let me talk to her that way. Bryson simply brushes off her remark by starting up a conversation with Santino. That's right. Even Bry knows when she's acting like the fucking queen bitch.

"Hold up," I yell out, running to catch up with Jenna. She doesn't look at me or stop; she keeps going at a quicker pace. "I hate her," Jersey Girl finally blurts out.

"I know. She's a bitch."

"A bitch is a nice description. She's a cunt."

She crosses her arms over her chest. I've never seen her this pissed off. I finally catch up and walk beside her until we reach the end of the dock. She steps close to the edge, looking down. I stand by. If I didn't know any better, I'd think she were about to jump in at any time.

"Don't let her get under your skin. She doesn't have a good bone in her body. She does shit like that just to get a rise out of you."

"Well, she sure knows how to hit a soft spot."

"Who's Eric?" I ask, my breath still a bit raspy from jogging.

Jenna drops her arms to her side, her hands tightening into fists.

"Who is he?" I ask again.

She squares her shoulders defensively.

"Jersey Girl." I grip her shoulder. "I'm not your enemy. You can talk to me."

Jenna shuts her eyes; her breathing calms and the tension in her body relaxes beneath my grip. Then she lets out a long sigh.

"He was someone I thought loved me."

"An ex-boyfriend?"

"Yeah."

I nod. "I see."

"He was my first."

"First?" I raise a brow. "As in first guy you ever slept with?"

She turns her head, eyes glistening. "Yeah, that too. But he was also the first guy I fell in love with, the first guy I ever trusted, and the first guy who broke my heart."

"What happened between the two of you?"

Jersey Girl turns her head away, her gaze skimming over the lake. She breathes in one deep breath, and then lets out a sigh, her shoulders deflating in the process. "I got sick."

"Sick?"

"Yeah, sick. There was a time where I was at my lowest point in my life. Well, at the time I thought it was my lowest—"

"Like, the flu sick?" I interrupt.

She brings her eyes back to me. "Just sick, Logan. The point that I'm trying to make is that Eric couldn't handle it and he left me. It was heartbreaking because it was when I needed him the most and he walked away from it all."

What kind of bastard does that to someone he claims to care for? "Do you know where he lives now?" I ask.

Her brows draw in. "No. Why?"

"So I can go kick his ass." I shrug at her wide-eyed expression. "I mean it's an instant reaction. Do you have a last name? Social security number?"

She laughs.

There it is—her smile. I grin along with her, but I'm dead

serious about hunting down this Eric guy. I put those thoughts aside and pull her into me. She nestles into my chest.

We stand there for a while before she pulls away and looks up. "So, there were a couple pretty girls at the party tonight."

I smile. She's talking about two girls that showed up. Jersey Girl caught Santino staring at them and overheard him tell me he thought they were hot. "Yeah, there were."

She looks down, lightly tapping her sneaks into the edge of my boots. "Well, maybe you should ask one of them out sometime," she says softly.

"Maybe," I say. *But they're not you.* That's what I really want to say.

"So," I say. "What's going on with you and Matthew? Are you guys a couple or something?" I ask.

She snorts. "Hell no. I told him I'd prefer to be friends. We have nothing in common."

You sure have a bad habit of putting guys in the friend zone, Jersey Girl. I make sure to keep that remark to myself.

Jenna lifts her chin. Her pouty lips twist into a gentle smile and her large cinnamon-brown eyes gleam. And that's when it hits me: the feeling. It feels like one hard shot to the chest, punching all the air from my lungs. They slowly struggle to expand as I try to catch my breath.

Jesus Christ, Jenna is beautiful. She's not the kind of beauty that you use for a one-night stand. She's also not a friendly, sisterly kind of beautiful. She's more than that.

Jenna is the kind of beautiful that I can get lost in. Lost from all the fucked-up-ness in my head. She's the kind of beautiful that laughs at all my nonfunny jokes because she gets me. She's the kind of beautiful that'll put me in my place without batting an eye. Jenna is the kind of beautiful that can transform a nonbelieving man like me into a man who wants more. A man who can fall hard, stumbling over his own two feet because he's so tangled up in her.

Fuck. Did I actually just admit that to myself?

Yes, I did. Because it's all true. I'm falling for her.

Jenna has me strung the fuck out and there's nothing I can do about it.

Maybe if I just tell her, maybe she feels the same.

But she's made it very clear we should remain friends. If I tell her, she'll just pull away. Do I risk our friendship over these feelings I have—feelings I'm not sure I can control any longer?

I know she feels it. She has to; there's no way I'm feeling every bit of this on my own, it's that damn powerful. Whatever is going on between us is definitely more.

I want to give her more of me, show her what I'm capable of. But I'm not even sure what the hell I'm capable of.

This is fucking frustrating.

"Are you okay?" Jenna asks. I nod. "Are you sure? You seem a little out of it."

"No. I'm fine." I take a step back, making sure to keep my eyes away from her. I can't bear to look at her with my thoughts racing like this.

"Logan?" she questions cautiously.

"Jenna, I'm fine. Just leave it at that," I say rather harshly.

"Okay," she stammers, shocked by my outburst.

Shit, I'm even surprised by how I'm acting.

"I'm sorry." Although it's an apology, my tone is still rough. "I need to... I'll be back. I just need to leave for a minute. I'll be back." I walk away.

I need to clear my fucking head.

chapter 21

Jenna

"Earth to Jenna," Charlie shouts with a snap of her fingers.

"Yes?" I ask, but continue to stare out my bedroom window.

"Here I am trying to tell you how my vacation went and you're ignoring me." She huffs.

It's Monday morning and I'm waiting for Logan to arrive for his work shift. He hasn't responded to any of my text messages or phone calls this entire weekend. It's as if he's dropped off the face of the earth. Thursday night he seemed off. The way he walked away from me, and then when he returned, he said things came up and he needed to go.

After I questioned his behavior, he assured me things were fine. But I knew they weren't. He didn't look at me at all, and he kept his distance in the car when he drove me all the way home. When I asked him questions or tried to lighten the mood, his responses were short and curt even.

I don't understand what I did wrong.

I thought maybe something bad had happened until Charlie stopped by and slept over last night, telling me all about her weekend at the lake house. She went straight there when she got back from vacation with her family, expecting to find me there. She mentioned how much fun the party this weekend was and how everyone—except me, of course—was there.

I questioned her about Logan, making sure to be discreet, to not sound like a pathetic stalker. She informed me he was, in fact, at the lake house this entire weekend. And not only was he present, but he was having the time of his life! She didn't use those *exact* words, but that's how I took it.

I'm furious. Here I am, worried sick that something might've happened to him, while he's busy having the time of his life.

Charlie keeps going on and on, but I can't hear a single word she says. My ears are blowing steam with the tick of each second that goes by as I wait for Logan to arrive.

And then, there he is.

He's laughing and smiling with Santino as they walk across the lawn toward the site of the guesthouse. More laughter. *What's so damn funny anyway?* Logan tosses his head back and howls in amusement again. This time whatever the joke is makes his body shake as he clenches his stomach. *Are they laughing about me?* How I spent the entire weekend stuck in my room, worrying about him? It's all just one big joke.

That's it. I can't take it anymore. My stomach knots as anger settles in. I turn and storm out of the room. Charlie's voice yells after me, but it's coming from a distance. The only thing I can think of is Logan and the way he acted with me on Thursday and how perfectly fine he seems now. He's a dick. How dare he treat me this way? I thought we were friends.

Finally through the sliding glass door—and with Logan's back to me—I yell out, "Hey!" He turns around. The large smile on his face instantly wipes clean, but that doesn't stop me. I continue forward, my fists clenched to my sides. He turns to Santino, mumbles something, and then Santino walks off. I reach him, but he won't look at me. He just keeps his eyes averted. His presence hits me strong.

I missed him.

I hate him.

I lift a hand and point my finger into his chest, poking against the thin fabric of his T. "What. Is. Your. Problem?" With each word I say, I dig my nail into his chest.

He brushes his hand over his pecs where I touched, as if it didn't faze him at all. This only adds fuel to my fire and makes me more pissed off. "Nothing. What's yours?" he retorts without a single look my way.

"What have I done for you to be such a dick right now?"

"Jenna, I have work to do. I don't have time for this." He adjusts the tool belt hanging over his shoulder and turns to walk away.

I grip his exceptionally large bicep, my thin fingers tightly fighting to hold on. He turns back around; still he doesn't look at me. "Logan why are you doing this? The past two months we were fine and now…now you're a complete asshole. Is it something I said? Or did you find someone else?"

Did I say that out loud?

Blue flaming eyes finally meet mine. "Find someone else?" *Yes, I did ask it out loud.* "We were only friends, remember?"

"Were?" How can a simple four-letter word hurt so damn much? That word cuts through me like a knife, splitting me in half.

"What do you want from me, Jenna? You're very confusing."

"*I'm* confusing?"

Logan looks down, huffs out a large sharp breath, and then grabs the back of his neck, rubbing it furiously. I wait for him to say something, anything, but instead he looks up and around to see who's nearby. Finally, he grabs my arm and drags me past the pool, past the guesthouse, and toward the far right of the yard, behind a large tree.

We're hidden.

He presses my back against the trunk of the tree, drops his tool belt, and leans his body against mine. I look up at him, confused. My mouth opens so I can say something, anything to figure out what the hell is going on, but he quickly places a finger along my lips to shut me up. "Before you say anything at all, just let me think for a second." *Think?* What does he need to think about? "Just let me say what I have to say first. Let me get it off my chest. Then you can say whatever you want. Okay?"

I nod.

His gaze falls to my mouth where his finger still rests. He traces the bow and curve of my lips, slowly, as if memorizing the shape of them. His touch feels warm, nice. The contact is… My breathing grows a bit ragged. Logan takes his other hand and runs his fingers through my hair, down my spine until his hand lands firmly at my lower back. "I've missed you all weekend," he confesses.

"If you missed me, then why—"

His finger silences me again. "I had to see if what I'm feeling is because we're spending so much time together or if it's real. But what does it matter if it's real or not? You won't accept it," he murmurs.

"Logan, I have no clue what you're talking about. Just tell me what's going on with you," I beg.

"I'm falling for you. Hard. And it's not some bullshit girl-next-door crush." He stumbles back two steps. "I mean a real fucking hardcore, madly-sinking-for-you kind of fall. I don't know." He shakes his head, bewildered. No. He can't be. I shake my head to tell him he's not, but he nods. "Yes."

"No. It's just because we spend a lot of time together, Logan. You're confused. Trust me, what you're feeling—"

"Don't tell me what I'm feeling!" His features distort into anger. He's struggling with this and I'm just making it worse. I let him go on. "I know what I'm feeling. I've been dealing with it for a long time now. I just kept ignoring it. Do you think this is easy for me? To stand in front of you and pour out my feelings like some chick? I feel pathetic right now." Logan bends his head, bringing a hand up to rub his forehead. "You're the worst distraction I've ever had. You're in all my thoughts, every single one. You have no idea how difficult it is to have something take over your mind like that. It's confusing and suffocating at the same time."

"You have no idea how much I know exactly what that's like," I say, my tone impassive.

Logan looks up. "Can you just do me a favor?" he asks.

I swallow back, staring at him, and then nod.

"Right now, right here—can you just be honest for once? I know I'm not the only one feeling this." He waves a hand at the empty space between us. "If I'm wrong, then fine, but I know I'm not. I know this is mutual. I know you feel it too."

I do feel it. I've felt it for a very long time now. For so long I just kept pushing it away, but I greedily kept Logan close. I want him for me, but I can't give him all of me. I step forward, meeting him. He leans in closer too, our breath intermingling. I reach up, resting my hand along his jawline. I'm battling with this internal feeling, and as usual my mind wins over my heart. I shake my head and force sincerity into my tone. "I'm sorry, Logan. I do care for you but not in the same way."

He laughs, but there's no humor in it. "Bullshit."

My brows knit together. "Excuse me?"

He chuckles, his lips twitching into a firm, thin line. I pull my hand away. He shakes his head. "Fucking bullshit. You know what your problem is, Jenna? You've worked so hard building this wall to keep everyone out. But when there's someone willing to tear down every brick because they want to be a part of your life, you freeze.

"You're scared to let anyone in. Don't push away the ones who care because in the end, there might be no one left, and you'll have exactly what you always wanted—to be alone. Sometimes the best thing to do is to just let go. If you don't, you'll never experience what you could've had. Instead, you'll wonder *what if*. And trust me, Jenna, when you're stuck wondering *what if*, it'll be too late for us."

His words tackle me full force. They ignite a fury inside because they're true. They're all true and I hate him for it. "You don't understand! There are things you don't know about me."

His arms swing in the air, frustration crashing between us. "Then tell me! Make me understand."

"No! You'll turn around and walk away. You'll see me differently. You'll—"

"Will you stop telling me how you *think* I'll react and give me the benefit of the doubt? Fuck! If I haven't proven myself to you in the last two months, then what have you learned about me at all?"

I swallow, not saying a word. How can I? What can I possibly say to change all of this?

"Do you realize what you're doing right now?"

I shake my head.

"You're treating me like one of your paintings. I'm human and I have feelings, Jenna. You can't just stuff me into a fucking cardboard box in hopes that everything will be fine. I'm here, standing in front of you, asking you to give us a shot, asking you to tell me everything and trust in me. But you just keep pulling away and shoving me aside."

Silence. Every word he speaks swims around in my head. Deeper. Further. Faster. Each word loud and clear. I'm speechless. My anxiety kicks up as fear creeps in. He's going to walk away once I tell him.

"I have another side of me, a darker side. You wouldn't understand," I whisper, bowing my head in shame. Tears prickle the rims of my eyes.

He huffs out, arms slamming to his side. "Everyone has a dark side. Everyone has secrets. Everyone suffers from something. You think in the past couple of months I didn't know you were keeping something from me? I know there's something you struggle with, but I waited and I was patient for a long time. I'm not going to judge you. I'm not going to walk away. The moment you realize that I'm not going anywhere, no matter what happened in your past, the better it'll be for us to just get over this hump."

I laugh, sniffing back the tears, and look up. "That's just the thing, Logan. It's not a past issue." I walk up to him, and our bodies almost touch. My head bends back so I can look him square in the eye. "My issue, my dark side, my problems...they're present. They're now. They are front and center."

"I'm not going to give up on what we have over whatever you're dealing with. We can take care of it together," he says, his voice adamant.

"I know you'll give up," I disclose.

He shakes his head, frustrated and angry and completely fed up. "I'm tired of this. None of this makes sense to me. Stop this bouncing back and forth and just tell me. If you don't tell me everything, and I mean everything that's going on with you, the feelings you have for me—*everything*—I'll walk. Right now. And as fucked-up as I'll be over it, I can't keep doing this. I can't keep playing these guessing games with you."

"I won't tell you…"

Logan laughs, his shoulders deflating. He looks me straight in the eyes, long and hard, and then turns on his boots, treading away.

"I'll show you," I yell out, my heart racing.

He stops, his back still facing me. I quickly go after him and walk around to stand before him, meeting his gaze. "Fine, Logan. I'll give you everything you want to know. All of it. The way I feel for you. My issues. But I can't just say it. It's better if I show you."

His features are stern, not giving in. I'm sure he doesn't believe it. "Meet me here tomorrow at eight in the morning."

"I have to work."

"Do you want to know?"

He nods after a few seconds in thought.

"Then call out sick or something. Meet me here at eight in the morning, and I'll take you where we need to go. By the end of tomorrow, you'll have all of your answers. And if you want me afterward," I choke back on the words, knowing he won't, "then at least you'll know the truth."

He nods. "All right. Okay. I'll be here at eight tomorrow morning." Logan presses his lips together to say one more thing, but I don't let him.

Instead, I turn around, walking past the lawn and the pool, through the sliding doors, and back up the stairs. Charlie's still in my room, cozy on my bed. She looks up from a magazine she's reading and raises a questioning brow.

"I'm going to tell Logan everything tomorrow."

"Are you sure that's a good idea?" she asks.

"He deserves to know, Charlie. I just hope after he finally knows it all, he'll be okay."

"I'm not worried about Logan," she says, placing the magazine aside. "I'm worried about you."

Logan

At 7:50 a.m. I pull up in front of Jenna's house. I cut the engine, lean my head back, and look out the passenger window, facing the double-door entrance where Jenna will soon exit from. My eyes are heavy and my head aches from lack of sleep. The entire night my head was spinning with what to expect today. Jenna says by tonight I'll have all of my questions answered, and if in the end I don't want her anymore, then at least I'll know the truth. What pisses me off is that I had to wait this long. The curiosity is ripping at me, and I hate that I have to wait another minute to know it all.

I had a talk with Bryson yesterday about not coming in today. I haven't been myself the past few days, so when I told him I had a personal issue that I needed to take care of, he didn't question me on it. Instead he said he'd talk to his dad if my whereabouts came up. Uncle George hasn't been at the site as much, only once a week to check on things. The guesthouse framing and bordering are all up and the exterior is already designed. We're now working on the interior, so me skipping a day isn't going to set us back.

Exactly at 7:58 a.m. Jenna steps out of her house. I'd be lying if I said I'm not nervous—I am. I have no idea where she's taking me, what she plans to tell me, or how I'll react to it all. Her biggest fear is how I'll perceive the information she's been holding back. Now my fear is exactly the same. How will I accept it? As much as I want to believe that nothing can keep us apart, not knowing how severe the issue is that she's keeping from me makes it hard to be sure.

Stepping out of my truck, I walk around and stand by the passenger side. I open the door, shove my hands into the front pockets of my jeans, and wait as Jenna makes her way down the path. With my head low, I try to focus on my breathing. Knowing this may be the last day we'll ever have together stings. It's the last thing I want to think about right now, but it's unavoidable.

I catch a whiff of her scent before I look up. "Hey," she says.

My gaze shifts from the pavement to her face. "Hey," I respond. The dark circles under her eyes prove that she had just as little sleep as me. The impulse to reach out and touch her face hits me, but I resist, and we both just stand there staring at each other. It's kind of awkward, and I sense that both of us have a lot running through our heads right now. I gesture for her to jump in the truck. She nods and I pull one hand out of my pocket, helping her to settle in.

After I hop back into the driver seat, I turn on the ignition. The truck roars to life as I crook my neck to face her. "Where to?"

She hands me her phone, the screen showing the

navigation to an unknown location.

"Where is this?" I ask.

"You'll see."

I grab the phone and place it on a holder on top of the dashboard. "It's a two-hour drive."

"Yep," she responds.

All right, then.

The music made up for the silence between us for the past two hours. There's no getting around it. We're both nervous about today, so I guess no conversation is necessary at this point.

Jenna shifts in her seat the moment her phone announces we've reached our destination. Making a left, I pull onto a long dirt driveway, driving until we approach a metal fence. I press on my breaks and roll down my window for the security guard.

Jenna leans over my lap, placing her hand against my thigh to keep herself balanced. "Good morning," she tells the guard. "Jenna McDaniel visiting Carol Peterson."

The guard looks over a list. He then presses a button and nods. The fence unlocks and slowly opens. I drive through, my eyes catching the large sign: Welcome to Brandy Mental Health Facility.

"Who's Carol Peterson?" I ask as I continue down the path, following the signs to the main building.

"My grandmother," she says softly.

I don't respond. I just keep going until I reach a large brick building. It looks like a small replica of a castle from London or someplace like that, something out of a brochure. After appreciating the exterior—after all, buildings and architectural structure is my thing—I pull into the first available parking spot. I shut off the ignition, unbuckle the seatbelt, and twist my body to face Jenna. She has her head low, her hair covering most of her face, and both of her hands fidget on her lap.

I reach over and toss dark brown waves of her hair over her shoulder. My fingers tug the remaining strands over her ear to view her profile. Then I trace down her jawline and tilt her face until she's looking at me.

"Jersey Girl," I say quietly. She shuts her eyes, huffing out a ragged breath.

"It feels like forever since you've called me that," she whispers. "Every time you say it, it feels right. Like everything is going to be okay. No matter how messed-up the world around me is, every time you call me Jersey Girl I feel safe somehow." Her tear-filled eyes pop open.

I smile. "Everything is going to be okay."

She sniffs back her tears, nods softly, and then hops out of the truck. Together, side-by-side, we step into the building.

It's not what you would expect a mental health facility to look like. This place is definitely for the upper class and privileged. It feels like I just walked into a hotel lobby. I shouldn't have expected anything less since Jenna comes from a wealthy family. Not that I've ever visited a mental facility, but I've seen my share of movies involving the mentally ill. Other than the distant moans and screams, I can't find any similarities, though. Jenna approaches the front desk and signs us in.

We're instructed to have a seat until they're ready to bring us into the visiting room. I sit next to Jenna and look around before bringing my gaze to her. "How long has your grandmother lived here?" I ask.

"I'm not exactly sure, but I believe over twenty years. It

was definitely after my mother and father got married. She's my maternal grandmother. My mother's side of the family isn't wealthy. I think my father put my grandmother in here so she could have the best care possible."

"Why do you say it like that? Like it's not the best care?"

She sucks in a lungful of air before slowly letting it out. "Because there was no saving her. She was already in a mental institute for at least ten years before my father had her moved here. When she was in the other one, they pumped her full of experimental drugs and other crap. She's older now and suffers from Alzheimer's as well."

"What is her diagnosis?"

Jenna's mouth twitches and moves around, like it always does when she's chewing the inside of her cheek. "Schizophrenia," she mutters.

"Is she one of the reasons why you want to teach art to teens with a mental health issue?"

"No, she's not the reason."

Before I can open my mouth to ask what the actual reason is, a nurse strolls out and waves us over. Jenna stands and I follow close behind. We step into an elevator, go to the second floor, and exit into an enclosed entryway. The nurse thumbs in a code, swipes a card, and the door unlocks. The three of us walk into a visiting room.

Now this looks more like the mental institutions I've seen on TV. There aren't a lot of people in here, probably around twenty. Half seem to be patients of different ages, races, and genders. The rest are visitors or nurses. I'm still following Jenna; she strolls straight to an elderly woman who's sitting in a wheelchair. Jenna takes a seat across from her. The nurse that led us up leaves to attend to another patient.

Not sure what else to do, I settle into a seat beside Jenna.

Her grandmother is incoherent; she's just sitting there, zoned-out, blankly staring straight ahead. Her grey hair is brushed back into a ponytail except for a few white, frizzy strands that stand out. I can't find any resemblance between Jersey Girl and her grandmother. Sure, Mrs. Peterson is older—streaks of wrinkles crease the corners of her slightly slanted eyes, thin lines are etched around her mouth, and dark spots dot the top of her stiff hands—but Jenna doesn't have the same light green eyes or pale, lifeless complexion as her grandmother.

"Good morning, Grandma. This is Logan," Jenna introduces. My eyes narrow, cautiously taking in every detail and potential movement from her grandmother. But...nothing. She doesn't move or say a word or even blink.

"Hi," I say awkwardly, low. This is weird. What does any of this have to do with Jenna's and my relationship? She said she wanted to show me something. I wonder if she comes here often, but in the past few months I've taken up most of her free time. "Do you volunteer here?" I ask.

Jersey Girl shakes her head with a smile. "No."

"Oh." I look around, spotting a young teen by the corner. She's standing there, facing the wall like she's a toddler on time-out as she mumbles to herself. "You visit her often?"

"Once a month. I usually take a cab up here."

"That's nice," I say, my gaze shifting over to a man seated on one of the couches. His legs are up against his chest as he bangs his head into his knee and slams a fist to his temple. He keeps going and going until he's yelling, "*Get out! Get out! Get out!*" A woman seated across from him—I assume she's visiting since she's not wearing scrubs—tries to soothe him by making hushing sounds, but that just makes it worse. He gets louder and punches harder. A nurse runs over and stabs his arm with a needle; he instantly calms. Then he's taken away.

"Are you okay, Logan?" Jenna prods, her hand at my arm.

"Yeah. I'm fine. How long is your visit for?"

"Only forty minutes."

I nod. I can handle forty minutes.

During our visit, there was no time for Jenna and me to talk. It was too noisy or something happened with a patient within those forty minutes. In a way I'm happy it's over. Jenna and I step out of the building in silence. I'm still just as confused as I was when I first walked in there. Nothing has been answered; nothing makes sense.

We both jump in my truck and sit there. No words are spoken. We just sit there, staring blankly ahead at the brick wall of the building, both of us a mirror image of her grandmother. I shake my head, releasing the thought, then turn to look at Jersey Girl. "Jenna, I'm glad you shared this part of your life, your grandmother, with me." I pause, pressing my lips together, and then continue. "But I don't understand what this has to do with us, with you. Is this the part where I get my answers to everything?"

She brings her head back, her gaze lingering on the ceiling of my truck. "Yes. Just bear with me, okay?" Her lips trembling, she tries to breathe smoothly. "This is hard for me to say."

I adjust in the driver seat so I'm fully facing her profile. I sit and I wait. I don't rush or push her. It's the longest six minutes of my life until she finally says, "Four years ago, I was diagnosed with a mental illness."

On the words *diagnosed* and *mental illness* my stomach drops. "What were you diagnosed with?"

"Schizoaffective disorder," she says, deadpan.

I rack my brain, trying to figure it out. "What is that? I've never heard of it. What is it?" I rush out.

Jersey Girl's eyes are still glued to the rooftop. "There are two types of schizoaffective disorder. The schizo side is when a person experiences schizophrenia-like symptoms like delusions or hallucinations, sometimes both. The affective side is where there are two types: there is a manic type, like bipolar symptoms, or the depressive type where a person struggles with depression." She says all of this like it's rehearsed. Then shaking her head, she goes on, "I've been diagnosed with schizoaffective depressive type by many psychiatrists."

"No," I shake my head.

She crooks her neck and finally lands her eyes on mine. "Yes, Logan."

I ignore her response. "No."

"*Yeeesss.*" She nods, stressing the word as if it will make me fully understand it.

"You are nothing like those people in there." I point toward the building.

She cocks her head to the side, studying me. "And how is that?"

"They—they're...*shit*. They were—"

"Crazy." She fills in the blank.

"I didn't say that."

"You didn't have to. I know that's exactly what you're thinking. It's okay if you are. That's what most people would say. I'm used to it. It's normal to hear what others perceive as crazy. But you have to understand that in my head, that's normal. I think everyone else around me are the crazy ones."

This can't be happening. It doesn't make any sense. "Jenna, you are not crazy. I spent two entire months with you—"

She cuts me off. "And within those two months, you didn't notice that I'm a bit off?"

I try to catch my breath as I look everywhere in the car frantically. *This is bullshit.* "You're shy."

"I'm paranoid."

I shake my head. "You sometimes make me repeat myself, but I always thought you had a lot going on."

"Yeah. In my head. Voices. I hear voices sometimes and it's distracting. It distracts me from my own thoughts."

What the fuck? What is happening right now? This is a lot to take in at once. I rub a hand over my head, my brain reeling with images of every moment we spent together. Everything I ever questioned about the way she acted toward certain things is now answered, and I still feel lost. I still don't fucking understand any of it. I've never heard of schizoaffective disorder. I've never met anyone with any mental illness other than depression—and it seems to me that everyone, at some point in their lives, has been depressed; it's normal. "So what does this mean for us? I don't understand."

Jenna lightly shrugs, her eyes filled with tears, her lips quivering. "I don't know," she chokes over her words. "I can't ask you to take this on. You say you want me, Logan, but my disorder is a part of me. I *wish* I could split myself in two, toss my damaged side away, and hand you over my perfect side. But I can't. It's either all of me or nothing."

"Jenna." I breathe out, lowering my head. I can't even fucking think straight right now. "I need to think. I mean, my feelings toward you haven't changed. I just need a day or two to process all of this. You know?" I look up. It kills me seeing her like this.

With tears running down her cheeks, she nods. "Yeah, I know. I understand."

I adjust in my seat, start the truck, and back out of the parking spot.

Jenna

The silence in the car is suffocating, like a dark fog seeping through the windows, wrapping its deadly cloud around me. I want to throw up. I knew it. I knew he'd react this way. I shouldn't have said anything at all. At least then we wouldn't be here right now, stuck in silence, in nothing but the sound of our breathing and the stupid broken love song playing in the background, which only shoves the knife in my chest deeper.

Instead I should've just told him about my feelings for him and never mentioned my disorder. I hate this disease, this chemical imbalance, as the medical field calls it. I hate myself even more for it because if I was normal, maybe, just maybe I could've been wrapped in Logan's arms right now. Maybe his lips would be covering mine. Or maybe we'd be laughing, joking over a bad impersonation. We could've been happy.

If only I were normal.

What is he thinking right now? My mind is self-destructing with the rejection. He's giving up on us after declaring that nothing could ever come between what we have. Yet it was me, my cancer of the mind, that finally destroyed what little hope there was for us.

"Are you okay?" he asks in a tender tone. I'm rocking in the seat. I stop and press my head firmly against the headrest, willing my mind to tell my body to stop it. I tell my mind to stop the tears. I tell my mind to look away. I tell my mind to close my eyes and just drift away.

And I do for the rest of the ride. No more words are spoken between the two of us. When he finally reaches my house, I spare us the awkwardness and just exit as quickly as possible.

I run as fast as I can up the pathway, through the door, up the grand spiral staircase and into my room. I lock it, staring at the doorknob as if it'll turn on its own at any second. When I realize it won't, that Logan isn't running after me, I let go. My body shudders as I allow the tears to shriek out.

"Jenna."

I spin around. Charlie. "What are you doing here?" I ask her.

She's sitting on top of my bed in the same clothes she was in when I left her here this morning. Her gaze takes me in, and her features distort into sympathy as her eyes water. They're tears of sadness for me. "I stuck around, just in case."

Just in case of this. She stuck around because she knew. Sobbing, I walk over to her, climb into the bed and lean into her open arms. "I'm so stupid." My words muffle against her pink blouse.

Charlie pulls me in closer and runs a hand over my hair. "You are not stupid, do you hear me? You're intelligent and beautiful and funny. You're many things, Jenna, but you are not stupid. He's the dumb fuck. Not you. You hear me?"

Sniffing back the tears, I lift my head to look at her. Charlie frames my face with her soft hands and thumbs over my moist cheeks.

"I'm the stupid one," I say, my voice drags. "For once, I thought maybe, just maybe I was worth someone's love. His love. And that it was possible he could love me back, Charlie," I choke over my words, straining to release my next confession. "I think I'm in love with him. I am *so* stupid. I'm falling in love with him, Charlie, and he doesn't love me. And it hurts." I press my hand to my chest. "I didn't think it could, but it hurts to even…" I crack, forcing myself to speak. "It hurts to even breathe."

"Oh, Jenna." She leans in, wrapping her arms around me again. I collapse in her arms and just cry. Hard, heavy sobs.

I don't ever want to see Logan Reed again.

chapter 22

Jenna

"Jenna, you have to eat something. It's been two days."

I tug the comforter back over my head. I don't bother to respond to Charlie. I don't bother to look at what she brought in for me to eat. I don't bother to open my eyes. I don't bother to do anything.

I'm just surprised that I'm still breathing.

It's the first time in the last few days that Charlie has left my side. She's been trying so hard to get me out of bed and I've been fighting her tooth and nail. She didn't say a word when she stormed out, slamming the door behind her. It made me feel like crap. I know she's frustrated with me and it isn't fair to her.

The guilt of disappointing my best friend seeps through me, so I carefully sit up. The slight movement causes a bout of dizziness. Breathing through it, I stand and slowly walk to the bathroom. I squint, covering my eyes as the natural light beaming down from the skylight blinds me. After a few seconds my eyes adjust and I turn on the showerhead. I brush my teeth and rinse my face at the sink as the mirror fogs, caused by the hot steam billowing out from the shower.

I breathe in the soothing mist, allowing my lungs to inhale and exhale easily for the first time in three days. Stripping off my clothes, I step into the shower. The searing raindrops splash along my skin, turning my flesh from its pale, golden complexion to a reddish tone. It burns, but I want it to. I let it strip away the pain on the surface, knowing nothing can ever rid the pain deep within.

If only I could peel away the top layer of my skin and continue to peel back each layer until there was nothing left beneath the scorching shower but my heart, still beating despite being ripped apart. Because that's where it hurts the most. The muscle that somehow keeps me living makes me feel nothing more than dead—dead without him, dead without his touch, and dead with the knowledge that I will never love again.

Logan

My life over the past two days has been on a repeating cycle. I wake up. I get ready. I go to work. I stare at Jenna's bedroom window, hoping she'll see me. But she never does. I finish my work shift. I stare at the window some more. I go home. I have a few beers while I search on the Internet until my eyes are heavy and I can't keep them open any longer. Then after the two-hour sleep I manage to get in, I wake up and do it all over again.

I'm a complete zombie on day three of this vicious cycle.

Bryson mumbles something along the lines of how shitty I look as I walk past him. I ignore his remark and go straight into the kitchen area, where I work for the first half of my day by installing oak cabinets.

As I finish adjusting the last cabinet for the top row, I hear an uproar in the living area. Santino yells, "You can't be in here!"

A female voice shouts over the loud sounds of hammers and saws going off throughout the house. "Fuck if I can't. Where is he?"

Santino shouts back, "Where is who?"

She replies, "Logan! Where is he?"

Santino screams, "The kitchen."

Before I have the chance to step forward and show myself, Charlie storms into the kitchen. My brows draw in as she struts up to me, her hand nudging my shoulder. "You're an asshole!"

"Excuse me?"

"You know, I really had hope for you. I thought you were different, that your feelings for Jenna were true. But you're just like the rest of them." She inspects me; her eyes narrow as she shakes her head disapprovingly. "God, did you prove me wrong. Were you just trying to get in her pants this entire time?"

"What?" *Who the hell does she think she is?* This time, I'm the one to narrow my eyes. "You have no idea what you're talking about. It was never that way with Jenna. I care for her."

Charlie crosses her arms, cocking a brow. "Oh? I couldn't tell because over the past three days I've been taking care of a brokenhearted girl. She's devastated, Logan. How could you do that to her?"

"You think I don't know that? My head has been fucked-up the past few days. I'm trying to understand it all!" I snap.

She takes two steps back, breathing out her anger and calming down a bit. "Understand what?" she asks mildly.

"Her illness." I calm too, defeated. I'm fucking tired and my head is pounding. "I've been up all night researching. I want to help her; I just don't understand it. I keep reading articles and medical websites." I huff out a laugh. "I've watched a dozen documentaries and even a fucking video blog with some guy who has the same disorder. I just don't know how to help her."

Charlie's expression softens. "Being there for her *is* helping her. Jenna doesn't have much support in her life. The most important piece of her recovery is for her to know she has a solid team backing her up. It's not easy all of the time, but she's worth it. She used to have Brooke and me; now she only has me. Jenna isn't close with her mother. Her father is barely around. So just being there for her, letting her know that you're not walking away, that you're not giving up, that's a step toward help. And that's what she needs."

"You're right."

She smiles. "Damn straight I'm right."

As much as I want to laugh, I can't. My shoulders deflate. "But how do I know if she's being triggered or if I am setting her off or something?"

Charlie places her hand on my shoulder. "Talk to her," she says kindly. "Once she sees that you haven't given up, that you were just afraid of not being enough to help her, she won't keep anything from you any longer."

"Does she tell you everything?"

"No. I don't push her. Well, except when she has her down days."

"Down days?" I ask.

"Yeah. She has her really low moments. It's difficult for her to do anything when she's suffering from the depressive side of her disorder. Like she is now. She won't eat. It's hard to get her out of bed. It's like she's a stone, just waiting for life to pass her by. Everything is hard for her to do. So I push her out of bed—literally. She tries to fight back and hates me for it, but in the end it's worth it. These past three days, though...they've been really hard."

Great. I feel like an even bigger asshole. "Do you think she'll see me?"

She shrugs. "We can try."

Placing the hammer on top of the counter, I wipe off the sawdust from my hands and then look up at Charlie. "Take me to her."

"Okay," Charlie says. "Oh, and Logan?"

"Yeah?"

"I'm glad you look like shit."

This makes me laugh. "Thanks."

"No, I mean it just further proves that I was wrong."

I raise a brow. "About what? I think you were pretty accurate on the asshole part."

She twirls around and starts walking. I follow behind her. "Oh no, you're still an asshole for not seeing Jenna sooner, but I admit I was wrong about your feelings and intentions toward her. I can tell now that you really care about her."

"Thanks," is all I can say. "Before we go in, I just need to grab something from my truck."

"Sure."

Jenna

Wrapping the towel around my chest, I stand before the mirror. I wipe away the fog and stare at my reflection. "What now?" I say to myself. I guess I just keep going. There's nothing else I can do. I don't know what will happen tomorrow, but I need to keep going for today. It's the only way to regain my strength.

Breathe. It's the first step, which I do.

After I'm done, I step into my room and freeze. My fingers grip the towel in place; my chest expands too quickly, trying to fight for air as my heart pounds away. I press my lips together, composing myself so as not to launch across the room and cling onto him. There's no way this can be real.

"Charlie let me in," he says, standing by the edge of my bed.

I close my eyes tight, willing my head to take the image away. When I open them he's still there.

He bows his head, looking down at an item held in his hand and then looks up at me. Red lines the rims of his stormy blue eyes, those eyes I've fallen in love with.

"What are you doing here, Logan?" I choke over the words scraping up from my dry throat and mouth. This is real. He's actually here.

Logan wets his lips, hesitant to say anything. We both just stand there, waiting. Finally he speaks first. "Jenna, I'm sorry."

"For?"

"For everything; the way I acted when you told me about your—" He pauses. "About your disorder. The last few days I've been trying to wrap my brain around all of it. And no matter how much I've researched and tried to figure out why ot1

 oothe

you suffer from this disorder, it hasn't changed the feelings I have for you."

"It hasn't?"

He shakes his head, taking a step forward; there's still so much space between us. He goes on, "No. I still care for you. I still want you."

"But—"

"No. There are no more *ifs, ands, or buts* between us. There's no mistaking any of it. I want us to be together. I want your struggles to be mine. I want you to be able to come to me for everything, Jersey Girl. I want to be there for *you*. You have to trust that I will never give up on us."

I look down. "I felt like you did, that you decided to just give up." My shoulders slowly lift into a shrug. "It's understandable. I couldn't blame you. I couldn't ask you to take this on. It's a lot to ask."

His boots slide across the floor until they're in my view. His closeness knocks the air out of my lungs. I continue to look down, staring at the round peep of his scuffed-up Tims. Logan crooks a finger under my chin, lifting my head back until he's fully gazing at every emotionally-shattered feature etched on my face, and I witness all the wretched pain stamped on his.

His eyes take on a look of sorrow, of compassion, of regret, of love. "I hate seeing you like this and I hate even more that I'm responsible for it." He releases the finger under my chin and frames the right side of my profile with his hand. I weaken against his touch, fluttering my eyes closed at the comfort found in the connection.

"I'm never giving up on what we have, Jenna."

I know it's wrong to ask this of him, but his closeness, his touch compels me to ask anyway. "Promise?"

"Promise."

Before I can utter another word, Logan's lips are on mine, binding our tiny pact. My breath, my lips, my tongue, my teeth, everything I have becomes a part of this kiss, inhaling and tasting and feeling and reveling in what I've been longing for since the very first time our lips disconnected so long ago. The first one was purely chemical, lust and desire. But this one? This one is passion and longing and promises and fireworks, fucking fireworks. As his tongue gently dives into my mouth, dancing with mine, my body falls into his. With one hand still on my face, he snakes his free arm around my waist to keep me in place, still gripping onto the item in his hand.

I try to keep my composure but fail as I moan against his mouth and lift onto my toes. My arms find their way around his neck. My towel—which hasn't fully dropped because it's pinched between us—has slipped, exposing the swell of my breast. We're hungry for more, starved by the time we've spent denying and repressing our feelings for one another. Logan drops whatever item was in his hand, his fingers gripping into the small of my back, tugging me ever closer to him.

The hand that was framed around my face is now gently fisting into my hair. Small gulps of air between kisses, our tongues twirl, entwine, and lash, growing thirstier for one another. He groans he wants me, and I moan I want him too. Our sounds turn this slow burn into an inferno. In one swoop he lifts me and carries me to the bed, our lips still molded to one another.

My back flush against the mattress, the towel loosens—exposing my breast and peaking nipples. A small groan rumbles deep within his throat. Logan drops his head; his tongue skims over my nipple before fully sucking in my small breast.

I tilt my head back, raking my teeth over the flesh of my bottom lip to savor the aching pleasure. My fingers dig into his scalp as his hand finds its way down between my thighs; teasing, he circles his palm over my nub.

We ignore the knock on the door. It's probably Charlie, checking in on us. I lift Logan's head with my hand and bring his lips back to mine. Another knock. I groan out, "Leave us alone, Charlie."

"It's not Charlie."

I freeze. My eyelids fly open. "Who's that?" Logan asks, whispering.

"My father," I say, scrambling out from beneath Logan. "Just a second, Daddy," I shout out, running over to the dresser and rummaging through a drawer. I grab the first ankle-length nightgown I can find and toss it on. I look over at Logan. He's up on his feet, his hand shoved in his jeans, trying to adjust himself. There's no helping him right now, and he curses under his breath when he realizes there's no hiding his erection. Then he lightly jogs over to the object he dropped earlier—it's a large, square-shaped item covered in newspaper. I smile at that little thought, and he holds onto it, using it to guard the bulge currently struggling against his jeans.

I calm my breathing, and then call for my father to come in. When he enters, his eyes widen. I'm not sure what's more shocking to him—the fact that I have a man in my room or the fact that there is *actually* a man in my room.

Dad straightens his shoulders before clearing his throat. "Jenna," he says in a fatherly tone.

"Daddy," I say, mocking his serious address. Logan snorts, which makes me giggle.

My father doesn't find this as amusing as we do; I can tell by the very high, arched brow.

"Dad, this is Logan. He's my…" I falter, looking over at Logan to see what we are exactly.

Logan smiles. "Boyfriend," he finishes for me. Logan then stands and walks over to Dad, extending his hand. "It's a pleasure meeting you, Mr. McDaniel."

My father shakes Logan's hand firmly. "Pleasure is all mine, son."

And then the awkward silence descends. I'm sitting on the edge of the bed. Logan is standing beside my father, still trying desperately to cover his boner. Dad is staring at me. "You needed something?" I finally ask him.

"Yes. I wanted to invite you to dinner Saturday night with your mother and me."

"Oh," I say. The thought of having dinner with my mother is not very appealing.

"You can bring Logan if you'd like," Dad adds.

Logan looks up at me for confirmation. I gently smile, indicating I'd like it if he joined me. He nods. Then he faces my father, straightening his stance. "I'll be there, sir. Thank you."

"Very well. Saturday at six. I'll have my assistant make the reservations and send you the information, Jenna."

I smile at him. "Thank you."

He gently grins at me, nods at Logan, and then pivots to leave my room. Then, as if he's forgotten something, he looks over his shoulder and grips the doorknob. "I'll just leave this open," he mumbles, then walks off.

Logan and I wait until we hear him halfway down the staircase before we finally look at one another and burst out laughing. "Oh my God, that was completely awkward," I force out, gasping for air.

"Tell me about it," Logan blows out, rubbing the back of

his neck with his hand. Then his shoulders relax as he lets out a sigh. "I should really get back to work anyway. I'm sure someone is looking for me."

As much as I don't want him to go—I just got him back—I know he has to. "You're probably right."

"This is for you." He walks over. "It came in yesterday." I grab the package he's been holding. It's pretty light, but large in size. Definitely not a CD. It's wrapped in an old newspaper article. "You really need to invest in some wrapping paper," I say.

He shrugs. "I figured I'd keep the tradition going."

Shaking my head, I focus back on the item in my hand. I shift on the bed, leaning back against the headboard, and then tear it open.

It's an eight-by-ten personalized photo album. The black gloss cover has a metallic silver inscription: Jenna's Art. I squint my eyes in confusion, wondering what that means as I open it. The first page is a personalized note in black ink from Logan.

You see what you did here?
You, my Jersey Girl, created art.
I told you. You're stronger than you think.
Love,
Logan

I flip to the next page. The first image is one I took when Logan and I were lying down on the trail looking up. The sun is casting down through the branches and leaves of the trees. It looks just as beautiful in the photo as it did in person. The next photo is a close-up of a baby deer, drinking by the creek. The fur of the deer is more vibrant than I remember; its reddish tone bursts out of the page. It is the focal point of the entire image.

Not able to contain myself, I flip to the next photo. I smile remembering this one. We were walking alone, side-by-side, and I had the urge to take a photo of the long, empty trail ahead of us. Trees, plants, branches, and leaves surround the pathway. You can't see the end, but even though it's leading to the unknown, it's still very welcoming, inviting. Like there's a captivating journey just waiting for you to follow it. I remember how when we pulled into that parking lot, I wanted nothing more than to run away from that place. Looking at these pictures now, I can't believe I ever felt that way.

I continue to flip through the pages, amazed by it all.

He managed to take the photos I took and brighten them, transform them into something more. He made them come alive. I feel like I could literally reach in and pluck a blueberry off of a bush. My heart expands in awe and gratitude as I take my time with each photo.

When I reach the very last picture, my breath catches in my chest. It's an image of the mother and daughter we ran into. They're walking away, and the focal point is their hands holding one another. A tiny dimpled hand nestles with its protective keeper. Everything around them blurs except for the hold the mother has on her daughter. This image speaks so much more to me than anyone will ever understand. It's something I've wished for, for so long—the relationship a mother and daughter should have. The one I will never have.

My eyes water. Sniffing back the tears, I close the album and look up at him. "You did this for me?"

"I didn't do a thing. You did."

"Logan, I'm—I don't know what to say. This is a beautiful gift. It's…" I wrap my arms around the album, bringing it to my chest and hugging it tightly. "It's something I will always cherish."

He bends at the knees, meeting me eye to eye. "I just wanted to show you that you're capable of doing what you love. It may not be with a paintbrush, but you captured something and created art, regardless."

I quickly pay the cab, climb out, and shut the door behind me. Unable to properly survey my surroundings, I dart for the apartment complex, clinging to the bag in my hand. It's too dark out, and even though the streets are quiet at this time of night, you can never be too careful. After entering the building, I climb the steps to the third floor and knock on apartment C-10.

I knock again and again and louder again until I'm banging on the heavy wooden surface, my knuckles reddening. "What the fuck?" He sneers. "I'm coming. I'm fucking coming," I hear distantly. A deadbolt unlocks, and the knob screeches as it turns before the door opens.

His sluggish blue eyes scrunch then widen when he recognizes it's me. "Jersey Girl? What are you doing here?"

"I couldn't sleep."

Logan opens the door, allowing me in. "So you came all the way down here at two in the morning?"

I nod, walking past him and straight into his living area.

He shuts the door, locking up. "How'd you get here?" Logan asks with a yawn, walking my way.

"Taxi."

He shakes his head. "You need to learn how to drive."

"Will you teach me?" I ask nervously.

A soft chuckle rumbles in his throat. "Yes, one day. But

for now can we sleep?" He reaches for my arm and drags me to his room.

"I've never been in here before." I look around, taking in his very plain bedroom. There's only a stream of streetlight shining through the blinds, so I can't make out much. The only thing I can see clearly is his grey comforter.

"You are wide awake." He yawns again, climbing into bed. He stretches on his back and waves me over. I place my duffle bag on the floor by the bed, then nestle and relax beside him. Logan snakes an arm around my shoulder, my head leaning against his chest. I wrap my leg over his and shut my eyes. This feels good. Peaceful. In his arms, just being held by him is where I always want to be.

I wake up to his touch, his hand softly stroking up and down my arm, his lips sliding along my hairline. I smile, inhale his natural scent, and exhale. My lashes flutter, struggling to open. "Morning," he whispers.

"Mmm," I moan.

Chuckling, he kisses my forehead. "I have to get ready for work. Do you want to stay here?"

I nod into his chest.

"Okay. I'll pick you up after my shift. Are we still going to the lake house or do you want to hang out here?"

Shrugging, I keep my eyes shut, too tired to pry them open. "Whatever you want."

His lips trace down, leaving a peck on my nose. "All right. We'll go to the lake house." His mouth leads back to my forehead where he leaves another caress. "We'll stay the night." I can sense him dip low before his lips touch my chin.

"Then we'll drive back Saturday to make it in time for dinner with your parents."

I smile, nodding and agreeing with the entire plan. "Now get some rest," he whispers. Leaving my side, he steps out of bed. As much as I'd prefer that he stay, I still feel like he's here. With his scent lingering, I breathe in the comfort and drift back into a peaceful sleep.

chapter 23

"How was work?" Jenna asks, climbing into my truck. She places her duffle bag on her lap, buckles the seatbelt, then leans over and kisses me. "What's the smile for?"

I nudge my head toward her lap. "What's in the duffle bag? Carrying deadly weapons or something?"

"Ha. Ha. Funny," she mocks. "No, I have my weekend stuff. It's better than dragging around my suitcase." She shrugs. "And I may have something for you in here."

"Lingerie?" I grin, wiggling my brows.

"I didn't know you were into wearing that kind of stuff. If I'd known, I would've purchased you a blue, skimpy lace number to bring out your eyes."

"All right, smartass."

She laughs. "You set yourself up for that one."

"This is true." I pull out of the parking lot and begin our drive to the lake house.

"It's nothing big, just a little something you can use in the future," she says as she unzips the black bag and starts rummaging through it. I reach a red traffic light and look over. Jenna hands me a clear plastic bag. I quickly peek in. Arching a brow, I meet her smile. "Gift bags and wrapping paper?"

She nods.

"You got me yellow gift bags and wrapping paper," I clarify.

She nods again.

"Well, aren't you the major wiseass."

Her laugh bounces around my truck. "Well, it does benefit me."

I steer with one hand, my other finds its way to hers. I bring our entwined fingers to my mouth and graze her soft knuckles against my lips. "Why yellow?" I mumble against her skin, my eyes on the road.

"It's my favorite color."

"Is that so?" I ask.

"Yep. It's bright and pretty and cheerful." She sighs. "It reminds me of the sun." Jersey Girl pauses. Squeezing her hand around mine, she whispers, "I spent most of my life in the dark. Yellow allows me to visualize the light. Even if it's just an image I paint in my head and not reality, I'll take it."

I press my lips firmly against her hand. Jersey Girl will probably never know this, but yellow will now and forever be my favorite color too—because I want her to be happy. I want her to be surrounded with brightness in her life. I want her to fight through the darkness and find *her* light someday.

Jenna

We're walking hand-in-hand into the lake house when a chorus of applause goes off. I tear my eyes away from Logan and see Santino, Charlie, Bryson, and Blair are all in the living area. Everyone, except for Blair, is smiling and clapping. "It's about damn time!" Santino hoots.

"You guys are dicks," Logan states. He shakes his head, smiling good-naturedly, and guides me up the stairs. More whistles and cheering trails up when the door to Logan's room closes behind us. "Sorry about that. If I'd known there was going be an audience, we would've stayed at my place," Logan says as he walks across the room and places our bags on the ground.

"It's okay." I look down and fiddle with the edge of my white camisole. I'm suddenly nervous. I desperately want to continue what we started in my room yesterday before my father intruded, but I know we have to get past a few things before that can happen.

"So, what do you want to do?" he says, removing his boots. "Want to go out by the dock? In the lake?" He goes on, stripping off his T-shirt, "I'm gonna hop in the shower, wash off this sweat and sawdust. You're more than welcome to join me," he jokes with a broad smile. But we both know there's seriousness hidden behind the humor.

"I'd like to talk."

His grin weakens. "Is everything okay?"

I cross my arms, hugging myself. "Yeah. I... I just figured you probably have a lot of questions for me and I want to answer them all."

"We have plenty of time for that. I don't want you to feel pressured to spell out everything at once."

"Logan, I've kept things from you for so long. I don't want to keep anything from you anymore. Can you honestly say you don't have any questions for me? About my disorder, my triggers, what started all of this?"

He bows his head, twisting the cotton fabric of his white

T in his hand. "I do."

"Well, I want to answer anything you might find confusing." I walk over to Logan and place my hand against his face, showing him the sincerity in mine. "In my opinion, the hardest thing anyone can do is accept someone else and all of the baggage that comes along with them. And you did that for me."

"Because I care for you."

"And I will never understand why. But the least I can do is be honest with you from here on out. It's challenging for me to tell you everything. I'm embarrassed about most of it, but I trust you and I know you won't judge me."

"I won't."

I smile. "I know. So take your shower. I'll wait for you by the dock. Okay?"

He nods, lowers his head, and lightly caresses my lips with his before turning and stepping into the bathroom.

I'm sitting by the edge of the dock, admiring the sunset, the crisp scent of the lake, and the light warm breeze crashing against the tall tree branches, when I hear footsteps from behind. There's no need to turn around. I catch a whiff of his fresh shower gel before he takes a seat beside me.

Logan scoots close enough so that the sides of our thighs are pressing against one another, and our feet are swinging in unison. He takes my hand in his, securely weaving his fingers between mine. "Let's talk," he says.

"What do you want to know?"

"Let's start with the beginning. Why did this happen to you?"

I shake my head; my gaze focuses on our hold. "I will

never know why, Logan. But I can tell you when and how it started."

"Okay. Let's start there." He brings our hands up to his mouth, gently kisses the back of my hand, and then places them back down on his thigh. I think it's his way of safeguarding me, of expressing in his own little way that no matter what I disclose to him today, it will never change his feelings toward me. A restful breeze whips by and instantly I'm okay.

Breathing in and out as calmly as possible, I begin. "It was senior year of high school. My grades weren't all perfect, so I was desperately trying to study my ass off so I could ace my SAT score. I wanted to be like Brooke.

"*God*, she managed to make everything seem effortless: school, getting into college, sports, and boys. Anything. You name it, she did it well. Nothing was difficult for her, which made my parents proud—especially my mother. I just wanted my mother to recognize me once in my life. Even before I was diagnosed with psychosis, our relationship was rocky.

"I think maybe she knew deep down I'd end up like this. I don't know. I was in therapy when I was younger, starting when I was about ten. I suffered from depression as well as lack of social skills, which freaked my mother right out. So maybe she knew." I shrug. "Anyway, back to senior year. I focused on trying to bring my grades up. They weren't bad—more than average, really—but not perfect.

"I spent months studying: at home, the library, even at Eric's place. I barely slept. I was a living, breathing zombie—if that's even possible. I became obsessed with academics just so I could be on the receiving end of that look of pride on my mother's face, just like she had given Brooke so many times before. Not even my talent impressed her. She never understood my art. It's funny. You know how some people say you're your biggest critic?" I chuckle, knowing that was never the case for me. "My mother was always mine."

I picture the me from four years ago, at seventeen: the scared girl I've tried to rid from my brain as she struggled, trying to comprehend why this disease chose her. I stretch and tighten my fingers around Logan's. My throat throbs with fear before I gain the courage to continue.

"It was a Sunday morning. I was in my bedroom, studying. The SAT exam was the next day and I was under a lot of stress. It was beautiful outside. Eric wanted to spend the day outdoors, but I just wanted to be locked in my room with no distractions. It's how I spent most of my summer that year and most of the beginning of the school year. Eric and I had gotten into a minor argument—nothing big, more of a disagreement.

"I didn't care. I just wanted to study. So there I was in my room with my nose in a book when I heard my name being called. It was so clear and loud. I looked up at the door, but there was no one there. I brushed it off as nothing and went back to studying. After a few seconds I heard my name again. I quickly looked up, searching around the room, but I was completely alone."

"What did the voice sound like? Like someone you knew?" Logan asks.

"No. It was a male voice I've never heard before. When I heard my name for the second time, I got out of bed and searched around my room. I opened the door to look out. No one was there. I closed it and then walked over to my bedroom window. I thought maybe the gardener or my father was in the yard. But from what I could see, there was no one.

"I sat back on the bed, confused but easily distracted by the way my mind was racing with how much more I had to do. There were just so many notebooks and textbooks and

highlighters and pens and scraps of paper. To say I was overwhelmed would be an understatement. Then the voice came
again. It was closer this time, so close I actually felt it coming
from behind me. It said, 'You'll never be good enough for
her.' I remember it like it was yesterday—how the goose
bumps rose on every inch of my skin, the fear lodged in my
throat, the sound of my breathing, its spastic rhythm matching
my heartbeat. I finally found the courage to look behind me,
but there was nothing there, only the headboard."

Logan lets out a deep breath. "That must've been fucking
scary for you. Especially at seventeen." He shakes his head.
"How long did you deal with the voice in your head before
you were diagnosed?"

"Voices. It started as one voice and then it multiplied.
They were getting louder and it was distracting. I couldn't focus on school. It was difficult to keep up with a conversation.
It was very scary. I just wanted them to go away, but it kept
getting worse, to the point where they were telling me to kill
myself. And then I had a breakdown with Eric.

"The voices were telling me he was seeing someone else.
I didn't know what was real or not. I didn't know the difference between my own thoughts and the voices at that point.
Everything began to blend together, and it drove me nuts. Finally, after three weeks of living through hell, I contacted
Brooke, who was away at college. I was hysterical over the
phone with her.

"She couldn't understand a word I was saying. She was
going to call our dad, but I begged her not to. So she did what
any loyal big sister would: she drove the five-hour trip from
her university to be by my side. When she got home, I told her
everything that was happening to me, and she encouraged and
finally convinced me to tell Dad. He took me to get assessed.

I had several evaluations done, and that's when I was diagnosed. At first they thought it was schizophrenia, but as my depression worsened, I was reexamined and my diagnosis was changed to schizoaffective."

I look over at Logan, expecting a reply or comment or something. He meets my gaze, and his hand reaches up and caresses my face. "Within the last four years, was there ever a time when you didn't hear the voices?"

I nod. "The first two years were very difficult for me. I didn't want to believe I was sick in the head. Eric and I had split up, Brooke was away at school, my mother grew more and more distant, and Dad was working on expanding the company. I'd never felt more alone in my life. I went to a local college because that was all I could handle, and my father felt it was best to stay close to home. The new medication I was taking at the time was making me zone out. It stopped the voices, but I felt dead. I had no feelings—highs or lows—and I didn't care about anything or anyone.

"So I stopped taking my medication. I lied to everyone, including my psychiatrist. They all thought I was still on my meds. I started to feel alive again, awake. I was able to focus more. But it only lasted a week. After that, the voices came back along with paranoia. I thought everyone was out to get me, that no one took my best interests to heart, and that they were all crazy and I was the sane one. And I definitely didn't want to continue on with the medication. I hated the way I felt and the person I was becoming. I didn't feel like *me* anymore.

"One day, I was told—by the voices—it would be best if I were dead, that it would be better for everyone who had to waste their lives taking care of me. And I thought they were right. I hated that Brooke drove back home every weekend just to be with me. I hated that Dad began to work from home on the weeknights that Charlie couldn't stop by because he was afraid to leave me alone. And I hated that I managed to drive my mother further away. So I did what the voices asked me to do."

"You tried to kill yourself?" Logan looks shocked, pained.

I nod.

"Jersey Girl," he lets out shakily, and I can tell that the news of how I attempted to take my own life is hitting him hard. And with those two words he mourns for the girl I was. They're an apology for the past, a thank you for the present, and a plea for the future.

"I know. Trust me, I know, Logan. I was at a really low point in my life."

"How did you do it?" He cringes for even asking.

"I stabbed myself. I took a big knife from the kitchen and I just jabbed myself in the middle of my stomach—it's what the voices instructed me to do." I lift my shirt just beneath my breast, revealing the three-inch scar. The scar is located where it's mostly hidden when I wear the thick strand of my bikini tops—which is probably why he's never noticed it before. Logan traces a finger over the clumpy skin, which is barely noticeable against my tan.

I roll my shirt back down, suddenly embarrassed by showing myself in the first place. I keep my eyes down as I continue my story, my voice lowering. "It went pretty far in. I remember it burned; it was a sharp burn, hurt like hell. But I wanted the voices to go away, so I twisted the knife deeper. And then I remember collapsing. I'd lost a lot of blood, but Brooke..." The ghost of a smile tugs at my lips. "I guess she was my guardian angel that day since she's the one who found me on my bedroom floor, covered in my own blood."

Logan brings both hands to my face and forces me to look at him. "You are never going to do that again." I nod, agreeing with him. "I'm serious, Jenna. If you ever feel that way again, if you ever feel the urge to harm yourself, come to me. Okay? I'd lose my fuckin' mind if I ever lost you."

"I'll try," I say truthfully. That's a promise I can never truly keep. When I'm triggered, pulled under and dragged into a dark place, it's difficult for me to come out of it. He presses his lips to my forehead, and then brings my head to lie on his shoulder.

"After Brooke found me, I was taken to the ER," I go on. "I was evaluated and placed on suicide watch in the psych ward. Then my parents felt it was best to send me away for a few months."

"You were taken to Brandy Mental Health?"

I shake my head. "No. My parents never told me about my grandmother. So I'm sure keeping me far away from Brandy was for a good reason. I was taken to a small, private 'rehabilitation' retreat, as my parents called it. They told family and friends I needed a break from all the stress of school and such." I roll my eyes. "But honestly, I didn't fight it. I let them take me there and I signed the admissions paperwork."

"Why?"

"Because I knew I was burden to all of them, so I didn't fight them on it. And at that point I was desperate to get better. The therapist at the retreat told my parents that because I was aware of my illness and willing to work on getting better, my chances of recovery were high."

"I don't understand the recovery process," Logan states, confusion evident in his tone. "I've heard of people who recover from drug and alcohol abuse and self-harm. How does someone recover from a mental illness?"

I draw small circles in the palm of his hand, allowing the comfort and calm to wash over me as I talk about my illness with him. "I know it's hard to believe. The word *recover* is sort of a misnomer. Someone who's recovering isn't miraculously cured. Just like an addict, sometimes when things get rough, it feels uncontrollable and they relapse. Think of it that way. I could relapse at any time.

"But with the proper treatment, good eating habits, and exercise—and most importantly a support team—there's a strong chance I can beat this. I've read stories of some people who were able to stop taking medication altogether without suffering from the hallucinations or delusions. And I did. For about a year, actually."

Logan shifts. I lift my head and meet his gaze. His eyes brighten with hope. "You were able to cope and deal with it without medication?" I nod in response. "Well, that's good, right? I mean that means you'll be able to again. Right?" he urges.

I shrug. "Maybe. Maybe not."

His brows crease then relax with understanding. "You relapsed."

"I did. Ten months ago, when Brooke died. It was difficult for me. See, before I only suffered from hearing voices. But I had my first hallucination about a month after her death."

"Of what?"

"Her."

Logan pulls his head back. "Brooke?"

"Yeah." I lower my head, ashamed. "My therapist said it had to do with the tragic loss. For most individuals, the loss of a loved one is an excruciating pain and they grieve, eventually moving on. But someone who already suffers from psychosis, someone like myself, tends to deal with things differently. Not everyone with my condition would have had the reaction I did. People with psychosis all have different triggers and such. But for me, I couldn't accept the fact that she was gone.

"Brooke was everything to me. She was my rock. She kept me on my toes. She cared for me, and never once did she make me feel like I was different. She always encouraged me, told me I could be a famous artist or a politician or a teacher. Whatever I wanted to be in life, in her eyes I was capable of being it. When others saw the glass half empty, she saw it three quarters of the way full. She was one of those annoying people who was always quirky but happy." I laugh, tears welling at the rim of my eyes.

"If you told her an image was ugly, she'd look at you as if you were nuts and show you how beautiful the picture truly was by pointing out details, the nuances in the color, the shading, the texture, the meaning behind it. Showing you that flaws could be stunning and intriguing and mind-blowing— that was Brooke. At the end, you'd be inspired by the portrait and even more by her. That's just the person Brooke was. That's the person who was taken away from me, and I couldn't handle it. I didn't know how to deal with it. I hated myself and everyone around me because I couldn't understand why she was taken away. Why wasn't it me?" Logan thumbs over my moist cheeks, wiping away the tears as I force my next words out. "The world needs more of her and less of me."

"Don't say that, Jersey Girl. You deserve to be here. Whatever happened to Brooke was out of your control. There was nothing you could do. You hear me?"

I shudder, tightly clamping my eyelids closed. As much

as my father and Charlie said it wasn't my fault, there's always something nudging at me that it was. Like maybe I could have saved her somehow. The thought reopens old wounds, and I burst into hard sobs. Logan pulls me into him, consoling me as I let it out.

And I do.

It's past midnight. Logan fails at TV surfing as he nods off in bed. He's seated up against the wooden headboard. I'm lying beside him, my head on his lap, looking up at him. His fingers gently comb through my hair, pausing midstride when he dozes off, then continuing when he comes to and flashes his eyes open.

After I cried my eyes out—when I thought there was no possible way I could shed another tear—Logan and I continued to sit by the lake. No words were spoken after that. None were needed. Logan had comforted me the only way he knew how: by holding me. His arms curled around me, his gesture silently reminding me that he wasn't going anywhere.

We didn't leave until it began to rain. Then we had dinner with the rest of the crew. It was a nice distraction from the haunted thoughts fighting for my attention.

When outside partiers began to trail indoors, Logan and I snuck into his room. For the past two hours, we've done nothing but lie here. Since Logan's room is located by the front of the house, the music and noise from out back is very distant.

I watch him doze in and out as I continue to trace his features. My eyes scroll over his, admiring the thickness of his lashes. They're not long, but they're dark enough to bring out the metallic cerulean hidden behind his hooded eyelids. I suck in air as my stare drops to his stubble-covered jawline, which could quite possibly be chiseled directly from granite. My gaze dashes to his full, soft lips. As quickly as it came, the air dissipates from my lungs, as I think of exactly how those lips taste. Although I've only fully felt them twice against mine, I'd recognize the owner of those lips on any given day.

Immersed in every inch of his rugged aspect, I try to memorize all of it, imprinting each and every fine detail of his features, and vault it deep within my head. A place where I can lock away the perfect image of the man—

Suddenly it hits me all at once.

I hope that there's a moment in *everyone's* life when everything around them just stops. There's no movement whatsoever, yet you *feel*...

Every. Single. Thing.

All of the emotions traveling through every cord, fiber, and thread of your existence—every muscle, *aching*. You want to cry. You want to laugh. You want to drop to your knees because you feel the weight deep within your chest. It's too difficult to bear, but you won't let it go.

You *can't* let it go.

Because deep down you know without it you're *nothing*. *Lifeless*.

This is madly, passionately, and without a doubt falling in love.

With every part of me, I'm falling in love.

And now that I have it, I just want to grip on to it for dear life. Because I know once it's gone, I'll be back to where I started: in a tomb, feeling *numb*. Before Logan, I thought if I stripped away any chance of feeling at all, I could keep myself from getting hurt. But I'd rather feel every single emotion, where it pains me so much to love, than feel nothing at all.

Logan makes me feel *alive*.

I've fallen in love with this man, this man that looks past my imperfections and accepts *me*.

I want to give him *all* of me. I'm in love with him. I am truly, without a doubt, deeply in love with Logan. It's a feeling I thought I had experienced before with Eric. A feeling I thought I knew. But I never really knew *this* feeling. What I have for Logan sits deep in my chest, rooted at the center of my heart, submerged and hidden for no one else but him. It's within my soul.

If I die today, my soul will forever be his.

So many emotions twirl deep within me. Tears filled with the love I have for this man obscure my vision. I'm unable to control it any longer. Sitting up, I lean in, shutting my eyes as I kiss him. The tears collect along my lashes and drip down my cheeks. Logan sucks in a breath as he awakens. It doesn't take him long before he registers what's happening and his lips respond, perfectly united with mine.

It's a kiss unlike any we've ever shared. It's sensuous yet obsessive and urgent. Though he's taken off guard, he doesn't pull away. His lips naturally mold to my mouth as if kissing me is the most natural thing in the world. He tenderly sucks on my bottom lip, gently tugging my flesh between his teeth. I lose control. I *need* to be near him, closer. Never breaking contact, I position myself across his lap, straddling him.

In the dark lit room, his hands find their way up and frame my tearstained face. He brushes his thumbs along my moist cheeks, but when he realizes I've been crying, he tries to pull away. I force our lips to hold. I don't want to lose his touch. "Why are you crying?" he mumbles against my mouth, his fingers gripping at my face.

"Because of *you*," I hum against his lips. "Because of you... I *love* you, Logan." Tears sting the corner of my eyes. I shut them tightly and dig my nails into the flesh of his shoulder blade, pulling his chest against mine.

He groans at my confession. Dropping his hold from my face, Logan grips my thighs and grinds me against him. I whimper as I feel his immense hard-on. The two thin cotton layers of our pajama bottoms are the only things interfering with what we both clearly desire.

Logan slightly lifts my shirt. His fingertips taunt the flesh of my hipbone, lingering, but he doesn't attempt to go farther up. He's trying not to lose control within our kiss. Our tongues savor this moment in slow, long licks. He tastes sweet and salty, and *I want more*. A strong pull, a tug deep below my waist, pushes me closer to him.

I *want* to feel his skin against mine.

I *want* to experience his touch.

I *want* his lips on every inch of my flesh.

My nails rake through his hair. My breathing grows rapid; I try to catch my breath, but our kiss intensifies. I weep over his mouth—with one hand, I grab his wrist and dare him to explore under the hem of my shirt; but he maintains his hold on my hips, his fingers digging into my skin there. *Does he not want this?*

I pull away, my lids flash open. His hooded eyes burn with want. I shake my head, confused. "Don't you want me?" I pant out.

Logan sucks in a breath and blows it out roughly between his words. "I want you so fuckin' bad"

His words kindle a throbbing pleasure below my waist. I grind, rubbing against him. I slowly rotate my hips, feeling the swell in his pants. He certainly wants me, and as wet as I am, I want him just as much. "Then why are you holding back?" In a bold gesture, I tug at his wrists. He releases his hold on my hips and allows me to guide him underneath my shirt. At the hint of my bare skin, he groans, and I match it with a charged exhale as his fingertips dust a scorching trail along my flesh. I guide him up my sides, around my back, and on to the clasp of my bra strap.

His fingers linger. "Jersey Girl." He hisses, sucking in a deep breath. "I don't think I'll be able to stop. I can't—"

"I want this, Logan," I cut him off. I gently rest the palm of my hands along his chest. "I want this more than anything."

Before we can utter any more words, we lose our breath as our lips collide. His hand still grazes the clasp of my bra, wavering. Within a heartbeat, he unclips it. Finally. My breath hitches.

This is it.

This is really happening.

Heart racing, I pull away, gripping the edge of my shirt and tugging it over my head. I moisten my lips and stare down at him. So much is written in his eyes. He's panting as his stormy blues dance around my face. It's as if he's mesmerized by every single carving of my features; and he seems to be analyzing what's going through my head at this moment. I lift my hands and remove the straps of my bra, slowly dragging them down my arms and exposing my swollen breasts.

Logan's struggling, fighting back the urge to lose control. He sucks in his bottom lip, stalling for time. His gaze drops down to my chest, but he doesn't make a move. He brings his eyes back up to mine as if he's seeking approval. I smile and lightly nod, wanting him to, needing him to. Desire has completely taken over. I need a stronger connection.

An intimate connection.

His hands softly slide up the side of my torso, and I arch my back, rocking against him as his fingers graze over my ribs. Logan stops just beneath my breasts. There's a long pause between us where nothing but the sound of our panting can be heard. His lustful stare penetrates through mine, shooting flames of longing deep into my belly. His tongue darts out over his dry lips and he traces his thumbs over my nipples. Before I can react, Logan rolls us over so that my back is flush against the mattress.

He quickly removes his clothes and kneels before me, totally naked, and without a doubt the most beautiful male I have ever laid eyes on. Aching for him, I reach down to remove my bottoms, but his hand stops me. I freeze. My heart's pounding and I'm trying to figure out what—he pulls at the string of my pants, hooking his fingers over the sides by my waist, and gently tugs them down along with my panties. They're on the floor in a matter of seconds.

Logan touches and caresses me with his eyes, learning every inch of my bare skin. And I allow him to. I'm entirely naked before him, embracing every part of this perfect experience. For so long, I wondered at what it would feel like to be exposed before Logan Reed, to bare it all and have him soak in every fragment of my being.

I thought I'd be scared or ashamed because of who I am, because of the darkness that is a part of me. But in this moment, as affection pools in his eyes and acceptance in his heart, I feel nothing but *free*. Until now I hadn't realized that Logan has been undressing me from the very first time we met. Slowly, layer-by-layer, he removed the facade that hid the real me beneath. The *me* I thought would always be concealed. But not anymore.

My love for him surges. The separation between us is too

much. I sit up, my hand wraps around his neck, and I pull him down to me, connecting our lips once again. Instantly, we're back in a trance, lost in our kiss, savoring each stride. I fall back onto the mattress, bringing his body down with mine, enthralled by the beat of his heart along my chest.

Logan slightly pulls away from our kiss. His lips flicker over my mouth—top, bottom, side… In a daze, I gradually open my eyes. I'm met with Logan's adoring stare. His hand frames my face and his thumb traces up and down my jawline. Our breathing is shallow, our hearts beating as one. The tenderness in his gaze gives me all the reassurance I'd ever need. "Say it again," he whispers. My brows draw in in confusion and I shake my head. He spreads my legs with his knee and sinks into me slightly—just the tip of him at my opening.

I gasp. Relief. Anticipation. Rapture. Ecstasy.

"Tell me again," he says, imploring me with his blue eyes. And then it registers through my haze of lust and love and passion and promises that my confession has touched him more deeply than I'd realized. I lift my head, the tip of my nose grazing his as the curve of my lips mold to the curve of his. My stare lingers as I emphasize each tiny word slowly, proving to him that I mean each one. "I. *Love*. You."

His lips ajar, a tiny groan escapes. My words encourage him, and he grinds his hips, inching himself farther into me. Thoughts flee my mind as air escapes my lungs. All I can feel is the delicious friction and pleasure coexisting within me. I shut my eyes, waiting for him to fill me completely, but he never does.

His face hovers over mine as his words drift over my lips. "I knew I was done for," he says, "the morning I drove by and saw you alone, staring at that house. I told myself to keep driving, but something told me to stop. And when I'd seen how lost and confused you were, something told me I was meant to be there." He kisses the corner of my mouth. "I was meant to be there so I could help you find your way."

Logan digs his hips farther into me. My breath hitches and my eyelids bolt open. Our lips agape, he fists his fingers into my hair. "The night we went to the diner, when I told you about my accident—" He thrusts. I arch into him, whimpering as he fills me with his length. "You didn't judge my past. That's when I knew I couldn't turn away from you even if I tried."

He pulls out slowly then fills me again. He continues with gentle strides, picking up the rhythm gradually. I join him, rotating my hips, my body shuddering at how incredible it all feels. Our bodies move together, pushing and pulling in perfect accord.

"The night of the beer pong game," he says roughly, struggling with his words. My breathing increases as he grips my thigh and tosses my leg over his waist, allowing him to push deeper into me. I toss my head back into the pillow, the desire burning in the pit of my stomach. "After we lost and I leaned into you. I wanted to fuckin' kiss those lips so bad." He grazes his lips over mine, sucking on my bottom one before taking a breath and mumbling, "But I saw how scared you were, so I gave you another kind of kiss."

"Special Logan kisses," I whisper.

His lips curl into a gentle smile, and he continues to drive into me. "Yeah, but you didn't know that I'd recited how I felt for you right then, in that moment, in my mind. The words flowed silently, so easily. There was no mistaking them. When I gave you those three kisses, I was telling myself and *you*..." He pecks my nose. "I..." He kisses my forehead. "Love..." My heart swells as he presses his lips to my chin.

Then he whispers, "You."

chapter 24

Logan

Jenna lies beside me on her side, propping her head up on one hand as she traces up and down my torso with the fingers of her other hand. I'm lying on my back, staring at the ceiling. We've lain this way, in silence, for what seems like forever. But it's a good silence. We enjoy each other's company. Her fingers glide over my chest, making their way to my arm.

She begins drawing over my tats, up my bicep, and over my ribcage. The tip of her finger goes over the lump on my skin. Curiosity spikes as she leans in closer to inspect my scars. Then she finds the rest of them, several scars on the side of my ribcage and hidden beneath the ink on my arms.

"What are these from?" she asks, tracing each one.

"Surgery. After the accident," I answer.

She doesn't say anything for a while; instead, she admires and continues to trace my scars with her fingertip. I'm neither embarrassed nor attached to my scars. They are the consequence of my shitty behavior from one messed-up night. "You don't ever question it?" she finally asks.

I tilt my head and look at her. With furrowed brows I ask, "Question why I didn't die?"

She shakes her head a little. "No. Question life. Why we turn out the way we do. Why we are the way we are. Why everything just falls out of place and seems screwed up eighty percent of the time. Why we're tested over and over again, like a vicious cycle. Just like this." She spreads her hand over my ribcage. "Why *you* lived and were brought back into a world that's more screwed up than we'll ever know. Why Brooke found me when I tried to take my life. Was it the universe's way of saying we were given another chance? And if so, for what?"

My stare lingers on her for a long time, taking in everything she said. Then I turn my head and focus back on the ceiling. "When I woke up in the hospital, my uncle George was the first person I saw. My mother was talking to the doctors or something. He was the only one in the room with me, right at my bedside. He looked like shit, bags under his bloodshot eyes. When he saw I was awake, he tried to fight back a sob. I'd never seen him like that before. My uncle is probably the toughest man you will ever meet. I didn't remember what happened to me or where I was. So I asked him. His response was, 'You were given a second chance at life, son. You were brought back for a purpose.' I had no idea what he meant by that."

"Did you ever figure it out?"

I shake my head. "No." I breathe in and blow out a sigh. "Life, Jersey Girl, sometimes pauses. It stops. Sometimes we don't even realize how everything around us is moving so quickly while we're standing in the middle of it, allowing it to pass us by. Most of us, if not all, just lose the *why*. Some of us never figure it out to begin with. We lose sight of the purpose that wakes us up every morning and pushes our day forward. We lose a sense of hope and the feeling of life in general. We view life as more of a test, one that's trying to beat us down every day to see if we're strong enough to keep going." I lightly shrug. "That's why I just live today and push for tomorrow."

"Live for today, push for tomorrow," she repeats. "I like it." She leans in and presses her lips to mine. Just like that, we're lost in one another for the second time in one night.

For the last hour, Jersey Girl has been fidgeting. Her hands twist in her lap and her leg bounces as she stares out the passenger window. I've tried to hold her hand to stop her shaking. She eases for a few minutes but then goes at it again. "Shouldn't I be the one nervous for dinner with your parents tonight?" I joke.

She shakes her head. "I'm not worried about my father. It's my mother. She always manages to ruin everything."

I continue to steer the wheel with one hand and reach out my other to hers. "You and I are in this together from now on. You know that, right?" I tear my eyes from the road and quickly glance her way. She's looking ahead, nodding.

"I know."

"So know this: I'm not going to let her hurt you. All right?"

"Okay."

Dinner isn't as bad as Jersey Girl had expected. Her mother is quiet for the most part. I've even caught her peeking over at Jenna from time to time. But mostly her father, Gregory—he asked me to call him that—keeps the conversation alive. We talk about the contracting business, his work, and even politics, which I don't care for, but he makes it an interesting topic.

Gregory couldn't get reservations for the restaurant he wanted, so he hired a private chef to come to the house and make us dinner instead.

I lean back in the chair, patting my stomach as the chef comes out with dessert. "I can't. I'm going to burst at the seams if I have anything else," I say.

Laura smiles. "I'm sure you can find some room for chocolate cake."

I don't want to seem rude, so I just nod. "I'm sure I can find room."

"You don't have to, Logan," Jersey Girl says. Her hand reaches over and clasps my shoulder. "We can take some for later."

Gregory nods. "Yes. Don't worry about it. Dessert is my wife's favorite part of dinner, so she always makes room for it."

"It was Brooke's as well," Laura mumbles.

That was random and awkward. I don't know what to say. I look between Jenna and her father. Gregory's jaw tightens as he focuses straight ahead, keeping his eyes away from Laura. Jersey Girl bows her head, looking at her lap.

"Very well," Laura spits out. "I guess I'll enjoy dessert on my own." She slides a plate closer to her, lifts her shoulders graciously, and then stabs her fork into the cake, bringing a crumb-sized bite to her lips. "Delicious."

Another awkward moment goes by before Jersey Girl announces, "I'm thinking of going back to school."

I smile. I know how hard it was for her to say that. We

talked about it at the lake house and on the drive back from there, and she was nervous to even mention the idea of going back to her parents.

I'm fuckin' proud of her right now.

"That's great, baby. Really great," her father encourages.

"You can't," Laura states.

"Why?" Jenna asks, her brows creasing.

Her mother raises a brow. "Because of your..." She glances over at me, then looks back to Jersey Girl. "Your condition."

Jersey Girl straightens her shoulders. A tiny smile pulls at her lips. "Logan knows."

Both Gregory and Laura shift their eyes my way. Her father's amused, maybe even impressed, but her mother... Well, her expression looks like a mix of disgust and shock. "Of your *mental illness*?" Laura hisses the words *mental illness*.

I nod. "Yes, ma'am. I'm aware of Jersey Girl's disorder, and it doesn't change how I feel about her."

"Jersey Girl?" her mother scoffs.

Gregory shifts in his seat, grinning at me. He nods in approval. "I think that deserves a drink. What do you say, son?" He stands. "Are you a whiskey man?"

"Sure." I move to stand, but he gestures for me to sit back down.

"I'll bring it to the table." He turns and walks in the direction of his office by the front entrance.

The table falls silent in his wake. Laura is staring between Jersey Girl and me, her expression seriously annoyed, maybe even angry. "You told him everything?" She locks eyes with Jenna.

Jenna nods.

"Even about Brooke?"

Jenna meets her mother's glare but doesn't answer.

I chime in, "Well, I know Brooke's life was taken from her."

"Logan," Jenna begins with a whisper.

Laura's eyes widen, a malicious smirk spreading across her face. "Ah, he doesn't know," she says.

"That's enough, Mother," Jersey Girl warns.

I'm very confused. "Doesn't know what?" I ask.

Laura tilts her head, gazing at me. Then she looks Jenna straight in the eye. She leans into the table, her stare hardening as she hisses, "It was all Jenna's fault."

What?

"No." Jenna shakes her head. "No, it wasn't." She continues moving her head side-to-side. Then she begins to rock in her chair.

"Yes, it was. You were there." Laura continues as she stands from her chair and taunts Jenna, "You watched them *rape* her and repeatedly *beat* her."

"Stop it," I say. This is fuckin' ridiculous. I pull away from the table and kneel beside Jersey Girl. "Look what you're doing to her." My tone sizzles. I grab both of Jersey Girl's hands. They're shaking; her entire body is fucking trembling.

"No," her mother continues, "I will not stop. She walks around as if she doesn't remember. Doctors said she blocked that memory out, but I know the truth. She remembers clearly. Don't you, Jenna?"

"I said stop it, dammit!" I stand and bring Jenna up with me, pulling her into my arms. Fuck. She's shivering. I look at her eyes to see if she's having a seizure that's how bad she's shaking. Her pupils are dilated, her eyes are filled with tears, and her face is ashen. She shakes her head, her mouth opening in shock. "Oh my God," she sobs out.

"You remember, don't you?" Laura accuses. "You're just as much a murderer as they were."

Jersey Girl's fingers clench at my chest, digging through my shirt as she tightens her grip. "Don't listen to her," I say. Jersey Girl shakes her head. "Don't listen to her," I repeat.

I pull her into my chest and guide her, storming out of the dining room and down the hall, past Gregory. His eyes widen as we pass, two whiskey-filled glasses in his hands. "What happened?" he asks.

"Ask your wife. She's a bitch," I bark out.

"Excuse me!" Laura shouts from behind. I stop, turn around, and glare at her.

"You heard me. You're despicable. You're scum. You're an evil bitch. I can't believe you have the audacity to call yourself a mother."

"What did you do, Laura?" Gregory demands.

Laura's eyes widen. "You're going to allow him to speak to me that way?"

"What did you do?" he booms.

Instead of sticking around for their back and forth, I turn with Jenna in my hold and guide us up the stairs and into her room.

"Jersey Girl, you're coming home with me, okay?"

She steps away and flattens her back against the wall. Her lashes and cheeks are soaked in tears, her face filled with pain. She brings a hand to her stomach as if she's going to be sick.

I quickly turn, searching for a suitcase or bag. Anything. I finally find her luggage by the closet and pack whatever I can find—clothes, shoes, her toothbrush. I rummage through her room, all while peeking over every few seconds to look at her. She's still in the same position, zoned out in space.

I zip up her case. Then I march over to her, watching her as I approach. With every step, I grow angrier. I can't believe her mother would do this. I tug at her chin and look her in the eyes, but she's not staring back. She's lost somewhere. "Jersey Girl," I say. "I'm going to take care of you." I rub my thumb over her jawline. "I'm going to make sure you never have to see her again. She's wrong. She doesn't know what she's talking about. Okay?"

She doesn't say anything.

Fuck.

I pull her into me, guiding her back down the stairs and out of the house while her parents argue in the background.

Jenna

Brooke spins around in the middle of her dorm room. The edge of her navy blue dress twists and hugs her curves as she whirls in place. Then she stops and looks at me. "Will you cheer up, buttercup!" she says, her smile brightening as she fists both hands on her hips. I force a smile, shifting uncomfortably on top of her roommate's bed, which is mine this weekend since her roommate is out of town "We're going to have a blast tonight! Who knows," she starts, lifting one shoulder into a slight shrug. "You might meet a boy."

"Oh my God," I cry out as I dig my fingers into the passenger seat. Logan reaches over.

"What's wrong?" he urges.

My head slams back against the headrest over and over again as every detail of that night whirls in my head. I remember. "I was there," I breathe out.

Music blasts in my ear the moment we step foot into the sorority house. I wrinkle my nose at the smell of piss beer and hard liquor floating through the air. Most of the ditzy girls are already drunk and stumbling around, throwing themselves at the first guy who walks by them. Brooke lets out a loud squeal, making me jump. She runs over to a guy who's dressed in skinny jeans the color of Pepto-Bismol, a fitted white T showcasing his lean figure, and—the only boyish piece of clothing on him—white slip-on sneakers. Brooke pulls him into a tight hug.

"T, this is my sister, Jenna. Jenna, this is T."

"Brooke has told me so much about you, honey." He smiles broadly at me and waves a large hand my way. "It's nice to finally put a face to a name."

I nod, raising both brows. Brooke's never mentioned him to me, but I don't say that to him. "Hi," I say.

"Well," Brooke says excitedly. "Let's party, shall we?" She wraps a hand through the crook of T's arm.

T searches around the room, narrowing his eyes as he takes in the scene before us. "Which men will be our victims tonight?" he purrs.

Brooke tosses her head back in laughter. I smile because I haven't seen her this happy in a long time. She looks over her shoulder, her smile expanding when she sees mine. She winks playfully and shimmies as she says, "Come on, Jenna. Let's dance."

Over the next few hours, I'm a wallflower as I watch Brooke and T dance the night away. They've had their fair share of shots of tequila and beer chugging. I'm sipping on my second can of Sprite when Brooke stumbles into me. "Jenna, you're no fun..." she slurs and wiggles a finger at the tip of my nose. "You need to live a little."

I place my Sprite down on a table beside me and grab Brooke by the elbows to balance her. "All right, I think you've had enough. Shall we go back to the dorm?"

"What? No. I'm having a blast!" *She quickly twirls, but sways side-to-side as she tries to stop.* "Whoa. That made me light-headed."

"Yep. We should go. Where's T?" *I ask, looking around.*

"He found a hottie to make out with. He's such a whore." *She giggles as she squints her eyes to search for him.* "There he is!" *She points to the middle of the dance floor. If it weren't for his pink pants, I would've missed him since his face is currently being smothered by another dude's. I shake my head.*

"Well, I can't drive, so how are we getting back to your dorm?"

"Walking. Duh."

"Walking?"

"Yes, Jenna. It's not a long drive..." *She hiccups.*

"Exactly, drive. How long is the walk?"

"About fifteen minutes."

"Okay, we can do that."

Fifteen minutes have come and gone and still no sign that we're near the dorm rooms. At this point I'm irritated. Brooke is singing along to God knows what as I sit her down on a bench in front of a graveyard. It's dark out and beginning to drizzle. I let out a frustrating sigh as I look around. The last thing I need is to get caught in the rain with my drunken sister.

"Jenna, we should make a musical!"

"Not now, Brooke."

Lively laughter echoes from behind me. I twirl around, my heart panicking as I hear noises coming from the graveyard—like boots crunching against fallen leaves or branches. The laughter grows and I hear muffled talking. It sounds like several voices, but I can't make out how many. "Brooke, come on. Let's keep moving," *I say anxiously.*

I pull at her arm, my eyes and ears alert to whatever may be beyond the cemetery fence.

"My feet hurt," *she whines.*

"I know they do, just come on—"

"Well, well, well. What do we have here?" *a low male voice asks amid chuckles.*

I look toward the voice. Three men step out of the grave-yard and onto the sidewalk beside the bench where Brooke and I are.

"Looks like we have a drunk one on our hands," *another one says, his cadence hinting at a southern accent. He takes a long pull of a joint. Then he steps forward, extending his arm and the butt toward me.* "Want a drag, little miss?" *he offers.*

I shake my head. My heart lurches as I take in all three men. The first one that spoke looks to be the youngest with blonde hair and honey-brown eyes. They might be attractive if they weren't so bloodshot, I'm sure from whatever drugs he enjoyed throughout the night. The second one, the one who offered me a smoke, looks like he might be the oldest. He has long, dark hair, dark eyes, and a poorly trimmed, long goatee. He stumbles a bit, which only proves he's just as stoned as his buddy. The third one, who hasn't uttered a word, stands far-ther behind them. His brown eyes seem gentle, as if he's si-lently apologizing to me.

Because of him, I ask, "Do any of you know where the university is by chance?"

"Do I look like I'm from here?" *The southerner chuckles again.*

The gentle-eyed man steps forward. "It's on the other side of the graveyard. Once you pass the gates, you'll see the *entrance for the university."*

"Thank you," I say emphatically.

Gathering Brooke, I lift her up and sling her arm over my shoulder. Side-by-side we step into the graveyard. It's dark and hard to see, but thankfully the moon is full and bright, which gives me enough light to find my way through. I continue down a pathway intended for cars to drive on instead of walking on the grass where the tombstones are.

Brooke and I pick up the pace when the drizzles turn into rain. Our clothes are beginning to soak through, and my feet squeak into my flats. I hear heavy footsteps behind us, so I stop and turn around. The three guys are running our way, yelling out for us—something about how we forgot something. The one with gentle eyes is waving a purse in the air as he jogs our way. I search over Brooke's body and, sure enough, she left her bag behind.

"You forgot this." He extends the purse.

"Thanks." I reach for it, but he pulls back. I look up at him, my chest clenching in fear.

"My friends and I were wondering if you girls were willing to have a little fun." The other two step forward, one on each side of gentle eyes.

"I'm just trying to get my sister home." I swipe away the soaked strands of hair plastered to the side of my face. With my other hand, I grip Brooke tightly and pull her behind me, shielding her from them.

The gentleness in his eyes instantly fades, replaced with something akin to hatred. Terror shivers up my spine. From the look in his eyes, I know we're in trouble. I step back, forcing Brooke to step back as well.

"I think you misunderstood," he says while his sidekicks quickly come over and grab Brooke.

"Let her go!" I go after them, but not-so-gentle eyes quickly yanks me to him. He pulls my back against his chest, sealing his arms around my shoulders and stomach, effectively locking my arms to my sides.

"We're going to have fun first," he insists, his lips touching the curve of my ear. I squirm beneath his hold.

"Let me go!" I struggle beneath him.

"No!" Brooke yells. I look over in the direction of her voice. The two men have her pinned down, her face against the mud. Tears burn my eyes.

"Stop it! Don't hurt her! Please!" I try to fight. I kick. I scream. But I'm not strong enough.

"You're going to watch." He tightens his arm around my stomach and brings his other hand to my face, keeping it steady.

Brooke tries to fight. Her fingers dig into the side of one man's face, but it only pisses him off. Groaning, he closes a fist and plows it into her nose. Blood gushes out as her head smacks into the ground.

"NO!" I buck, trying to break free. No. No. No.

The one who punched her tears her dress open and laughs. He laughs! How could he be enjoying this? The other man pins Brooke's hands over her head. Her panties and bra are torn off.

I can't.

I can't.

I want to throw up.

I shut my eyes tight.

Grunts from him. Cries from her. She continues to fight. Another crunch of her bones, cracking from a blow. More groaning. More punches. More cries.

"My turn," the other says excitedly. There's shuffling as

they switch positions. And then the noises begin again.

Brooke cries.

I collapse into the evil man, my eyelids fixed shut. I never want to see again.

I can't.

I can't.

My stomach churns, bile rises up in my throat, and then I jerk, vomiting over and over again.

Then a heavy blow to the back of my head from my captor's fist. "You fuckin' cunt!" he spits out. "Don't worry your little heart out. You're next."

Sobs escape me as I hear the two men take Brooke over and over again until her cries die down to whimpers. After they have their way with her, I'm tossed to ground, my shoes flying off in the process. I dig my fingers into the muddy grass, trying to grip onto something and pull myself up. A kick to my stomach forces all the air out of my lungs, and I collapse back to the ground.

Finally I have the courage to open my eyes. I choke over a sob when I see her. Brooke is to my right about an arm's length away. I barely recognize her. Her face his drenched in blood. Her nose is brutally broken. Her cheekbones are so swollen she can barely open her eyes. Her breath wheezes. She tries to speak through her split, puffy lips. "Get..." she struggles.

I can hear my captor's zipper pull open. "Help," she manages. "Run," she whispers.

Before I can respond, I'm dragged down by my feet, screaming out for help. But it's not enough. I'm flipped over, and my back slams against the sodden, filthy ground. My attacker's eyes are dark now as an evil smirk spreads along his face. One of the guys is over by Brooke, putting his pants back on. The other is on standby, keeping an eye out for anyone coming.

I hear Brooke's words in my head over and over again. To run. To get help. My chest heaves and without hesitating, as the evil bastard bends at the knees, I lift my foot and kick him in the balls with as much strength as I can manage. He screams, grabbing his crotch, and I waste no time scrambling away from him to stand and run.

I dart through the graveyard, my lungs burning for air. I continue, pushing harder, one foot in front of the other. The rough terrain cuts my feet, but I keep going. I need to get help. I need to find help.

I can hear someone yelling behind me, a familiar voice. My captor. I sprint for my life, for Brooke's life. I'm almost near the cemetery exit. I see the large black metal fence and a guard in a golf cart patrolling. I flail my arms, screaming and yelling as I keep going. A flash of light shines my way, reflecting through the heavy rain. It makes me scream louder, run harder. The guard sees me!

Then I slip and fall. My head bangs against a tombstone, splitting open as blood gushes down my eye. I can't move. Everything is a daze. I try to get up, but I can't. My eyes shift to the side. A tombstone inscribed with 'Beloved Woman, Sister, and Friend' swims before me. The letters fade into one another, and then a light. I squint and hear a voice asking me if I'm okay. The guard's voice.

I shut my eyes and drift.

Logan

I cut off the ignition and lean back, staring out the windshield. I didn't want to leave Jenna behind at my place all alone. It's been two days since the dinner with her parents and the memory of what happened the night Brooke died resurfaced. When she told me what happened, in full-blown tears, I could barely understand anything she said. Her words were unintelligible.

After calming her down a bit, she was finally able to explain it to me. For the past two days, I've told her over and over again that none of what happened that night was her fault. There was nothing she could've done. But she feels if she'd never ran, the men wouldn't have continued to beat Brooke to death out of anger that she got away. There was nothing I could do but hold her and allow her to shed all the tears she needed.

But yesterday she wouldn't do anything. She wouldn't eat. She wouldn't get out of bed. She wouldn't watch TV. She stayed in bed with the blankets wrapped around her all day. Then last night, in the middle of the night, I found her on the bathroom floor, curled up in a ball by the corner. She was slamming her head back against the tile wall and mumbling to herself. When I approached her, it was like she snapped out of a trance and woke up. Then she burst into tears because she didn't know how she'd gotten in there.

It fucking scared me. So much shit ran through my head after that. I watched her sleep. I wondered if she'd be okay if I left for work. Would she hurt herself? So this morning I packed up any and all sharp items—knives, tools, anything she could use to harm herself. I'm still on the fucking fence about it all. I shouldn't have left her this morning.

Bryson storms down the driveway. He looks pissed off. I bunch my brows as he walks over to my truck, opens the door, and hops into the passenger seat. "What the fuck happened between you and the McDaniels?"

"What are you—"

"Don't fuck with me, Logan. Mrs. McDaniel called Pop this morning in a rage. She was threatening not to pay the balance. When Pops told her that the job is ninety percent done and he'd take her to court if she doesn't pay, she said fine. But she refuses to have you on her property. What happened?" he demands.

Fuck. I slam my head back, groaning.

"It's all just one big fuckup. That's what happened."

"Well, tell me. Pop is pissed off right now."

I run a hand over my face and sigh. I tell Bryson everything: about Jenna's disorder; about how Blair isn't a megabitch after all and Laura takes the fucking cake on that one; about how Brooke died and how Jenna was there. I tell it all.

"What the hell." Bryson huffs.

"I know."

"What are you gonna do?"

"I'm going to take care of her."

"Logan—"

"No. Before you give me this long spiel bullshit, I love her and that's that."

He sighs. "I know you want to help her, but she needs more help than just you. You can't save her. It's impossible. She's sick, dude."

"She's fine."

"Logan. We kept saying that Sean was fine, and look what happened. If you really want to help her, get her *professional* help."

"I'm not fucking sending her off."

He shakes his head, opens the door, and says, "I'll talk to Dad about having you start on the Royersford place. At least you'll have some work."

I nod. Then he hops out and slams the door behind him.

August

*Each day is unexpected. No matter how hard you try,
you can never prepare for the life ahead.*

chapter 25

Logan

"Where the hell is she?" I mumble under my breath, pacing up and down the narrow hallway. The screams and sounds of items crashing and breaking ring loud and clear from behind my apartment door. So far three neighbors have stepped out to complain and said if I don't get her to stop, then they're calling the cops. I gave them my fucking death glare, and they stepped back into their apartments without another word.

I huff out in relief when Charlie—in her sleepwear—storms down the hallway. She narrows her eyes as she passes me. Without a single word spoken, she enters my apartment, shutting the door behind her.

Silence.

It's like clockwork. I don't fucking understand it. What am I doing wrong?

Forty minutes later Charlie steps out. "She's sleeping now," she says, deadpan. Then she moves to walk away.

"I'm sorry," I say. Because there is nothing else I can say.

She turns around, her features distort into anger, and then she steps forward until she's front and center. "Six times this month, Logan. Six times!" she stresses. "I can't keep taking midnight runs over here every time Jenna has a breakdown."

"I'm trying."

"No, you're not! I told you what's best for her, but you're so against it. She needs *help*, Logan."

My nostrils flare. "I am helping her."

"Keeping her locked in this apartment"—she points toward my closed door—"with no medication and no therapy is not helping her. She just remembered that she witnessed her sister being brutally attacked, that she was almost raped as well. That's not even a trigger, that's a fucking nuclear bomb that just exploded in her world, and that's why she's been getting worse."

"Then get her medication."

She laughs, shaking her head at my ridiculousness. I know I am, but I'm desperate. "She needs them prescribed."

I shut my heavy eyes. This past month has been fucking hard. I've never felt this lost in my life. I want to help her, I just don't know how. It's as if she's hanging from the edge of a cliff and I'm the one holding on to her hand. She's begging for me to help her, to not let go, and I'm fucking trying the best I can. But she's slowly slipping.

Every time I think of what happened to Jenna and Brooke I get pissed off all over again. "I wish I could find the bastards who did this and kill each one of them. I swear to God I would, Charlie."

Charlie looks down. Her shoulders deflate as she crosses her arms over her chest. "I would too. I just keep telling myself they'll get what's coming to them someday." She shakes her head, disgusted with it all. Then she looks up at me, a pathetic smile pulling at the corner of her mouth.

"Look at you. You look like shit. You don't have to do this," she says.

"Yes, I do."

"Why?"

"Because I love her."

"So do I," she says. "And because of that we need to get her the best help right now."

My shoulders drop. "I promised her I wouldn't give up. Every time I suggest that maybe she should get help, she thinks I'm giving up on her, and then she spazzes out."

Charlie reaches both hands up and grips my shoulders. I look down at her. "I'm not going to lie to you. She's going to hate you at first. She'll even refuse to see you in the beginning. And it's the worst feeling. You'll feel guilty that you may have done something wrong, that you didn't try hard enough. But that won't be true. And when she's treated and better, she'll thank you. Trust me."

I swallow hard, nodding. "Okay."

Charlie lets out a sigh of relief. "Thank God. I'll call you tomorrow. You can meet with her father and me and then we'll set it all up. You're doing the right thing, Logan."

I nod. If this is the right thing, then why do I feel like shit right now?

"Let me have ten minutes with her before you come in," I say. They nod. I step out of the car, knowing this is it. There's no turning back. I'm going to break the heart of the one person I love.

With each step I take, my chest rips open a little more. How does someone look in the eyes of the person they love and say good-bye? Is this even love? I'm going to break her heart, tear it right out of her chest, because I claim to *love* her so much. How do I explain the reason why I'm going to hurt her? That it's what's best for her?

The reality is I can't help her. No matter where we are—whether it's the lake house or in our own little world in my shitty apartment—it doesn't help. No matter how hard I try, I *can't* help her. She needs more than what I can offer.

I swallow back the nerves lodged in my throat and open the door leading to my fate.

Jenna's in the kitchen by the stove, her back facing me. I look around. My eyes scan the table filled with pots, pans, and food remnants. The counter is just about the same. The fridge door is open and a gallon of milk is spilling out all over the floor. I step forward, my boots squishing against the spilled liquid. Jenna spins around, spatula in hand. "You scared me!" She jumps, a smile settling on her face.

"What's going on here?" I ask, taking in the mess.

"I wanted to make you something special to apologize about last night, and I didn't know what to make. At first I was thinking of a cake, but you didn't have any baking pans, and then I thought of something healthy, but there's nothing healthy in the fridge. And I forgot how to get to the supermarket." She shakes her head. "I didn't want to leave the house anyway, so I settled for pancakes, but I couldn't find the pan to cook it on, so I searched all over until—"

"Jenna," I cut off her rambling. "It's fine." I take two steps, stand the milk container back up in the fridge, and step over the contents spilled on the floor.

"What are you doing?" she asks, her eyes roaming over me as I remove the spatula from her hand and turn off the gas range.

"We need to talk."

"I know. I'm sorry about last night. I promise I'll get

better. It's just some days are really bad, and I don't know how to control them. I promise, Logan, I'll get better." She reaches her hand to my face, pulling my stare from the counter to look at her face. I was trying to avoid making eye contact. I knew it'd be difficult.

I wet my lips nervously. "I'm so sorry."

"For what?"

My lips crush into hers. I pull her in, kissing her hard. "I'm sorry," I mumble over her mouth.

Jersey Girl tries to pull away from my hold, her eyes wide "What are you talking about?"

I silence her again, tasting her, devouring every bit of her mouth before she leaves, before she'll never speak to me again.

"Logan!" She pushes at my chest. I stumble back, my breathing heavy. Her eyes are zoomed in on me. "What are you sorry about?"

I raise my hands to caution her. "Before I tell you, please let me explain that I'm only looking out for your best interest."

Jenna shifts, her mouth slightly open as if reading my mind. "What did you do?" I shake my head and step forward. "No. What did you do, Logan?" My gaze shifts to the curtain. Her eyes leave mine, lingering over the window. Her chest expands, and then she looks at me again. "You didn't," she pleads. Jenna storms over to the window. Flinging back the curtain, she looks out. "No. No. Logan. Why? Why would you call them?"

"Jenna, you need help. More than I can give you."

She marches over, her fingers digging into her chest as if her heart hurts. Tears forming in her beautiful eyes, she cries, "Please don't do this. I beg you, *please*. I need *you*, Logan. I don't need them. You have to believe me, I'll get better…" I feel small and pathetic. She's begging me not to send her away. The pain in her voice and in her eyes stabs at my chest, breaking me apart.

My vision blurs as I fight back my own tears. "I'm sorry, Jenna. I... I... dammit!... you need this."

She lifts a hand. "No!" Tears streaming down her cheeks, she yells, "I can't believe you're doing this to me. You said you'd never give up on me." Her voice sounds rough through hard sobs.

Fuck. I feel useless. My chest feels heavy. I step forward and grip her face with my hands. Hoarsely I say, "I'm not giving up on you, Jenna. I will never give up on you. I love you. I'm only helping you."

Her features fill with pain and her lip quivers as she shakes her head. "How can you say you love me but hurt me at the same time? If you loved me so much, I wouldn't feel this broken."

"Jenna." My eyes scan her face. I'm hurting her. "I'll always love you." Her eyes shut tight and her body quivers as she lets out hard sobs.

The front door opens. Jenna's father and Charlie storm through along with an assistant. I pull Jenna into me for one last hold, but I don't want to let go.

What am I doing?

This is ridiculous. She's fine. She can get better with me. "I changed my mind," I say, my words muffled against Jenna's hair while her face buries into my chest.

She clings to me. "Don't let them take me. Please," she cries out.

"Jenna, you need help," Charlie says.

No, this wrong.

"Let go of her, son," her father urges.

"We'll probably need to sedate her if she doesn't cooperate," the assistant says.

"No!" Jenna lets out, her fingers digging into my flesh.

I look all around. Everyone's talking at once. Jenna whimpers. I shake my head. "No. Just leave. I made a mistake."

The assistant grips Jenna's left arm. "Take her other arm, Mr. McDaniel." Jenna's father grips her right arm and they both try to pull her away from me. Jenna looks up at me, waterworks flowing. She tries to hold onto me for dear life.

"Son… Son," I look at Mr. McDaniel. "You're only making things worse. Trust me. You're doing the right thing. She needs to get better. Don't you want her better?"

I look down at Jenna, her head shaking furiously for me not to let go. But I don't see my Jersey Girl anymore. All I see is a sick girl. One with dark circles around her sunken eyes, one with pale skin, and one who's almost skin and bones from lack of nourishment. And as much as she's still beautiful to me, she's not Jersey Girl anymore.

I let go.

"NO!" She screams, shouts, kicks, and swings. She tries her hardest to tear away from their hold, but they pull her down to the floor. "Get off me, get off me. No!"

I stumble back and watch as it all takes place in slow motion. The assistant pulls out a needle, stabs Jenna in the arm, and pumps her with a clear liquid. I grip my head. *What the fuck have I done?*

"No… No… Noo…" Jenna mumbles, then her eyes shut.

Everything else is a blur. They carry her outside. Charlie pats my shoulder and tells me I did the right thing. They drive away.

And I'm just here.

In my apartment right back at a fucking standstill.

Jenna

Love is the devil in disguise. He sweeps in and seduces you when you're at your weakest, when you've lost all hope. But he gives you a sense of want and desire. He whispers sweet words, wrapping you into a world of existence, because before *Love*, you didn't exist. Then, when you give in fully, when you're lost in *Love* and when he has you exactly where he wants you, he takes over completely, possessing your mind, body, and soul.

That's when he snatches your heart, rips it to shreds, and leaves you with nothing left to give.

Logan was *Love*. He was the devil in disguise. He gave me everything I wanted and more, and then he ripped it away.

Just. Like. That.

I allowed myself to get lost in him. I believed every single word he said.

For what?

Nothing.

Because eventually, he gave up on us.

"How are you feeling today, Jenna?"

I continue to stare out the window. This new doctor should know how I feel. What's the point at explaining, anyway?

He goes on, "Do you know how long you've been in

here?"

"Twenty-six days."

"That's right. Twenty-six days, Jenna. Don't you want to get better so you can go home?"

I turn my head and stare blankly at him. "What's the point?" I shrug.

"What do you mean?"

I stand, "No one wants me at home. I'm a burden. So what's the point?" I turn, walking out the door and into the rec room with the other patients.

This is the first time in the eight weeks that I've been here that I've agreed to meet with my visitors. My father tried to visit, but I just couldn't bear to see the disappointment on his face. Logan tried, but I definitely couldn't see him. Period. My mother hasn't bothered. She was called in to have a therapy session with me and she refused.

I walk into the visiting area. My eyes scan the room until I spot Charlie. I walk over and take a seat on the couch across from her. She smiles.

"You look so good, Jenna."

"Thanks." I swallow back a sob. It's been two months since I've seen her and I miss her so much. "You do too."

Her smile softens. "How are you doing?"

I shrug. "Okay, I guess."

She nods. "That's great. Really great."

"You?"

"Oh, I'm okay. I found work in the city. You are looking at the new fashionista for an up-and-coming small magazine. They want me to find all of the latest fashion trends. Can you believe it?"

I wish I could jump for joy for my friend. That is what I feel right now—pleasure for her—but I just can't find the motivation to show it. "That's awesome."

"Listen, your father and I were talking and we thought maybe when you get out of here, you and I can share an apartment. Maybe in the city? Get a fresh start? You could go back to school, while I focus on my new job. It could be fun."

"Yeah. Sounds fun," I say, knowing it's not going to happen. I'm never getting out of here because I'm never getting better.

"Jenna," She leans in, "I miss you."

I nod, sniff back the tears, and look out the window. "Yeah, that's nice."

"Logan misses you too." She had to go there. My chest aches and suddenly it's difficult to breathe. "He asked me to give you something."

I tilt my head to look at her. She digs into her purse and pulls out a small yellow gift bag—one of the ones I'd given him. My lips tremble as I see it dangle from her fingertips. I don't move or reach for it, so instead she places it down on the table between us. She digs into her purse again and removes an envelope, placing it beside the gift bag.

"I'll just leave it here. You can open it whenever you're ready." She stands from her seat. "Jenna?" I look up at her. "You really do look good. Think about what I said. You can start fresh. A clean slate."

I nod. Then she turns and walks away. I stare at the door she exited for what seems like a long time, wishing she'd come back, but she never does.

Then I stare at the small yellow bag and envelope for the rest of my visiting hour. When time is up, I pick both up and take them with me to my room. I sit cross-legged in the middle of my bed as I continue to stare at both side-by-side.

Finally, I dig into the bag and pull out a small box. A tiny tug pulls at the corner of my lip. The box is wrapped in newspaper. Tearing it open, I flip the lid and remove a necklace. Hanging from the silver chain is a clear locket with floating charms in it. I shake the locket, scattering the charms so I can have a better look at each one.

Still holding the locket in my hand, I grab the envelope and remove a letter. My throat closes and my chest tightens at just reading the first two words. I can hear him saying them. Then I keep reading.

Jersey Girl,

I'm probably the last person you ever want to see again, let alone read a letter from, but I figured it's worth a shot. I just hope you can find it in your heart to fully read this letter before throwing it away.

I know you feel as if I have given up on you, and for a while I thought maybe I had. But the more I think of it, the more I know I was never giving up. Instead it was the complete opposite. I'd never thought I would fall in love, but you changed that for me. I now know that it's possible for anyone to feel and be loved. Even if it was just for the short summer we had together, you have no idea how much you changed my life. You saved me from the standstill I lived in for so long. I truly feel my purpose was to find you, and if we never see one another again, I know loving you was the reason I was given a second chance at life.

You have given me so much, and for that I want to give you something in return. If you haven't already opened the present, you'll find a locket with a few charms. Each one represents what I want to give to you and what I hope for you in life:

The coin with the word 'believe' inscribed on it, represents my hope that one day you can believe in yourself and your talents just as much as I do.

The paintbrush charm signifies the hope that when you do paint again, you'll capture every moment, both good and bad, and every emotion without feeling stuck or shoving them away. If you can do that, Jersey Girl, you can paint the world.

The heart-shaped charm symbolizes my love for you and the love we shared. As long as you want it, my heart will always be yours. But most of all, I hope that you can learn to love yourself. You will never know how special and beautiful and intelligent you are until you can love the person I fell in love with.

And lastly, the yellow stone charm reflects the light you shine on so many lives, mine included. And I hope that no matter how many demons you struggle with, you will always find your way out of the dark.

I love you, Jersey Girl.

Always,

Logan

Tears are freely flowing down my cheeks as I try to blink them away. With one hand I grip the letter, allowing the words to wrap around and soothe my heart. With my other hand I clench my fingers around the locket, forming a fist and bringing it to my chest.

The last three months we shared together begin to whirl in my head: me flowing beneath the water in the pool, the first time I saw his blue eyes when he jumped in after me, our first kiss on the porch, the day I ran away and he found me on the street corner barefoot, weekends at the lake house sitting together on the dock, us laying by the lake watching the stars.

My thoughts continue, lingering briefly on each memory. The park. The laughs. The hugs. The special Logan kisses. The day I realized I fell in love with him. The day I told him about my illness. The day he accepted me—all of me. The first time we made love. The fear I felt when he moved me in with him. The day I thought he'd given up—my hand reaching for him, begging him not to let them take me away. The look of fear and confusion in his eyes after realizing what he'd done.

And now.

This.

The letter. The locket.

Through it all, I still love him. I will always love him, but he's right. I need to learn how to love myself before I can *fully* love him.

I can slowly work on it.

Starting with today.

chapter 26

Six Months Later.

Jenna

I remove the books from of the last box and place them on the bookshelf. There's something about emptying the last box that's relieving. Looking around, I inspect my new place and smile. It's definitely different than my bedroom, but now that I'm sharing a space with Charlie we had to compromise on décor.

I hear a knock at the door and rush over to open it. My father steps in with a large box in his hand. "I was just thinking how great it felt to empty the last box. Thanks, Dad," I joke. He leans in, pressing his lips against my forehead.

"Well, I thought you'd like to have some of Brooke's things," he says, dropping the box on top of the dining table.

I walk over and search through, smiling at the filled picture frames, a few of her favorite books, and a few other favorite things of hers. "Thank you, Daddy." I hug him.

He nods.

"Would you like anything?" I ask, walking into the open kitchen.

He scoots onto a stool by the island. "I'll have coffee."

While the coffee is brewing, I turn and face him. My handsome father looks run-down. "Have you heard from Mom?" I ask him.

He shakes his head. "No. Like I said to you, I know it's difficult for your mother to handle this separation, but until she gets professional help, I can't continue going on with her like this."

I nod in understanding. "Do you know if she is?"

"I've spoken with Dr. Rosario. She won't give me specifics, but she has mentioned she's been in the office. I'm just hoping it works out for her." He pauses. "Jenna, I do love your mother. We have a history of twenty-eight years and I can't erase that, even if I tried. But the way she treated you was uncalled for, and I couldn't stand by and let her think it was acceptable."

I know this has been as hard on him as it has been on me. I haven't spoken to my mother in over eight months. I'd be lying if I said she hasn't crossed my mind because she has. I wonder if she's getting the help she needs, or if she even thinks of me, but I don't dwell on it for too long. I've learned not to focus on the things I can't control. Instead I focus on waking up each morning and continuing to push throughout the day. "Thank you," I say, then slide a filled mug his way.

Charlie walks in just on time. "Hey, Mr. McDee."

"Charlie." My father smiles.

"Guess who I just ran into at the market?" she says, placing the groceries on the counter.

"Who?" I ask.

"Bryson." My body stills at hearing his name. It's the closest I've gotten to Logan in a long time. And since Santino and Charlie haven't been a thing for a while, I haven't heard anything about any of the guys. "He is getting hotter, by the way, and guess what? He finally dumped Blair. For good this time! Thank God."

"How is he?" I ask, slowly scooting onto a stool. What I really want to ask is *How is Logan doing*?

"He's okay. His father is ill."

"George?" I breathe out in disbelief.

She nods, digging into the bags and removing a carton of milk. "Yeah. Poor guy. Cancer. They found out last month, and he's going through chemo. Bryson has been handling the business on his own. Since Logan left he's been so busy."

"Left? What do you mean Logan left?"

"I think I'm going to go now." My father stands, heads my way, and leaves a kiss on my cheek. "Enjoy your new apartment, baby."

"Thank you, Dad." He waves bye to Charlie and leaves. I focus back on Charlie. "Logan left?"

She stops, her hands resting over the counter, and then she looks at me. "Yes. Logan quit months ago. He said he needed a new start. He moved to the Poconos and has been staying at the lake house. He began working on small projects around there."

I swallow hard. "Why didn't you tell me?"

"Because you were finally getting yourself together. And he thought it was best."

I shake my head. "He? The two of you have been talking?"

"Not much, just through text. He only texts me to check in on you. I didn't even know about his uncle until today."

"How could you keep that from me, Charlie?" I stand, pacing in the kitchen as I reach for the locket secured around my neck.

"Like I said, he wanted to keep it that way."

Wetting my lips, I stop my pacing. "Does he not want to see me?"

"Jenna, he loves you. He always has. He asked me to respect his wishes and not mention him to you. I thought it was ridiculous and that the two of you need each other, but he made me promise."

I rush to the closet, grab my jacket, and snatch my keys from the counter.

"Where are you going?" Charlie shouts out.

"To the lake house."

After the longest two and a half hour drive of my life, I finally reach the lake house. I stop and admire it for a moment. It looks different. Quiet. There's no music or people partying or Ping-Pong games set up. It's simply peaceful and beautiful.

Instead of using the front entrance, I walk around the back. My heart skips a beat when I see Logan's truck. He's here. I find the courage to climb the stairs of the deck and gently knock on the door.

Nothing.

My knuckles scrape against the door as I knock louder this time. Still there's no answer.

Air leaves my lungs in frustration. I've come too far to just walk away. Turning, I head for the swing bench by the large tree, thinking I could wait there for him. That's when I see him. He's on the dock by the lake. I take in a lungful of air, hoping it will give me the confidence to face him.

I slowly travel down the long path that leads to the dock. My legs tremble as I continue down the wooden boards. His back is facing me. He's standing by the edge, looking over the lake, his hands shoved in the front pockets of his khaki shorts. A white T-shirt hugs his figure, exposing his broad shoulders, and he's wearing the Phillies cap.

"It's beautiful, isn't it?" I say as I get closer.

His body stiffens; slowly, he tilts his head and looks over his shoulder. I freeze in place and take this second to appreciate the sight of him. He looks down and then turns around so he's facing me.

I take a few steps forward until we're arm's length away from one another. "Hey," I say, my eyes glued to his.

"Hey," he says back, swallowing.

We both stand here for a long time, trying to figure out if this is real. Both our chests and shoulders move rapidly with our breathing.

"You look really good," he finally says.

"So do you," I say quietly.

His brows furrow. "How did you get here?" he asks.

"I drove."

His face lights up. "You're finally driving, huh?"

I let out a nervous chuckle. "No. Actually I took a taxi."

He laughs, which makes me smile. For a moment everything is back to normal until he bows his head, breaking our connection.

"I heard about your uncle. I'm sorry."

He looks up. "Thanks. He's strong. He's going to beat this."

I nod. "I know he will."

Another round of silence. Then his gaze drops to my neckline. "I see you got the necklace."

I lift my hand and touch it. "Yeah. I love it. Thank you. This necklace and your letter got me through a lot during my recovery."

His lips slant, eyes tearing up a bit. "I'm glad to hear that. I meant everything in that letter."

"I know." I break out into tears. Then laugh. "I'm sorry. *God,* I didn't want to cry." I wipe my eyes.

Logan closes the three steps between us, and before I know it, his hands are on my face, wiping my tears away. "So, what's new with you?" he asks, his eyes tracing my features.

"I'm painting again," I admit, blinking away my tears so I can see him.

A smile tugs at the corner of his lips. "I'm glad to hear that."

I nod. "And I applied to school. I'll be starting in the fall, and over the summer I'll be teaching art at a day camp."

His face shows so much pride. "That's good. Real good."

I moisten my lips. "You? What have you been up to?" I manage to ask.

"You know." He shrugs. "A little of this, a little of that. And missing you." His smile fades. "I've missed you, Jersey Girl."

"I missed you too," I choke out. "So, so much."

He shuts his eyes.

"Logan?"

"Yeah?"

"Thank you," I say.

"For what?"

"For believing in me. For loving me. For looking past the ugly and finding the beauty hidden beneath. You know, I'm learning a lot, and there are times when it's hard to love myself, but every time I think of you, I always think, if someone else can dig deep and fall in love with even my damaged side, then there is hope for me after all."

358

His fingers graze my face. "I didn't have to dig deep to love you, Jersey Girl. Digging takes work. Falling in love with you was the simplest thing I've ever done."

I look up at him; his eyes are filled with sincerity and love. I reach out and frame his face with my hands. I miss this—the way he feels, the way I feel around him. I just miss *him*. Logan loves me...for who I am. He's never looked at me any different, he's never judged me, and never ran away when I was at my worst; he's always been here, even when I tried to push him away.

I stand on my tiptoes and touch my lips to his. For the first time, I don't allow the voices or fear of loving someone to take over. I allow my heart to.

He pulls away, his forehead resting on mine. "Where do we go from here?" he asks.

"Let's just take it one day at a time."

He smiles. "I like that."

I smile too. My gaze looks past him and I take in the scenery.

Have you ever stepped outside and looked around, and even though it's very familiar territory—you've seen it a dozen times before—it instantly looks different? The trees are more vibrant, the view is clearer, the sky is bluer, and every-thing is just brighter. That's what I feel right now. It's sooth-ing and breathless and beautiful.

I want to keep it like this forever.

"Everything okay?" he asks.

I smile up at him. "Yes, it's just..." I sigh. "Look around you." I breathe out in awe. Logan lifts his head, his eyes scan-ning the view that surrounds us. His wrinkled brow relaxes, as if he knows my thoughts exactly, and he pulls me into him. I nestle my head into the side of his chest and loop my arms around his waist while he snakes his arm over my shoulder. We just stand there, holding one another, and admiring the view.

I know it won't stay this way. I know there will be days when this view is covered with grey and gloomy clouds. I don't know what tomorrow will bring. But for right now, I enjoy this moment. I breathe, I feel free, and I'm thankful that for today…

I am *living*.

Author Note

Thank you so much for reading *Perfectly Damaged*. I only ask if you enjoyed reading Jenna and Logan's story that you take five minutes out of your time to help others enjoy it as well. You can share it with a friend by using the lending feature. You can also write a small (non-spoiler please) review from the site you purchased the book from. Word of mouth is key, and the more you spread to family and friends the more others will have the chance to experience *Perfectly Damaged*.

Also, after you write a review and you would like to discuss the story with me, please email me at auth.el.montes@gmail.com. I would love to hear your thoughts!

Thank you again!

Xo,

E.L. Montes

Acknowledgements

Alex, not enough words could ever express how appreciative I am of you, and all that you do for me. I know it can be stressful at times: dealing with my emotional breakdowns when I'm going out of mind. But thank you for sticking by me and supporting my dream. It means the world to me. I love you, baby. Always and forever.

Mom, although you live thousands of miles away, our phone calls allows me to feel like you are right by my side holding my hand the entire step of the way. Thank you for always pushing me and believing in me. I said it before and I will always say it: you're the reason I'm living my dream. I love you!

To my family, friends and M7: Wow. Your continued support and encouraging words truly gets me through my toughest days. Thank you so much. I love you all with all of my heart.

Jessica, my sister, you said that you're proud of me. Just know that I am and will always be proud of you and woman you've grown to be. I love you.

Beta readers: Missy Swain and Dana Caponi. You ladies have no idea how grateful I am for your hard work and feedback on *Perfectly Damaged*. Thank you. Thank you. Thank you!

Emmy's Entourage Group: Thank you all for always pimping me out and supporting me. I'm forever grateful.

A HUGE shout out to: Richelle Robinson, Jennifer Wolfel, Holly Malgieri, Jennifer Diaz, Missy Swain, Sandy Borrero and Tasha Burkowski. I love all so HARD. Even on days where I feel down I know I can open my laptop and see something from one of you that brightens my day. Whether it's a private message with an encouraging word, or a tag/notification for being pimped, or just simply being there for me. Thank you for it all. I love you, girls!

Megan Ward, thank you for your outstanding work on editing *Perfectly Damaged*. Our long talks about the characters and storyline kept me sane. I loved that you were invested with the story and characters as much as I was. I appreciate all of your hard work. SIGH. I <3 you big time!

Alison Duncan, thank you for going over the second round of edits. Your final touches truly completed the story. I appreciate the hard work and THANK YOU for going over it a second time when I screwed up and sent you the wrong Manuscript. *face palm* In my defense I had a lot going on that week. LOL. You're the best!

Regina Wamba, I absolutely love the cover for *Perfectly Damaged* and I love your face! You are extremely talented. Thank you for being patient with me. In the end it all worked out. The final cover is beautiful.

Becca Manuel, you've done it again! The book trailer on YouTube for *Perfectly Damaged* is perfect. Seriously, you managed to take my story and transformed it visually. You talented, woman, you. ;) ;)

To all Book Bloggers: Thank you so much for everything. You take time out of your life, work, and family to support and spread the word of your favorite authors. I'm in *awe* of you, for just being so committed and loving a story that has touched you. In turn all you want to do is simply share your passion about the story with others. Thank you for that! If not for you, many readers would lose out on the opportunity in finding a story that they might fall in love with as well. Thank you!

Last but certainly not least my, Author Groups, you girls keep me sane. Seriously, you girls made me laugh when I wanted to cry, allowed me to feel pride when I was discouraged, and allowed me to believe in myself when I had doubt. A special thank you to Melissa, Syreeta, Claribel, Gail, Madeline, Karina, Cindy, Amy, Gretchen, Rebecca, Renee, Hadley, Julie, Toni, Nikki, Jessica and Jennifer L. You girls rock! Thank you for listening to my everyday rants. <3

about the author

USA Today Bestselling Author, E.L. Montes (Emmy Luz Montes) lives in Pennsylvania with her husband, Alex, and their English Bulldog name Butters. She has a Bachelor of Science in Legal Studies.

Ms. Montes worked several years as a paralegal for a mid-size law firm. She had always loved the legal field and found it to be interesting. She more so "secretly" loved to write. Disastrous was her debut novel which was released October 2012. After the release of her second novel Ms. Montes took a huge leap, by leaving her fulltime job to focus on her writing career. She has and continues to write characters with flaws. Ms. Montes said, "No one is perfect and neither are my characters. It makes the storyline a bit more realistic, in my opinion. But I also feel no matter who you are or the life you have lived, everyone deserves someone to love and be loved. I'm a hopeless romantic, and enjoy writing a story where my readers feel like they're living and feeling every emotion."

Media Links

Website: http://www.booksbyelmontes.com/

Facebook:
https://www.facebook.com/E.L.MontesAuthor

Twitter: https://twitter.com/emmymontes

Instagram: http://instagram.com/el_montes

Goodreads:
https://www.goodreads.com/author/show/6538202.E_L_Mo
ntes

CPSIA information can be obtained at www.ICGtesting.com
Printed in the USA
LVOW10s1033290614

392203LV00017B/785/P